NIGHTWORK

Douglas Grimes finds his fortune one day quite
by accident when he comes across a man lying
dead in the corridor of the hotel where he
works. And so from the life of a night clerk in
the dingy St Augustine hotel he becomes a
member of a jet-set racy world of fast cars,
fancy women, blue movies, gambling and gold.

How long is this newly acquired wealth going
to last? And how long can Grimes survive
before his sins catch up with him? In this
highly entertaining story, the adventures of a
lovable rogue are as inventive as they are
comic.

**Also by the same author,
and available from New English Library**

About the Author

Born in New York in 1913, Irwin Shaw began his
literary career writing plays for radio and also short
stories. He found success early and many of his
short stories were published in magazines, including
THE NEW YORKER, HARPER'S and PLAYBOY.

During World War II Shaw served as a private, then
as a Warrant Officer in North Africa, the Middle East
and all over Europe. Drawing on first-hand
observation, he published his first novel, THE
YOUNG LIONS, after the war and achieved instant
acclaim. He has now written more than a dozen
novels all of which are worldwide bestsellers. His
books have been enormously successful as feature
films and TV serials and have been translated into
twenty languages. Irwin Shaw died in 1984.

Nightwork

Irwin Shaw

NEW ENGLISH LIBRARY
Hodder and Stoughton

Copyright © Irwin Shaw 1975

First published in Great Britain by
Weidenfeld and Nicolson

First published in paperback by Pan Books Ltd 1976

New English Library Paperback Edition 1987

British Library C.I.P.

Shaw, Irwin
  Nightwork.
  I. Title
  813'.52[F]   PS3537.H384
  ISBN 0-450-39752-1

Printed and bound in Great Britain for
Hodder and Stoughton Paperbacks, a
division of Hodder and Stoughton Ltd.,
Mill Road, Dunton Green, Sevenoaks,
Kent (Editorial Office: 47 Bedford
Square, London WC1B 3DP) by
Richard Clay Ltd, Bungay, Suffolk

To Gerda Nielsen

1

It was night and I was alone, behind the locked door, the bulletproof glass. Outside, the city of New York was in the black grip of January. For the last two years, six times a week, I'd come in an hour before midnight and left at eight in the morning. I was neither content nor discontent. The room I worked in was warm, the work untaxing, the necessity to speak infrequent.

My duties left me time for my own amusements, with no one to give me orders or change the routine of the night. I spent an hour on the *Racing Form*, preparing my bets for the next day. It was a lively paper, written with brio, confident of the future, renewing hope with each edition.

Finished with my calculations of times, weights, distances, sunshine, and rain, I read, making sure always to have a supply of books on hand to suit my tastes. For other nourishment there was a sandwich and a bottle of beer that I picked up on the way to work. Twice during the night I did isometric exercises, for the arms, the gut, the legs. Despite my sedentary occupation, at the age of thirty-three I was stronger and in better condition than I had been at twenty. I'm just short of six feet tall and weigh one hundred and eighty-five pounds. People are surprised when they hear I weigh that much. I'm vain enough to be pleased by this. But I wish I were taller. Some women have told me I look boyish, which I don't take as a compliment. I have never longed for a mother. Like most men I would prefer to resemble the sort of man who is cast on television as a captain in the Marines or the leading figure in a desperate enterprise.

*

I was working on an adding machine, preparing the previous day's accounts for the day staff. The machine made a noise like a large, irritated insect as I hit the keys. The sound, which had at first annoyed me, was now familiar and rhythmic, soothing. Beyond the glass, the lobby of the hotel was dark. The management saved on electricity, as on everything else.

The bulletproof pane had been put in over the front desk after the last night man had been held up for the second time. Forty-three stitches. The night man had taken up another profession.

I owed my position to the fact that, at the urging of my mother, I had taken a year's course in business procedures in college. She had insisted that I learn at least one useful thing, as she put it, in those four years. I had finished college eleven years ago and my mother was now dead.

The name of the hotel was the St Augustine. What yearning for the South the name represented for the original owner or what obscure religious whim would have been hard to say. There were no crucifixes on any of the walls, and only the four potted rubber plants in the worn lobby had any conceivable connection with the Tropics. Although it looked respectable enough on the outside, the hotel had seen better days. As had its clientele. They paid modestly for their accommodations and expected little in return. Except for two or three guests who wandered in late, I hardly had to talk to anybody. I hadn't taken the job for its opportunities for conversation. Often whole nights went by without a single light showing on the switchboard.

I was paid one hundred and twenty-five dollars a week. Home was one room with kitchenette and bath on East Eighty-first Street.

*

Tonight I had been interrupted only once, by a prostitute who had come down from upstairs a little after one o'clock and had to be let out the front door. I hadn't been on duty when she came in so I had no idea which room she had been visiting. There was a buzzer by the side of the door that was designed to open it automatically, but it had been broken for a week. I sniffed the cold night air briefly and was happy to close the door and get back to the office.

The *Racing Form* was open on my desk to the next day's program at Hialeah. The warm holidays of the South. I had made my choice earlier. *Ask Gloria* in the second. The filly had finished out of the money in its last three outings, but had had a good race up North in the autumn and was dropping down in class. The probable odds were fifteen to one.

I had always been a gambler. I had paid a good part of my way through college in fraternity poker games. When I still was working in Vermont, I played in a weekly poker game and figured I was ahead by several thousand dollars by the time I left. Since then I had not been particularly lucky.

In fact, it was my devotion to gambling that had led me to the Hotel St Augustine. When I first drifted into New York, I had happened to meet a bookie in a bar. He lived in the hotel, and paid off there. He gave me a line of credit and we settled at the end of each week. The hotel was cheap and convenient, and my financial situation did not permit me to demand luxury. When I ran up a five-hundred-dollar debt to the bookie, he had cut me off. Luckily, he said, the old night clerk had just quit his job and the manager was looking for a new man. I looked and sounded like a college graduate, the bookie said, and he knew I could add and subtract. I took the job, but moved out to a place of my own. Twenty-four hours a day at the St Augustine was more than anybody could stomach. I paid the bookie off in weekly installments from my salary. I had cleared my original debt with him and was on credit again. I was only a hundred and fifty dollars down on this night.

As we had arranged in the beginning, I would write out my choice or choices for the day, and put them in an envelope in the bookie's box. He never awoke before eleven in the morning. I decided to bet five dollars. If the filly came in it would cut my debt by half.

Lying on top of the *Racing Form* was a Gideon Bible, open to the Psalms. I came from a religious family and had been reared on the Bible. My faith in God was not what it once was, but I still enjoyed reading the Bible. Also on the desk were *Vile Bodies*, by Evelyn Waugh and Conrad's *Almayer's Folly*. In the two years I had been working behind the desk, I had given myself a liberal education in English and American literature.

As I sat down once more in front of the adding machine, I glanced over at the Bible lying open on top of the *Racing Form*. 'Praise him for his mighty acts,' I read; 'praise him

*according to his excellent greatness, praise him with the
sound of the trumpet; praise him with the psaltery and harp.
Praise him with the timbrel and dance; praise him with
stringed instruments and organs.'*

All right for Jerusalem, I thought. Could a timbrel be
found in New York? High above, penetrating stone and steel,
there was the whining noise of a jet, crossing New York.
Descending from the pole, outward bound to Karachi. I
listened, thinking of the quiet flight deck, the silent men at
the controls, the flicker of the dials, the radar scanning the
night sky. 'Christ,' I said aloud.

Finished with the adding machine, I pushed my chair back,
took a sheet of paper, held it on my thighs, looked straight
ahead at a calendar on the wall. Then I moved the sheet of
paper up, bit by bit. Only when it was high up on my chest,
almost to my chin, did it come within the limit of my vision.
No miracle had happened that night. 'Christ,' I said again
and crumpled the sheet of paper and threw it into the waste-
basket.

I made a neat, small pile of the bills I had prepared and
began filing them in alphabetical order. I had been working
automatically, my mind on other things, and I hadn't paid
any attention to the date on the bills on my desk. Now it
struck me. The date on the bills was 15 January. An anniversary. Of a kind. I grinned. Painfully. Three years ago, to
the day, it had happened.

2

It had been overcast in New York, but when we passed Peek-
skill, flying north, the skies cleared. The snow glistened in the
sunshine on the rolling hills below. I had flown the little
Cessna down to Teterboro Airport early to pick up the New
Jersey charter, and I could hear my passengers behind me

congratulating each other on the blue skies and the fresh powder. We were flying low, only six thousand feet, and the fields made clearly defined checkerboard patterns, with stands of trees black against the clean white of the snow. It was a flight I always liked to make. Recognizing individual farm-houses and road intersections and the course of a small stream here and there made the short voyage cozy and familiar. Upstate New York is beautiful at ground level, but on a fine day in early winter, from the air, it is one of the loveliest sights a man can hope to see. Once again, I was grateful that I had never been tempted to take a job on one of the big airlines, where you spent the best part of your life at an altitude of over thirty thousand feet, with the world below you just a vast sea of cloud or a remote and impersonal map unrolling slowly beneath you.

There were only three passengers, the Wales family, mother and father and a plump girl with buck-teeth of about twelve or thirteen called Didi. They were enthusiastic skiers and I had flown them up and back four or five times. There was a regular airline to Burlington, but Mr Wales was a busy man, he said, and took off when he could find the time and didn't like being tied down to a schedule. He had an adver-tising firm of his own in New York and he didn't seem to mind throwing his money around. Flatteringly, when he called for a charter, he always asked for me. Part of the reason, or maybe the whole reason for this, was that I skied with them from time to time at Stowe and Sugarbush and Mad River and led them down the trails, which I knew better than they did, and occasionally threw in a little tactful in-struction about how they could improve their performance. Wales and his wife, a hard-looking, athletic New York woman, were fiercely competitive with each other and went too fast, out of control a good deal of the time. I predicted to myself that there would be a broken leg in the family one of these days. I could tell when they were furious with each other by the different tones in which they called each other 'Darling' at various moments.

Didi was a serious and unsmiling child, always with a book in her hands. According to her parents, she started reading as soon as she was strapped into her seat and only stopped when the plane rolled to a halt. On this flight she was engrossed in *Wuthering Heights*. I had been an omnivorous reader, too, as a boy – when my mother was displeased with me she would say, 'Oh, Douglas, stop acting like a character in a book' – and it amused me to keep track of what Didi was reading from one winter to another.

She was by far the best skier in the family, but her parents made her bring up the rear on all descents. I had skied alone with her one morning, in a snowstorm, when the older Waleses were hung over from a cocktail party, and she had been a changed girl, smiling blissfully and fleeing joyfully down the mountain with me, like a small wild animal suddenly let loose from a cage.

Wales was a generous man and made a point of giving me a gift after each flight – a sweater, a new pair of fancy poles, a wallet, things like that. I certainly made enough money to be able to buy anything I needed, and I didn't like the idea of being tipped, but I knew he would have been insulted if I had ever refused to take his offerings. He was not an unpleasant man, I had decided. Just too successful.

'Beautiful morning, isn't it, Doug?' Wales said behind me. He was a restless man and even in the small plane seemed always on the prowl. He would have made a terrible pilot. He brought a smell of alcohol into the cockpit. He always traveled with a small, leather-bound flask.

'N ... not bad,' I said. I had stuttered ever since I was a boy and as a result tried to talk as little as possible. Sometimes I couldn't help but speculate about what my life would have been like if I hadn't suffered from this small affliction, but I didn't allow myself to sink into gloom because of it.

'The skiing ought to be marvelous,' Wales said.

'Marvelous,' I agreed. I didn't like to talk while I was at the controls, but I couldn't tell Wales that.

'We're going up to Sugarbush,' Wales said. 'You going to be there this weekend?'

'I ... I ... b ... believe so,' I said. 'I t ... told a girl I'd ski with her up ... up there.' The girl was Pat Minot. Her brother worked in the airline office and I had met her through him. She taught history at the high school, and I had arranged to pick her up at three o'clock, when school let out. She was a good skier and very pretty besides, small and dark and intense. I had known her for more than two years and we had had what was a rather desultory affair for fifteen months now. At least it was desultory as far as she was concerned, since for weeks on end she would put me off with one excuse or another and hardly notice me when we met by accident. Then suddenly she would relent and suggest we go off together somewhere. I could tell by the particular kind of smile on her face when, for whatever reason, she was entering into a non-desultory phase.

She was a popular girl, stubbornly unmarried; at one time or another, according to her brother, almost every friend of his had made a pass at her. With what success I never did find out. I have always been shy and uneasy with girls and I could not say that I pursued her. I couldn't say, either, that she had pursued me. It had just, well, happened, when we found each other skiing together on a long weekend at Sugarbush. After the first night, I had said, 'This is the best thing that ever happened to me.'

All she had said was, 'Hush.'

I never made up my mind whether or not I was in love with her. If she hadn't badgered me continually about curing my stutter, I think I would have asked her to marry me. The coming weekend, I felt, was going to rise – or fall – to some sort of climax. I had decided to be cautious, leaving all options open.

'Great,' Wales was saying. 'Let's all have dinner together tonight.'

'Thanks, G ... George,' I said. He had insisted from the first time I met him that I call him and his wife by their first names. 'Th ... that w ... would be very nice.' Dinner with another couple would postpone decisions, give me time to sound out Pat's mood and re-assess my own feelings.

'We're driving up as soon as we land,' Wales said. 'We can get in a few runs this afternoon. How about you? Should we wait for you at the inn?'

'I ... I'm afraid n ... not. I have my six-m ... month

13

physical checkup at the doc's and ... and I don't know when I c ... can split.'

'Dinner, then?' Wales said.

'D ... dinner.'

'Doug,' Wales said, 'do you ever get three weeks off at a time? In the winter, I mean?'

'N ... not really,' I said. 'It's a busy season. Wh ... Why?'

'Beryl and I're going over on a charter flight to Zurich the first of February.' Beryl was his wife. 'We always try to manage three weeks in the Alps.... You ever ski in the Alps?'

'I've never b ... been out of the country. Except Canada for a f ... few days.'

'You'd flip,' he said. 'The slopes of Heaven. We've been talking it over and we'd love to have you with us. There's this club I belong to. It's surprisingly cheap. Under three hundred dollars round trip. The Christie Ski Club. It's not just the money, of course. It's the people. The nicest bunch of people you could ever travel with and all the free booze you can drink. And no worrying about a baggage allowance or Swiss customs. They just wave you through with a smile. You're supposed to belong at least six months in advance, but they're not sticky about it. There's a girl in the office I know, her name's Mansfield, and she fixes everything. Just tell her you're a friend of mine. They have flights just about every week in the winter. We made St Moritz last year and we're doing St Anton this year. You'll dazzle the Austrians.'

I smiled. 'I b ... bet,' I said.

'Think it over,' Wales said. 'You'd have the time of your life.'

'S ... stop tempting a working man,' I said.

'What the hell,' Wales said. 'Everybody needs a vacation.'

'I ... I'll think it o ... over,' I said.

He went back to his seat, leaving the smell of whiskey in the cockpit. I kept my eyes on the horizon, sharp against the bright blue of the winter sky, trying not to be jealous of a man who was as untalented on the slopes as Wales, but who could take three weeks off from work to spend thousands of dollars to ski in the Alps.

*

After I checked into the office and confirmed that there was nothing for me that weekend, I drove into town in my Volkswagen for the biannual ritual of the physical examination. Dr Ryan was an eye-specialist, but kept up a limited general practice on the side. He was a slow-moving, gentle old man who had been listening to my heart, taking my blood pressure, and testing my eyes and reflexes for five years. Except for one occasion when I had come down with a mild case of *grippe*, he had never prescribed as much as an aspirin for me. 'In shape for the Derby,' he would say each time when he finished with me. 'Ready to run for the roses.' He shared my interest in the horses and was an impressive student of form. Every once in a while he would call me at my home when he would discover a horse that was outrageously underpriced or carrying, in his opinion, much too little weight.

The examination followed its usual routine, with the doctor nodding comfortably after each stage. It was only when he came to my eyes that his expression changed. I read the charts all right, but when he used his instruments to look into my eyes, his face became professionally sober. His nurse came into the office twice to tell him that there were patients in the waiting room with appointments, but he brusquely waved her aside. He gave me a whole series of tests that he had never used before, making me stare straight ahead while he kept his hands in his lap, then slowly lifting his hands and asking me to tell him when they came into my field of vision. Finally, he put away his instruments, sat down heavily behind his desk, sighed, and passed his hand wearily across his face.

'Mr Grimes,' he said finally, 'I'm afraid I have bad news for you.'

The news old Dr Ryan had for me on that sunny morning in his big, old-fashioned office changed my whole life.

'Technically,' he said, 'the name of the disease is retinoschisis. It is a splitting of the ten layers of the retina into two portions, giving rise to the development of a retinal cyst. It is a well-known condition. Most often it does not progress, but as far as it goes it's irreversible. Sometimes we can arrest it by operating by laser beam. One of its manifestations is a blocking out of peripheral vision. In your case downward peripheral vision. For a pilot who has to be alert to a whole array of dials in front of him, below him, around him on all sides, as well as the horizon toward which he is speeding, it is essentially disabling. . . . Still, for all general purposes, such as reading, sports, et cetera, you can consider yourself normal.'

'Normal,' I said. 'Boy, oh boy, normal. You know the only thing that's normal for me, Doc. Flying. That's all I ever wanted to do, all I ever prepared myself to do. . . .'

'I'm sending the report over today, Mr Grimes,' Ryan said. 'With the greatest regret. Of course, you can go to another doctor. Other doctors. I don't believe they can do anything to help you, but that's only my opinion. As far as I'm concerned, you're grounded. As of this minute. For good. I'm sorry.'

I fought to hold back the surge of hatred I felt for the neat old man, seated among his shining instruments, signing papers of condemnation with his scrawly doctor's handwriting. I knew I was being unreasonable, but it was not a moment for reason. I lurched out of the office, not shaking Ryan's hand, saying, 'Goddamnit, goddamnit,' aloud over and over to myself, paying no attention to the people in the waiting room and on the street who stared curiously at me as I headed for the nearest bar. I knew I couldn't face going back to the airfield and saying what I would have to say without fortification. Considerable fortification.

*

The bar was decorated like an English pub, dark wood and pewter tankards on the walls. I ordered a whiskey. There was a thin old man in a khaki mackinaw and a hunter's red cap leaning against the bar with a glass of beer in front of him. 'They're polluting the whole lake,' the old man was saying in a dry Vermont accent. 'The paper mill. In five years it'll be as dead as Lake Erie. And they keep putting salt on the roads so those idiots from New York can go eighty miles an hour up to Stowe and Mad River and Sugarbush, and, when the snow melts off the salt goes into all the ponds and rivers. By the time I die there won't be a fish left anywhere in the whole state. And nobody does a goddamn thing about it. I tell you, I'm glad I won't be around to see it.'

I ordered another whiskey. The first one hadn't seemed to do anything for me. Nor did the second. I paid and went out to my car. The thought that Lake Champlain, in which I had swum every summer and on which I had spent so many great days sailing and fishing, was going to die, somehow seemed sadder than anything that had happened to me for a long time.

*

When I got to the office I could tell by the look on Cunningham's rough old face that Dr Ryan had already called him. Cunningham was the president and sole owner of the little airline and was a World War II vintage fighter pilot, and I guess he knew how I felt that afternoon.

'I'm ch . . . checking out, Freddy,' I said. 'You know wh . . . why.'

'Yes,' he said. 'I'm sorry.' He fiddled uncomfortably with a pencil on his desk. 'You know, we can always find something for you here. In the office, maybe . . . maintenance . . .' His voice trailed off. He stared at the pencil in his big hand.

'Thanks,' I said. 'It's nice of you, but forget it.' If there was one thing I knew it was that I couldn't hang around like a crippled bird, watching all my friends take off into the sky. And I didn't want to get used to the look of pity I saw on Freddy Cunningham's honest face, or on any other face.

'Well, anyway Doug, think it over,' Cunningham said.

'No n . . . need,' I said.

'What do you plan to do?'

'First,' I said, 'leave town.'

'For where?'

'Anywhere,' I said.

'Then what?'

'Then try to figure out what I'm going to do with the rest of my life.' I stuttered twice on the word life.

He nodded, avoiding looking at me, deeply interested in the pencil. 'How're you fixed for dough?'

'Sufficient,' I said. 'For the time being.'

'Well,' he said, 'if you ever . . . I mean you know where to come, don't you?'

'I'll keep that in mind.' I looked at my watch. 'I have a date.'

'Shit,' he said loudly. Then stood up and shook my hand. I didn't say good-bye to anyone else.

*

I parked the car and got out and waited. There was a peculiar muted hum coming from the big, red-brick building with the Latin inscription on the facade and the flag flying above it. The hum of learning, I thought, a small, decent music that made me remember my childhood.

Pat would be in her classroom, lecturing the boys and girls on the origins of the Civil War or the succession of the kings of England. She took her history seriously. 'It is the most relevant of subjects,' she had told me once, using the word that cropped up in every conversation about education in those days. 'Every move we make today is the result of what men and women have been doing with each other and to each other since before recorded time.' As I remembered this, I grinned sourly. Had I been born to stutter or lived to be a discarded airman because Meade had repulsed Lee at Gettysburg, or because Cromwell had had Charles beheaded? It would be an interesting point to discuss when we had an idle moment to spare.

Inside the building a bell clanged. The hum of education swelled to a roar of freedom, and a few minutes later the students began to pour out of the doors in a confused sea of brightly colored parkas and brilliant wool hats.

As usual, Pat was late. She was the most conscientious of teachers, and there were always two or three students who clustered around her desk after class, asking her questions that she patiently answered. When I finally saw her, the lawn was deserted, the hundreds of children vanished as if melted away by the pale Vermont sun.

She didn't see me at first. She was nearsighted, but out of vanity didn't wear her glasses except when she was working or reading or going to the movies. It had been a little joke of mine that she wouldn't find a grand piano in a ballroom.

I stood, leaning against a tree, without moving or saying anything, watching her walk down the cleared walk toward me, carrying a leather envelope that I knew contained test papers, cradled against her bosom, schoolgirl-fashion. She was wearing a skirt and red wool stockings and brown suede after-ski boots and a short, blue cloth overcoat. Her way of walking was concentrated, straight, uncoquettish, always brisk. Her small head with its dark hair pulled back was almost half obscured by the big, upraised collar of her coat.

When she saw me, she smiled, a non-desultory smile. It was going to be even more difficult than I had feared. We didn't kiss. You never knew who was looking out of a window. 'Right on time,' she said. 'My stuff's in the car.' She waved toward the parking lot. She had a battered old Chevy. A good part of her salary went for Biafra refugees, starving Indian children, political prisoners in various parts of the world. I don't think she owned more than three dresses. 'I hear the skiing's great,' she said, as she started toward the parking lot. 'This ought to be a weekend to remember.'

I put my hand out and held her arm. 'W ... wait a min ... minute, Pat,' I said, trying not to notice the slight strained look that invariably crossed her face when I stuttered. 'I have some ... something to tell you. I ... I'm not going up there th ... this weekend.'

'Oh,' she said, her voice small. 'I thought you were free this weekend.'

'I am f ... free,' I said. 'But I'm not going skiing. I'm leaving town.'

'For the weekend?'

'For good,' I said.

She squinted at me, as though I had suddenly gone out of focus. 'Has it got something to do with me?'

'N ... nothing.'

'Oh,' she said harshly, 'nothing. Can you tell me where you're going?'

'No,' I said. 'I don't know wh ... where I'm g ... going.'

'Do you want to tell me *why* you're going?'

'You'll hear s ... soon enough.'

'If you're in trouble,' she said, her voice soft now, 'and I could help ...'

'I'm in t ... trouble,' I said. 'And you can't help.'

'Will you write me?'

'I'll try.'

She kissed me then, not worrying who might be at a window. But there were no tears. And she didn't tell me that she loved me. It might have been different if she had, but she didn't. 'I have a lot of work to catch up on over the weekend anyway,' she said, as she stepped back a pace. 'The snow'll last.' She smiled a little crookedly at me. 'Good luck,' she said. 'Wherever.'

I watched her walk toward the old Chevy in the parking lot, small and neat and familiar. Then I got into the Volkswagen and drove off.

*

I was out of my small furnished apartment by six o'clock that evening. I had left my skis and boots and the rest of my skiing equipment except a padded parka, which I liked, in a duffel bag to be delivered to Pat's brother, who was just about my size, and had told my landlady that she could have all my books and whatever else I left behind me. Traveling light, I headed south, leaving the town where, I realized now, I had been happy for more than five years.

I had no destination. I had told Freddy Cunningham that I was going to try to figure out what I was going to do with the rest of my life and one place was as good as another for that.

3

Figure out my life. I had plenty of time to do it. As I drove south, down the entire East Coast of America, I was alone, unfettered, free of claims, with no distractions, plunged in that solitude that is supposed to be the essential condition of philosophic speculation. There was Pat Minot's cause and effect to be considered; also not to be overlooked was the maxim I had been taught in English lit courses that your character was your fate, that your rewards and failures were the result of your faults and virtues. In *Lord Jim*, a book I must have read at least five times since I was a boy, the hero is killed eventually because of a flaw in himself that permitted him to leave a shipload of poor beggars to die. He pays for his cowardice in the end by being killed himself. I had always thought it just, fair, inevitable. At the wheel of the little Volkswagen, speeding down the great highways past Washington and Richmond and Savannah, I remembered *Lord Jim*. But it no longer convinced me. I certainly was not flawless, but, at least in my opinion, I had been a decent son, an honorable friend, conscientious in my profession, law-abiding, careful to avoid cruelty or spite, inciting no man to be my enemy, indifferent to power, abhorring violence. I had never seduced a woman – or cheated a shopkeeper, had not struck a fellow human being since a fight in the schoolyard at the age of ten. I had definitely never left anyone to die. Yet ... Yet there had been that morning in Dr Ryan's office.

If character was fate, was it the character of thirty million Europeans to die in World War II, was it the character of the inhabitants of Calcutta to drop in the streets of starvation, was it the character of thousands of citizens of Pompeii to be mummified in a flood of lava?

The ruling law was simple – accident. The throw of dice, the turning of a card. From now on I would gamble and trust to luck. Maybe, I thought, it was in my character to be a gambler and fate had neatly arranged it so that I could play out my destined role. Maybe my short career as a man who traveled the Northern skies was an aberration, a detour and only now, back to earth, was I on the right path.

*

When I got to Florida, I spent my days at the tracks. In the beginning, all went well; I won often enough to live comfortably and not have to worry about taking a job. There was no job that anyone could offer me that I could imagine accepting. I kept by myself, making no friends, approaching no women. I found, mildly surprised, that all desire had left me. Whether this was temporary or would turn out to be permanent did not bother me. I wanted no attachments.

I turned with bitter pleasure into myself, content with the long sunny afternoons at the track and the solitary meals and

the evenings spent studying the performances of thoroughbreds and the habits of trainers and jockeys. I also had time
now for reading, and I indiscriminately devoured libraries of
paperbacks. As Dr Ryan had assured me, the condition of my
eyes did not interfere with my ability to read. Still, I found
nothing in any of the books I read that either helped or
harmed me.

I lived in small hotels, moving on from one to another
when other guests, to whom I had become a familiar presence, attempted to approach me.

I was ahead of the game by several thousand dollars when
the season ended and I drifted up to New York. I no longer
went to the track. The actual running of a race now bored
me. I continued betting, but with bookies. For a while I went
often to the theater, to the movies, losing myself for a few
hours at a time in their fantasies. New York is a good city
for a man who prefers to be alone. It is the easiest city in the
world to enjoy solitude.

My luck began to change in New York and with the onset
of winter I knew that I would have to look for some kind of
job if I wanted to continue eating. Then the night man at the
St Augustine was held up for the second time.

*

I put the last of the 15 January bills in the file. It was now
three hours into 16 January. Happy Anniversary. I got up
and stretched. I was hungry and I got out my sandwich and
the bottle of beer.

I was unwrapping my sandwich when I heard the sound of
the door from the fire emergency stairs opening into the
lobby and quick woman's footsteps. I reached for the switch
and the lobby was brightly lit. A young woman was hurrying,
almost running, toward the desk. She was unnaturally tall,
with those thick soles and exaggerated high heels which
made women look like so many displaced Watusis. She had
on a white, fake fur coat and a blonde wig that wouldn't fool
anybody. I recognized her. She was a whore who had come in
just after midnight with the man in 610. I glanced at my
watch. It was just after three o'clock. It had been a long
session in 610 and the woman looked it. She ran to the front

door, pushed futilely at the broken buzzer, then clattered over to the desk.

She knocked sharply on the glass over the desk. 'Open the door, mister,' she said loudly. 'I want to get out of here.'

I took the key from the drawer under the desk in which the pistol was kept and went through the little room next to the office where there was a huge old safe against the wall, lined with safety-deposit boxes. The safety-deposit boxes were relics of a richer day. None was in use now. I unlocked the door and stepped out into the lobby. The woman followed me across the lobby toward the front door. She was gasping for breath. Her profession didn't keep her in shape for running down six flights of steps in the middle of the night. She was somewhere around thirty years old, and by the look of her they hadn't been easy years. The women who came in and out of the hotel at night made a strong argument for celibacy.

'Why didn't you take the elevator down?' I asked.

'I was waiting for the elevator,' the woman said. 'But then this crazy, naked old man popped out of the door, making all kinds of funny noises, grunting, like an animal, and waving something at me....'

'Waving wh ... wh ... *what*?'

'Something. It looked like a club. A baseball bat. It's dark in that hall. You bastards certainly don't waste much money on lights in this hotel.' Her voice was whiskey-hoarse, set in city cement, praising nothing. 'I didn't wait around to see. I just took off. You want to find out, you go up to the sixth floor and see for yourself. Open the goddamn door, will you? I have to go home.'

I unlocked the big, plate-glass front door, reinforced by a heavy, cast-iron grill. For a shabby old hotel like the St Augustine, the management was nervously security-conscious. The woman pushed the door open impatiently and ran out into the dark street. I took a deep breath of the cold night air as the clatter of heels diminished in the direction of Lexington Avenue. I stood at the door another moment, looking down the street, on the chance that a prowl car might be cruising past. I would have felt better about going up to see what was happening on the sixth floor if I had a cop with me. I was not paid for solitary heroics. But the street was empty. I heard a siren in the distance, probably on Park Avenue, but that was no help. I closed the door and locked it and walked slowly back across the lobby toward the office, thinking, am I going to spend the rest of my life ushering whores to and from anonymous beds?

Praise him with stringed instruments and organs.

In the office I took the pass-key out of the drawer, looked for a moment at the pistol. I shook my head and shut the drawer. Having the pistol there wasn't my idea. It hadn't helped the other night man when the two junkies came in and walked off with all the cash in the place, leaving the night man lying in his blood on the floor with a bump the size of a cantaloupe on his head.

I put my jacket on, somehow feeling that being properly dressed would give me more authority in whatever situation I would find on the sixth floor, and went out into the lobby again, locking the office door behind me. I pushed the elevator button and heard the whine of the cables and the elevator started down the shaft.

When the door creaked open, I hesitated before going in. Maybe, I thought, I just ought to go back into the office, get my overcoat and my sandwich and my beer, and walk away from here. Who needs this lousy job? But just as the door began to slide shut, I went in.

When I reached the sixth floor, I pushed the button that kept the elevator door open, and stepped out into the corridor. Light was streaming from the doorway of the room diagonally across from the elevator, number 602. On the worn carpet of the corridor, half in and half out of the light, was a naked man, lying on his face, his head and torso in shadow, old man's wrinkled buttocks and skinny legs sharply, obscenely illuminated. The left arm was stretched out, the fingers of the hand curled, as though the man had been trying to grab at something as he fell. His right arm was under him. He lay absolutely still. Even as I bent to turn him over, I was sure that nothing I could do and nobody I could call would do any good.

The man was heavy, with a big loose paunch that belied the

24

thin legs and buttocks, and I grunted as I pulled the body over onto its back. Then I saw what the whore had said the man had been waving at her, that might have been a club. It wasn't a club, but a long cardboard tube tightly wrapped in brown paper, the kind artists and architects use to carry rolled-up prints and building plans. The man's hand was still clutching it. I didn't blame the whore for being frightened. In the dim light of the corridor, I'd have been frightened, too, if a naked man had suddenly sprung out waving the thing menacingly at me.

I stood up, feeling a chill on my skin, nerving myself to touch the body once more. I stared down at the dead face. The eyes were open, staring up at me, the mouth in a last tortured grimace. Grunting animal sounds, the whore had said. There was no blood, no sign of a wound. I had never seen the man before, but that was not unusual with my working hours, coming in after guests had checked in for the night and leaving before they came down in the morning. It was a round, fat, old man's face, with a big, fleshy nose and wispy gray hair on the balding skull. Even in the disarray of death, the face gave the impression of power and importance.

Fighting down a rising feeling of nausea, I knelt on one knee and put my ear to the man's chest. His breasts might have been those of an old woman, with just a few straggles of damp white hair and nipples that were almost green in the bare light. There was the sour, living odor of sweat, but no movement, no sound. Old man, I thought, as I stood up, why couldn't you have done this on somebody else's time?

I bent down again and hooked my hands under the dead man's armpits and dragged him through the open doorway into room 602. You couldn't just leave a naked body lying in the corridor like that. I had been working in the hotel business long enough to know that death was something you kept out of the sight of paying guests.

As I pulled the body along the floor of the little hallway that led into the room proper, the cardboard tube rolled to one side. I got the body into the room, next to the bed, which was a tangle of sheets and blankets. There was lipstick smeared all over the sheets and pillows. The lady I had let out around one o'clock, probably. I looked down with something like pity at the old body naked on the threadbare carpet, the flaccid dead flesh outlined against a faded floral pattern. One last erection. Joy and then mortality.

There was a medium-sized but expensive-looking leather suitcase open on the little desk. A worn wallet lay next to it and a gold money clip, with some bills in it. In the bag three clean shirts were to be seen, neatly folded.

Strewn on the desk were some quarters and dimes. I counted the money in the clip. Four tens and three ones. I dropped the clip back on the desk and picked up the wallet. There were ten, crisp, new, hundred-dollar bills in it. I whistled softly. Whatever else had happened that night to the old man, he had not been robbed. I put the ten bills back into the wallet and carefully placed it back on the desk. It never occurred to me to take any of the money. That was the sort of man I used to be. *Thou shalt not steal.* Thou shalt not do a lot of things.

I glanced at the open suitcase. Along with the shirts there were two pairs of old-fashioned button shorts, a striped necktie, two pairs of socks, some blue pajamas. Whoever he was, number 602 was going to stay in New York longer than he had planned.

The corpse on the floor oppressed me, made uncertain claims on me. I took one of the blankets from the bed and threw it over the body, covering the face, the staring eyes, the mutely shouting lips. I felt warmer, death now only a geometric shape on the floor.

I went back to the corridor to get the cardboard tube. There were no labels or addresses or identification of any kind on it. As I carried it into the room, I saw that the heavy brown paper had been torn raggedly away from the top. I was about to put it on the desk, next to the dead man's other belongings, when I caught a glimpse of green paper, partially pulled out of the opening. I drew it out. It was a hundred-dollar bill. It was not new like the bills in the wallet, but old and crumpled. I held the tube so that I could look down into it. As far as I could tell, it was crammed with bills. I remained immobile for a moment, then stuffed the bill I had taken out back in and folded the torn brown paper as neatly as I could over the top of the tube.

Holding the tube under my arm, I went to the door, switched off the light, stepped out into the corridor and turned the pass-key in the lock of room number 602. My actions were crisp, almost automatic, as though all my life I had rehearsed for this moment, as though there were no alternatives.

*

I took the elevator down to the lobby, went into the little windowless room next to the office, using the key. There was a shelf running along above the safe, piled with stationery, old bills, ragged magazines from other years that had been recuperated from the rooms. Pictures of extinct politicians, naked girls who by now were no longer worth photographing – the momentarily illustrious dead, the extremely desirable women, monocled assassins, movie stars, carefully posed authors – a jumble of recent and not-so-recent American miscellany. Without hesitation I reached up and rolled the tube back toward the wall. I heard it plop down onto the shelf, out of sight, behind the dog-eared testimony of scandals and delights.

Then I went into the lighted office and called for an ambulance.

After that I sat down, finished unwrapping my sandwich, opened the bottle of beer. While I ate and drank, I looked up the register. Number 602 was, or had been, named John Ferris, had booked in only the afternoon before, and had given a home address on North Michigan Avenue, Chicago, Illinois.

I was finishing my beer when the bell rang and I saw the two men and the ambulance outside. One of them was in a white coat and was carrying a rolled up stretcher. The other was dressed in a blue uniform and was carrying a black bag, but I knew he wasn't a doctor. They don't waste doctors on ambulances in Manhattan, but dress up an orderly who is something of a medical technician and good enough to give first aid and who can usually be depended upon not to kill a patient on the spot. As I was opening the door, a prowl car drove up and a policeman got out.

'What's wrong?' the policeman asked. He was a heavy-set, dark-jowled man, with unhealthy rings under his eyes.

'An old man croaked upstairs,' I said.

'I'll go along with them, Dave,' the policeman said to his partner at the wheel. I could hear the car radio chattering, dispatching officers to accidents, cases of wife beating, suicides, to streets where suspicious-looking men had been reported entering buildings.

Calmly, I led the group through the lobby. The technician was young and kept yawning as though he hadn't slept in weeks. People who work at night all look as though they are being punished for some nameless sin. The policeman's shoes on the bare floor of the lobby sounded as though they had lead soles. Going up in the elevator nobody spoke. I volunteered no information. A medicinal smell filled the elevator. They carry the hospital with them, I thought. I would have preferred it if the prowl car hadn't happened along.

When we got out on the sixth floor, I opened the door to 602 and led the way into the room. The technician ripped the blanket off the dead man, bent over him, and put his stethoscope to the man's chest. The policeman stood at the foot of the bed, his eyes taking in the lipstick-smeared sheets, the bag on the desk, the wallet and money clip lying next to it. 'Who're you, Jack?' he asked me.

'I'm the night clerk.'

'What's your name?' The way he asked was full of accusation, as though he was sure whatever name I gave would be a false one. What would he have done if I had answered, 'My name is Ozymandias, King of Kings'? Probably taken out his black book and written, 'Witness asserts name is Ozymandias. Probably an alias.' He was a real night-time cop, doomed to roam a dark city teeming with enemies, ambushes everywhere.

'My name is Grimes,' I said.

'Where's the lady who was here with him?'

'I have no idea. I let a lady out around one o'clock. It

might have been this one.' I was surprised that I wasn't stuttering.

The technician stood up, taking the stethoscope plugs out of his ears. 'DOA,' he said flatly.

Dead on arrival. I could have told that without calling for an ambulance. I was discovering that there is a lot of waste motion about death in a big city.

'What was it?' the cop asked. 'Any wounds?'

'No. Coronary, probably.'

'Anything to be done?'

'Not really,' the technician said. 'Go through the motions.' He bent down again, rolled back the dead man's eyelids and peered into the rheumy eyes. Then he felt around the throat for a pulse, his hands gentle and expert.

'You seem to know what you're doing, friend,' I said. 'You must get a lot of practice.'

'I'm in my second year in medical school,' he said. 'I only do this to eat.'

The policeman went over to the desk and picked up the money clip. 'Forty-three bucks,' he said. 'And in the wallet—' His thick eyebrows went up as he inspected it. He took out the bills and riffled them, counting. 'An even grand,' he said.

'Holy man!' I said. It was a good try, but from the way the cop looked at me, I wasn't fooling him.

'How much was there in it when you found him?' he asked. He was not a friendly neighborhood cop. Maybe he was a different man when he was on the day shift.

'I haven't the faintest idea,' I said. Not stuttering was a triumph.

'You mean to say you didn't look?'

'I didn't look.'

'Yeah. Why?'

'Why what?' This was a good time to look boyish.

'Why didn't you look?'

'It didn't occur to me.'

'Yeah,' the cop said again, but let it go at that. He riffled the bills again. 'All in hundreds. You'd think a guy with that much dough on him would pick a better place to knock it off than a creep joint like this.' He put the bills back into the wallet. 'I guess I better take this into the station,' he said. 'Anybody want to count?'

'We trust you, Officer,' the technician said. There was the faintest echo of irony in his voice. He was young, but already an expert at death and despoliation.

The policeman looked through the wallet compartments. He had thick hairy fingers, like small clubs. 'That's funny,' he said.

'What's funny?' the technician asked.

'There's no credit cards or business cards or driver's licence. A man with more than a thousand bucks in cash on him.' He shook his head and pushed his cap back. 'You wouldn't call that normal, would you?' He looked aggrieved, as though the dead man had not behaved the way a decent American citizen who expected to be protected in death as in life by his country's police should have behaved. 'You know who he is?' he asked me.

'I never saw him before,' I said. 'His name is Ferris and he lived in Chicago. I'll show you the register.'

The policeman put the wallet into his pocket, went quickly through the shirts and underwear and socks in the bag, then opened the closet door and searched the pockets of the single dark suit and overcoat that were hanging there. 'Nothing,' he said. 'No letters, no address book. Nothing. A guy with a bad heart. Some people got no more sense than a horse. Look, I got to make a inventory. In the presence of witnesses.' He took out his pad and moved around the room, listing the few possessions, now no longer possessed, of the body on the floor. It didn't take long. 'Here,' he said to me, 'you have to sign this.' I glanced at the list. One hundred and forty-three dollars. One suitcase, brown, unlocked, one suit and overcoat, gray, one hat . . .' I signed, under the patrolman's name. The cop put his thick black pad into a back pocket. 'Who put the blanket over him?' he asked.

'I did,' I said.

'You find him there on the floor?'

'No. He was out in the corridor.'

'Starkers – like that?'

'Starkers. I dragged him in.'

'What did you want to do that for?' The policeman sounded plaintive now, faced with a complication.

'This is a hotel,' I said. 'You have to keep up appearances.'

The policeman glowered at me. 'What are you – trying to be smart?' he said.

'No, Officer, I'm not trying to be smart. If I'd left him out where I found him and somebody had come along and seen him, I'd have had my ass chewed down to the bone by the manager.'

'Next time you see a body laying anyplace,' the policeman said, 'you just let it lay until the law arrives. Just remember that, see?'

'Yes, sir,' I said.

'You alone in this hotel all night?'

'Yes.'

'You work in the office all by yourself?'

'Yes.'

'How'd you happen to come up here? He telephone down or something?'

'No. A lady was leaving the building and she said there was a crazy old naked man up on the sixth floor who was making advances toward her.' Objectively, almost as though I were listening to myself on a tape, I noted that I hadn't stuttered once.

'Sexual advances?'

'She implied that.'

'A lady? What sort of lady?'

'I would think she was a whore,' I said.

'You ever see her before?'

'No.'

'You get a lot of lady traffic in this hotel, don't you?'

'Average, I would say.'

The policeman stared down at the contorted bluish face on the floor. 'How long you think he's been dead, Bud?'

'Hard to tell. Anywhere from ten minutes to a half hour,' the technician said. He looked up at me. 'Did you call the hospital as soon as you saw him? The call came in at three-fifteen.'

'Well,' I said, 'first I listened to see if I could get a heartbeat, then I pulled him in here and covered him and then I had to go down to the office and phone.'

'Did you try mouth-to-mouth resuscitation?'

'No.'

'Why not?' The technician wasn't being inquisitive; it was too late at night and he was too tired for that; he was just going through a routine.

'It didn't occur to me,' I said.

'A lot of things didn't occur to you, mister,' the policeman said darkly. Like the technician he was going through a routine. Suspicion was his routine. But his heart wasn't in it and he sounded bored already.

'Okay,' the technician said, 'let's take him away. No sense wasting any time. When you find out what the family wants to do with the body,' he said, addressing me, 'call the morgue.'

'I'll send a telegram to Chicago right away,' I said.

The two ambulance men lifted the body onto the stretcher. 'He's a heavy old sonofabitch, isn't he?' the driver said, as he let the cadaver down. 'I bet he ate good, the old goat. Sexual advances. With a droopy old cock like that.' He draped a sheet over the body and strapped the ankles to the foot of the stretcher while the technician buckled a strap across the chest. The elevator was too small to handle the body lying flat and they would have to stand the stretcher up to fit it in. They took the stretcher out into the hall, followed by the policeman. I took a last look around the room and put out the light before closing the door.

'Had a busy night?' I asked the technician pleasantly, as the elevator started down. Be matter-of-fact, normal, I told myself. Obviously it was perfectly normal for all three of these men to carry dead men out of hotels in the middle of the night, and I tried to fit into their standards of behavior.

'This is my fourth call since I came on,' he said. 'I'll trade jobs with you.'

'Yeah,' I said. 'I'll still be sitting here all night working an adding machine while you're raking in the loot year after year.' Now, I thought, why did I use the word loot? 'I read the papers,' I said quickly; 'doctors make more than anybody else in the country.'

'God bless America,' the technician said as the elevator came to a stop and the door opened. He and the driver picked up the stretcher and I led the way across the lobby. I opened the door for them with my key and watched as they put the body into the ambulance. The policeman at the wheel of the car was asleep, snoring softly, his cap off and his head lolling back.

The technician got into the ambulance with the corpse, and the driver slammed the door shut. He went around to the front and started the motor, revving it loudly. He had the siren going while he was still in first gear.

'What the hell is his hurry?' said the policeman standing on the sidewalk with me. 'They're not going anywhere.'

'Aren't you going to wake your pal up?' I asked.

'Nah. He wakes up if a call comes for us. He's got the instinct of a animal. Might as well let him get his beauty rest. I wish I had his nerves.' He sighed, weighed down by cares which his own nerves were not strong enough to support. 'Let's get a look at the register, mister.' He followed me back into the hotel, his tread heavy, the law weighty.

I unlocked the office door. I didn't look up at the shelf over the safe, where the cardboard tube lay hidden behind the boxes of stationery and the piles of old magazines. 'I have a bottle of bourbon in here, if you'd like a slug,' I said, as we went into the front office. Even as I spoke I admired the absolutely matter-of-fact way in which I was behaving. I was running on computers; all the cards were correctly punched. Data input. But it had been an effort not to look up at the shelf.

'Well, I'm on duty, you know,' the policeman said. 'But one small slug...'

I opened the register and pointed out the entry for room 602. The policeman slowly copied it out into his black book. The history of the city of New York, faithfully recorded in twenty thousand handwritten pages by the graduates of the police academy. An interesting archaeological discovery.

I got out the bottle and uncorked it. 'Sorry, I don't have a glass,' I said.

'I drunk out of bottles before this,' the policeman said. He raised the bottle. 'Well, *L'chaim*,' he said, and took a long swig.

'You Jewish?' I asked as the policeman gave me the bottle.

'Nah. My partner. I caught it from him.'

L'chaim. To life, I remembered from the song in *Fiddler on the Roof*. 'I think I'll join you,' I said, raising the bottle. 'I can use it. A night like this can leave a man a little shaky.'

'This is nothing,' the cop said. 'You oughta see some of the things we run into.'

'I can imagine,' I said. I drank.

'Well,' the policeman said, 'I gotta be going. There'll be an inspector around in the morning. Just keep that room locked until he gets here, understand?'

'I'll pass the word on to the day man.'

'Night work,' the policeman said. 'Do you sleep good during the day?'

'Fair.'

'Not me.' The policeman shook his head mournfully. 'Look at the rings under my eyes.'

I looked at the rings under the policeman's eyes. 'You could use a good night's sleep,' I said.

'You ain't kidding.' The man dug a knuckle into his eyes, viciously. *If the eye offend thee* ... 'Well, at least there ain't been no crime committed. Be thankful for small mercies,' he said surprisingly. Unsuspected depths, a vocabulary that included the word mercy.

I accompanied him to the front door, opened it politely.

'Have a good day,' the policeman said.

'Thanks. You too.'

'Hah,' he said.

I watched the heavy, slow-moving man climb into the prowl car and wake up his partner. The car went slowly down the silent street. I locked the door and went back to the office. I picked up the telephone and dialed. I had to wait for at least ten rings before the connection came through. This country is in full decay, I thought, waiting. Nobody moves.

'Western Union,' the voice said.

'I want to send a telegram to Chicago,' I said. I gave the

name and address, spelling out Ferris slowly and clearly.
'Like wheel,' I said.

'What's that?' The voice of Western Union was irritated.

'Ferris wheel,' I said. 'Amusement parks.'

'What is the message, please?'

'Regret to inform you that John Ferris, of your address,' I
said, 'died this morning at three-fifteen am. Please get in
touch with me immediately for instructions. Signed, H. M.
Drusack, Manager, Hotel St Augustine, Manhattan.' By the
time the reply came in, Drusack would be on duty and I
would be somewhere else, safely out of the way. There was
no need for the family in Chicago to know my name. 'Charges, please.'

The operator gave me the charges. I noted them on a sheet
of paper. Good old Drusack would put them on Ferris' bill. I
knew Drusack.

I took another slug of bourbon, then settled down in the
swivel chair and picked up the Bible. I figured I could get well
into Proverbs before the day man came on to relieve me.

4

I took a taxi home after telling the day man what had happened, or most of what had happened. I left the envelope for
my bookie friend, as usual, with the note inside telling him I
was betting five dollars on *Ask Gloria* at Hialeah in the
second. For as long as possible it was wise to make it seem
that today was just like every other day.

Even in the East Eighties, where I lived, muggings, at all
hours, were not infrequent. The taxi was a luxury, but this
was no day to be mugged. I had gotten the tube down from
the shelf when the day man was busy in the front office.
There had been no one in the lobby when I went out, and,
even if there had been, there was nothing remarkable about a

man carrying a cardboard tube wrapped in brown paper in broad daylight.

My head was clear and I wasn't in the least bit sleepy. Ordinarily, when the weather was good I would walk the thirty-odd blocks to my apartment, stopping for breakfast at a coffee shop on Second Avenue, before getting into bed and sleeping until two o'clock in the afternoon. But today I knew I couldn't sleep, no need of sleep.

When I opened the door of the one-room apartment, its windows gray in the cold north light, I went to the refrigerator in the kitchenette and took out and opened a bottle of beer. I didn't bother to take off my overcoat. Then, occasionally taking a sip of beer, I tore the paper from the cardboard tube. Using a knife, I managed to slit the tube down one side. It was stuffed from top to bottom with one-hundred-dollar bills.

I took the bills out one by one, smoothed them, and arranged them in piles of ten on the kitchen table. When I finished, there were a hundred piles. One hundred thousand dollars. They covered the table.

I stared silently at the bills spread out on the table. I finished the beer. I wasn't concious of feeling any emotion, not fear, or exhilaration, or regret. I looked at my watch. It was just eight-forty. The banks wouldn't open for another twenty minutes.

I got a small bag from the closet and stacked the money in it. There was no one else who had a key to the apartment, but there was no sense in taking any chances. Carrying the bag, I went downstairs and walked to the avenue. There was a stationery store on the next block and I bought a packet of rubber bands and three thick manila envelopes, the largest in the shop.

Then I went back to the apartment, locked the door, took off my overcoat and jacket, and methodically slipped the rubber bands around each batch of bills before putting it into one of the manila envelopes. I kept one thousand dollars, which I put in my wallet, for immediate use.

I sealed the envelopes, grimacing at the taste of the glue as

I licked the flaps. Then I took another bottle of beer from the refrigerator, poured the beer into a glass, and sipped at it, sitting in front of the table, in front of the neat pile of thick brown envelopes.

I had taken the apartment furnished and only the books in the room were mine. And there weren't many of those. When I finished a book, I usually threw it away. There was never enough heat and when I sat in the one frayed easy chair to read, I usually wore the padded ski-jacket that hung on a hook on the back of the front door. This morning, while it was as cold as usual, and even though I was now in my shirt-sleeves, I felt perfectly comfortable.

I knew that I was going to have to move out. And quit the job. And get out of the city. I had no plan beyond that, but I knew that one day or another somebody was going to appear, looking for one hundred thousand dollars.

*

At the bank I had to write out two specimen signatures on separate cards. My hand was absolutely steady. The sealed manila envelopes with the money in lay on the desk at which I was sitting, facing the young assistant manager who was serving me. He had the bland, sexless face of a seminarian. The conversation between us was short and businesslike. I'd shaved and was neatly dressed. I still had a couple of decent suits left over from the old days, and today I had put on a sober, quiet, gray Glen plaid with a blue Oxford shirt and solid blue tie. I wanted to give the impression of being a solid citizen, perhaps not wealthy, certainly not wealthy, but modestly prosperous, a careful, industrious man who might have some bonds and some legal papers that were too valuable to leave lying around the house.

'Your address, please, Mr Grimes,' the assistant manager was saying.

I gave him the address of the St Augustine. If anybody got as far as the bank in the search for me, which was unlikely in any case, there would be no useful information to be found.

'Will you be the sole person authorized to have access to the safety-deposit box?'

That's for sure, brother, I thought. But all I said was, 'Yes.'

'That will be twenty-three dollars for the year. Do you wish to pay by cash or by check?'

'Cash.' I gave him a hundred-dollar bill. His expression did not change. Obviously, he thought that I looked like a man who might normally carry a hundred-dollar bill loose in his pocket. I took this as a good sign. The assistant manager smoothed the bill carefully, with a churchly gesture, went over to a teller's window to break the bill down into smaller denominations.

I sat relaxedly at the desk, touching one of the manila envelopes with the tips of my fingers. I hadn't stuttered once all morning.

The assistant manager came back and handed me my change and made out a receipt. I folded it neatly and put it into my wallet. Then I followed the man down to the vault. There was a hygienical, almost religious hush there that made you hesitate to speak above a whisper. Stained-glass windows would not have been out of place. The parable of the talents. The vault attendant gave me a key and led me down a silent aisle of money.

With the three thick manila envelopes under my arm, I couldn't help wondering how all the treasure lying in those locked boxes, the greenbacks, the stocks and bonds, the jewelry, had been accumulated, what sweat expended, what crimes enacted, through whose hands all those stones and all that luxuriously printed paper had passed before coming to rest in this sanctified cold steel cave. I looked at the attendant's face as he used the two keys, his and mine, and pulled out a box for me. He was an old man, pale from his underground existence. He didn't look as though he had ever speculated about anything. Perhaps such people were chosen for their lack of curiosity. A curious man would go mad here. I followed the attendant back to a little curtained cubbyhole with a desk in it, and the attendant left me there with my box, respecting the privacy of wealth.

I tore open the manila envelopes and laid the piles of bills in the box. I looked at the neatly stacked notes, trying without success to foresee what they finally would mean for me.

It was like looking at a huge engine, quiet now, but capable of sudden, brutal force. I closed the box with a decisive little click. I tossed the envelopes into a wastepaper bucket and went back along the row of safes with the attendant and watched him slide the box into my own slot. The attendant used both keys once more to lock the safe. I dropped my key into my pocket, said 'Thank you,' to the man. 'Have a good day,' courteous as any policeman.

'Hah,' the man said. He hadn't had a good day since he was twelve.

I went up the steps and out onto the sunny, cold avenue. Okay for today, I thought. Chemical Bank and Trust, with all my worldly goods I thee endow.

I walked home briskly and packed. Beside the small bag I had carried the money in, I had a flight bag and everything I owned fitted in, with room to spare. I left the old parka hanging in the closet. Whoever moved in next would need it more than I. Then I wrote a note to the landlord saying that I was giving up the apartment. I had no lease and was on a month-to-month arrangement, so there wouldn't be any difficulties there. I folded the note and stuck it in an envelope and dropped the key in with the note. Downstairs I put the envelope in the landlord's mailbox. Carrying the two bags, I left the building without looking back. I wouldn't ever again have to worry about keeping warm at that particular address.

I hailed a cab and gave the driver the name of a hotel on Central Park West. It was a neighborhood I had never lived in and had only rarely visited. Even with my night-time job and my reclusive habits, in my old neighborhood on the East Side there were bound to be people who had come to recognize me, my bookie, the bartender in the saloon around the corner I sometimes drank in, a waitress in a nearby Italian restaurant, others, who could point me out to someone who might come around making inquiries about me. Eventually, I knew, I would put a great deal more distance behind me, but for the time being crossing Central Park would have to do. But I didn't want to flee blindly. I knew that I needed at least one day to think and plan.

The hotel was a busy one, but middle-class and commercial, and not the sort of place a man who had entered into sudden wealth would choose to celebrate in.

I asked for a single room with bath, registered under the name of Theodore Brown, gave as my home address Camden, New Jersey, a city I had never visited, and followed the bellboy with the bags into the elevator. On the way up, I studied the man's sullen, narrow face. He was young, but there was no trace of innocence in the guarded eyes, the tightly closed lips. It was a face designed specifically by nature for corruption. What wonders a man with a face like that could perform with a hundred thousand dollars.

In the room, which overlooked the park, the bellboy put the big bag in a chair, turned on the light in the bathroom, ostentatiously earning his tip.

'I wonder if you could do me a favor,' I said, taking out a five-dollar bill.

The bellboy eyed the bill. 'Depends on what the favor is,' the bellboy said. 'The management don't like whores coming in and out.'

'Nothing like that,' I said. 'I'd just like to make a bet on a horse and I'm new in town and...' I had entered a new life, but I was taking some baggage along with me. *Ask Gloria* cantered out of the stables of my past.

The bellboy showed his teeth in what he imagined was an accommodating smile. 'We have a house bookie,' he said. 'I can have him up here in fifteen minutes.'

'Thanks.' I gave him the five-dollar bill.

'Very good of you, sir,' the bellboy said. The bill disappeared. 'Do you mind telling me what you're going to play?'

'*Ask Gloria* in the second,' I said. 'At Hialeah.'

'It's a fifteen-to-one shot,' he said. He was a student of the sport.

'So it is,' I said.

'Interesting,' he said. There was no doubt about what he was going to do with my five dollars. Dishonest as he was, he would live and die a poor man.

When he left the room, I loosened my tie and lay down on the bed, although I still wasn't tired. Try money, I thought grinning, for that run-down feeling, that midmorning sag.

More and more, thinking these days is in the form of a television commercial.

The house bookie appeared promptly. He was a huge fat man in a rumpled suit, with three ball-point pens slipped into the breast pocket of his jacket. He panted when he moved and spoke in a high, almost soprano voice, surprising coming out of all that bulk. 'Hi, pal,' he said as he came into the room. He looked around the room swiftly, taking everything in. He was a man prepared for ambush. Although he performed in daylight, he lived in the same world as the cop in the prowl car. 'Morris said you were looking for a little action.'

'A little,' I said. 'I like *Ask Gloria*...' I hesitated for a moment. 'For three hundred to win in the second at Hialeah. The morning line has her at fifteen to one.' I had a peculiar feeling of lightheartedness, as though I were in an open plane, without oxygen, and had suddenly climbed from the deck to twenty thousand feet.

The fat man took a creased sheet of paper from his pocket, unfolded it, ran a finger down it. 'I can give you twelve to one,' he said.

'Okay,' I said. I gave him three bills.

The bookie took the bills, examined them closely, glanced briefly at me. I detected respect, a certain delicate wariness.

'My name is...' I started to say.

'I know your name, Mr Brown. Morris told me,' the bookie said. He made a note with one of the pens on the sheet of paper. 'I pay off at six o'clock in the bar downstairs.'

'See you at six,' I said.

'You hope,' the fat man said, without smiling. He placed the notes that I had given him on the outside of a roll of bills, snapped a rubber band deftly around it. He had small, fat, nimble hands. 'Morris always knows where to find me, Mr Brown,' he said as he went out.

After that, I unpacked and started to put my clothes away. As I was taking my toothbrush and shaving things out of the kit, my razor fell to the floor and skidded beneath the chest of drawers. I knelt to retrieve it, running my hand under the chest. Along with the razor and a small pile of dust, I brought out a coin. It was a silver dollar. I blew the dust off the coin and put it in my pocket. They don't clean very thoroughly in this hotel, I thought. Good for them. Today, I was definitely ahead of the game.

I looked at my watch. It was almost noon. I picked up the telephone and gave the number of the St Augustine to the operator. As usual, it was nearly thirty seconds before there was an answer. Clara, the operator, regarded all calls as wanton interruptions in her private life, which consisted, as far as I could ever tell, of reading magazines on astrology. She used delay as a means of protest and punishment for electronic interrupters of her search for the perfect horoscope, wealth, fame, a young and handsome dark stranger.

'Hello, Clara,' I said. 'Is Mr Drusack there?'

'He sure is,' Clara said. 'He's been on my neck all morning to call you. What the hell is your number anyway? I couldn't find it anywhere. I called the hotel we have here as your address and they say they never heard of you.'

'That was two years ago. I moved.' Actually, I had moved four times since then. A typical American, I had continually pushed toward new frontiers, always farther north. The wealth of the Yukon, by way of the East Eighties, Harlem, Riverdale, the frozen tundra. 'I don't have a number, Clara.'

'What do you mean, you don't have a number?'

'I don't have a telephone.'

'You're a lucky man, Mr Grimes.'

'You can say that again, Clara. Now give me Mr Drusack.'

'My God, Grimes,' Drusack said when he got on the phone, 'you sure left me a mess. You better get right on down here and help me straighten it out.'

'I'm very sorry, Mr Drusack,' I said. I tried to sound genuinely grieved. 'I'm busy today. What's the matter?'

'What's the matter?' Drusack was shouting now. 'I'll tell you what's the matter. The goddamn Western Union called at ten o'clock. There's no John Ferris at that address you gave them, that's what's the matter.'

'That's the address he registered under.'

'You come and tell that to the police. They were in here for an hour this morning. And there were two characters in here asking for him, and if they weren't packing guns I'm Miss Rheingold of 1983. They talked to me as if I was hiding the sonofabitch or something. They asked me if the guy left a message for them. *Did* he leave a message?'

'Not that I know of.'

'Well, they want to talk to you.'

'Why me?' I asked, although I knew why.

'I told them the night man found the guy. I told them you'd be in at eleven pm, but they said they couldn't wait that long, what was your address. Grimes, do you know that nobody in this goddamn hotel knows where you live? Naturally, those two fuckers wouldn't believe *that*. They said they're coming back here at three o'clock and I'd better damn well produce you. Scary. They weren't any small-time hoods. Short hair, dressed like stockbrokers. Quiet. Like spies in the movies. They weren't kidding. Not at all kidding. So you be here. Because I'm going to be out on a long, long lunch.'

'That's what I wanted to talk to you about, Mr Drusack,' I said smoothly, enjoying a conversation with the manager for the first time since I started working for him. 'I called to say good-bye.'

'What do you mean, good-bye?' Drusack was really shouting now. 'Good-bye, good-bye, who says good-bye like that?'

'I do, Mr Drusack. I decided last night I don't like the way you run your hotel. I'm quitting. . . . I *have* quit.'

'Quit! Nobody quits like that. For Christ's sake, it's only Tuesday. You got things here. You got a half bottle of bourbon, you got your goddamn Bible, you . . .'

'I'm donating it to the hotel library,' I said.

'Grimes,' Drusack roared. 'You can't do this to me. I'll have the police bring you in. I'll . . .'

I put the telephone gently down on its cradle. Then I went out to lunch. I went to a good sea-food restaurant near Lincoln Center and had a large grilled lobster that cost eight dollars, with two bottles of Heineken.

As I sat there in the warm restaurant, eating the good food and drinking the imported beer, I realized that it was the first moment since the whore had come running down from the sixth floor of the hotel that I had time to think about what I was doing. Everything up to now had been almost mechanical, act following act unhesitatingly, my movements ordered and precise, as though I had been following a program learned, assimilated, long ago. Now I had to make decisions, consider possibilities, scan the horizon for danger. Even as I was thinking this, I saw that something in my subconscious had made me choose a table where I could sit with my back against the wall, with a clear view of the entrance to the restaurant and of everybody who came in. I was amused by the realization. Given half a chance, every man becomes the hero of his own detective story.

Amusement or not, the hour had come to take stock, think about my position. I could no longer depend on simple reflexes or on anything in my past to guide me for the future. I had always been completely law-abiding. I had never done anything to make enemies. Certainly not enemies like the two men who had frightened Drusack that morning. Naturally, I thought, men who came to a hotel where they expected to receive a hundred thousand dollars in cash from someone who was registered most probably under a false name and certainly with a false address might very likely be carrying guns or at least *look* like men who were in the habit of carrying guns. Drusack might have been a little hysterical that morning, but he was no fool and he had been in the hotel business a long time and had a feeling about who meant trouble when he arrived at the front desk and who didn't. Drusack couldn't possibly know just what trouble the two men represented and in all probability would never know.

One thing was sure, or almost sure – the police wouldn't be brought in, although an individual crooked policeman here or there might be in on it. So I wouldn't have that to worry about. There was no possibility that the man who had registered under the name of John Ferris and the two men who had come to meet him at the hotel were engaged in a legal business transaction. It had to be bribery of some sort, a payoff, blackmail. This was when the scandals of the second Nixon administration were just beginning to surface, when we all discovered that perfectly respectable people, pillars of the community, had developed the habit of secretly carrying huge sums of money around in attaché cases and stuffing hundreds of thousands of dollars in office desks, so it didn't occur to me, as it could have later, that I might have stumbled on an amateurish and comparatively undangerous political technique. What I had to deal with, I was sure, was grim professionalism, men who killed for money. Like spies in the movies, Drusack had said. I discounted that. I had seen the body.

Gangsters, I thought. The Mob. Despite the occasional movies and magazine pieces about the underworld I had seen and read, like most people, I had only the vaguest notion of what was meant by the Mob and a perhaps exaggerated respect for its omnipotence, its system of intelligence, its power to seek out and destroy, the lengths it was likely to go to exact vengeance.

One thing I was sure of. I was on its side of the fence now, whoever it might turn out to be, and I was playing by its rules. In one moment in the tag end of a cold winter night, I had become an outlaw who could look only to himself for safety.

Rule one was simple. I could not sit still. I would have to keep moving, disappear. New York was a big city and there were undoubtedly thousands of people hiding out in it successfully for years, but the men who even now were probably on my trail would have my name, my age, a description of my appearance, could, without too much trouble and with a minimum of cunning, discover where I had gone to college, where I had worked before, what my family connections were. Lucky me, I thought, I am not married, there are no children, neither my brothers nor my sister have the faintest notion of where I am. Still, in New York, there was always the chance of running into someone I knew, who would somehow be overheard saying the wrong thing to the wrong man.

And just this very morning there was the bellboy. I had made my first mistake there. He would remember me. And from the look of him, he would sell his sister for a twenty-dollar bill. And the bookie in the hotel. Mistake number two. I could easily imagine what sort of connections *he* had.

I didn't know what I was eventually going to do with the money now lying in the hush of the vault, but I certainly intended to enjoy it. And I wouldn't enjoy it in New York. I had always wanted to travel, and now traveling would be both a pleasure and a necessity.

Luxuriously, I lit a cigar and leaned back in my chair and thought of all the places I would like to see. Europe. The words London, Paris, Rome rang pleasantly in my mind.

But before I could cross the ocean I had things to do, people to see, closer to home. First I would have to get a passport. I had never needed one before, but I was going to need one now. I knew I could get it at the State Department office in New York, but whoever might be looking for me could very well figure out that that would be the first place I would go to and could be there waiting for me. It was an outside chance but I was in no mood to take even that much of a chance.

Tomorrow, I decided, I would go to Washington. By bus.

I looked at my watch. It was nearly three o'clock. The two men who had confronted Drusack that morning would be approaching the St Augustine, eager to ask questions and no doubt with the means to compel answers. I flicked the ashes off the end of my cigar and smiled gently. Why, this is the best day I've had in years, I thought.

*

I paid my bill and left the restaurant, found a small photographer's shop and sat for passport photos. The photographer told me that they would be ready at five-thirty, and I spent the time watching a French movie. I might as well start getting used to the sound of the language, I thought, as I settled comfortably in my seat, admiring the views of the bridges across the Seine.

When I got back to my hotel with the photographs in my pocket (I looked boyish), it was nearly six o'clock. I remembered the bookie and went into the bar to look for him. The bookie was in a corner, alone, sitting at a table, drinking a glass of milk.

'How'd I do?' I asked.

'Are you kidding?' the bookie said.

'No. Honest.'

'You won,' the bookie said. The silver dollar had been a reliable omen. Speak again, Oracle. My debt to my man at the Hotel St Augustine was reduced by sixty dollars. All-in-all a useful afternoon's work.

The bookie did not look happy. 'You came in by a length and a half. Next time tell me where you get your information from. And that little shit, Morris. You had to let him in on it. That's what I call adding insult to injury.'

'I'm a friend of the working man,' I said.

'Working man,' the bookie snorted. 'Let me give you a piece of advice, brother, about that particular working man. Don't leave your wallet where he can spot it. Or even your false teeth.' He took a few envelopes out of his pocket, shuffled through them, gave me one and put the rest back in his pocket. 'Thirty-six hundred bucks,' the bookie said. 'Count it.'

I put the envelope away. 'No need,' I said. 'You look like an honest man.'

'Yeah.' The bookie sipped at his milk.

'Can I buy you a drink?'

'I can only stand so much milk,' the bookie said. He belched.

'You're in the wrong business for a man with a bad stomach,' I said.

'You can say that again. You want to bet on the hockey game tonight?'

'I don't think so,' I said. 'I'm not really a gambling man. So long, pal.'

The bookie didn't say anything.

I went over to the bar and had a Scotch and soda, then went out into the lobby. Morris, the bellboy, was standing near the front desk. 'I hear you hit it big,' he said.

'Not so big,' I said airily. 'Still, it wasn't a bad day's work. Did you take my tip?'

'No,' the bellboy said. He was a man who lied for the sheer pleasure of lying. 'I was too busy on the floors.'

'That's too bad,' I said. 'Better luck next time.'

I had a steak for dinner in the hotel dining room, and

another cigar with the coffee and brandy and then went up to my room, undressed, and got into bed. I slept without dreaming for twelve hours and woke up with the sun streaming into the room. I hadn't slept that well since I was a small boy.

5

In the morning I packed my bags and carried them myself to the elevator. I didn't want to have any more conversations with Morris, the bellboy. I checked out, paying with some of the money I had won on the second race at Hialeah. Under the hotel canopy I looked around carefully. There was nobody as far as I could see who was waiting for me or who might follow me. I got into a cab and drove to the bus terminal where I could board a bus to Washington. Nobody would dream of looking in a bus terminal for a man who had just stolen a hundred thousand dollars.

I tried the Hotel Mayflower first. As long as I was in Washington I thought I might as well take the best of what the city had to offer. But the hotel was full, the man at the desk told me. He gave me the impression that in this center of power one had to be *elected* to a room by a large constituency, or at least appointed by the President. I resolved to buy a new overcoat. Still, he was polite enough to suggest a hotel about a mile away. It usually had rooms, he said. He said it the way he might have said of an acquaintance that he usually wore soiled shirts.

He turned out to be right. The building was new, all chrome and bright paint and looked like a motel on any highway in America, but there were vacancies. I registered under my own name. In this city, I felt, I didn't have to go to extreme lengths to remain anonymous.

Remembering what I had heard about crime in the streets of the capital, I prudently put my wallet in the hotel's vault, keeping out only a hundred dollars for the day's expenses.

Avoid the chambers of the mighty. Danger lurks at their doorsteps. The Saturday night pistol lays down the final law.

The last time I had been in Washington had been when I'd flown a charter of Republicans down from Vermont for the inaugural of Richard Nixon in 1969. There had been a lot of drinking among the Republicans on the plane, and I had spent a good part of the flight arguing with a drunken Vermont State Senator who had been a B-17 pilot during World War II and who wanted to be allowed to fly the plane after we crossed Philadelphia. I hadn't gone to the Inaugural or to the ball for which the Republicans had found me a ticket. At that time I considered myself a Democrat. I didn't know what I considered myself now.

I had spent the day of Inaugural at Arlington. It seemed a fitting way to celebrate the installation of Richard Nixon as President of the United States.

There was a Grimes buried in the cemetery, an uncle who had died in 1921 from the effects of a dose of chlorine gas in the Argonne Forest. Myself, I would never be buried in Arlington. I was a veteran of no wars. I had been too young for Korea and by the time Vietnam came around I was set in the job with the airline. I had not been tempted to volunteer. Walking among the graves, I experienced no regret that I finally would not be laid to rest in this company of heroes. I had never been pugnacious – even as a boy I had only one fistfight at school – and, although I was patriotic enough and saluted the flag gladly, wars had no attraction for me. My patriotism did not run in the direction of bloodshed.

When I went out of the hotel the next morning, I saw there was a long line of people waiting for taxis, so I started to walk, hoping to pick up a taxi along the avenue. It was a mild day, pleasant after the biting cold of New York, and the street I was on gave off an air of grave prosperity, the passersby well-dressed and orderly. For half a block I walked side by side with a dignified, portly gentleman wearing a coat with a mink collar who looked as though he could be a Senator. I amused myself by imagining what the man's reaction would be if I went up to him, fixed him, like the Ancient Mariner, who stoppeth one of three, and told him what I had been doing since early Tuesday morning.

I stopped at a traffic light and hailed a cab which was slowing to a stop there. It was only after the cab had come to a halt that I saw that there was a passenger in the back, a woman. But the cabby, a black man with gray hair, leaned over and turned down the window. 'Which way you going, Mister?' he asked.

'State.'

'Get in,' the cabby said. 'The lady is on the way.'

I opened the back door. 'Do you mind if I get in with you, ma'am?' I asked.

'I certainly do,' the woman said. She was quite young, no more than thirty, and rather pretty, in a blonde, sharp way, less pretty at the moment than she might ordinarily have been, because of the tight, angry set of her lips.

'I'm sorry,' I said apologetically and closed the door. I was about to step back on the curb, when the cabby opened the front door. 'Get in, suh,' the cabby said.

Serves the bitch right, I thought, and, without looking at the woman, got in beside the driver. There was a bitter rustle from the back seat, but neither the cabby nor I turned around. We drove in silence.

When the cab stopped in front of a pillared government building, the woman leaned forward. 'One dollar and forty-five cents?' she said.

'Yes ma'am,' the cabby said.

The woman yanked open her purse, took out a dollar bill and some change, and put it down on the back seat. 'Don't expect to find a tip,' she said as she got out. She walked towards the big front doors, her back furious. She had nice legs, I noted.

The cabby chuckled as he reached back and scooped up his fare. 'Civil servant,' he said.

'Spelled c-u-n-t,' I said.

The cabby chuckled again. 'Oh, in this town you learn to take the fat with the lean,' he said.

As he drove, he shook his head, chuckling to himself, over and over again.

At State, I gave the man a dollar tip. 'I tell you, suh,' the cabby said, 'that little blonde lady done made my day.'

I went into the lobby of the building and up to the information desk.

'I'd like to see Mr Jeremy Hale, please,' I said to the girl at the desk.

'Do you know what room he's in?'

'I'm afraid not.'

The girl sighed. Washington, I saw, was full of tight-assed women. While the girl thumbed through a thick alphabetical list for Jeremy Hale, I remembered how I had once said to Hale, long ago, 'With a name like that, Jerry, you *had* to wind up in the State Department.' I smiled at the memory.

'Is Mr Hale expecting you?'

'No.' I hadn't spoken to Hale or written him in years. Hale certainly wasn't expecting me. We had been in the same class at Ohio State and had been good friends. After I took the job in Vermont we had skied together several winters, when Hale wasn't on a post overseas.

'Your name, please?' the girl was saying.

I gave her my name and she dialed a number on the desk telephone.

The girl spoke briefly on the phone, put it down, scribbled out a pass. 'Mr Hale can see you now.' She handed me the pass and I saw she had written on it the number of the room I was to go to.

'Thank you, miss,' I said. Too late, I saw the wedding ring on her finger. I have made another enemy in Washington, I thought.

I went up in the elevator. The elevator was nearly full, but it rose in decorous silence. The secrets of state were being well-guarded.

Hale's name was on a door that was exactly the same as a long row of identical doors that disappeared in diminishing perspective down a seemingly endless corridor. What can all these people possibly be doing for the United States of America eight hours a day, two hundred days a year? I wondered, as I knocked.

'Come in,' a woman's voice called.

I pushed the door open and entered a small room where a

beautiful young woman was typing. Good old Jeremy Hale.

The beautiful young woman smiled radiantly at me. I wondered how she behaved in taxicabs. 'Are you Mr Grimes?' she said, rising. She was even more beautiful standing than sitting down, tall and dark, lissome in a tight blue sweater.

'I am indeed,' I said.

'Mr Hale is delighted you could come. Go right in, please.' She held the door to the inner office open for me.

Hale was seated at a cluttered desk, peering down at a sheaf of papers in front of him. He had put on weight since I had last seen him, and had added statesmanlike solidity to the mild polite face. On the desk, in a silver frame, was a family group, a woman and two children, a boy and a girl. Everything in moderation. Zero population growth. An example to the heathen. Hale looked up when I came in and stood, smiling widely. 'Doug,' he said, 'You don't know how glad I am to see you.'

As we shook hands, I was surprised at how moved I was by my friend's greeting. For three years now, no one had been genuinely glad to see me.

'Where've you been, where've you been, man?' Hale said. He waved to a leather sofa along one side of the spacious office and, as I sat down, pulled a wooden armchair close to the sofa and sat down himself. 'I thought you'd disappeared from the face of the earth. I wrote three times and each time the letters came back. Haven't you learned anything about forwarding addresses yet? And I wrote your girl friend, Pat, asking about you and she wrote back and said she didn't know where you'd gone.' He scowled at me. He was agreeable-looking, tall, comfortably built, soft-faced, and the scowl was incongruous on him. 'And you don't look so almighty great, either. You look as though you haven't been out in the open air for years.'

'Okay, okay,' I said, 'one thing at a time, Jerry. I just decided I didn't like flying anymore and I moved on. Here and there.'

'I wanted to ski with you last winter. I had two weeks off and I heard the snow was great....'

'I haven't been doing much skiing, to tell the truth,' I said.

Impulsively, Hale touched my shoulder. 'All right,' he said. 'I won't ask any questions.' Even as a boy in college he had always been quick and sensitive. 'Well, anyway, just one question. Where're you coming from and what're you doing in Washington?' He laughed. 'I guess that's two questions.'

'I'm coming from New York,' I said, 'and I'm in Washington to ask you to do a little favor for me.'

'The government is at your disposal, lad. Ask and ye shall receive.'

'I need a passport.'

'You mean you never had a passport?'

'No.'

'You've never been out of the country?' Hale sounded amazed. Everybody *he* knew was out of the country most of the time.

'I've been in Canada,' I said. 'That's all. And you don't need a passport for Canada.'

'You said you were in New York,' Hale looked puzzled. 'Why didn't you get it there? Not that I'm not delighted you finally had an excuse to visit me,' he added hastily. 'But all you had to do was go to the office on Six thirty. . . .'

'I know,' I said. 'I just didn't feel like waiting. I'm in a hurry and I thought I'd come to the fountainhead, from which all good things flow.'

'They *are* swamped there,' Hale said. 'Where do you intend to go?'

'I thought Europe, first. I came into a little dough and I thought maybe it was time I ought to get a dose of Old World culture. Those postcards you used to send me from Paris and Athens gave me the itch.' Deception, I found was coming easily.

'I think I can run the passport through for you in a day,' Hale said. 'Just give me your birth certificate. . . .' He stopped when he saw the frown on my face. 'Don't you have it with you?'

'I didn't realize I needed it.'

'You sure do,' Hale said. 'Where were you born – Scranton, wasn't it?'

'Yes.'

He made a face.

'What's the matter?' I asked.

'Pennsylvania's a bore,' he said. 'All the birth certificates are kept in Harrisburg, the state capital. You'd have to write there. It'd take at least two weeks. If you're lucky.'

'Balls,' I said. I didn't want to wait *anywhere* for two weeks.

'Didn't you get your birth certificate when you applied for your first driver's license?'

'Yes,' I said.

'Where is it now? Have you any idea? Maybe somebody in your family. Stashed away in a trunk somewhere.'

'My brother Henry still lives in Scranton,' I said. I remembered that after my mother died he had taken all the accumulated family junk, old report cards, my high school diploma, my degree from college, old snapshot albums and stored them in his attic. 'He might have it.'

'Why don't you call him and have him look. If he finds it tell him to send it to you special delivery, registered.'

'Even better,' I said. 'I'll go down there myself. I haven't seen Henry for years and it's about time I put in an appearance, anyway.' I didn't feel I had to explain to Hale that I preferred not to have Henry know where I was staying in Washington or anywhere else.

'Let's see,' Hale said. 'This is Thursday. There's a weekend coming up. Even if you find it, you couldn't get back in time to do anything until Monday.'

'That's okay,' I said. 'Europe's waited this long I guess it can wait another couple of days.'

'You'll need some photographs, too.'

'I have them with me.' I fished the envelope out of a pocket.

He slid one out of the envelope and studied it. 'You still look as though you're just about to graduate from high school.' He shook his head. 'How do you manage it?'

'A carefree life,' I said.

'I'm glad to hear they're still available.' Hale said. 'When I look at pictures of myself these days, I seem to be old enough to be my own father. The magic of the cameraman's art.' He put the photograph back in its envelope, as though the one glimpse of it would do him for a long, long time. 'I'll have the application ready for you to sign Monday morning. Just in case.'

'I'll be here.'

'Why not come back and spend the weekend here?' Hale said. 'Washington is at its best on the weekends. We have a poker game on Saturday night. You still play poker?'

'A little.'

'Good. One of our regulars is out of town and you can have his place. There're a couple of eternal pigeons in the game who'll donate their dough with a pathetic generosity.' He smiled. He hadn't been a bad poker player himself in college. 'It'll be like old times. I'll arrange everything.'

The phone rang and Hale went over to the desk, picked up the instrument, and listened for a moment. 'I'll be right over, sir,' he said and put the phone down. 'I'm sorry, Doug, I have to go. The daily eleven am crisis.'

I stood up. 'Thanks for everything,' I said, as we walked toward the door.

'*Nada*,' Hale said. 'What are friends for? Listen, there's a cocktail party at my house tonight. You busy?'

'Nothing special,' I said.

'Seven o'clock.' We were in the outer office now. 'I've got to run. Miss Schwartz will give you my address.' He was out of the door, moving fast, but still preserving a statesmanlike decorum.

Miss Schwartz wrote on a card and gave it to me, smiling radiantly, as though she were ennobling me. Her handwriting was as beautiful as she was.

*

I awoke slowly as the soft hand went lightly up my thigh. We had made love twice already, but the erection was immediate. The lady in bed with me was profiting from my years of abstinence.

'That's better,' the lady murmured. 'That's much better. Don't do anything for the moment. Just lie back. Don't move.'

I lay back. The expert hands, the soft lips, and lascivious tongue made remaining motionless exquisite torture. The lady was very serious, ritualistic almost, in her pleasures, and was not to be hurried. When we had come into her bedroom at midnight, she had made me lie down and had undressed me slowly. The last woman who had undressed me had been my mother, when I was five, and I had the measles.

It was not the way I had expected the evening to end. The cocktail party in the nice Colonial house in Georgetown had been polite and sober. I had arrived early and had been taken upstairs to admire the Hale children. Before the other guests came, I had chatted desultorily with Hale's wife, Vivian, whom I had never met. She was a pretty, blondish woman, with an overworked look about her. It turned out that through the years Hale had told her quite a bit about me. 'After Washington,' Mrs Hale had said, 'Jerry said you were like a breath of fresh air. He said he loved skiing with you and your girl – Pat – am I right, was that her name?'.

'Yes.'

'He said – and I hope you won't think it's condescending – he said that you, both of you were so transparently decent.'

'That's not condescending,' I said.

'He was worried about you when he found out that you weren't well – together – anymore. And that you'd just vanished.' Mrs Hale's eyes searched my face, looking for a reaction, an answer to her unspoken question.

'I knew where I was,' I said.

'If I hadn't met Jerry,' Mrs Hale said, candor making her seem suddenly youthful, 'I'd have nothing. Nothing.' The doorbell rang. 'Oh, dear,' she said, 'here comes the herd. I do hope we'll see a lot of you while you're here....'

The rest of the party had been something of a blur, although not because of drink. I never drank much. But the names had been flung at me in such quick succession, Senator So-and-So, Congressman This, Congressman That, His Excellency, the Ambassador of What country, Mr Blank, he works for *The Washington Post*, Mrs Whoever, she's ever so important at Justice, and the conversation had been about people who were powerful, famous, despicable, conniving, eloquent, on the way to Russia, introducing a bill that would make your hair stand on end.

Even though I knew next to nothing about the social structure of the capital, I could tell that there was a lot of power assembled in the room. By Washington standards everybody there was more important than the host, who, while obviously on the way up, was still somewhere in the middle ranks of the Foreign Service, and who couldn't have afforded many parties like this on his salary. But Vivian Hale was the daughter of a man who had been a senator for two terms and who owned a good part of North Carolina besides. My friend had married well. I wondered what I would have turned into if I had married a rich wife. Not that I ever had the offer.

I had merely stood around, wincing a little as the drinks began to take effect on the rising curve of conversation, a glass tactfully in my hand at all times, smiling manfully, like a small boy at dancing school. I wondered how Hale could bear it.

*

Mrs Whoever, whose hand and lips were now caressing me, had turned out to be the lady who was ever so important at Justice. She looked thirty-five years old, but a very handsome thirty-five, full bodied, with glowing skin, large dark eyes, and soft dark blonde hair, almost the color of mine, that fell to her shoulders. We had found ourselves in a corner together and she had said, 'I've been watching you. Poor man, you look marooned. I take it you're not an inmate.'

'An inmate?' I had asked, puzzled. 'Of what?'

'Washington.'

I had grinned. 'Does it show that badly?'

'It does, man, it does. Don't worry about it. I leap at the opportunity to talk to someone who isn't in the government.' She had looked at her watch. 'Forty-five minutes. I have done my duty. Nobody can spread the rumor that I don't know how to behave in polite society. Time for chow. Grimes, are you busy for dinner?'

'No.' I was surprised that she had remembered my name.

'Shall we leave together or leave separately?'

I laughed. 'That's up to you, Mrs. . . .'

'Coates, Evelyn.' She had smiled widely. I decided she had a mouth for smiling. 'Together. I'm divorced. Do you consider me forward?'

'Yes ma'am.'

'Excellent man.' She had touched my arm lightly. 'I'll wait for you in the front hall. Say good-bye to your hosts, like a good boy.'

I had watched her sweep through the crowded room, imperious and confident. I had never met a woman like that before. But even then I hadn't imagined for a moment that the evening would end up as it did. I had never in my life gone to bed with a woman the first time I had met her. What with my stutter and ridiculously youthful appearance, I had always been rather shy, not sure that I was particularly attractive, and had felt that I was clumsy with women. I was resigned to the fact that other men got the beauties. I had never gotten over wondering why Pat, who was exceptionally attractive, had had anything to do with me. Luckily for my ego, I had no taste for the ordinary kind of male conquest, and the remnants of my religious upbringing had kept me from promiscuity, even if I could have indulged in it.

The restaurant Mrs Coates had taken me to was French and, as far as I could tell, very good. 'I hope you're enormously wealthy,' she had said. 'The prices here are ferocious. Are you enormously wealthy?'

'Enormously.'

She had squinted at me across the table, studying me. 'You don't look it.'

'It's old money,' I had said. 'The family likes to pretend to be slightly shabby.'

'What old family?'

'Some other time.' I had turned her off.

She had talked about herself, though, without any urging from me. She was a lawyer, she worked in the antitrust division of the Justice Department, she had been in Washington eleven years, her husband had been a commander in the Navy and was an absolute beast, she had no children and wanted none, she went to the Hamptons, on Long Island, whenever she could and swam and pottered around a garden, her boss had been trying to lay her for five years, but otherwise was a dear, she was determined to run for Congress before she died. Along with all that, all spoken in an incongruously low, melodic voice, she had entertained me through dinner by interrupting herself to point out other guests and describing them by function and character in short, malicious sketches. There was a senator with whom a girl wasn't safe if they were in an elevator together, a second secretary at an embassy who ran dope in the diplomatic pouches, a lobbyist who had blocs in both Houses in his pocket, a CIA operator who was responsible for murders in several South American countries. I had enjoyed myself, allowing her to pick the wine, although I would have preferred beer, and order for both of us, saying, 'I'm just a simple country boy and I trust myself to your hands.' It was exhilarating to be able to talk to a handsome woman without stuttering. A whole new world seemed to be opening up before me.

'Is your entire, enormously wealthy, slightly shabby family composed of simple country boys like you?'

'More or less,' I had said.

She stared at me quizzically. 'Are you a spook?'

'A what?'

'A spook. CIA?'

I had shaken my head, smiling. 'Not even.'

'Hale told me you were a pilot.'

'Once. Not anymore.' I wondered when she had had time, in all the confusion of the party, to question Hale about me. For a moment, the woman's inquisitiveness had bothered me and I half-decided to put her in a cab after dinner and let her go home herself. But then I had thought, I mustn't get paranoid about the whole thing and settled back to enjoy the evening. 'Don't you think we need another bottle?' I had asked.

'Definitely,' she had said.

We had been the last ones left in the restaurant, and I was pleasantly drunk from the unaccustomed wine when we got into the taxi. We sat in the taxi without touching each other, and, when the taxi stopped in front of the apartment building in which Mrs Coates lived, I had said, 'Hold it, driver, please; I'm just seeing the lady to the door.'

'Forget it, driver,' Mrs Coates had said. 'The gentleman is coming in for a nightcap.'

'That's just what I need,' I had said, trying not to mumble, 'a nightcap.' But I had paid the driver and gone in with her.

I hadn't discovered what the apartment was like, because she didn't switch on the lights. She merely put her arms around me as I shut the door from the hall and kissed me. The kiss was delicious.

'I am now seducing you,' she had said, 'in your weakened state.'

'Consider me seduced.'

Chuckling, she had led me by the hand through the dark living room and into the bedroom. A thin shaft of light from the partially open door to a bathroom was enough so that I could make out the shapes of pieces of furniture, a huge desk piled with papers, a dresser, a long bookcase against one wall. She had led me to the bed, turned me around, then given me a sharp push. I had fallen backward on the bed. 'The rest,' she had said, 'is my job.'

If she was as good at Justice as she was in bed, the government was getting its money's worth.

*

'Now,' she said, sliding up on me, straddling me, using her hand to guide me into her. She moved on me, first very slowly, then more and more quickly, her head thrown back, her arms rigid behind her, her hands spread out on the bed, supporting her. Her full breasts loomed above me, pale in the dim light reflected off a mirror. I put up my hands and caressed her breasts and she moaned. She began to sob, loudly, uncontrollably, and when she came she was weeping.

I came immediately after, with a long, subdued sigh. She rolled off me, lay on her stomach beside me, the weeping slowly coming to an end. I put out my hand and touched the firm, rounded shoulder. 'Did I hurt you?' I asked.

She laughed. 'Silly man. Lord, no.'

'I was afraid I . . .'

'Didn't a lady ever cry while you were fucking her?'

'Not that I remember,' I said. And none of the ladies ever called it that either, I could have added. They obviously called a spade a spade at Justice.

She laughed again, twisted around, sat up, reached for a cigarette, lit it. Her face was calm and untroubled in the flare of the match. 'Do you want a cigarette?'

'I don't smoke cigarettes.'

'You'll live forever. So much the better. How old are you anyway?'

'Thirty-three.'

'In the prime of life,' she said. 'The dear prime of life. Don't go to sleep. I want to talk. Do you want a drink?'

'What time is it?'

'Drink time.' She got out of bed and I saw her put a dressing gown on. 'Whiskey okay?'

'Whiskey is fine.'

She went into the living room, her robe making a soft rustling sound. I looked at my watch. She had taken it off, the last item, when she had undressed me and put it neatly on the bedside table. She was an orderly woman. The luminous dial of the watch showed that it was past three. Everything in its time, I thought, lying back luxuriously, remembering other three o'clocks, the noise of the adding machine, the bullet proof glass, the bedraggled women asking me to unlock the front door.

She came back with the two glasses, handed me mine, sat on the edge of the bed, her profile outlined against the light from the bathroom. The silhouette was bold and sharp. She drank heartily. She was a hearty as well as an orderly woman. 'Most satisfactory,' she said. 'You were, too.'

I laughed. 'Do you always rate your lovers?'

'You're not my lover, Grimes,' she said. 'You're a nice-looking, youngish man with good manners whom I happened to take a slight shine to at a party and who had the great virtue to be passing briefly through town. Briefly is the operative word in that sentence, Grimes.'

'I see,' I said, sipping at the whiskey.

'You probably don't and I won't bother to explain.'

'You don't have to explain anything to me,' I said. 'Sufficient unto the night are the pleasures thereof.'

'You don't do this sort of thing often, do you?'

'Frankly, no.' I laughed again. 'Frankly, never. Why – does it show?'

'Like a neon sign. You're not at all like what you look like, you know.'

'What do I look like?'

'You look like those young men who play the villains in Italian movies – bold and dark and unscrupulous.'

Nobody had ever said anything like that to me before. I had gotten used to hearing that I reminded people of somebody's kid brother. Either I had changed drastically or Evelyn Coates was not deceived by surfaces, could see through to the wished-for inner man. 'Is that a good way to look?' I asked. I was a little worried by the 'unscrupulous.'

'It's a very nice way to look. In certain situations.'

'Like tonight, for example?'

'Like tonight.'

'I might be coming back to Washington in a few days,' I said. 'Should I call you?'

'If you have nothing better to do.'

'Will you see me again?'

'If *I* have nothing better to do.'

'Are you as tough as you pretend to be?'

'Tougher, Grimes, much tougher. What would you be coming back to Washington for?'

'Maybe for you.'

'Try that once more, please.'

'Maybe for you.'

'You *do* have nice manners. Maybe for what else?'

'Well,' I said slowly, thinking, this is as good a place and as a good a time to dig for information, 'supposing I was looking for somebody ...'

'Somebody in particular?'

'Yes. Somebody whose name I know, who's dropped out of sight.'

'In Washington?'

'Not necessarily. Somewhere in the country, or maybe even out of the country....'

'You *are* a mysterious man, aren't you?'

'Someday I may tell you the whole story,' I said, sure that I never would, but pleased that luck had put me into the bed of a woman who was in on the secrets of government, and whose job, partially, at least, must involve tracing people down, people usually who did not want to be traced down. 'It's a private, delicate matter. But suppose I had to find this hypothetical friend, how would I go about it?'

'Well, there are a lot of places you could look,' she said. 'The Internal Revenue Service – they'd know his address at the time he sent in his last return. The Social Security people. They'd have a record of whom he was working for. The Selective Service people, although that would probably be outdated. The FBI. You never know what you can pick up in *that* factory. The State Department. It would all depend upon whether or not you knew the right people.'

'Take it for granted that I would get to know the right people,' I said. For a hundred thousand dollars, I could take it for granted *somebody* would be able to reach the right people.

'You probably would eventually be able to pick up your friend's trail. Say, are you a private detective or something!'

'Or something,' I said ambiguously.

'Well, everybody comes to Washington eventually,' she said. 'Why not you? It's America's *real* living theater. Standing room only at every performance. Except that it's a peculiar audience. The good seats are all filled by actors.'

'Are you an actress?'

'You bet your life. I'm playing a role that can't be beat. The dauntless Portia striking deadly blows at the malefactors of great wealth. Women's Lib at Justice and Injustice. I've gotten rave reviews in the best beds in town. Do I shock you?'

'A little.'

'While on the subject,' she said, 'let me give you a t.l.'

'What's a t.l.?'

'Where have you been, you poor innocent?' She reached over and pinched my cheek. 'T.l. stands for trade last. A compliment. You gave almost the best performance of anyone I've slept with in this town. You were even as good as a certain Senator from a Western state whom I shall not name, who used to be at the head of the list. Until the poor dear was beaten at the last election.'

'I didn't realize I was giving a performance.' I had no desire to hear the defeated Senator's name.

'Of course you were. Otherwise you wouldn't be in Washington. And every performance calls on enormous talent here. We all have to pretend we love our roles.'

'Are you like that, too?'

'You must be kidding, honey. Of course. I'm a big, grown woman. Do you think that, if I went into that office every day for the next hundred years, it would make the slightest difference to you or General Motors or the United Nations or anybody's pet dog? I just play the game, honey, and have fun like everybody else, because this town is the best place to have fun anybody's found for people like us. Actually, what I believe is that, if everyone here, from the President down to the janitor at Indian Affairs, would only be allowed to operate two weeks a year, America would turn out to be the greatest country in the world.'

I had finished the whiskey by now and felt an overwhelming desire to sleep. I barely suppressed a yawn.

'Oh,' she said, 'I'm boring you.'

'Not at all,' I said truthfully. 'But aren't you tired?'

'Not really.' She put her glass down, slipped out of her robe, and got into bed beside me. 'Sex invigorates me. But I have to get up early and it doesn't do for me to look debauched when I get to the office in the morning.' She snuggled up to me and kissed my ear. 'Good night, Grimes. Of course call me when you come back.'

*

When I awoke, it was nearly ten o'clock and I was alone. The curtains let enough sun through for me to see that it was a nice day. There was a note on the dresser, where she had put my money clip the night before. 'Dear Guest: Off to work.

You were sleeping like a baby and I hadn't the heart to wake you. I am happy to see such evidence of a clear conscience in this naughty world. There's a razor and shaving cream in the medicine cabinet and a big glass of orange juice in the refrigerator and a pot of coffee on the stove. The good servant deserves his hire. I hope you find your friend. E.C.'

I grinned at the last sentence, then went into the bathroom and shaved and showered. The cold shower woke me up completely and I felt fresh and cheerful. And, I had to admit, pleased with myself. I looked carefully at myself in the mirror. My color had improved.

As I went into the living room, I smelled bacon frying. I pushed open the door to the kitchen and saw a young woman sitting at a table in slacks and a sweater, with a scarf around her head, reading the newspaper and munching on a piece of toast.

'Hi,' the young woman said, looking up. 'I wondered if you were going to sleep all day.'

'I ... I'm terribly sorry ...' I said, flustered. 'I didn't mean to disturb you.'

'You're not disturbing me.' She got up and opened the refrigerator and took out a glass of orange juice. 'Evelyn left this for you. You must be thirsty.' She didn't say why she thought I must be thirsty. 'Do you want bacon and eggs?'

'I don't want to be any trouble.'

'No trouble. Breakfast comes with the deal.' She stripped off three slices of bacon from an open package and put it in the pan with the others. She was tall and slender in her slacks. 'Sunny side up?'

'Any way you're having them.'

'Sunny side up,' the woman said. She put a slab of butter in another pan and cracked four eggs into the pan, her movements swift and authoritative. 'I'm Brenda Morrissey,' she said. 'I share the apartment with Evelyn. Didn't she say anything about me?'

'Not that I remember,' I said. I sipped at the chilled orange juice.

'I guess Evelyn was busy at the time,' she said flatly. She poured two cups of coffee, indicated the cream and sugar on the table. 'Sit down. You're not in a hurry, are you?'

'Not really.' I sat down.

'Neither am I. I run an art gallery. Nobody ever buys a picture before eleven o'clock in the morning. It's a dream job for a girl like me. Evelyn neglected to tell me your name.'

I told her my name.

'How long have you known Evelyn?' she asked, as she stood at the stove, shaking the pan with the eggs in it with one hand and feeding slices of bread into the toaster with the other hand.

'Well,' I said, embarrassed, 'the truth is we just met last night.'

She gave a short, sharp chuckle. 'That's Washington. You collect votes wherever you can find them. Any kind of votes. Maybe this is the nicest kind. Dear Evelyn,' she said, but without malice. 'I heard you at your revels.'

I felt myself blushing. 'I had no idea there was anyone else in the house.'

'That's all right. Actually, I keep meaning to buy earplugs and then I forget from one time to the next.' She slid the eggs onto plates and put the bacon over them. She sat across from me on the other side of the little table, clear greenish eyes staring at me steadily. She was wearing no lipstick and her lips were light pink, her cheeks just a little flushed from the heat of the stove. She had a long face, the bones all showing, and the scarf around her head made her look severe. 'Evelyn's not one to keep her enjoyment to herself when she's being amused,' she said, as she broke a piece of bacon and started eating it with her fingers. 'I had to use all my maidenly restraint to keep from coming and joining the fun.'

I felt my face go rigid and I ducked my eyes. The woman laughed. 'Don't worry,' she said, 'it hasn't happened yet. Whatever else we do around here, we do not go in for orgies. Still,' she said evenly, 'if you're going to be in Washington tonight and if you tell me what hotel you're staying at, you might like to buy me a drink.'

I won't say that I wasn't tempted. The night had re-awakened all the sensuality in me that had lain dormant for so long. And the cool impersonality of the invitation was intriguing. At least for its novelty. Things like that had happened to friends of mine, or at least so they had said, but never to me. And after what I had done in room 602 of the St Augustine Hotel, I could hardly refuse on moral grounds to sleep with the friend of a lady I had only just met the night before. Let the accidents happen. But there was the business of the birth certificate. 'I'm sorry,' I said. 'I'm leaving town this morning.'

'What a pity,' the woman said tonelessly.

'But I'll be back at my hotel . . .' I hesitated, remembering Jeremy Hale's poker game on Saturday night. First things first. 'I'll be back on Sunday.'

'What hotel are you staying at?'

I told her.

'Perhaps I'll call on Sunday,' she said. 'I have nothing against Sundays.'

Money in the bank, I thought, as I was leaving the apartment building, even money in a bank two hundred and fifty miles away must give off an irresistible sexual aroma.

I tried to examine just how I felt that morning. Springy and light-footed. Lighthearted, I decided. Wicked. It was an old-fashioned word, but it was the word that came to mind. Was it possible that for thirty-three years I had miscalculated absolutely what sort of man I was? I looked carefully at the ordinary faces of the men and women on the street. Were they all on the edge of crime?

At the hotel I rented a car and took my wallet out of the vault. I was beginning to feel deprived if I wasn't carrying a certain number of hundred-dollar bills on me.

The roads through Pennsylvania were icy and I drove carefully. A car crash was one accident I wanted to avoid. This was no time to be laid up immobilized and helpless, in a hospital for weeks or maybe months on end.

6

'May I speak to Mr Grimes, please,' I said to the girl on the phone. 'Mr Henry Grimes.'

'Who's calling, please?'

I hesitated. I was getting more and more reluctant to give my name to anyone. 'Say his brother is calling,' I said on the phone. Since there were three brothers in the family, this could leave at least a small margin of doubt.

When I heard my brother's voice on the phone, I said, 'Hello, Hank.'

'Who's this? No, I don't believe it! Doug! Where the hell are you?' Once again I felt the same quick gratitude that had swept over me in Jeremy Hale's office because someone was so obviously glad to hear the sound of my voice. My brother was seven years older than I and when we had been growing up had regarded me as a pest. Since I had moved away from Scranton, we had only seen each other rarely, but there was no mistaking the warmth in the greeting.

'I'm in town. At the Hilton Hotel.'

'Take your bag and come on over to the house. We've got a guest room. And the kids won't wake you until six thirty in the morning.' Henry laughed at his own invitation. Behind the deep, remembered voice, there was the clatter of office machines. Henry worked in a firm of accountants and the mechanical noise of the symbols of money coming in and going out was the music of his working day. 'I'll call Madge,' Henry was saying, 'and tell her to expect you for dinner.'

'Hold it a minute, Hank,' I said. 'I have to ask you for a favor.'

'Sure, kid,' he said. 'What is it?'

'I'm applying for a passport,' I said, 'and I need my birth certificate. If I write Harrisburg it'll take three weeks and I'm in a hurry...'

'Where you going?'

'Abroad.'

'Where abroad?'

'No matter. Do you think that in the stuff you took from Mom's house you might find my birth certificate?'

'Come on over to the house for dinner and we'll look for it together.'

'I'd rather Madge didn't know I was in town, Hank,' I said.

'Oh.' The worry set in immediately.

'Do you think you might see if you could find it this afternoon and then come over to the Hilton and have dinner with me. Alone?'

'But why...?'

'I'll explain later. Can you manage it?'

'I'll be there a quarter after six.'

'In the bar.'

'That's no hardship.' Henry chuckled. It was a drinker's chuckle.

'See you then,' I said and hung up. I sat on the edge of the single bed in the nondescript hotel room, my hand on the telephone, wondering if it wouldn't have been better to have written Harrisburg and waited the two weeks and never have come back to Scranton, never have said anything to my brother. I shook my head. If you wanted to figure out what your future was going to be, you had to have a firm grasp on your past. And my brother Henry was a big part of my past.

Because our father had died when Henry was twenty and all the other children much younger, and Henry had taken on the responsibility of the male head of the family automatically, without fuss, I had learned to respect him and depend on him. It was easy to depend on Henry. He was an outgoing, uncomplicated, clever boy, quick in his studies (he always led his class, always was elected class president, and got a scholarship to the University of Pennsylvania). He had a knack for business, too, and was generous to the other children, especially to me, with the money he made after school and in the summers. As our mother kept repeating, he was the one of her children who was born to be rich and successful. It was Henry who fought our mother and overcame her objections when I decided I wanted to learn to fly. Henry had also financed the flying school. By that time he was a certified public accountant, doing fairly well for his age, and already married.

Through the years, I had paid back the money Henry had lent me, although Henry had never once asked me for a penny. But we had not seen each other often. We lived in different parts of the world, and Henry was involved with his growing family and his wife, Madge. Because of the scandal of my younger brother, Bert, the few times that we had all been together Madge had been uncomfortably persistent in trying to find out why I was not yet married.

Because of everything, my brother Henry was one of the people in my life who somehow made me feel guilty, lacking in feeling. I knew that I had received much more than I had given and the imbalance disturbed me. I was glad now that the bureaucracy in Harrisburg had forced me to come to my home town and once more ask my brother to help me.

*

I was shocked when I saw him come into the bar. I had not seen him for five years, and Henry had been a powerfully built, erect, confident-seeming man then. Now he looked as though the five years had ravaged him. He seemed diminished, bent. His hair had thinned and what was left was stringy, yellowish-gray. He wore thick, gold-rimmed spectacles that bit deep into the bridge of his nose. He had always had fine eyes, deep-colored, like all the family, and keen of sight, and the glasses did not become him. Even in the half-light of the bar, Henry reminded me of a small, worried animal peering fearfully out of a hole, ready to scuttle back at the first sign of danger.

'Over here, Hank,' I said, standing up.

We shook hands wordlessly. I was sure Henry knew the changes that had taken place in him were apparent and that I was trying to hide my reaction to them.

'You're in luck,' Henry said. 'I found it right off.' He reached into his pocket and took out a yellowed envelope and gave it to me. I slipped out the certificate. There it was. My identity was confirmed. Douglas Traynor Grimes, citizen, born in America, male, son of Margaret Traynor Grimes, heir to the continent.

While I was examining the frail piece of aging paper, Henry was fussily taking off his coat and folding it on a chair. The coat was worn at the cuffs and elbows.

'What'll it be, Hank?' I asked, overly hearty, false.

'An old-fashioned will do it.' His voice had somehow remained the same, full and deep, like a cherished and lovingly polished relic from better days.

'The same,' I said to the waiter, who was standing at the table.

'Well, boy, well,' Henry said. 'The Prodigal returns.' If I closed my eyes the voice was still my brother.

'Not exactly. More of a refueling stop, I would say.'

'You're not flying anymore?'

'I wrote you that.'

'*That's* the only thing you wrote me,' Henry said. 'I'm not complaining, you understand.' He spread his hands in a placating gesture. I noticed that the hands shook a little. Holy God, I thought, he's only forty years old. 'The world's a busy place,' Henry said. 'Communication is difficult. Time passes. Brothers go their different ways.'

We toasted each other when the drinks came. Henry drank greedily, half the glassful in one gulp. 'After a day in the office,' he said, catching my glance. 'Those're long days in that office.'

'I can imagine,' I said.

'Now tell me the news,' Henry said.

'You tell *me* the news,' I said, 'Madge, the kids et cetera, et cetera.'

There were two more drinks for Henry while he told me about Madge and the kids. Madge was fine, a little run down taking care of everything with no help and the PTA and teaching a stenographic course at night, the three daughters were lovely, the oldest at fourteen something of a problem, high-strung, the way kids that age these days were likely to be, and having a little psychiatric help. The photographs came out of the wallet, the family beside a lake in the Poconos, all the females brown, robust, and cheerful, Henry, in a pair of bathing trunks that were too big for him, pale and worried-looking, as though a drowning was imminent. The news of our brother Bert was not surprising. 'He's a fag radio announcer out in San Diego,' Henry said. 'We should have seen it coming. Did you see it coming?'

'No.'

'Well, these days, it's not so bad, I suppose,' Henry said with a sigh. 'Still, in our family ... Pa would have split a gut. He's got a good heart, Bert, he always sends the kids gifts on Christmas from California, but I wouldn't know what to do with him if he ever showed up here.'

Our sister Clara, the youngest of the family, was married, in Chicago, with two kids, did I know that?

'I knew about her being married. Not about the kids.'

'We don't see much of her either,' Henry said. 'Families sort of just disintegrate, don't they? In a few years I suppose my kids'll go off, too, and Madge and I'll be sitting home looking at the television together.' He laughed ruefully. 'Happy thoughts. Still, there's one good thing. The bastards'll never be able to drag any son of mine off and kill him in one of their goddamn wars. What a country, where you thank God you don't have a son. More happy thoughts.' He shook himself, as though the conversation had gotten away from him onto subjects that would have been better left unexamined. 'Don't you think it's time for another drink?'

I still had my first glass almost full in front of me, but he ordered two more. In a little while Henry would be drunk. Maybe that explained it all, although I knew it never explained it all.

'Clara's doing all right,' Henry was saying. 'At least that's what she writes us. *When* she writes us. Her husband's a big shot in a brokerage firm out there. They have a boat on the lake. Imagine that – a Grimes with a yacht. Okay, enough about all of us. What about you?'

'Over dinner,' I said. By now it was obvious that Henry had to get some food in him – fast.

In the dining room, Henry ordered a big meal. 'How about a bottle of wine?' he said, smiling widely, as though he had just thought of a brilliant and original idea.

'If you want,' I said. I knew that Henry would be much the worse for the wine, but I had been in the habit all my boyhood and youth of taking orders from him, not the other way round, and the habit, I saw, persisted.

Henry neglected his food, but paid a great deal of attention to the wine during dinner. He had flashes of sobriety, when he would sit very erect and peer fiercely across the table at me and speak almost sternly, as though suddenly remembering his position as the head of the family. 'Now let's have it, son,' he said, during one of these periods. 'Where've you been, what have you done, what brings you here? You need help, I imagine. I don't have much, but I guess I could manage to scrape up a couple of ...'

'Nothing like that, Hank,' I said hastily, 'Really. Money isn't the problem.'

'That's what you think, brother.' Henry laughed bitterly. 'That's what you think.'

'Listen carefully, Hank,' I said, leaning forward, speaking in a low voice, trying to freeze his attention, 'I'm going away.'

'Going away? Where?' Henry asked. 'You've been going away all your life.'

'This is different. Maybe for a long time. To Europe first.'

'Do you have a job in Europe?'

'Not exactly.'

'You don't have a job?'

'Don't ask any questions, please, Hank,' I said. 'I'm going away. Period. I don't know when I'll ever be able to see you again. Maybe never. I wanted to touch some of the bases before I took off. And I want to thank you for what you've always done for me. I want to tell you that I realize it and that I'm grateful for it. I was a snotty little kid and I guess I used to think gratitude was effeminate or degrading or un-British or something equally idiotic.'

'Oh, shit, Doug,' Henry said. 'Forget it, will you?'

'I won't forget it. Another thing. Pa died when I was thirteen years old ...'

'He left a nice little piece of insurance.' Henry nodded approvingly. 'Yessiree, a very nice little piece of insurance. You'd never have expected it – a man who worked as a foreman in a machine shop. A man who worked with his hands. His thought was only for his family. Where would we all be today if it wasn't for that nice little piece of insurance...?'

'I'm not talking about that part of it.'

'Talk about that part of it. Listen to an accountant when it comes to death and insurance.'

'What do you remember about him? That's what I want to talk about. I was just a kid; it seems to me I hardly ever saw him; he was just somebody who came in for meals mostly. I still have dreams about him, but I never get the face right. But you were twenty....'

'His face,' Henry said. 'His face was the face of an honest rough man who never had any doubt about himself. It was a face out of another century. Duty and honor were written plain on those simple features.' Henry was mocking himself, mocking our father's memory now. 'And he gave me bad advice,' Henry said, almost sober for the moment. 'Also out of another century. He said, "Marry early, boy." You know how he was always reading the Bible, and making us all go to church. It's better to marry than to burn, he said. I married early. I have a bone to pick with good old dad; insurance or no insurance, burning is better.'

'Will you for Christ's sake stop talking about insurance?'

'Whatever you say, boy. It's your dinner. I take it it *is* your dinner?'

'Of course.'

'Forget Pa. He's dead. Forget Mom. She's dead. They worked their fingers to the bone and worried night and day and got the old royal American screwing and raised a family, one who's a fag radio announcer in San Diego, the other who's a drunken accountant in Scranton working *his* fingers to the bone to raise a family, who in turn will work *their* fingers to the bone to raise *their* families. I'll say this for our dad, he had his religion. Clara has her yacht. Bert has his beach boys. I have my bottle.' He smiled owlishly. 'What have you got, brother?'

'I don't know yet,' I said.

'You don't know yet?' Henry cocked his collapsed, pale head to one side and grimaced. 'You're what – thirty-two, thirty-three? And don't know yet? You're a lucky man. The future is all ahead of you. I got something beside the bottle. I got a pair of eyes that are no good for anything and steadily getting worse.'

'What?'

'You heard me. Did you ever hear of a blind accountant? In five years I'll be out in the street on my naked ass.'

'Jesus,' I said, shaken by the coincidence. 'That's why *I* was grounded. My eyes started to go bad.'

'Aha,' Henry said. 'I thought you'd run a plane into a hill or screwed the boss's wife.'

'No. Just a little failure of the retina. Nothing much,' I said bitterly. 'Just enough.'

'We none of us ever did see clearly, I guess.' Henry laughed foolishly. 'The fatal flaw of the Grimeses.' He took off his glasses and wiped his eyes, which were watering. The marks of the frames on his nose were like small deep wounds. His eyes without the glasses looked almost blank. 'But you said you were traveling, you were going to Europe. What've you got – a rich woman to support you?'

'No.'

'Take my advice. Find one.' Henry put his glasses on. They fitted automatically into the slots on each side of his nose. 'Romance yourself no romance. That's another thing I have.' He was off ranting again. 'I have a wife who despises me.'

'Oh, come on now, Hank.' In the photograph Madge hadn't looked like a woman who despised anyone, and the few times I had met her she had seemed like a good-natured, even-tempered woman, solicitous at all times of her husband's welfare.

'Don't say come on now, brother,' Henry said. 'You don't know. *I* know. She despises me. You know *why* she despises me? Because by her high American standards I am a failure. She does not get new dresses when her friends get new dresses. I can't afford to pay for a psychiatrist for the older kid *and* send her off to a private school and she's afraid the Blacks at the high school will rape her between lunch and gym class. The house hasn't been painted for ten years. We're behind on our payments for the television set. Our car is six years old. I am not a partner in my firm. I keep track of other people's money. You know what the worst thing in the world is? Other people's money. I . . .'

'That's enough, Hank, please.' I couldn't stand the wave of self-hatred at the dinner table, even though there was nobody near enough but myself to hear any of it.

'Permit me to continue, brother,' Henry said. 'My teeth are bad and they smell, she says, because I can't afford to go to the dentist. I can't afford to go to the dentist because all three goddamn kids go to the dentist every week to have their braces worked on so that they'll all look like movie stars when they grow up. And she despises me because I haven't been able to fuck her for five years.'

'Why not?'

'I'm impotent,' Henry said with a crazy smile. 'I have every reason to be impotent and I'm impotent. Do you remember when you came home that Saturday afternoon and you found me in bed with that girl? What was her name?'

'Cynthia.'

'That's it – Cynthia. Cynthia of the big tits. She let out a shriek when she saw you that I can hear to this day. And she slapped me because I laughed. What did you think of your big brother then?'

'I didn't think anything. I didn't know what you were doing.'

'You know now, don't you?'

'Yes.'

'I wasn't impotent then, was I?'

'How the hell would I know?'

'Take your brother's word for it. Glad you came back to Scranton, Doug?'

'Listen to me, Hank.' I grabbed both his hands and pressed them hard. 'Are you sober enough to understand what I'm saying?'

'Approximately, kid, approximately.' Henry chuckled, then frowned. 'Give me back my hands.'

I let go of his hands. I took out my wallet and counted out ten bills. 'This is a thousand dollars, Hank,' I said. I leaned over and stuffed it into my brother's breast pocket. 'Don't forget where I put it.'

Henry let out his breath noisily. He fumbled at his pocket,

took out the bills, smoothed them out on the table. 'Other people's money,' he said. He sounded dead sober.

I nodded. 'There's more where that came from. Now, I'm going away tomorrow. Out of the country. I won't tell you where, but from time to time you'll hear from me, and if you need more there'll be more. Do you understand that?'

Henry slowly folded the bills and put them in his wallet. Then the tears started, silently rolling down the pallid cheeks out from under the glasses.

'For Christ's sake, Hank, don't cry,' I pleaded.

'You're in trouble,' Henry said.

'Maybe,' I said. 'Anyway, I have to keep on the move. If anybody ever comes to you and asks you if you know where I am, you don't know anything. You got that?'

'I got it.' Henry nodded. 'Let me ask you a question, Doug.' He *was* sober now, sobered by money. 'Is it worth it? Whatever you're doing?'

'I don't know yet. I'll let you know when I find out. I think we can skip coffee, can't we?'

'I don't need any coffee. I can get coffee in my happy home from my happy wife.'

We stood up and I helped Henry put on his coat. We walked out together, after I had paid the waiter. Henry walked in a straight line, a bent, oldish figure, then stopped for a moment, as I was pushing at the door. 'Just before he died,' Henry said, 'do you know what Pa said to me? He said, of all his sons he loved you best. He said you were the purest.' His voice sounded petulant, almost childish. 'Now why would a man on his deathbed want to tell his oldest son something like that?' He started walking again, and I opened the door for us, thinking, I am an opener of doors.

It was cold outside, the night wind gusting. Henry shivered a little, settling deeply into his coat. 'Beautiful old Scranton, where I live and die,' he said.

I kissed him on the cheek, hugging him, feeling the wetness of his tears. Then I put him in a cab. But before the cabby could start off, Henry tapped him on the shoulder to stop him and rolled down the window on my side. 'Hey, Doug,' he said. 'I just noticed; I knew something was peculiar about you all evening and I couldn't put my finger on it. You don't stutter anymore.'

'No,' I said.

'How'd it happen?'

'I went to a speech doctor,' I said. It was as good an explanation as any.

'Why, that's great, that's wonderful. You must be a happy man.'

'Yep,' I said. 'I'm a happy man. Get a good night's sleep, Hank.'

He rolled up the window and the cab started away. I watched its tail-lights go down the street, disappear around a corner, carrying away the brother of whom our mother had said that of all her children he was the one who was born to be rich and successful.

I took a deep breath of the icy night air, shivered, remembered the warm beds of Washington. Then I went in and took the elevator to my room and watched the television for hours. Many objects were advertised that I would never buy.

I slept badly that night, tantalized by fleeting visions of women and funerals.

The ringing of the telephone on the bedside table put a welcome stop to my dreams. I looked at my watch. It was only seven-thirty. 'Doug...' It was Henry on the phone. It couldn't have been anyone else. Nobody else in the whole world knew where I was. 'Doug ... I have to see you.'

I sighed. I felt as though we had exhausted each other the night before, that there was no need to see each other for another five years. 'Where are you?' I asked.

'Downstairs. In the lobby. Have you had your breakfast?'

'No.'

'I'll wait for you in the dining room.' He hung up before I could say yes or no.

*

He was drinking a cup of black coffee, alone in the neon-lit dining room. It was still dark outside. Henry had always been an early riser. It was another one of his virtues that my parents had praised.

'I'm sorry if I woke you,' he said, as I sat down across

78

from him. 'I wanted to make sure I got hold of you before you left town.'

'That's okay.' Half-remembering my dreams, I said, 'I wasn't particularly enjoying my sleep.'

The waitress came over to us and I ordered breakfast. Henry asked for a second cup of coffee.

'Listen, Doug,' he said, when the waitress had gone, 'last night, you said something. When you ... when you gave me all that money. Don't think that I'm not grateful...'

I waved my hand impatiently. 'Forget it,' I said. 'Let's not talk about it.'

'You said ... and I can't forget it ... you said, if I needed it, there's more where that came from.'

'That's what I said.'

'Did you mean it?'

'I wouldn't have said it if I didn't mean it.'

'Did you mean as much as twenty-five thousand?' He flushed, as though the effort of getting the question out had been enormous.

I hesitated only a moment. 'Yes,' I said. 'I meant that. If you need it.'

'Don't you want me to tell you what I'm going to do with it?'

'Only if you want to tell me,' I said. I was sorry I hadn't left town last night.

'I want to tell you. It's not only for me, it's for both of us. It's a ...' he began, then stopped, as the waitress came over with my juice and coffee and toast. He watched her tensely as she poured him a second cup. When she'd finished and moved off, he gulped a steaming mouthful. I saw that he was sweating.

'Here it is,' he said. 'There's an account I handle in the office. A small new company. A couple of very smart young guys. Two kids out of MIT. They're on to something. Something that can be very big. Big, *big*. They've got a patent pending for a new system of miniaturization. For all sorts of electronic systems. But they're just about busted. They need about twenty-five thousand to tide them over. They've been to the banks and they've been refused. I know their situation because I know their books inside out. And I've talked to them about it. I can buy in. With a little pushing, for twenty-five thousand, I could have a third of the stock. And I could become an officer of the company, treasurer, to protect our interests. Once they go into production, they'd go on the board on Amex...'

'What's Amex?' I asked.

'American Exchange.' He looked at me oddly. 'Where the hell have you been all these years?'

'No place,' I said.

'There's no limit to how high the stock would go. I'd take a third of the thirty-three percent and you'd get two-thirds. Does that seem unfair to you?' he asked anxiously.

'No.' I had already kissed the twenty-five thousand good-bye. None of it was real to me anyway. Stacks of paper in a vault.

'You're noble, Doug, noble.' Henry's voice was quivering with emotion.

'Oh, cut it out, Hank,' I said sharply. I didn't feel noble. 'Can you be in New York Wednesday?'

'Sure.'

'I'll have the money ready for you. In cash. I'll call you at your office Tuesday and tell you where to meet me.'

'In cash?' Henry looked puzzled. 'What's the matter with a check? I hate to carry that much cash around with me.'

'You'll just have to bear the burden,' I said. 'I don't write checks.' I could see his face working. He wanted the money – badly, badly – but he was an honest man and no fool and there was no doubt in his mind that whatever else the money was, it wasn't honest. 'Doug,' he said, 'I don't want you to get into trouble on my account. If it means . . .' He was pushing himself and I appreciated what it cost him. 'Well, I'd rather do without it.'

'Let me handle my end,' I said curtly. 'You handle yours. Just be in your office Tuesday morning for my call.'

He sighed, an old man's resigned, weary sigh, honesty too difficult a position to maintain. 'Baby brother,' was all he said.

*

I was glad to get out of Scranton and back on the icy road to Washington. At the wheel, I thought of the poker game that night and touched the silver dollar in my pocket.

I was stopped for speeding in Maryland, where the ice ran out, and bribed the cop with a fifty-dollar bill. Mr Ferris, or whatever his name really was, was spreading the wealth all through the American economy.

7

It was late in the afternoon when I arrived in Washington. The monuments to Presidents, generals, justice, and law, all the ambiguous Doric-American pantheon, were wavery in a soft, twilight Southern mist. Scranton could have been in another climate zone, another country, a distant civilization. The streets were almost empty, and the few people walking there in the quiet dusk moved slowly, peacefully. Jeremy Hale had said Washington was at its best on weekends, when the mills of government ground to a halt. In the capital, between Friday afternoon and Monday morning, it was possible to believe in the value and decorum of democracy. I wondered idly what the blonde lady whose taxicab I had shared was doing with her holiday.

There was no message for me at the desk of the hotel, and, when I went up to my room, I called Hale at his home. A child answered, her voice bell-like and pure, and I had a sudden, unexpected moment of jealousy because there was no child to answer for me and to call, with uncomplicated love, 'Daddy, it's for you.'

'Is the game still on?' I asked Hale.

'Good,' Hale said. 'You got back. I'll pick you up at eight.'

It was only five o'clock and I played with the idea of calling Evelyn Coates' number to see which one of the ladies was at home. But then what would I say? 'Listen, I have two hours to spare.' I was not that sort of a man and never would be. So much the worse for me.

I shaved and took a long hot bath. Lying there, luxuriously steaming myself, I counted my blessings. They were not insignificant. 'Peter Piper picked a peck of pickled peppers,' I said aloud in the clouded bathroom. I hadn't stuttered once in five days and nights. In a minor way it was like being able to throw down your crutches and stride away from the spring at Lourdes. Then there was the money in the vault in New York, of course. Again and again, I found myself thinking of it, the neat stacks of bills lying in the steel box, laden with infinite promise. The twenty-five thousand dollars I was going to give Hank was a small price to pay for freeing me from the guilt about my brother that had lain somewhere in my subconscious for so many years. And Evelyn Coates . . . Old man, I thought, remembering the flaccid body in the corridor, you have not died in vain.

I got out of the bath, feeling fit and rested, put on some fresh clothes and went down and had a leisurely dinner by myself, without liquor. Not before a poker game.

I made sure I had the silver dollar in my pocket when Hale came to get me. If there ever was a gambler, dead or alive, who was not superstitious, I haven't heard of him.

Silver dollar or no silver dollar, Hale nearly got us killed driving to the hotel in Georgetown, where the weekly poker game was played. He went through a stop sign without looking and there was a wild screech of brakes as a Pontiac swerved to avoid hitting us. From the Pontiac somebody screamed, incomprehensibly, 'Goddamn niggers.'

Hale had been a careful driver in college. 'Sorry,' he said. 'People drive like maniacs on Saturday night.' If gambling did that to me, I thought, I wouldn't play. But I didn't say anything.

There was a big round table covered by a green cloth set up in one of the small private dining rooms of the hotel, and an array of bottles, ice, and glasses on a sideboard, all under a strong light. Very professional. I looked forward to the evening. There were three other men already in the room and one woman, standing with her back to the door fixing herself a drink as we came in. Hale introduced me to the men first. I found out later that one of them was a well-known columnist, one a congressman from upstate New York, who looked like Warren Gamaliel Harding, white-haired, benign, falsely presidential. The last player was a youngish lawyer by the name of Benson who worked at the Department of Defense. I had never met a columnist or a congressman before. Was I going up or down on the social scale?

When the woman turned around to greet us, I saw that it was Evelyn Coates. Somehow, I wasn't surprised. 'Yes,' she said, without smiling, as Hale started to introduce us. 'I know Mr Grimes. I believe I met him at a party the other night at your house, Jerry.'

'Of course,' Hale said. 'I must be losing my mind.' He did seem distracted. I noticed that he kept rubbing the side of his jaw with the palm of his hand, as though he had an intermittent itch there. I made a small bet with myself that he would wind up losing that night.

Evelyn Coates was dressed in dark blue slacks, not too close-fitting, and a loose beige sweater. Working clothes, I thought. Dyke? I dismissed the idea. Probably when she was younger she was one of those girls who played touch football with the boys on the block. I wondered if her room-mate had told her about me.

She was the only one in the room who had a drink in her hand as we sat down at the table and started counting our chips. She piled her chips expertly, her long hands deft, pale fingers, pale polished nails.

'Evelyn,' Benson said as the congressman began to throw cards for the first ace to deal, 'tonight you must be merciful.'

'Without fear or favor,' she said.

The lawyer, I noticed, seemed to have a special, teasing relationship with her. I put it out of my mind. I didn't like his voice either, round and self-satisfied. I put that out of my mind, too. I was there to play cards.

Everybody took the game very seriously, and there was almost no conversation except for the usual postmortems between hands. Hale had told me the game was a moderate one. Nobody had ever lost more than a thousand dollars on any one night, he said. If he hadn't been married to a rich wife, I doubt that he would have called it moderate.

Evelyn Coates was a tricky player, unpredictable and hard-nosed. She won the second biggest pot of the night on a pair of eights. In other days you would have said she played like a man. Her expression was the same whether she won or lost, cool and businesslike. It was hard for me to remember, as I faced her across the table, that I had ever been in her bed.

I won the biggest pot of the night on a low straight. I had never had as much money to back me up in any of the games I had been in before, but, as far as I could tell, I played as I always did. My new-found fortune wasn't reflected in my betting. I folded early a good deal of the time.

The newspaper columnist and the congressman were the eternal pigeons Hale had promised me. They played out of hope and optimism, and were around at the end of almost every pot. Inevitably, it made me doubt their wisdom in other fields. I knew I would read the columnist from then on with great reservations, and I trusted the congressman wasn't in on any important legislative decisions.

It was a friendly game and even the losers were good-natured about their bad luck. I enjoyed playing poker again after the three-year hiatus. I would have enjoyed it more if Evelyn Coates hadn't been there. I kept looking for a wink, a secret, conspiratorial smile, but it never came. I couldn't help beginning to feel resentful. I didn't let it affect my game, but I felt a little extra satisfaction when I took a pot away from her.

She and I were the only winners at two o'clock, when we finished. While the congressman, as banker, bent over the accounts, I fingered the silver dollar in my pocket. The go-ahead sign from Central Park West.

A waiter had brought in some sandwiches, and we started on them while the congressman worked at the table. I couldn't help but think how pleasant it all was, a game that continued, in the same room, with the same friends, week after week, everybody knowing everybody's telephone number, everybody's address, everybody's mannerisms and jokes. Whom would I be seeing next week, what numbers would I dare call, what game would I be playing? For a moment I was on the verge of saying that I would be available next week to give them all the chance to get back their money. Put down my roots in a deck of cards, in the mulch of government. How fast did I have to run? If Evelyn Coates had as much as smiled at me, I believe I would have spoken. But she didn't even glance in my direction.

To give her a chance to say a few words to me away from the others, I went over to a window at the far corner of the room and opened it, pretending I was warm and the cigarette smoke was bothering me, but she still did not make a gesture toward me, didn't even seem to notice that I had moved.

The bitch, I thought, I won't give her the satisfaction of calling when I get back to my hotel. I imagined her in her place with the young lawyer, smooth and tallow-faced, and the phone ringing and Evelyn Coates saying, 'Hell, let it ring,' and knowing who it was on the other end and smiling secretly to herself. I wasn't used to hard women. To any kind of women, if I wanted to be honest with myself. One thing, I decided, as I closed the window with a sharp little click, insisting on my presence, one thing I'm going to do from now on is learn how to handle women.

The columnist and the lawyer began a long discussion about what was happening in Washington. The columnist accused the President of trying to destroy the American press, raising postal rates to drive newspapers and magazines into bankruptcy, jailing reporters for not disclosing their sources, threatening to lift the franchises of television stations that broadcast material which displeased the Administration, all stuff that I had read in his columns whenever I had happened to come across them. Even I, who barely read any newspaper but the *Racing Form*, was overexposed to all possible opinions. I wondered how anyone in that room, battered by arguments from all sides, ever managed to vote yes or no on anything. The congressman, working on a scratch pad, his forehead sweating from the effort, never even looked up. He had showed himself an amiable man throughout the game, and I supposed he voted as he was told, his attention always on party instructions and on the next election. He had said nothing to indicate whether he was a Republican, a Democrat, or a follower of Mao.

When Evelyn Coates brought up the subject of the Watergate break-in and said it meant grave trouble ahead for the President, the columnist said, 'Nonsense. He's too smart for that. It'll all just be kicked under the rug. Mark my words. By May, if you ask anybody about it, they'll say, "Watergate? What's that?" I'll tell you,' said the columnist, his deep voice and meticulous speech resonant with the assurance of a man who was accustomed to being listened to attentively at all times, 'I tell you we're witnessing the opening moves toward Fascism.'

As he spoke, he munched on a corned beef sandwich, washed down with Scotch. 'The skinheads are preparing the ground. I won't be surprised if they're not called in to run the whole show. One morning we'll wake up and the tanks will be rolling down Pennsylvania Avenue and the machine guns will be on every roof.' *That* hadn't been in any of his columns that I had read. Come to Washington and get the real, authentic, scary dope.

The lawyer didn't seem to be at all ruffled by the charges. He had the calm, good-natured imperturbability of the pliant Company Man. 'Maybe it wouldn't be such a bad idea,' he said. 'The press is irresponsible. It lost the war in Asia for us. It churns up the public against the President, the Vice President, it holds up all authority to scorn, it's making it more and more impossible to govern the country. Maybe putting the skinheads, as you call them, in control for a few years might be the best thing that happened to this country since Alf Landon.'

'Oh, Jack,' Mrs Coates said, 'the true believer. The voice of the Pentagon. What crap!'

'If you saw what passed over my desk day after day,' the lawyer said, 'you wouldn't call it crap.'

'Mr Grimes...' She turned toward me, a little cool smile on her lips. 'You're not in the mess here in Washington. You represent the pure, undefiled American public here tonight. Let's hear the simple wisdom of the masses....'

'Evelyn,' Hale said warningly. I half-expected to hear him

say, 'Remember, he's our guest.' But he let it go with the 'Evelyn'.

I looked at her, annoyed with her for taunting me, feeling that she was testing me somehow, for some not quite innocent purpose of her own. 'The pure, undefiled representative of the American public here tonight,' I said, 'thinks it's all bullshit.' I remembered the speech she had made to me, naked, a glass of whiskey in her hand, sitting on the side of the big soft bed in the darkened room, about everybody in Washington being an actor. 'You people aren't serious,' I said. 'It's all a game for you. It's not a game for me, the pure, undefiled etcetera; it's life and death and taxes, and other little things like that for me, but it's just a pennant race for you. You depend upon each other to have different opinions, just the way baseball teams depend upon other teams to have different color uniforms. Otherwise, nobody would know who was leading the league. In the end, though, you're all playing the same game.' I was surprised at myself even as I spoke. I didn't even know that I had ever thought like this before. 'If you get traded to another team, you'll just take off the old suit and put on another one and you'll go out there and try to boost your batting average so you can ask for a raise the next year.'

'Let me ask you something, Grimes,' the lawyer said affably. 'Did you vote in the last election?'

'I did,' I said. 'I got fooled. The papers printed the sports news on the editorial pages. I don't intend to vote again. It's an undignified occupation for a grown man.' I didn't tell them that, where I expected I'd be by the time of the next elections, there wouldn't be a chance I'd be able to vote.

'Forgive me, folks,' Evelyn Coates said, 'I didn't realize I had introduced a homespun political philosopher into our midst.'

'I'm not absolutely against what he said,' the lawyer said. 'I don't see where it's so wrong to be loyal to the team. If the team's winning, of course.' He chuckled softly at his own joke.

The congressman looked up from his accounts. If he had heard a word of the discussion, or any discussion for the last ten years, for that matter, he didn't show it. 'Okay,' he said, 'it all comes out even. Evelyn, you won three hundred and fifty-five dollars and fifty cents. Mr Grimes, you won twelve hundred and seven dollars. Everybody else get out their checkbooks.'

While the losers were finding out how much they owed, there were the usual jokes, directed at Hale, for bringing a ringer, me, into the game. Evelyn Coates made no jokes. There was no hint in the way anyone else talked that anything like an argument had just taken place.

I tried to look offhand as I put the checks into my wallet. Luckily, they were all on Hale's Washington bank. He endorsed them for me so that I wouldn't have any trouble cashing them.

We all left together, and there was a jumble of good-byes as the congressman and the columnist got into a taxi together. The lawyer took Evelyn by the arm, saying, 'You're on my way, Evelyn, I'll drop you.' Hale was inside getting a pack of cigarettes from the machine, and I stood alone for a moment watching the lawyer and Evelyn Coates walk off into the darkness of the parking lot. I heard her low laugh at something he had said as they disappeared.

*

Hale drove silently for a little while. 'How long do you plan to stay in town?' he asked, as we were stopped for a light.

'Just until I get my passport. Monday, Tuesday . . .'

'Then where?'

'Then I'll look at a map. Somewhere in Europe.'

He started the car with a jerk as the light changed. 'God I wish I was coming along with you. Wherever you're going.' The intensity in his voice was disturbing. He sounded like a prisoner speaking to a man who was about to be freed in the morning. 'This town,' he said. 'Total swamp.' He turned a corner recklessly, the tires squealing. 'That miserable, smooth, molasses-talking Benson bastard ... It's a lucky thing you're not in the government. . . .'

'What're you talking about?' I was really honestly puzzled.

'If you were – in the government, I mean – by Monday night, somebody in your department – *higher* in your department – would get a little poison in his ear about you.'

'You mean because of what I said about voting and changing uniforms, that stuff?' I tried not to sound incredulous, as though I were really taking him seriously. 'Actually, I hardly meant it. I was joking, or, anyway, half-joking.'

'You don't joke in this town, friend,' Hale said somberly. 'At least not in front of guys like him. I've been trying to get him out of the game for six months and nobody's got the guts to do the job. Including me. You may have been joking, but he for sure wasn't.'

'At one point in the evening,' I said, 'I was on the point of saying I'd hang around till next Saturday.'

'Don't. Blow. Blow as fast as you can. I wish to hell I could.'

'I don't know how it works in your department,' I said, 'but can't you ask for an assignment someplace else?'

'I can ask,' Hale said. 'That's about as far as it would go.' He fumbled at a cigarette. 'They have me pegged as unreliable in the service, and they're making sure they can keep an eye on me twenty-four hours a day....'

'You? Unreliable?' It was the last thing I'd ever guess anybody would think about him.

'I was in Thailand for two years. I sent you a letter. Remember?'

'I never got it, I've been moving around a lot....'

'I wrote a couple of reports that didn't exactly go through channels.' He laughed bitterly. 'Channels! Sewers. Well, they yanked me – politely – and gave me a nice office with a beautiful secretary and a raise in salary and some memos to shuffle that you might just as well paper the walls with. And the only reason they're being so kind to me is because of my goddamn father-in-law. But the message was clear – and I got it. Be a good boy or else ... God!' He laughed again, a harsh, croaking sound. 'When I think that I celebrated when I found out I passed the Foreign Service exam! And it's all so senseless – those reports I wrote ... I was patting myself on the back – the intrepid truth-seeker, the brave little old truth-announcer. Christ, there wasn't anything in those pages that hasn't been spread over every newspaper in the country since then.' He scraped his cigarette out savagely in the ash-tray on the dashboard. 'We live in the age of the Bensons, the smooth poison-droppers, who know from birth that the way up is through the sewer. I'll tell you something peculiar – a physiological phenomenon – somebody ought to write it up in a medical journal – I have days when I have the taste of shit in my mouth all day. I wash my teeth, I gargle, I get my secretary to put a bowl of narcissus on my desk – nothing helps. . . .'

'Jesus,' I said. 'I thought you were doing great.'

'I put on a good act,' Hale said lifelessly. 'I have to. I'm a dandy little old liar. It's a government of liars and you get plenty of practice. Happy civil servant, happy husband, happy son-in-law, happy father of two. . . . Ah, Christ, why am I letting it all out on you? I imagine you have troubles enough of your own.'

'Not at the moment,' I said. 'If it's so bad, why don't you quit? Go into something else?'

'Into what?' he said. 'Selling neckties?'

'Something would be bound to turn up.' I didn't tell him that there might be a job open as a night clerk in New York. 'Take a few months off and look around and . . .'

'On what?' He made a derisive sound. 'I haven't a penny. You saw how we live. My salary's just about half of it. My sainted father-in-law kicks in the rest. He nearly had apoplexy when I got sent home from Asia. He'd burn the house down over my head if I told him I was quitting. He'd have my wife and the kids back living with him in two months after I went out the door. . . . Ah, forget it, forget it, I don't know why I suddenly went off the handle like this. That sonofabitch Benson. I see him multiplied by a thousand every time I come to work in the morning. What the hell – I don't *have* to play in that poker game anymore. At least that'll be *one* Benson I won't have to talk to.' He laughed softly. 'Maybe if I'd won tonight, I'd be telling you what a great life it is right this minute in this dandy little old town of Washington.' He was driving more and more slowly, as though he didn't want to be left alone or have to go home and face the concrete facts of his wife, his children, his career, his father-in-law. I wasn't so anxious to get to my hotel room either. I didn't want to put on the light and look at the telephone on the bedside table and fight down the temptation to pick it up and ask for Evelyn Coates's number.

'I wonder if you'd do me a favor, Doug?' he said, as we neared my hotel.

'Of course.' But even as I said it, I made strong mental reservations. After the conversation in the car, I didn't have any inclination to get mixed up more than was absolutely necessary with the life and problems of my old college buddy, Jeremy Hale.

'Come out to dinner tomorrow night,' he said, 'and somehow get onto the subject of skiing and say you're thinking of going skiing in Vermont the first two weeks next month and why don't I join you?'

'I don't think I'll even be in the country by then,' I said.

'That makes no difference,' he said calmly. 'Just say it. Where my wife can hear it. I have some time coming to me and I can get away then.'

'You mean you have to make excuses to your wife if you want to . . .?'

'Not really.' He sighed, at the wheel. 'It's more complicated than that. There's a girl . . .'

'Oh.'

'That's it.' He laughed uneasily. 'Oh. That doesn't sound like me either, does it?' He said it pugnaciously, as though somehow he was accusing me of something.

'Frankly, no,' I said.

'It *isn't* like me. This is the first time since I've been married . . . I never thought it would happen. But it *did* happen and it's driving me crazy. We've just had a few times . . . a few minutes, an hour, here and there. Sneaking around. It's killing both of us. In a town like this, with people snooping around like bird dogs after everybody. We need some time together – *real* time. God knows what my wife would do if anybody ever said anything to her. I didn't want it to happen, I swear to God, but it happened. I feel as though the top of my head is going to blow off. I can't talk to anyone in this town. It's like living with a stone on my chest, day in, day out. I never knew I could feel like this about any woman. . . . You might as well know who it is. . . .'

I waited. I had the terrible feeling that the name he was going to come out with would be Evelyn Coates.

'It's that girl in my office,' he said, whispering. 'Miss Schwartz. Miss Melanie Schwartz. God, what a name!'

'Name or no name,' I said, 'I can understand. She's beautiful.'

'She's a lot more than that. I'm going to tell you something, Doug – if it keeps going on the way it's been going – I don't know what I'm liable to do. We've got to get out of this town together . . . a week, two weeks, a night . . . But we've got to . . . I don't want a divorce. I've been married ten years, I don't want . . . Oh, hell, I don't know why I should drag you into it.'

'I'll come to dinner tomorrow night,' I said.

Hale didn't say anything. He stopped in front of the hotel. 'I'll expect you around seven,' he said calmly, as I got out of the car.

In the elevator on the way up to my floor, I thought, Scranton isn't all that far from Washington after all.

As I got ready for bed I kept away from the telephone in my room. I took a long time getting to sleep. I guess I was waiting for the phone to ring. It didn't ring.

*

I couldn't tell whether it was the telephone that awoke me or if I had opened my eyes just before it began to ring. I had had a nasty, jumbled dream in which I was hiding out, running, from unseen and unknown pursuers, through dark, forested country, then suddenly in glaring sunlight between rows of ruined houses. I was glad to be awake and I reached over gratefully for the telephone.

It was Hale. 'I didn't get you up, did I?' he asked.

'No.'

'Listen,' he said, 'I'm afraid I have to cancel the dinner tonight. My wife says we're invited out.' He sounded offhand and untroubled.

'That's okay,' I said, trying not to let my relief show in my voice.

'Besides,' he said, 'I talked to the lady in question and—'
The rest of the sentence was muffled by a deep crescendo of
sound.

'What's that noise?' I asked. I remembered what he had
said about phones being tapped in Washington.

'It's a lion roaring,' he said. 'I'm in the zoo with my kids.
Want to join us?'

'Some other time, Jerry,' I said. 'I'm still in bed.' After the
outburst in the car after the poker game, I didn't relish the
idea of watching him play the role of the dutiful father de-
voting his Sunday morning to his children. I have never been
expert at complicity and didn't relish the thought of being
used to deceive infants.

'See you in the office tomorrow,' he said. 'Remember to
bring your birth certificate.'

'I'll remember,' I said.

The lion was roaring as I hung up.

I was in the shower when the phone rang again. Streaming
and soapy, grabbing a towel to wrap around my middle, I
picked up the phone.

'Hello,' the voice said. 'I waited as long as I could.' It was
Evelyn Coates. Her voice was half an octave lower on the
phone. 'I have to leave the house. I thought you might have
been tempted to call last night, after the game. Or this morning.' Her self-confidence was irritating.

'No,' I said, leaning back, trying to keep the water from
dripping onto the bed. 'It didn't occur to me,' I lied. 'Anyway, you seemed somewhat preoccupied.'

'What are you doing today?' she asked, ignoring my
complaint.

'At the moment I'm taking a shower.' I felt at a disadvantage trying to cope with that low, bantering voice, the
water dripping coldly down my back from my wet hair and
my eyes beginning to smart because I had gotten some soap
in them.

She laughed. 'Aren't you polite?' she said. 'Getting out of a
shower to answer the phone. You knew it was me, didn't you?'

'The thought may have crossed my mind.'

'Can I take you to lunch?'

I hesitated, but not for long. After all, I had nothing better to do that afternoon in Washington. 'That would be fine,' I said.

'I'll meet you at Trader Vic's,' she said. 'It's a Polynesian place in the Mayflower. It's nice and dark, so you won't see the poker-rings under my eyes. One o'clock?'

'One o'clock,' I said. I sneezed. I heard her laugh.

'Go back to your shower and then dry yourself thoroughly, like a good boy. We don't want you spreading cold germs among the Republicans.'

I sneezed again as I hung up. I fumbled my way back to the bathroom with my eyes smarting from the soap. A dark room would suit me, too, because I knew my eyes would be bloodshot the better part of the afternoon. Somehow, I was beginning to have the feeling that I would have to be at my best physically and mentally, anytime I had anything to do with Evelyn Coates.

*

'Grimes,' she said to me as we were finishing lunch in the dimly lit room, watching the Chinese or Malayan or Tahitian waiter pour flaming rum into our coffee, 'you give me the impression of being a man with something to hide.'

It came as a complete surprise to me. Until then our conversation had been almost absolutely impersonal – about the food, the drinks (she had had three enormous rum concoctions, with no apparent effect) – about the poker game the night before (she had complimented me on the way I played and I had complimented her) – about the various social strata in Washington and where the people of the night before fitted in, all the small polite kind of talk with which a courteous and worldly woman might fill an hour to entertain a visitor from afar who had been asked to look her up by some mutual friend. She was dressed charmingly, in a loose tweed suit and plain blue blouse, high at the throat, and had her dark blonde hair pulled back and tied with a blue ribbon in girlish fashion. I had spoken little, and, if I wondered why she had bothered to call me, I hadn't shown it. She hadn't mentioned the night we had spent together, and I had made up my mind not to be the first to bring it up.

'Something to hide,' she repeated. My questions to her the night I had met her, I realized, had not been forgotten. Had been filed away in that sharp, suspicious mind for future reference.

'I don't know what you're talking about,' I said. But I avoided her eyes.

'Yes, you do,' she said. She watched the waiter finish with his performance and place the mugs of hot coffee, smelling of rum and orange and cinnamon sticks, in front of us. 'I've seen you three times now – and this is what I don't know about you – where you come from, where you're going, what you're doing in town, what business you're in, why you didn't call me after the other night.' She sipped at her drink, smiling demurely over the rim of the mug. 'Every other man I've ever seen three times in one week has regaled me with his complete biography – how his father didn't communicate with him, how important he is, what stocks he's bought, all the influential people he knows in town, what problems he has with his wife . . .'

'I'm not married.'

'Bravo,' she said. 'I am in possession of a fact. Mind you, I'm not digging for information. I'm not all that curious about you. It just occurred to me all of a sudden that you must be hiding something. Please don't tell me what it is' – she held up her hand as though to stop me from saying anything. 'You might turn out to be a lot less interesting than I think you are. There's only one thing I'd like to ask you, if you don't mind.'

'I don't mind.' I could hardly say less.

'Are you staying in Washington?'

'No.'

'According to Jerry Hale you're going abroad.'

'Eventually,' I said.

'What does that mean?'

'Soon. In a week or so.'

'Are you going to Rome?'

'I imagine so.'

'Are you prepared to do me a favor?'

'If I can.'

She looked at me consideringly, tapping a fingernail absently on the wood surface of the table. She seemed to come to some decision. 'In the course of my duties,' she said, 'I have come across certain private memorandums of considerable interest. I've taken the liberty of Xeroxing them. The Xerox is Washington's secret weapon. No man is safe if there's one in the office. I happen to have a small sampling of records of delicate negotiations that someday may prove very useful to me. And to a friend – a very good friend. He used to work with me, and I'd like to protect him. He's in the embassy in Rome. I want to get some papers to him – some papers very important to me and to him – safely. I don't trust the mails here. And I certainly don't trust them in Rome. My friend has told me he thinks his correspondence is being tampered with, both in the embassy and at his home. Don't look so surprised. If you'd been in this city as long as I have...' She didn't finish the sentence. 'There's not a soul here I really trust. People talk incessantly, pressures are applied, mail is opened, as I said, phones are bugged ... I imagine your good friend Jeremy Hale intimated as much to you.'

'He did. You think you can trust me?'

'I think so.' Her voice was hard, almost threatening. 'For one thing, you won't be in Washington. And if you're hiding something important of your own, as I believe ... Do you deny it?'

'Let it pass,' I said. 'For the moment.'

'For the moment.' She nodded, smiling pleasantly at me. 'As I said, if you're hiding something important of your own, why couldn't you undertake a little secret errand for a friend? Something that wouldn't take up more than a half hour of your time – and keep quiet about it?' She dug in the big leather handbag that she had on the floor under the table and produced a thick, business-size envelope, sealed with Scotch tape. She slapped it down on the table between us. 'It doesn't take up much space, as you can see.'

'I don't know when I'm going to be in Rome,' I said. 'Maybe not for months.'

'There's no rush,' she said deliberately. She pushed the

envelope a half-inch closer to me across the table with her fingernail. She was a hard woman to say no to. 'Any time before May will do.'

There was no name or address on the envelope. She took out a small gold pencil and a notebook. 'Here's the address and telephone number of my friend,' she said. 'Call him at home. I'd rather you didn't deliver this at the embassy. I'm sure you'll like him. He knows everybody in Rome and you might meet some interesting people through him. I'd appreciate it if you dropped me a line after you've seen him to let me know the deed's been done.'

'I'll write you,' I said.

'There's a nice boy.' She pushed the envelope still closer to me. 'From all indications,' she said evenly, 'you would like to see me from time to time. Am I right?'

'Yes, you're right.'

'Who knows?' she said. 'If I knew where you were and I had a few weeks of holiday, I might just turn up . . .'

It was pure blackmail and we both knew it. But it was more than that, too. I was going abroad with the intention of losing myself. I had told Hank that I would get in touch with him from time to time, but that was different. He would never know where I was. Looking across the table at this baffling, desirable woman, I realized that I did not want to lose myself completely, cut all ties to America, have no one in my native country who could, *in extremis*, reach me with a message, even if the message were only 'Happy Birthday' or, 'Will you lend me a hundred dollars?'

'If you're tempted to open this' – she touched the envelope – 'and read what's in it, by all means do so. Naturally, I'd rather you didn't. But I promise you there is nothing there that'll make the slightest sense to you.'

I picked up the envelope and put it in my inside pocket. I was connected to her, even if it was only by the memory of a single night, and she knew it. Just how deeply she was connected to me was another matter. 'I won't open it.'

'I was sure I could depend on you, Grimes,' she said.

'Use my first name, please,' I said, 'the next time we meet.'

'I'll do that,' she said. She looked at her watch. 'If you're finished with your coffee,' she said, 'I'll pay and we'll leave. I have a date in Virginia.'

'Oh,' I said, trying not to sound disappointed. 'I thought we might spend the afternoon together.'

'Not this time, I'm afraid,' she said. 'If you're lonely, I believe my room-mate, Brenda, isn't doing anything this afternoon. She said she thought you were very nice. You might give her a call.'

'I might,' I said. I was glad the room was dimly lit. I was sure I was blushing. But I was stung by the callousness of her offer. 'Do your lovers always go with the apartment?' I asked.

She looked at me evenly, undisturbed. 'I think I told you once before that you are not my lover,' she said. Then she called to the waiter for the check.

*

I didn't phone Evelyn's room-mate. By some perverse reasoning that I didn't really try to understand, I decided that I would not give Evelyn Coates *that* satisfaction. I spent the afternoon walking around Washington. Now that I knew, at least fragmentarily, what went on behind those soaring columns, off the long corridors, in those massive copies of Grecian temples, I was not as impressed as I otherwise would have been. Rome, I thought, just before the arrival of the Goths. It occurred to me that I probably was never going to vote again, though I was not saddened by the idea. But for the first time in three years I felt unbearably lonely.

As I entered the lobby of my hotel in the dusk, I made up my mind to leave Washington that night. The sooner I arranged to get out of the country the better. As I packed my bags I remembered George Wales' ski club. What was its name? The Christie Ski Club. No worrying about baggage allowance, no worrying about the Swiss customs, all the free booze you could drink. I had no intention of arriving economically drunk when I set foot on European soil, but with the freight I would be carrying, being waved through Swiss customs with a smile had obvious attractions. Besides, if anybody was watching for the clerk who had fled the Hotel St Augustine with a hundred thousand dollars in hundred-dollar bills, I reasoned, the last place they'd think to look would be the counter where some three hundred and fifty hilarious suburbanites were embarking for a holiday in the snow from which they would all return en masse in three weeks to the United States.

I was just about to close my second bag when the phone rang. I didn't want to speak to anybody and I let it ring. But it rang persistently and finally I picked it up.

'I know you're there ...' It was Evelyn Coates's voice. 'I'm in the lobby and I asked at the desk if you were in.'

'How was Virginia?' I said flatly.

'I'll tell you when I see you. May I come up?' She sounded hesitant, uncertain.

'I suppose so,' I said.

She chuckled, a little sadly, I thought. 'Don't punish me,' she said. And hung up.

I buttoned the collar of my shirt, pushed the tie into place, and put on my jacket, ready for all formalities.

*

'Ghastly,' she said, when she came through the door and looked around her at my room. 'Chromium America.'

I helped her off with her coat, because she stood there with her arms out as though expecting it. 'I don't intend to spend the rest of my life here,' I said.

'I see,' she said, glancing at the packed bag on the bed. 'Are you on your way?'

'I thought I was.'

'Past tense.'

'Uh-huh.' We were standing stiffly, confronting one another.

'And now?'

'I'm not in all that much of a hurry.' I did nothing to make her comfortable. 'I thought you said you were busy today.... In Virginia.'

'I was,' she said. 'But during the course of the afternoon, it occurred to me that there was one person I desperately wanted to see and that he was in Washington. So here I am.' She smiled experimentally. 'I hope I'm not intruding.'

'Come in,' I said.

'Are you going to ask me to sit down?'

'I'm sorry,' I said. 'Of course. Please.'

She sat down, with neat, womanly grace, her ankles primly crossed. She must have been walking in the cold in Virginia because the color was heightened along her cheekbones.

'What else occurred to you?' I asked, still standing, but at a good distance from her.

'A few other things,' she said. She was wearing brown driving gloves, and she pulled them off and dropped them in her lap. Her long fingers, nimble with cards, deft with men, shone in the light of the lamp on the desk beside her. 'I decided I didn't like the way I talked to you at lunch.'

'I've heard worse,' I said.

She shook her head. 'It was pure, hard-boiled Washingtonese. Defend yourself at all times. Professional deformation of speech habits. No reason to be used on you. You don't have to be defended against. I'm sorry.'

I went over to her and kissed the top of her head. Her hair smelled of winter countryside. 'There's nothing to be sorry about. I'm not as tender as all that.'

'Maybe I think you are,' she said. 'Of course you didn't call Brenda.'

'Of course not,' I said.

'What a stupid, patronizing thing for me to have said.' She sighed. 'On weekends,' she said, 'I must learn to leave my armor at home.' She smiled up at me, her face soft and young in the subdued glow of the lamp. 'You'll forget I said it, won't you?'

'If you want. What else occurred to you in Virginia?'

'It occurred to me that the only time we made love, we both had had too much to drink.'

'That's for fair.'

'I thought how nice it would be if we made love stone-cold sober. Have you had anything to drink since lunch?'

'No.'

'Neither have I,' she said, standing up and putting her arms around me.

This time she allowed me to undress her.

Sometime in the middle of the night she whispered, 'You

must leave Washington in the morning. If you stay another day, maybe I'll never let you out of the city again. And we can't have that, can we?'

When I woke in the morning, she was gone. She had left a note on the desk in her bold, slanted handwriting. 'Weekend blues. It's Monday now. Don't take anything the lady said seriously, please. E.'

She had put on her armor for the day's work. I crumpled the note and threw it in the waste-basket.

8

I got my passport the next day. Mr Hale was not in his office, but he had left all the necessary instructions, Miss Schwartz said. I was fairly certain that Mr Hale was not in his office because by the end of the weekend he had come to the conclusion that he wouldn't be comfortable seeing me again. Not in the presence of Miss Schwartz. It was not the first time that a man had regretted in daylight the dark confidences of midnight.

Miss Schwartz was as beautiful and melodious as ever, but I didn't envy Jeremy Hale.

I cashed the checks from the poker game, and with the bills in my pocket went to a department store and bought two strong, but lightweight suitcases. They were handsome pieces of luggage, dark blue with red piping, one large, the other an overnight bag. They were expensive, but I was looking for security, not bargains, at the moment. I also bought a roomy leather attaché case, with a sturdy lock. The case fitted snugly into the larger of the two bags. I was now armed for travel, Ulysses with the black ships caulked and a fair wind behind him, unknown perils beyond the next promontory.

The salesman asked what numbers I wanted to put into the combination. 'It's advisable,' he said, 'to use a number that means something to you, that you won't forget.'

'Six-O-Two,' I said. It was a number that meant quite a bit to me and I doubted that I ever would forget it.

With the new bags in the trunk of the rented car, I was on my way toward New York by three o'clock in the afternoon. I had called my brother and told him to meet me outside my bank at ten o'clock the next morning.

I stopped at a motel on the outskirts of Trenton for the night. I wasn't going to stay in New York any longer than I had to.

Knowing that I was doing the wrong thing, accumulating regrets for the future, I called Evelyn's number in Washington. I didn't know what I could say to her, but I wanted to hear the sound of her voice. I let the phone ring a dozen times. Luckily, there was no one home.

*

When I drove through the New York City traffic up Park Avenue, toward the bank, I was stopped at a light at the corner of the cross street on which the St Augustine was located. On an impulse, when the light turned green, I turned down the street. I could feel the skin on the back of my neck prickling as I drove slowly past the falsely impressive canopied entrance, and I even played with the idea of going in and asking for Drusack. It was not a case of nostalgia. There were some questions that he might be able to answer by now. And his predictable rage would have brightened my morning. If there had been a place to park, I think I would have been foolish enough to go in. But the whole street was solidly blocked and I drove on.

Hank was huddled down into his overcoat, with the collar turned up, looking cold and miserable in the biting wind, when I walked up to the bank. If I were a policeman, I thought, I would suspect him of *something*, a small, mean crime, petty forgery, abuse of widow's confidence, peddling fraudulent jewelry.

His face lit up when he saw me, as though he had doubted that I would ever arrive, and he took a step toward me, but I didn't stop. 'Meet me at the next corner uptown,' I said as I passed him. 'I'll only be a minute.' Unless someone had been standing near and watching closely, it couldn't have seemed that there was any connection between us. I had the uncomfortable feeling that the city was one giant eye, focused on me.

In the vault, the same old man, paler than ever, took my key and, using his own along with it, opened my safe and handed me the steel box. He led me back to the curtained cubicle and left me there. I counted out the two hundred and fifty hundred-dollar bills and put them in a manila envelope that I had bought in Washington. I was becoming an important consumer of manila envelopes and was no doubt giving a lift to the entire industry.

*

Hank was waiting for me at the corner, in front of a coffee shop, looking colder than ever. He eyed the manila envelope under my arm fearfully, as though it might explode at any instant. The plate-glass window of the shop was steamed over, but I could see that the place was almost empty. I motioned for Hank to follow me and we went in. I chose a table in the rear and put the manila envelope down and took off my coat. It was suffocatingly hot in the restaurant, but Hank sat down opposite me without taking off his coat or the old, sweat-stained gray slouch hat he was wearing, set squarely and unfashionably on his head. His eyes behind the glasses that dug into the sides of his nose were leaking tears from the cold. He had an old commuter's face. I thought, the kind of face, weathered by years of anxiety and stale indoor air, that you see on men standing on windy station platforms on dark winter mornings, patient as donkeys, weary long before the day's work ever begins. I pitied him and could hardly wait to get rid of him.

Whatever happens, I thought, I am not going to look like that when I'm his age. We still didn't say a word to each other.

When the waitress came over, I asked for a cup of coffee. 'What I need is a drink,' Hank said, but he settled for coffee, too.

Against the partition at the end of the small table, there was a small slot for coins and a selector for the juke box near the entrance. I put in two dimes and jabbed the selector at random. By the time the waitress came back with our coffees, the juke box was playing so loudly that nobody could have heard me at the next table unless I shouted.

Hank drank his coffee greedily. It did not smell of cinnamon or rum or oranges. 'I puked twice this morning,' he said.

'The money is in there.' I tapped the envelope.

'Christ, Doug,' Hank said, 'I hope you know what you're doing.'

'So do I,' I said. 'Anyway, it's yours now. I'll leave first. Give me ten minutes and then you can go.' I didn't want him to see my rented car and note the license number. I hadn't planned any of this and didn't believe it was really necessary, but caution was becoming automatic with me.

'You'll never regret this,' he said.

'No, I won't,' I said.

With a crumpled handkerchief he wiped at the cold-tears streaming from his eyes. 'I told the two fellows that I was coming up with the money this week,' he said. 'They're delirious with joy. They're going for the deal. They didn't say boo.' He opened his overcoat and fished past an old gray muffler that hung around his neck like a dead snake. He brought out a pen and a small notebook. 'I'll write a receipt.'

'Forget it,' I said. 'I know I gave you the money and you know you got the money.' He had never asked for a receipt for any of the sums he had lent me or given me.

'Inside of a year you'll be a rich man, Doug,' he said.

'Good,' I said. His optimism was forlorn. 'I don't want anything on paper. Not anything. As an accountant, I imagine you know how to arrange to check off whatever may be coming to me without any records being kept.' I remembered what Evelyn Coates had said about Xeroxes. I was reasonably sure there were Xeroxes in Scranton, too.

'Yes, I imagine I do.' He said it sadly. He was in the wrong profession, but it was too late now to do anything about it.

'I don't want the Internal Revenue Service looking for me.'

'I understand,' he said. 'I can't say I like it, but I understand.' He shook his head somberly. 'You're the last man in the world I'd . . .'

'That's enough of that, Hank,' I said.

The first record on the juke box ended with an ear-shattering climax, and the voice of the waitress giving an order to the counterman sounded unnaturally loud in the lull. 'Eggs and bacon, up. One English.'

I took another gulp of my coffee and got up, leaving the envelope on the table. I put on my coat. 'I'll be calling you. From time to time.'

He smiled up at me wanly as he put his hand on the envelope. 'Take care of yourself, kid,' he said.

'You, too,' I touched his shoulder and went out into the cold.

*

The flight wasn't scheduled to leave until eight Wednesday night.

On Wednesday afternoon, at two-thirty, I left a hundred-dollar bill in the safety-deposit box and walked out of the bank with seventy-two thousand, nine hundred dollars in the attaché case I had bought in Washington. I was through with manila envelopes. I couldn't have explained, even to myself, why I had left the hundred dollars behind. Superstition? A promise to myself that one day I would come back to the country? In any event, I had paid in advance for the rental of the box for a year.

This time I was staying at the Waldorf Astoria. By now, anybody who was looking for me must have decided that I had left the city. I went back to my room and opened the attaché case and took out three thousand dollars, which I put into the new sealskin wallet I had bought for myself. It was large enough to hold my passport and my round-trip charter ticket. At the Christie Ski Club office on Forty-seventh Street, where I had gone after I left Hank in the coffee shop, I had asked for Wales' friend Miss Mansfield, and the girl had filled out my application form and predated it automatically. She told me I had been lucky to come in just then, as they had two cancellations that morning. Offhandedly, I asked her if the Waleses were also making the flight. She checked her list and to my relief said that they weren't on it. I still had plenty of cash from my winning on *Ask Gloria* and the

Washington poker game. Even without the money in the attaché case and after the expenses of the hotels in Washington and Scranton and what it had cost me when I returned the rented car, I still had more money on me than I ever had carried at one time in my whole life. When I checked in at the desk at the Waldorf, I didn't bother to ask what the room cost. It was a pleasant experience.

I gave Evelyn Coates's address in Washington as my residence. Now that I was completely alone, all my jokes had to be private ones.

There had been very little opportunity for any kind of laughter at all in the last few days. Washington had been a sobering experience. If, as so many people believed, wealth made for happiness, I was a neophyte at the job. I had made a poor choice of companions in my new estate – Hale, with his blocked career and nervous love affair, Evelyn Coates, with her complex armor, my poor brother.

In Europe, I decided, I was going to seek out people without problems. Europe had always been a place to which the American rich had escaped. I now considered myself a member of that class. I would let others who had preceded me teach me the sweet technique of flight. I would look for joyful faces.

On Tuesday night I stayed in my room alone, watching television. On this last night in America there was no sense in taking unnecessary risks.

As a last gesture, I put a hundred and fifty dollars in an envelope with a note to the bookie at the St Augustine that read, 'Sorry I kept you waiting for your money,' and signed my name. There would be one man in America who would vouch for my reputation as an honest man. I mailed the note as I checked out of the hotel.

*

I got to the airport early, by taxi. The attaché case, with the money inside it, was in the big blue bag with the combination lock. The money would be out of my hands, in the baggage compartment, while we crossed the Atlantic, but there was nothing to be done about it. I knew that every passenger was searched and his hand luggage opened and examined before boarding the plane, as a precaution against hijackers, and it would have been awkward, to say the least, to have to try to explain to an armed guard why I needed more than seventy thousand dollars for a three-week skiing trip.

Wales had been right about the overweight, too. The man at the desk never even looked at the scale as the skycap swung my two bags onto it.

'No skis or boots?' he asked.

'No,' I said. 'I'm going to buy them in Europe.'

'Try Rossignols,' he said. 'I hear they're great.' He had become an expert on equipment at a departure desk at Kennedy.

I showed him my passport, he checked the manifest list and gave me a boarding pass and the formalities were over. 'Have a good trip,' he said. 'I wish I was going with you.' The other people on the line with me had obviously started celebrating already, and there was a loud holiday air about the entire occasion, with people embracing and calling to each other and skis clattering to the floor.

I was early and went into the restaurant for a sandwich and a glass of beer. I hadn't eaten lunch and it would be a long time before they served us anything on the plane and I was hungry.

As I ate and drank my beer, I read the evening paper. A policeman had been shot in Harlem that morning. The Rangers had won the night before. A judge had come out against pornographic films. The editors were firmly in favor of impeaching the President. There was talk of his resigning. Men who had had high positions in the White House were being sent to jail. The envelope Evelyn Coates had given me to deliver in Rome was in my small bag, now being stowed into the hold of the airplane. I wondered if I was helping to put someone in jail or keep him out. America. I reflected on my visit to Washington.

There was a pay telephone on the wall near where I was sitting and I suddenly had the desire to speak to someone, make one last statement, make one ultimate connection with a familiar voice, before I left the country. I got up and dialed the operator and once more called Evelyn Coates's number.

Again, there was no answer. Evelyn was a woman who was more likely to be out than in at any given moment. I hung up and got my dime back. I was about to return to my table, where my half-eaten sandwich was waiting for me, when I stopped. I remembered driving down the street past the St Augustine Hotel and nearly stopping. This time there would be no danger. I would be climbing into international jet space within forty minutes. I put the dime back into the machine and dialed the number.

As usual, the phone rang and rang before I heard Clara's voice. 'Hotel St Augustine,' she said. She could manage to get her discontent and her irritation with the entire world even into this brief announcement.

'I'd like to speak to Mr Drusack, please,' I said.

'Mr Grimes!' My name came out in a shriek. She had recognized my voice.

'I would like to speak to Mr Drusack, please,' I said, pretending that I hadn't heard her or at least hadn't understood her.

'Mr Grimes,' she said, 'where are you?'

'Please, miss,' I said, 'I would like to speak to Mr Drusack. Is he there?'

'He's in the hospital, Mr Grimes,' she said. 'Two men followed him in his car and beat him up with a pistol. He's in a coma now. They think his skull is fractured and . . .'

I hung up the phone and went back to my table and finished the sandwich and the beer.

*

The seat belt and no smoking signs went on and the plane started the descent from the zone of morning sunlight. The snow-capped peaks of the Alps glittered in the distance as the 747 slanted into the gray bank of fog that lay on the approaches to Kloten Airport.

The large man in the seat next to mine was snoring loudly. By actual count, between eight and midnight, when I had given up keeping track, he had drunk eleven whiskies. His wife, next to him on the aisle, had kept her own pace, at the ratio of one to his two. They had told me they planned to catch the early train from Zurich to St Moritz and intended to ski the Corvatch that afternoon. I was sorry I couldn't be there to watch their first run down the hill.

The flight had not been restful. Since all the passengers were members of the same ski club, and a great many of them made the trip together every winter, there had been a good deal of loud socializing in the aisles, accompanied by hearty drinking. The passengers were not young. For the most part they were in their thirties or forties, the men seeming to belong to that vague group that goes under the label of the executive class and the women carefully coiffed suburban housewives who were damned if they couldn't hold their liquor as well as their husbands. A certain amount of weekend wife-swapping could be imagined. If I had to make a guess, I would have said that the average income per family of the passengers on the plane was about thirty-five thousand dollars a year and that their children had nice little trust funds set up by Grandpa and Grandma, craftily arranged to avoid the inheritance tax.

If there were any passengers on the plane who were reading quietly or looking out the windows at the stars and the growing dawn, they were not in my part of the aircraft. Sober myself, I regarded my boisterous and boozy fellow-travelers with distaste. In a more restrictive state than America, I thought, they would have been prevented from leaving the country. If my brother Hank had been on the plane, I realized with a touch of sorrow, he would have envied them.

It had been warm in the plane, too, and I hadn't been able to take off my jacket, because my wallet with my money and passport was in it and the wallet was too bulky to fit in my trouser pocket.

The plane touched down smoothly and I had a moment of envy of the men who piloted those marvelous machines, confidently at work on the flight deck forward. For them only the voyage mattered, not the value of the cargo. I made sure that I was one of the first travelers out of the plane. At the terminal building I went through the door reserved for passengers with nothing to declare. I was lucky enough to see my two bags, both blue, one large, one small, come out in the first batch. I grabbed one of the wire carts and threw the bags on it and rolled the cart out of the customs room without being stopped. The Swiss, I saw, were charmingly tolerant toward prosperous visitors to their country.

I got into a waiting taxi and said, 'The Savoy Hotel, please.' I had heard that it was a good hotel in the center of the business district.

I had not changed any money into Swiss currency, but when we arrived at the hotel, the driver agreed to accept two ten-dollar bills. It was two or three dollars more than it would have been if I had had francs, but I didn't argue with the man.

While I was registering, I asked the clerk for the name and telephone number of the nearest private bank. Like most Americans of this age I had only the vaguest notions of just what Swiss private banks might be like, but had a firm belief, nourished by newspaper and magazine articles, in their ability to conceal money safely. The clerk wrote down a name and a number, almost as if that were the first service demanded of him by every American who signed in at his desk.

Another clerk showed me up to my room. It was large and comfortable, with heavy, old-fashioned furniture, and as clean as I had heard Swiss hotel rooms were likely to be.

While waiting for my luggage to come up, I picked up the phone and gave the operator the number the clerk had given me. It was nine-thirty, Swiss time, four-thirty in the morning New York time, but even though I had not slept at all on the plane, I wasn't tired.

A voice on the phone said something in German. 'Do you speak English?' I asked, regretting for the first time that my education had not equipped me even well enough to say 'Good morning' in any language but my own.

'Yes,' the woman said. 'Whom do you wish to speak to?'

'I would like to make an appointment to open an account,' I said.

'Just a moment, please,' she said. Almost immediately a man's voice said, 'Dr Hauser here. Good morning.'

So. In Switzerland men who were entrusted with money were doctors. Why not? Money was both a disease and a cure.

I gave the good doctor my name and explained once more

that I wanted to open an account. He said he would expect me at ten-thirty and hung up.

There was a knock on the door and the porter came in with my bags. I apologized for not having any Swiss money for his tip, but he merely smiled and said, 'Thank you,' and left. I began to feel that I was going to like Switzerland.

I twirled the three tumblers on the lever to open it. The lever did not budge. I tried once more. It still didn't open. I tried again, with the same result. I was sure I was using the correct numbers. I picked up the small bag, which had the same combination, and twirled the tumblers and pushed at the lever. It opened smoothly.

'Damn it,' I said under my breath. The big bag had probably been handled roughly at one end of the flight or the other and the lock had jammed. I had nothing with me with which to force the lock. I didn't want anyone else meddling with the bag, so I went down to the desk and asked for a big screwdriver. The concierge's English vocabulary did not include the word screwdriver, but I finally got him to understand by the use of elaborate gestures what I wanted. He said something in German to an assistant and two minutes later the man reappeared with a screwdriver.

'He can go up with you,' the concierge said, 'and assist you, if you want.'

'That won't be necessary, thank you,' I said, and went back to my room.

It took five minutes of scraping and prying to force the lock, and I mourned for my handsome, brand-new bag as it broke open. I would have to get a new lock put on, if that were possible.

I lifted the lid. On the top of whatever else was in the bag there was a loud, houndstooth sports jacket. I had never owned a jacket like that in my life.

I had taken the wrong bag at the airport. One that looked exactly like mine, the same size and make, the same color, dark blue with red piping. I swore softly at the chain-belt system of manufacturing and selling in America, where everybody makes and sells a million identical copies of everything.

I let the lid drop on the bag and flipped the clasps on each side of the lock shut. I didn't want to disturb anybody else's belongings. It was bad enough that I had broken open the lock. Then I went down to the concierge's desk again. I gave him back the screwdriver and explained what had happened and asked him to call the airport for me to find out if one of the other travelers on my plane had reported that a mistake had been made and, if so, where and how I could pick up my own bag.

'Do you have your baggage checks?' he asked.

I searched through my pockets while the concierge looked on condescendingly. 'Accidents happen. One must foresee,' he said, 'When I travel, I always paste a large, colored etiquette with my initials on it on all my luggage.'

'A very good idea,' I said. 'I will remember it in the future.' I didn't have the baggage checks. I must have thrown them away when I went through customs and saw I didn't need them. 'Can you call, now, please? I don't know any German and ...'

'I shall call,' he said. He picked up the phone and asked for a number.

Five minutes later, after a good deal of agitated Swiss-German, interrupted by long waits which the concierge filled with rapid drumming of his fingertips on his desk, he hung up. 'Nothing has been reported,' he said. 'They will call you here when there is any news. When the passenger who has your bag gets to his hotel, he will undoubtedly discover that there has been an exchange and will make inquiries at the airport.'

'Thank you,' I said.

'For nothing.' He bowed. I did not bow back. I went up to my room.

When the passenger gets your bag to his hotel, the concierge had said. I had overheard some of the conversations on the plane. There were probably five hundred ski resorts in Europe, and from what I had heard my bag might even at that minute be on its way to Davos or Chamonix or Zermatt or Lech or ... I shook my head despairingly. Whoever it was who had my bag might not try to open it until the next morning. And when he did, he probably would do exactly as I had done and break open the lock. And he might not be as fastidious as I had been about disturbing a stranger's affairs.

I lifted the lid of the bag on the bed and stared down at the houndstooth jacket. I had a premonition that I was going to have trouble with the man who would wear a jacket like that. I knocked the lid back hard.

I picked up the telephone and gave the number of the bank. When I got an answer, I asked for Dr Hauser again. He was very polite when I told him that I found that I could not come in today. A specialist in the fever regions of international currency, he was calm in the face of ups and downs. I said I would try to call him tomorrow for an appointment. 'I will be in my office all day,' he said.

After he had hung up, I sat staring at the telephone for a long time. There was nothing I could do but wait.

Accidents happen, the concierge had said. One must foresee.

He had been a little late with his advice.

9

In the next two days I had the concierge call the airport half a dozen times. The conversation was always the same. No one from the ski club had reported having taken a wrong bag.

Pacing up and down in the gloomy room, my nerves twanging like overtuned guitar strings, I remembered the old saw – accidents go in threes. There had been Ferris on the floor, Drusack in the hospital, now this. Should I have been more wary? I knew I was a superstitious man and I should have paid more honor to superstition. The hotel room, which had seemed at first glance to be cozy and welcoming, now only added to my depression, and I took long random walks around the city, hoping to tire myself at least enough so that I could sleep at night. The climate of Zurich in the winter is not conducive to gaiety. Under the leaden sky, even the lake looked as though it had lain in a vault for centuries.

On the second day I recognized defeat and finally unpacked the suitcase I had carried away from Kloten. There was nothing in it to identify its owner, no address books, no checkbooks, no books of any kind, with or without a name on the flyleaf, no bills or photographs, signed or unsigned, and no monograms on anything. The owner must have been inordinately healthy – in a leather shaving kit, there were no medicine bottles that might have had a name on a label – just toothpaste, toothbrush, a safety razor, a bottle of aspirin, after-shaving talcum powder, and a bottle of eau de cologne.

I began to sweat. It was room 602 all over again. Was I going to be haunted forever by ghosts who slipped into my life for a moment, changed it, and then slipped out, eternally unidentified?

Remembering detective stories I had read, I looked for tailors' labels on the jackets of suits. While the clothes were presentable enough, they all seemed to come from big clothing manufacturers who distributed to stores all over the United States. There were laundry symbols on some of the shirts. Perhaps, given time, the FBI would have been able to track them down, but I couldn't see myself approaching the FBI for help.

There was a pair of crimson ski pants and a lemon yellow, nylon, lightweight parka. I shook my head. What could you expect of a man who would appear on the slopes looking like the flag of a small hot country? It was in keeping with the houndstooth jacket. I would keep my eyes open for bright spots of color coming down the hill.

There was one clue, if it could be called that. Along with the two suits and the flannel slacks and the houndstooth sports jacket, there was a tuxedo. It might mean that my man had intended to spend at least part of his time at a plush resort where people dressed for dinner. The only place I had ever heard of like that was the Palace Hotel in St Moritz, but there probably were a dozen others. And the presence of the tuxedo could also mean that its owner intended to go to London or Paris or some other city where dress might occasionally be formal while he was in Europe. Europe was just too goddamn enormous.

I thought of calling the ski club office in New York, explaining that there had been an innocent mix-up at the Zurich airport and asking for a copy of the manifest with the names of the people on board my plane and their home addresses. For a little while I entertained the notion of sending letters to each and every one of the more than three hundred passengers with my story of the mistake about the luggage and asking the recipients of the letter to let me know whether or not they had lost theirs, so that I could return the bag in my possession to its rightful owner. But thinking about this plan for just a minute or two, I realized how hopeless it would be. After the two fruitless days, I was sure that whoever had my bag would not be inclined to advertise.

Trying to get some idea of what the thief (which was how I now described the man to myself) might look like, I tried on some of his clothes. I put on one of his shirts. It fit me around the neck. I have a sixteen-and-a-half-inch neck. The sleeves were about an inch too short for me. Could I carry a tape measure and invent some plausible reason for measuring the necks and arms of all the Americans in Europe for the winter? There were two pairs of good shoes, one brown, one black, size ten. Whitehouse & Hardy. Stores in almost every big city in the United States. No footprint there. I tried them on. They fit me perfectly. My feet would be dry this winter.

The houndstooth jacket fit me well enough, too – a little loose around the middle but not much. No middle-aged paunch there, but then, again, the man was a skier and probably in good condition, no matter how old he was. The slacks were a little short, too. So the man was slightly shorter than I, say five foot ten or eleven. At least I wouldn't have to waste my time on giants or fat men or midgets.

I hoped that the thief would turn out to be as thrifty as I intended to be and wear the clothes he had no doubt by now found in my bag, even though they would only fit him approximately, as his fit me. I was sure that if I saw a suit of mine go past I would recognize it. I realized I was grasping at straws – with seventy-thousand dollars in his pocket, he was probably being measured at that moment by some of the best tailors in Europe. I had the same sense of pain that I imagined a husband might have knowing that at that moment his beautiful wife was in bed with another man. With anguish I realized I was *married* to a certain number of hundred-dollar bills. It wasn't rational. After all, I was richer than I had been only two weeks before. But there it was. I was beyond rationality.

Meanwhile I had about five thousand dollars in cash on me. I had five thousand dollars worth of time to find a man with a sixteen-and-a-half-inch neck, thirty-four-inch arms, a size ten shoe, and no intention of returning seventy thousand dollars that had fallen, almost literally, from the heavens into his hands.

As I repacked the bag carefully, putting the gaudy jacket on top, the way I had found it, I thought, well, at least there's one consolation – I won't have to spend any money on a new wardrobe to replace the one I had lost. The Lord giveth and the Lord taketh away. I don't know what I would have done if the bag had been full of women's things.

*

I paid my bill and took a taxi to the Bahnhof and bought a first-class ticket for St Moritz. The only people I had spoken to on the plane coming over were the couple who were going to ski the Corvatch at St Moritz. They hadn't told me their names or where they were going to stay. I knew the chances of their being able to give me any useful information if I did find them were almost infinitesimal. But I had to start somewhere. Zurich had no further charms for me. It had rained the two days I had been there.

At Chur, an hour-and-a-half ride from Zurich, I had to change for the narrow-gauge railroad that mounted into the Engadine. I went down the first-class car until I saw an empty compartment and went in and put my coat and two bags on the rack over the seats.

The atmosphere on the new train was considerably different from the one on the express from Zurich, which had been businesslike and quiet, with solid, heavy types reading the financial pages of the *Zürcher Zeitung*. Getting into the toy-like cars *en route* to the Alpine resorts, there were a lot of young people, many of them already in ski clothes, and expensively dressed pretty women in furs, with appropriate escorts. There was a feeling of holiday that I was in no mood to share. I was hunting and I wanted to think and I hoped that no one would come into my apartment to disturb me. Undemocratically, I closed the sliding door of the compartment, as a deterrent to company. But just before the train started, a man pulled the door open and asked, in English, politely enough, 'Pardon me, sir, are those seats taken?'

'I don't think so,' I said as ungraciously as possible.

'Honey,' the man called down the corridor. 'In here.' A fluffy blonde, considerably younger than the man, wearing a leopard coat and a hat to match, came into the compartment. I grieved briefly for all prowling animals threatened with extinction. The lady was carrying a handsome leather jewel case and smelled strongly of a musky perfume. A huge diamond ring graced the finger over her wedding band. If the world were better organized, there would have been a riot of porters and any other workers within a radius of ten blocks of the station platform. Unthinkable in Switzerland.

The man had no luggage, just some magazines and a copy of the *International Herald Tribune* under his arm. He dropped the magazines and paper on the seat opposite me and helped the lady off with her coat. Swinging it up to put it on the rack, the hem of the coat brushed against my face, tickling me and swamping me in a wave of scent.

'Oh,' the woman said, 'excuse, excuse.'

I smiled glumly, restraining myself from scratching at my face. 'It's a pleasure,' I said.

She rewarded me with a smile. She couldn't have been more than twenty-eight years old, and up to now she had obviously had every reason to feel that a smile of hers was indeed a reward. I was sure that she was not the man's first wife, maybe not even the second. I took an instant dislike to her.

The man took off the sheepskin coat that he was wearing, and the green, furry Tyrolean hat, with a little feather in the band, and tossed them up on the rack. He had a silk foulard scarf tied around his throat, which he didn't remove. As he sat down he pulled out a cigar case.

'Bill,' the woman said, complaining.

'I'm on a holiday, honey. Let me enjoy it.' Bill opened the cigar case.

'I hope you don't mind if my husband smokes,' the woman said.

'Not at all.' At least it would kill some of the overpowering aroma of the perfume.

The man pushed the cigar case toward me. 'May I offer you one?'

'Thank you, no. I don't smoke,' I lied.

He took out a small gleaming clipper and cut off the end. He had thick, brutal, manicured hands that went with his high-flushed, fleshy face and hard blue eyes and jaw. I would not have liked to work for him or be his son. I figured he was over forty years old. 'Pure Havana,' he said, 'almost impossible to find back home. The Swiss are neutral about Castro, thank God.' He used a thin gold lighter to start the cigar and leaned back, puffing comfortably. I looked out the window morosely at the snowy countryside. I had thought I was going to be on holiday, too. For the first time it occurred to me that perhaps I ought to turn around at the next station and start for home. Except where was home? I thought of Drusack, who was not going to St Moritz.

The train went into a tunnel and it was absolutely dark in the compartment. I wished the tunnel would go on forever. Self-pityingly, I remembered the nights at the St Augustine and thought, darkness is my element.

Sometime after we emerged from the tunnel, we were in sunlight. We had climbed out of the gray cloud that hung over the Swiss plain. The sunlight was somehow an affront to my sensibility. The man was dozing now, his head thrown back, the cigar dead in an ashtray. His wife had the *Herald Tribune* and was reading the comic strips, a rapt expression on her face. She looked foolish, her mouth pursed, her eyes childish and bright under the leopard hat. Was that what I had thought money was going to buy for me?

She became conscious that I was staring at her, looked up at me, giggled coquettishly. 'I'm a pushover for comic strips,' she said. 'I'm always afraid Rip Kirby is going to get killed in the next installment.'

I smiled inanely, looked at the diamond on her finger, earned, I was sure, in honest matrimony. She peered obliquely at me. I guessed that she never looked at anyone straight-on. 'I've seen you someplace before,' she said. 'Haven't I?'

'Perhaps,' I said.

'Weren't you on the plane Wednesday night? The club plane?'

'I was on it,' I said.

'I was sure I knew you from someplace before that. Sun Valley maybe?'

'I've never been in Sun Valley,' I said.

'That's the wonderful thing about skiing,' she said, 'you get to meet the same people all over the world.'

The man groaned a little, awakened by the sound of our voices. Coming out of sleep. his eyes stared at me with blank hostility. I had the feeling that hostility was his natural and fundamental condition and that I had surprised him before he had time to arrange himself for the ordinary traffic of society.

'Bill,' the woman said, 'this gentleman was on the plane with us.' From the way she said it, it sounded as though it had been an extraordinary pleasure for us all.

'Is that so?' Bill said.

'I always feel it's lucky to find Americans to travel with,' the woman said. 'The language and everything. Europeans make you feel like such a dummy. I think this calls for a drink-drink.' She opened the jewel case, which she had kept on the seat beside her, and brought out an elegant silver flask. There were three small chromium cups, one inside the other, over the cap, and she gave one to me and one to her husband and kept one for herself. 'I hope you like cognac,' she said, as she poured the liquor carefully into our cups. My hand was shaking, and some of the cognac spilled over on it. 'Oh, I'm so sorry,' she said.

'Nothing,' I said. The reason my hand was shaking was that the man had taken off the foulard scarf around his neck and for the first time I saw the tie he was wearing. It was a dark red woolen tie. It was either the tie that I had packed in my bag or one exactly like it. He crossed his legs and I looked down at his shoes. They were not new. I had had just such a pair of shoes in my bag.

'Here's to the first one to break a leg this year,' the man said, raising his chromium cup. He laughed harshly. I was sure he had never broken anything. He was just the sort of man who had never been sick a day in his life and didn't carry anything stronger than aspirin with him when he traveled.

I drank my cognac in one gulp. I needed it. And I was glad when the lady refilled my cup immediately. I raised the cup gallantly to her and smiled widely and falsely, hoping the train would be wrecked and both she and her husband crushed, so that I could search them and their baggage thoroughly. 'You people certainly know how to travel,' I said, with an exaggerated, admiring shake of the head.

'Be prepared in foreign lands,' the man said. 'That's our motto. Say...' He extended his hand. 'My name's Bill. Bill Sloane. And the little lady is Flora.'

I shook his hand and told them my name. His hand was hard and cold. The little lady (weight one twenty-five, I figured) smiled winsomely and poured some more cognac.

By the time we reached St Moritz we were a cosy threesome. I had learned that they lived in Greenwich, Connecticut, that Mr Sloane was a three-handicap golfer, that he was a building contractor and a self-made man, that, as I had guessed, Flora was not his first wife, that he had a son at Deerfield, who, thank God, did not wear his hair long, that he had voted for Nixon and had been to the White House twice, that the Watergate fuss would die down in a month and the Democrats sorry they had ever started it, that this was their third visit to St Moritz, that they had stopped over in Zurich for two days so that Flora could do some shopping, and that they were going to stay at the Palace Hotel in St Moritz.

'Where're you staying, Doug?' Sloane asked me.

'The Palace,' I said without hesitation. I certainly couldn't afford it, but I was not going to let my new friends out of my sight at any cost. 'I understand it's fun.'

*

When we got to St Moritz, I insisted on waiting with them until their luggage came out of the baggage car. Neither of them changed expression when I swung the big blue bag off the rack. 'Do you know your bag's unlocked?' Sloane asked.

'The lock's broken,' I said.

'You ought to get it fixed,' he said, as we left the compartment. 'St Moritz is full of Italians.' His interest could mean something. Or nothing. The two of them might be the best actors in the world.

They had eight bags between them, all brand new, none of them the twin of mine. That again could mean nothing. We had to hire an extra taxi for the baggage, and it followed us up the hill through the busy, snowy streets of the town to the hotel.

The hotel had a tantalizing, faint, indefinable aroma. Its source was money. Quiet money. The lobby was like an extension of the bank vault in New York. The guests were treated by the help in a kind of reverential hush, as though they were ikons of great age and value, frail and worthy of worship. I had the feeling that even the small, exquisitely dressed children with their English nannies, who walked decorously along the deep carpets, knew I didn't belong there.

Everybody at the reception desk and at the concierge's desk shook Mr Sloane's hand and bowed to Mrs Sloane. The tips had obviously been princely in the preceding years. Would a man like that, who could afford a wife like Flora and a hotel like the Palace, walk off with somebody else's seventy-thousand dollars? And wear his shoes in the bargain? The answer, I decided, was probably yes. After all, Sloane had confessed he was a self-made man.

When I told the clerk at the reception desk that I had no reservation, his face took on that distant no-room-at-the-inn look of hoteliers in a good season. He had pierced my disguise instantly. 'I'm afraid, sir,' he began, 'that ...'

'He's a friend of mine,' Mr Sloane said, coming up behind me. 'Fit him in, please.'

The clerk made an important small business of checking the room chart and said, 'Well, there's a double room. I might ...'

'That's fine,' I said.

'How long will you be staying, Mr Grimes?' the clerk asked.

I hesitated. Who knew how long five thousand dollars would last in a place like that? 'A week,' I said. I would skip orange juice in the mornings.

We all went up in the elevator together. The clerk had put me in the room next to the Sloanes. It would have been convenient if the walls had been thinner or I had been trained in electronic bugging equipment.

My room was a large one, with a great double bed with a pink satin spread and a magnificent view of the lake and the mountains beyond, pure and clear in the late afternoon sunlight. Under other conditions it would have been exhilarating. Now it merely seemed as if nature was being callous and expensive. I closed the blinds and in the gloom lay down fully dressed on the soft bed, the satin rustling voluptuously under my weight. I still seemed to smell Flora Sloane's perfume. I tried to think of some way in which I could find out quickly and surely if Sloane was my man. My mind was flat and tired. The two days in Zurich had exhausted me. I felt a cold coming on. I could think of nothing except to hang on and watch. But then if I *did* find out that it was my tie he was wearing, my shoes he was walking around in, what would I do? My head began to ache. I got up off the bed and dug in the leather shaving kit for the tin of aspirin and swallowed two.

I dozed fitfully after that, dreaming disconnectedly. There was a man who appeared and disappeared at the edge of my dreams who might have been Sloane or Drusack, jangling keys.

*

I was awakened by the ringing of the telephone. It was Flora

Sloane, inviting me to dinner. I made myself sound enthusiastic as I accepted. I didn't have to dress for dinner, she said; we were dining in town. Somehow, Bill had forgotten to pack his tuxedo, and it was being flown from America but hadn't arrived yet. I said I preferred not dressing myself and went in and took a cold shower.

We met for drinks at the bar of the hotel. Sloane was wearing a dark gray suit. It was not mine. He had changed his shoes. There was another couple at the table who had been on our plane coming over and who were also from Greenwich. They had been out skiing that day and the wife was already limping. 'Isn't it marvelous?' she said. 'I can just go up to the Corveglia Club every day for the next two weeks and just lie in the sun.'

'Before we were married,' her husband said, 'she used to tell me how much she loved to ski.'

'That was before we were married, dear,' the woman said complacently.

Sloane ordered a bottle of champagne. It was finished quickly and the other man ordered a second one. I would have to get out of St Moritz before it was my turn to reciprocate. It was easy to love the poor in that atmosphere.

We went to dinner in a restaurant in a rustic chalet nearby and drank a great deal more champagne. The prices on the menu were not rustic. During the course of the meal I learned more than I ever wanted to know about Greenwich – who was nearly thrown out of the golf club, what lady was doing it with what gynaecologist, how much the new addition to the Powell's house cost, who was leading the brave fight to keep black children from being bussed into the town schools. Even if I had been guaranteed that I would get my seventy thousand dollars back before the end of the week, I wondered if I could endure the necessary dinners.

It was worse after dinner. When we got back to the hotel, the two men went to play bridge and Flora asked me to take her dancing in the Kings Club downstairs. The lady with the limp came along with us to watch. When we were seated at a table, Flora asked for champagne, and this time it was fairly and truly on my bill.

I never liked to dance, and Flora was one of those women who clutch their partners as if to cut off any possible movement to escape. It was hot in the room and infernally noisy and my flannel blazer was heavy and too tight under the arms and I was swamped in Flora's perfume. She also hummed amorously into my ear as we danced.

'Oh, I'm so glad we found you,' she whispered. 'You can't *drag* Bill onto a dance floor. And I'll bet you're a great skier, too. You move like one.' Sex and all other human activities were clearly inextricably entwined in Mrs Sloane's mind. 'Will you ski with me tomorrow?'

'I'd love to,' I said. If I could have chosen a list of people whom I could suspect of having stolen my suitcase, the Sloanes would have been far down at the bottom.

It was after midnight, with two bottles of champagne gone, when I finally managed to call a halt. I signed the check and escorted the two ladies upstairs to where their husbands were playing bridge. Sloane was losing. I didn't know whether I was glad or sorry. If it was my money, I would have wept. If it was his, I'd have cheered. Aside from his friend from Greenwich, there was a handsome, graying man of about fifty at the table, and an old lady encrusted with jewelry, with a harsh Spanish accent, like the cawing of a crow. The Beautiful People of the International Set.

While I was watching, the handsome, gray-haired man made a small slam. 'Fabian,' Sloane said, 'every year I find myself writing out a check to you.'

The man Sloane had called Fabian smiled gently. He had a charming smile, almost womanish in sweetness, with laugh wrinkles permanently around his liquid dark eyes. 'I must admit,' he said, 'I'm having a modest little run of luck.' He had a soft, husky voice and an accent that was a little strange. I couldn't tell from the way he spoke where he came from.

'Modest!' Sloane said. He wasn't a pleasant loser.

'I'm going to bed,' Flora said. 'I'm skiing in the morning.'

'I'll be right up,' Sloane said. He was shuffling the cards as though he was preparing to use them as weapons....

I escorted Flora to her door. 'Isn't it comfy,' she said,

'We're just side-by-side?' She kissed my cheek good night, giggled, and said, 'Night-night,' and went in.

I wasn't sleepy and I sat up and read. I heard footsteps about a half hour later and the door to the Sloanes' room open and shut. There were some murmurs through the wall that I couldn't make out and after a while silence.

I gave the couple another fifteen minutes to fall asleep then opened the door of my room silently. All along the corridor, pairs of shoes were placed in front of bedroom doors, women's and men's moccasins, wing tips, patent leathers, ski boots, in eternal sexual order. Two by two, entries to the Ark. But in front of the Sloanes' door, there were only the dainty leather boots Flora Sloane had worn on the train. For whatever reason, her husband had not put out the brown shoes with the gum soles, possibly size ten, to be shined. I closed my door without a sound, to ponder the meaning of this.

10

'I'm worried about my husband,' Flora Sloane said to me. We were having a drink before lunch, seated in the sunshine on the terrace of the Corveglia Club, among the maritime Greeks, the Milanese industrialists, the people who were photographed beside pools at Acapulco, and the ladies of various nationalities who preyed on them all. Flora Sloane, who obviously had not been what has in other times been called 'gently reared' and who lapsed, when excited, into a language and an accent you might expect to hear from a waitress in a diner in New Jersey patronized almost exclusively by truck drivers, was completely at home here and accepted all attention or deference with regal aplomb. I, on the other hand, felt like a man who had just been dropped behind enemy lines.

The temporary membership had cost me a hundred and

twenty francs for two weeks, but where the Sloanes went I
had to follow. Not that Sloane himself was very much in
evidence. In the mornings, according to Flora, he was on the
phone back to his office in New York for hours on end and in
the afternoon and evening he played bridge.

'He won't even have a *tan* when we get back to Greenwich,' she complained. 'People won't believe he's ever *seen* an
Alp.'

Meanwhile, I had the honor of leading Flora Sloane down
the hill and buying her lunch. She was a fair skier, but one of
those women who squealed when she came to a steep bit and
constantly complained of her boots. I spent quite a bit of time
kneeling in the snow, loosening the hooks, then tightening
them again after three turns. I had refused to be seen in the
red pants and the lemon parka I had found in the suitcase
and had bought myself a sensible navy blue outfit. At great
expense.

At night, there was the inevitable sweaty dancing and the
champagne. Madame Sloane was becoming progressively
more amorous, too, and had a nasty habit of sticking her
tongue in my ear while we danced. I wanted to get into the
Sloanes' room and search it, but not that way. There was a
choice of reasons for my coolness, not the least of which was
the total lack of all response to any sexual stimulation, dating
from the moment I had realized that my seventy thousand
dollars had disappeared. Money was power. That I knew. It
had not occurred to me that its absence involved impotence.
Any attempt at performance on my part, I was sure, would
be grotesquely inadequate. Flora Sloane's flirtatiousness was
trying enough. Her derision would be catastrophic. I foresaw
years of psychiatry ahead of me.

My efforts at detective work had been pathetically useless.
I had knocked at the Sloanes' door several times on one
pretext or another in the hope of being invited in so that I
could at least take a quick, surreptitious look around their
room, but whether it was the wife or the husband who re-
sponded, all conversations took place on the threshold, the
door just barely ajar.

I had opened my door every night when the hotel slept, but

the brown shoes had never been in the corridor. I had begun to feel that I had been the victim of a hallucination in the train compartment – that Sloane had never worn brown shoes with gum soles and never had a red wool tie around his neck. I had brought up the subject of the confusion of luggage at airports these days, but the Sloanes had shown no interest. I would stay the week, I had decided, on the off chance that something would happen, and then I would leave. I had no idea of where I would go next. Behind the Iron Curtain, perhaps. Or Katmandu. Drusack haunted me.

'Those miserable bridge games.' Flora Sloane sighed over her Bloody Mary. 'He's losing a fortune. They play for five cents a point. Everybody knows Fabian's practically a professional. He comes here for two months each winter and he walks away rich. I try to tell Bill that he's just not as good a bridge player as Fabian, but he's such a stubborn man he refuses to believe that anybody is better than him at *anything*. Then when he loses he gets furious at me. He's the worst loser in the world. You wouldn't believe some of the things he says to me. When he comes up to the room after one of those awful games, it's nightmare time. I haven't had a decent night's sleep since I came up here. I have to *drive* myself to put on my ski boots in the morning. By the time I leave here, I'll be a worn-out old hag.'

'Oh, come now, Flora.' I made the awaited objection. 'You couldn't look like a hag if you tried. You look blooming.' This was true. At all hours of the day and night, in no matter what clothes, she looked like an overblown peony.

'Appearances are deceiving,' she said darkly. 'I'm not as strong as I look. I was *very* delicate as a child. Frankly, honey, if I didn't know you were waiting for me downstairs every morning, I think I'd just stay in bed all day.'

'Poor girl,' I said sympathetically. The thought of Flora staying in bed was delicious, but not for the reason that Flora herself might have believed. With her off the hill I could give back my rented skis and boots and never have to go up the mountain again that winter. Even with the welcome discovery that my eyes served me adequately when skiing, after Vermont the sport had no joys for me.

'There's a gleam of hope,' Flora said. She looked at me obliquely in that sidelong, automatically provocative way I had learned to hate. 'Something has come up and Bill may have to go back to New York next week. Then we could spend *all* the time together.' The *all* had a thunderous emphasis that made me look around uneasily to see if anyone happened to be listening to us. 'Wouldn't that be just beautiful?'

'B ... bu ... beautiful,' I said. It was the first time I had stuttered since I had left the St Augustine. 'Let's ... let's go in for lun ... lunch.'

*

That afternoon she presented me with a watch. It was a great thick model, guaranteed for accuracy under three hundred feet of water or when dropped from the roofs of tall buildings. It had a stopwatch attachment and all sorts of dials. It did everything but play the Swiss national anthem. 'You shouldn't have,' I said faintly.

'I want you to think of this marvelous week whenever you look at the time,' she said. 'Don't I get just a little kiss for it?'

We were in a *stübli* in the middle of town where we had stopped on the way to the hotel after the afternoon's skiing. I liked it because there wasn't a bottle of champagne in the house. The place smelled of melted cheese and wet wool from the other skiers who crowded the room, drinking beer. I pecked at her cheek.

'Don't you like it?' she asked. 'The watch, I mean.'

'I love it,' I said 'Hon ... honestly. It's just so extravagant.'

'Not really, honey,' she said. 'If you hadn't come along and just *pampered* me, I'd have had to hire a ski teacher and you know what ski teachers cost in a place like this. And you have to buy them lunch besides. And the way they eat! I think they just dine on potatoes all the rest of the year and stock up in the winters.' She was a flighty woman, but she had a strong feeling for economics. 'Here,' she said, 'let me put it on you.' She slipped it on my wrist and clipped on the heavy silver band. 'Isn't it just absolutely *male*?'

'I suppose you could describe it like that,' I said. When I

finally rid myself of the Sloanes, man and wife, I would take it back to the jeweler's and sell it back. It must have cost at least three hundred dollars.

'Just don't tell Bill about it,' she said. 'It's a little secret between you and me. A little darling secret. You'll remember, won't you, honey?'

'I'll remember.' That was one promise I definitely would keep.

*

The crisis arrived the next morning. When she came down into the hall where I was waiting for her as usual at ten o'clock, she wasn't in ski clothes. 'I'm afraid I can't ski with you this morning, honey,' she said. 'Bill has to go to Zurich today and I'm taking him to the train. The poor man. With all this beautiful snow and gorgeous weather and all.' She giggled. 'And he has to stay overnight, too. Isn't it just too bad?'

'Awful,' I said.

'I hope you won't be lonesome, skiing by yourself,' she said.

'Well, if it can't be helped, it can't be helped,' I said manfully.

'Actually,' she said, 'I don't feel much like skiing today either. I have an idea. Why don't you go up now and get your exercise and come down by one o'clock and we'll have a cozy little lunch somewhere? Bill's train leaves at twenty to one. We can have a perfectly dreamy afternoon together...'

'That's a great idea,' I said.

'We'll start with a scrumptious cold bottle of champagne in the bar,' she said, 'and then we'll just see how things work out. Does that sound attractive to you?'

'Scrumptious.'

She gave me one of her significant smiles and went back upstairs to her husband. I went out into the cold morning air feeling a frown beginning to freeze on my face. I had no intention of skiing. If I never saw a pair of skis again it would be all the same to me. I regretted ever having listened to Wales about the ski club plane, which was the beginning of the chain of events that was leading Mrs Sloane inexorably into my bed. Still, I had to admit to myself, if I had crossed the ocean on a regular flight and my bag had been stolen, I'd have *no* notion at all of where I might look for it. And through the Sloanes I had met quite a few of the other passengers on the plane and had been able to try my lost luggage gambit on them. True, it had yielded nothing so far, but one could always hope that on the next hill or in the next Alpine bar, a face would leap out, an involuntary gasp or heedless word would put me on the track of my fortune.

I thought of leaving St Moritz on the same train with Sloane, but when we got to Zurich what could I do? I couldn't trail him around the city spying on him.

I contemplated the perfectly dreamy afternoon ahead of me, starting with a scrumptious bottle of champagne (on my bill) and groaned. A young man, swinging ahead of me down the street on crutches, his leg in a cast, heard me and turned and stared curiously at me. Everyone to his own brand of trouble.

I turned and looked into a shop window. My reflection stared back at me. A youngish-looking man in expensive ski clothes, on holiday in one of the most glamorous resorts in the world. You could have taken my picture for an advertisement for a chic travel magazine. Money no object. The vacation of your dreams.

Then I grinned at myself in the window. An idea had come to me. I started down the street, after the man on crutches. I was limping a little. By the time I passed him I was limping noticeably. He looked at me sympathetically. 'You, too?' he said.

'Just a sprain,' I said.

By the time I reached the small private hospital conveniently located in the center of town, I was giving a fair imitation of a skier who had fallen down half the mountain.

*

Two hours later I came out of the hospital. I was equipped with crutches and my left leg was in a cast above the knee. I sat in a restaurant for the rest of the morning, drinking black coffee and eating croissants, happily reading the *Herald Tribune* of the day before.

The young doctor at the hospital had been skeptical when I told him I was sure I had broken my leg – 'A hairline fracture,' I told him. 'I've done it twice before.' He was even more skeptical when he looked at the X-rays, but when I insisted he shrugged and said, 'Well, it's *your* leg.'

Switzerland was one country where you could get any kind of medical attention you paid for, necessary or not. I had heard of a man who had a slight fungus growth on his thumb and had become obsessed with the idea that it was cancer. Doctors in the United States, England, France, Spain, and Norway had assured him it was only a slight fungus infection that would go away eventually and had prescribed salves. In Switzerland, for a price, he had finally managed to have it amputated. He now lived happily in San Francisco, thumbless.

At one o'clock I took a taxi back to the Palace. I accepted the sympathy of the men at the desk with a wan smile, and I fixed a look of stoic suffering on my face as I clumped into the bar.

Flora Sloane was seated in a corner near the window, with the unopened bottle of champagne in a bucket of ice on the table in front of her. She was dressed in skintight green slacks and sweater that made the most of her generous, and I must admit, well-shaped bosom. Her leopard coat was on a chair beside her, and the aroma of her perfume made the bar smell like a florist's shop full of exotic tropical plants.

She gasped when she saw me stagger in, using the crutches clumsily. 'Oh, shit,' she said.

'It's nothing,' I said bravely. 'Just a hairline fracture. I'll be out of the cast in six weeks. At least that's what the doctor says.' I collapsed on a chair, with a sound that sensitive ears would have distinguished as a smothered groan, and put the cast up on the chair across from me.

'How in hell did you do it?' she asked crossly.

'My skis didn't open.' That much was true. I hadn't touched them that day. 'I crossed my skis and they didn't open.'

'That's damned peculiar,' she said. 'You haven't fallen once since you've been here.'

'I guess I wasn't paying attention,' I said. 'I guess I was thinking about this afternoon and ...'

Her expression softened. 'You poor dear,' she said. 'Well, anyway, we can have our champagne.' She started to signal the barman.

'I'm not allowed to drink,' I said. 'The doctor was most specific. It interferes with the healing process.'

'Everybody else I know who's broken bones went right on drinking,' she said. She was not a woman who liked to be deprived of her champagne.

'Maybe,' I said. 'I have brittle bones, the doctor said.' I grimaced in pain.

She touched my hand lightly. 'It hurts, doesn't it?'

'A little,' I admitted. 'The morphine's beginning to wear off.'

'Still,' she said, 'we can at least have lunch....'

'I hate to have to disappoint you, Flora,' I said, 'but I'm a bit woozy. Actually, I feel like throwing up. The doctor said I'd better stay in bed today, with my leg up on some pillows. I'm terribly sorry.'

'Well, all I can say is you sure picked the wrong day to crash.' She brushed at her cashmere bosom. 'And I got all dressed up for you.'

'Accidents happen when they're fated to happen,' I said philosophically. 'And you *do* look beautiful.' I heaved myself to my feet. Or rather my foot. 'I think I'd better go upstairs now.'

'I'll come with you and make you comfy.' She started to rise.

I waved her back. 'If you don't mind, for the moment I'd rather be alone. That's the way I've always been when something is wrong with me. Ever since I was a kid.' I didn't want to be lying helpless on a bed with Flora Sloane loose in the room. 'Drink the champagne for both of us, dear. Please put this bottle on my bill,' I called to the barman.

'Can I come and see you later?' she asked.

'Well, I'm going to try to sleep. I'll call you later if I wake up. Just don't worry about me, dear.'

I left her there, the brightest and fullest flower in the

garden, splendid and pouting in her tight green slacks and snug sweater, as I maneuvered out of the bar.

Just as the last light of the afternoon was dying in a pink glow on the farthest peaks I could see from my window, the door of my room opened softly. I was lying in bed merely staring brainlessly but comfortably at the ceiling. I had had lunch sent up and had eaten heartily. Luckily, the waiter had been in to take the tray, because it was Flora Sloane who poked her head around the door.

'I didn't want to disturb you,' she said. 'I just wanted to see if you needed anything.' She came into the room. I could barely see her in the dusk, but I could smell her. 'How are you, honey?'

'Alive,' I said. 'How did you get in here?' Being an invalid excused me from gallantry.

'The floor maid let me in. I explained.' She came over to the side of my bed and touched my forehead in a Florence Nightingale gesture. 'You have no fever,' she said.

'The doctor says I can expect it at night,' I said.

'Did you have a good afternoon?' she asked, seating herself on the edge of the bed.

'I've had better.' This was not true – at least for the time I had been at St Moritz.

Suddenly, she swooped down and kissed me. Her tongue, as ever, was active. I twisted, so as to be able to breathe, and my bad leg (as I now considered it) dropped off the edge of the bed. I groaned realistically. Flora sat up, flushed and breathing hard. 'I'm sorry,' she said. 'Did I hurt you?'

'Not really,' I said. 'It's just ... well, you know ... sudden movements.'

She stood up and looked down at me. It was too dark in the room for me to see her face clearly, but I got the impression of the birth of suspicion. 'You know,' she said, 'a friend of mine picked up a young man on the slopes at Gstaad and they arranged to meet that night and, well ... *do* it, and he broke his leg at three o'clock, but he didn't let it stop him. By ten o'clock that night, they *did* it.'

'Maybe he was younger than I am,' I said lamely. 'Or he had a different kind of break. Anyway, the first time ... with

133

you, I mean ... I wouldn't like it to be anything but perfect.'

'Yeah,' she said. Her voice was flat and unconvinced. 'Well, I better be going. There's a party tonight and I have to get ready.' She leaned over and kissed me chastely on the forehead. 'If you want, though,' she said, 'I can look in after the party.'

'I don't think it would be a wise idea, really.'

'Probably not. Well, sleep well,' and she left the room.

I lay back and stared once more at the dark ceiling and thought of the heroic young man at Gstaad. One more day, I thought, and I'm getting out of here, crutches or no crutches. Still, Flora Sloane had given me an idea. Without a key to my room, she had had the door opened. The floor maid ...

*

That evening I dined alone, late. I had seen Flora Sloane, in a blazing evening gown, at a distance, sweeping off to her party with a group of people, some of whom I recognized, some of whom I didn't, anyone of whom might have my seventy thousand dollars in the bank. If Flora saw me, she gave no sign. I took my time over dinner, and, when I went up to my floor, I deliberately avoided asking for my key at the desk. The corridor on which my room was located was empty, but after a moment I spied the night maid coming out of a room farther down. I stepped in front of the Sloanes' door and called to the maid. 'I'm terribly sorry,' I said, moving heavily toward the woman on my crutches, 'but I seem to have forgotten my key. Will you let me in, please?' I had never seen her before.

She took a key out of her apron pocket and opened the door. I said thank you and went in, closing the door behind me. The room had already been made up for the night, and the bed was turned down, two bedside lamps softly lit. The scent of Flora Sloane's perfume was everywhere. Except for that, it could have been any room in the hotel. I was breathing heavily, moving with care. I went over to the big wardrobe and opened the door. Women's clothes. I recognized various dresses, ski outfits. I opened the next door. A long array of suits, stacked shirts. On the floor six pairs of shoes. The brown shoes Sloane had worn on the train were the last in line. I bent down clumsily, nearly toppling, and picked up the right shoe. Then I sat on a little straight-backed chair and took off my right shoe. My left foot was encased in plaster. I tried to put my foot into the brown shoe. I could hardly get halfway in. It must have been two sizes smaller than mine – size eight. I sat there for a moment, holding the shoe in my hand, staring at it numbly. I had wasted almost a week, precious time, and a small fortune, on a false trail, I was sitting like that, in the softly lit room, stupidly holding the shoe in my hand, when I heard the rattle of a key in the door. The door opened and Bill Sloane, dressed for traveling and holding a small bag in his hand, came into the room.

He stopped when he saw me and dropped the bag. It made a small, luxurious thump on the thick carpet. 'What the hell ...?' he said. He didn't sound angry. He hadn't had time to be angry.

'Hello,' I said foolishly. 'Hello, Bill. I thought you were in Zurich.'

'I'll bet you did.' His voice was beginning to rise. 'Where the hell is Flora?' He switched on the overhead light, as though his wife might be lurking in the shadows.

'She went to a party.' I didn't know whether I ought to get up or stay where I was. Getting up presented problems, with the cast and my stockinged foot.

'Went to a party.' He nodded grimly. 'And what the fuck are you doing in here?'

'I forgot my key,' I said, realizing as I said it how improbable the whole scene was. 'I asked the maid to open the door to my room and I wasn't looking ...'

'What're you doing with my shoe?' Each question was an arc on a constantly rising curve.

I looked at the shoe as though I had never seen it before. 'I honestly don't know,' I said. I dropped it to the floor.

'The watch,' he said. 'The goddamn watch.'

I looked at it automatically. It was ten minutes past ten.

'I know where you got that goddamn watch.' There was no mistaking the menace in his tone now. 'My wife. From my stupid, goddamn wife.'

'It was ... well ... a kind of private little joke.' Nothing in my life until then had prepared me for a situation like this, and I realized bitterly that my improvisations at the moment were far from brilliant.

'Every year she gets a crush on some idiotic ski teacher and she gives him a watch. For openers,' he said. 'Just for openers. So – this year, you're elected. This is her year for amateurs. The St Moritz Open.'

'It's only a watch, Bill,' I said.

'She's the shiftiest little bitch in the business,' Sloane said, looming over me. 'And I thought, well, this year, finally, she's out there with someone I can trust.' He began to cry. It was terrifying.

'Please, Bill,' I pleaded. 'Don't cry. I swear nothing's happened.' I wished I could explain to him that I hadn't had the slightest twinge of sexual desire or the least hope of consummation in the last seven days.

'You swear,' he growled, weeping. 'You swear. They all swear.' With a surprisingly swift movement he bent and grabbed my arm and yanked at it. 'Give me back that goddamn watch, you son of a bitch.'

'Of course,' I said, with considerable dignity. I unclasped it and gave it to him. He glared down at it, then strode over to the window, opened it, and hurled the watch out into the night. I took advantage of his trip to get up and balance on my crutches. He wheeled and came back to me, very close to me. I could smell the whiskey on his breath. 'I ought to hammer you into the deck. Only I don't hit cripples.' He kicked my cast, not very hard, but enough to make me teeter. 'I don't know what the fuck you were doing in here and I don't want to know. But if you're not out of this hotel and out of this town by tomorrow morning, I'm going to have you thrown out bodily. When the Swiss police get through with you, you'll be sorry you ever saw a mountain.' He swooped down again and grabbed my single shoe from the floor and swept across the room with it and threw it out of the window after the watch. It was the weirdest act of revenge I'd ever heard of. He was still weeping. There was no doubt about the fact that, appearances to the contrary (all that telephoning in the morning and all that bridge), he was linked with a high and unusual passion, for a man of his age and temperament, to his wife.

He was seated, like a great tragic bear, his head bent into his hands, sobbing, as I left the room on my crutches.

11

The next morning, early, I was on the train to Davos. Davos is a ski resort some two hours away from St Moritz, famous for long runs that I had no intention of exploring. I had begun to hate winter and the sight of ruddy, happy faces, the sound of boots on snow, the tinkle of sleigh bells, the bright colors of ski caps. I yearned for the comfort of soft Southern weather, a climate where decisions could be put off until tomorrow. Before I bought my ticket at the railroad station, itself a loathsomely picturesque structure on the valley floor, I had played with the idea of surrender, of heading for Italy, Tunisia, the Mediterranean coast of Spain, in one last destructive splurge. But the first train into the station was going in the direction of Davos. I had taken it as an omen and, helped by a porter, had clambered aboard. I was doomed for the winter to cold country.

The train wound its way through some of the most magnificent mountain scenery in the world, soaring peaks, dramatic gorges, high spidery bridges across foaming streams. The sun shone brightly over it all in a clear blue sky. I appreciated none of it.

*

When I reached Davos I got into a taxi and went directly to the hospital and had the cast taken off my leg, resisting all attempts by two doctors to have me X-rayed. 'Just when and where, sir,' one of the doctors asked, as he saw me hop jauntily off the table, 'was this cast put on?'

'Yesterday,' I said. 'In St Moritz.'

'Ah,' he said, 'St Moritz.' He and the other doctor exchanged significant looks. Obviously *they* would never choose St Moritz for medical attention.

The younger of the two doctors accompanied me to the cashier's desk at the door to make sure I paid for the operation. One hundred Swiss francs. A bargain. The doctor watched me puzzled as I opened the big bag that I had left at the entrance and took out a sock and a shoe and put them on. As I went out the door, carrying my bags, I was sure I heard him say, '*Amerikanish*,' to the cashier, as though that explained all eccentricities.

There was a taxi at the door, discharging a child in a cast. I was in the zone of broken bones. It suited the mood I was in. I got into the taxi and, after a short struggle with the German language, managed to make the driver understand that I wanted to be taken to a reasonably priced hotel. Driving through the town, we passed one hotel after another, with large individual balconies for each room, which at other times had been used to air the invalids who had made prewar Davos the tuberculosis capital of the world. Now, the institutions had all been renamed sport hotels, but in my present circumstances all I could think of as we drove past these endless empty balconies was the vanished thousands of bundled figures, lying in rows in the cold sunlight, coughing blood.

The chauffeur of the taxi drove me to a small place, owned by his brother-in-law, with a good view of the railroad tracks. The brother-in-law spoke English and our negotiations were amiable. The price of a single room with a bath down the hall was not exactly amiable, but after the ravages of the Palace it was friendly.

The narrow bed was not covered in silk and the room was so small that there was no place in it for my big bag. The owner explained that, after I unpacked, I could leave it out in the hall, with whatever clothes would not fit into the tiny closet and the minute dresser. It would be safe, he said, there were no thieves in Switzerland. I did not laugh.

I unpacked haphazardly, cramming the stranger's suits into the closet. I left the tuxedo in the bag. I had worn it several times in St Moritz, when necessary, and the memories associated with it were not of a nature to induce nostalgia. If a thief finally showed up in Switzerland and happened to take a liking to it, he would be welcome to it.

I took a hot bath, scrubbing the shaved leg that had been in the cast. The leg had begun to itch. Back in my room, I put on a pair of the shorts I had found in the bag. They were made of silk and were pale blue and I had to fold them over at the top to keep them on me, but I had refused to send any laundry out at the Palace, and the few pieces of clothing I had had in my small bag all needed washing. The jacket I had worn across the ocean and in Zurich and St Moritz, when I hadn't worn the tuxedo, was crumpled. I hesitated for a moment, then picked the houndstooth jacket off the hanger and put it on, hoping nobody I knew would chance to be in Davos to see it on me. I put my wallet, containing all that was left of my fortune, into the inside breast pocket. There was a small crinkling sound as I did so. I reached down and pulled out a folded sheet of paper. It was rose colored and perfumed and was covered with a woman's handwriting.

My hands began to shake and I sat down heavily on the bed and began to read.

There was no address or date on the luxuriously tinted sheet of paper.

'Love,' the letter began, 'Oh, dear! I hope you won't be too frantically disappointed. I can't make it to St Moritz this year....' I felt a tremor go through my body as I read this, as though an avalanche had dropped down the side of one of the surrounding peaks and shaken the foundations of the city. 'Poor old Jock fell off his trusty steed hacking home from a hunt three days ago and broke his hip and has been in *agony* ever since. The local witch doctor, whose practice dates back to the Crimean War, just made pitiful little cries when asked for a diagnosis, so we've moved Jock down to London. The surgeons here are debating whether or not to operate and don't seem to be able to make up their minds and meanwhile the poor old darling just lies there groaning on his bed of pain. Naturally, dear little wifey can't go swinging off to the Alps while the drama is so hideously fresh. So I'm back and forth to the hospital, carrying flowers and gin and soothing the fevered brow and telling him he'll be able to hunt again next year, which, as you know, is his chief and practically single occupation in life.

'However, all is not lost. I have promised to visit my sweet old Aunt Amy in Florence, arriving on Feb Quatorze. The situation should have subsided by then and I'm sure dear old Jock will insist I go. Aunt Amy has a house full of guests, so I'll be staying at the Excelsior. Which is just as well. Or even better. I'll look for your beaming, welcoming face in the bar. Longingly, L.'

I read the letter again, getting a clear and not very flattering impression of the lady who had written it. I considered it an affectation on her part not to put an address or a date on her letter, writing Quatorze instead of the honest English fourteen and signing it only with her initial. I tried to picture what she probably looked like. A cold, fashionable English beauty between thirty and forty, with lofty airs, and a manner that owed a great deal to the works of Sir Noel Coward and Michael Arlen. But whatever she looked like and however she behaved, I would be at the Hotel Excelsior in Florence to greet her, along with her paramour, on February fourteenth. St Valentine's Day, I remembered, anniversary for lovers and massacre.

I tortured myself briefly with the thought that I might have brushed shoulders with the adulterer in the dining room of the Palace Hotel or on the slopes of St Moritz and even thought for a moment of returning there. The idea of Madam L's friend squandering my money undisturbed in St Moritz for another full week was harrowing. But if I hadn't found him there before, there was no reason to suppose that I could find him now. The only clue to his identity in the letter was that he was probably not married or at least was not accompanied by a wife on this trip to Europe, that he could count in French, at least up to fourteen, and that in the presence of his partner in sin he would be expected to have a beaming and welcoming face. It was information that was of no practical value at the moment. I would have to be patient and wait seven days.

*

I left Davos, with its regiments of coughing ghosts, happy to be able to get out of the regions of snow. The train from Zurich to Florence passed through Milan, and I got off and spent the night there, using my time to go see *The Last Supper*, fading sadly into the past on its stone wall in the ruined church. Leonardo da Vinci helped me feel that there was an escape possible from comedy. Milan was covered in fog and I soaked myself in healing melancholy.

I had one moment of uneasiness, when I was followed through the vaulted gallery which presides over the center of Milan by a swarthy youngish man in a long overcoat, who waited across from the door of a café I went into for an *esprésso*. I had felt safe, although uncomfortable, in Switzerland, but here I couldn't help remembering what I had read about the Italian connections to organized crime in America. I ordered another *esprésso* and drank it slowly, but the man didn't budge. I couldn't wait in the café forever, so I paid and left the place, walking rapidly.

The man in the long overcoat crossed the arcade swiftly and cut me off. He grabbed my elbow. He had one wall-eye, which somehow made him seem extremely menacing, and the grip on my elbow was like a steel clamp.

'Hey, boss,' he said, walking along with me. 'What's a da hurry?'

'I'm late for an appointment.' I tried to tug away, but it was useless.

He put his other hand in his pocket and I feared the worst.

'Wanna buy beautiful piece genuine jewelry?' he said. 'Big bargain.' He let go of me then and produced something that clinked and was wrapped in tissue paper. 'Beautiful gift for lady.' He pulled back the tissue paper and I saw a gold chain.

'I have no lady,' I said, beginning to walk again.

'Interesting piece.' Now he was pleading. 'You would pay twice, three times, in America.'

'Sorry,' I said.

He sighed, and I left him rewrapping the chain and putting it back in his pocket.

As I walked away, I realized that any hope I might have had of fading unnoticed into the populations of Europe was derisive. Wherever I went I would be picked out, by anyone who had the slightest interest in me, as an American. I considered growing a beard.

The next day, feeling that perhaps I would never pass this way again, I took the *rapido* to Venice, a city that I believed, rightly as it turned out, would be even sadder at that season than Milan. The misty canals, the sad hooting of boat-horns, the black water and mossy pilings in the gray Adriatic winter light did much to restore the sense of my own dignity and erase the memory of the athletic frivolity of St Moritz. I read, with satisfaction, that Venice was sinking into the sea. I lingered on, in a cheap pensione, visiting churches, drinking a light white wine called Soave in bare cafés along the sides of the Piazza San Marco and watching Italians, an occupation that I found I enjoyed. I avoided Harry's Bar, which I feared would contain a hard core of Americans, even at that season. There was only one American I wanted to see and I had no reason to believe he would be found in Venice that week.

The little excursion had done me a great deal of good. My nerves, which had been shattered in Switzerland, now seemed dependable. I arrived at the Hotel Excelsior in Florence on the evening of the thirteenth of February confident that I would handle myself capably when the moment of confrontation arrived.

After an excellent dinner I wandered through the streets of Florence, stood awhile before the monumental copy of Michelangelo's statue of David in the Piazza della Signoria, musing on the nature of heroism and the defeat of villainy. Florence, with its history of plots and vendettas, its Guelphs and Ghibellines, was a fitting city in which to meet my enemy.

Not unnaturally, I slept badly and was up before the light of dawn broke over the swollen Arno beneath my window.

Even before I had my breakfast I questioned the concierge about the schedules of flights from London to Milan and the most convenient rail connection from Milan to Florence. By my calculation the lady would arrive at five-thirty-five.

I would be in the lobby of the hotel at that hour, strategically placed so as to be able to observe any female who signed

142

in at the reception desk. And any man, slightly shorter than myself, who might accompany her or move to greet her.

I drank a great deal of black coffee all that day, but no alcohol, not even a beer. Out of a sense of duty to my role as a tourist, I wandered through the Uffizi Gallery, but the glorious display of Florentine art spread through the great halls made no impression on me. I would come back at another time.

I made one purchase, at a little souvenir shop, a letter opener, shaped like a stiletto, with a chased silver hilt. I refused to think of the exact reasons for the purchase, and pretended to myself that I had merely taken an idle and innocent fancy to it when I had happened to see it lying in the display window.

Late in the afternoon I bought the *Rome Daily American* and installed myself in one of the ornate chairs in the hotel lobby, not too ostentatiously close to the entrance and the reception desk, but with a clear view of the critical area. I was wearing my own clothes. I didn't want to warn anyone off with the houndstooth jacket or any of the brightly striped shirts that had come along with it.

By six o'clock, I had read the newspaper over twice. The only arrivals at the hotel had been an American family, stout, loud father, weary mother in sensible shoes, three lanky, pale children in identical red, white, and blue anoraks. They had driven up from Rome, I overheard; the roads were icy. By an act of will, I restrained myself from going over to the concierge to ask him to find out if the train from Milan was running late.

I was reading the column of social notes, which I had skipped before, and learned that in Parroli someone I had never heard of had given a party for someone else I never had heard of, when a hatless blonde woman of about thirty came through the door, followed by a quantity of expensive-looking luggage. I made a conscious effort to control my breathing. The woman, I noted automatically, was pretty, with a long, aristocratic nose and a bright slash of a mouth and was wearing a heavy, wrap-around, brown cloth coat that was, even to my inexperienced eye, beautifully tailored.

143

She strode over to the reception desk with the air of a woman who had been used to five-star hotels all her life, but just as she was about to give her name to the clerk behind the desk, two of the three American children, who had remained in the hall, broke into a loud argument about whose turn it was to go up to their room and take the first bath. So I couldn't hear the name that the lady gave the clerk. If I ever had children, I thought grimly, I would never travel with them.

I sat glued to my chair while the lady signed the hotel registration card and threw down her passport. I could not see its color. Finished at the desk, the lady didn't go towards the elevators, but strode directly into the bar. I touched the silver coin in my pocket and stood up and started toward the bar. But just as I reached it, she came out. I stepped back to let her pass me, and made a little hint of a polite bow, but she paid no attention to me. I could not tell what the expression on her face meant.

I sat in a corner of the bar and ordered a Scotch and soda. The bar was empty and dark. There was nothing I could do for the moment but wait.

*

I was still there at seven o'clock, when she came back. She was wearing a severe black dress with two strands of pearls looped around her throat and was carrying her brown coat. Obviously she intended to go out. She stopped at the door and scanned the room. The American family was seated around a table, the mother and father drinking martinis, the children Coca-Colas, the father from time to time saying, 'For God's sake, will you kids stop yelling?'

An elderly English couple was seated across the room from me, the gentleman reading a three-day-old copy of the London *Times*, the woman, in a billowing flowered print, staring vacantly into space.

An Italian group near the bar itself chattered continuously, and I could make out the word *disgrazia* which they had been using over and over again, with great intensity, ever since they had sat down fifteen minutes before. There was no way of my telling who or what was disgraceful.

No one but myself was sitting alone.

A little grimace twisted the generous red mouth of the woman at the door. Her skin was pale, with a delicate pink flush over the prominent cheekbones. The eyes were dark blue, almost violet, the figure, frankly revealed by the sober dress, willowy, the legs slender and finely shaped. I decided she was not pretty, but beautiful. Just the sort of woman a man who was bold and shameless enough to steal seventy thousand dollars at the Zurich airport would be likely to take away on an illicit holiday from an adoring and crippled husband.

She noticed me looking at her and frowned slightly. Frowning became her. I lowered my eyes. Then she came across the room and sat down at the table next to mine, throwing her coat over the other chair at her table and dragging a pack of cigarettes and a heavy gold lighter out of her bag.

The waiter on duty hurried over to her and lit her cigarette. She was the sort of woman who is served immediately on all occasions. The waiter was a handsome, dark young man with the soft, watchful eyes of a fighting bull, and he showed splendid teeth in a wide smile as he bent gracefully over the lady's table to take her order.

'A pink gin, *per favore*,' she said. 'No ice.' British.

'Another Scotch and soda, please,' I said to the waiter.

'*Prego?*' The smile on the waiter's face vanished as he faced me. He had not questioned me when I had ordered before.

'*Ancora un whiskey con soda*,' the lady said impatiently.

'*Si Signora.*' The smile appeared once more. '*Molto grazia.*'

'Thank you for helping out,' I said to the lady.

'He understood you perfectly well,' she said. 'He was just being Italian. You're American, aren't you?'

'I guess it sticks out all over,' I said.

'Not to be ashamed,' she said. 'People have a right to be American. Have you been here long?'

'Not long enough to learn the language.' I felt my pulse quickening. Things were going along infinitely better than I had dared hope. 'I just arrived last night.'

She made an impatient gesture. 'I mean here in the bar.'

'Oh. For about an hour.'

'An hour.' She had a clipped manner of talking but the

voice was musical. 'Did you by any chance see another American gentleman wander through? A man of about fifty, though he looks younger. Very fit. A little gray in the hair. Perhaps with a questing look in his eyes. As though he was looking for someone.'

'Well, let me think,' I said craftily. 'What would his name be?'

'You wouldn't know his name.' She looked hard at me. Adulteresses, even British ones, I had just discovered, weren't anxious to broadcast the names or exact locations of their lovers.

'I wasn't paying any particular attention,' I said innocently, 'but I seem to have noticed somebody who might answer to your description at the door. Around six thirty, I would guess.' I wanted to keep the conversation going at any cost, and I wanted to keep the lady in the bar as long as possible.

'What a bore,' she said impatiently. 'The mails these days!'

'I'm sorry,' I said, touching the letter in my pocket, 'I didn't quite get that. I mean, what about the mails?'

'No matter,' she said. The waiter was putting the drink on the table in front of her. I would not have been surprised if he had knelt to do so. My own drink was put before me without ceremony. The lady raised her glass. 'Cheers,' she said. She plainly had no girlish prejudices against talking to strangers in bars.

'Are you here for long?' I asked.

'One never knows, does one?' She left a lipstick stain on her glass. I longed to ask her name, but something told me not to rush matters. 'Beautiful old Firenze. I've been in gayer towns.' As she talked, she kept turning her head toward the door. A German couple came in and she frowned again. She looked impatiently at her watch. 'You're sunburned,' she said to me. 'Have you been skiing?'

'A little.'

'Where?'

'St Moritz, Davos.' It was a small lie.

'I adore St Moritz,' she said. 'All those amusing cheap people.'

146

'Have you been there?' I asked. 'This season, I mean.'

'No. Disaster intervened.' I would have liked to ask her about the health of her husband, to keep the conversation going on a friendly basis, but thought better of it. She looked around her with distaste. 'This place *is* gloomy. They must have buried Dante in the front hall. Do you know of any brighter spot in town?'

'Well, I had a very good meal in a restaurant called Sabattini's last night. If you'd care to join me tonight I'd be...'

At that moment a page came in, calling, 'Lady Lily Abbott, Lady Lily Abbott...'

Longingly, L., I remembered, as she crooked a finger at the page. *'Telephono per la signora,'* the page said.

'Finalmente,' she said loudly and stood up and followed the boy into the lobby. She left her handbag on the chair, and I wondered how I could manage to look through it while she was busy on the phone without being arrested for theft. The German couple kept staring at me. Oddly, I thought. They would certainly report all suspicious activities to the proper authorities. I didn't touch the bag.

She was gone about five minutes, and, when she came striding back into the bar, her expression could have been described as peevish if it had been on the face of another woman. On her it was noble displeasure. She slumped down in her chair, her feet sticking out straight under the table.

'I hope it wasn't bad news,' I said.

'It wasn't good.' She sounded grim. 'Absent me from felicity awhile. Rearrangements of schedules. Someone will suffer.' She slugged down her gin and began to stuff her cigarettes and lighter into her bag.

'If that means you're free...' I began. 'What I was saying, when you were called to the phone, Lady Abbott...' It was the first time in my life that I had called anybody Lady Anything and I nearly stuttered over the words. 'Well, I was about to invite you to have dinner with me at this very nice...'

'Sorry,' she said. 'That's sweet of you. But I'm not free. I'm taken for dinner. There's a car waiting for me outside.' She stood up, gathering in her coat and bag. I stood up gallantly. She looked hard at me, squarely in the eyes. A decision was made. 'The dinner will be over early,' she said. 'All the poor old dears have to go beddy-bye. We can have a nightcap, if you'd like that.'

'I'd like it very much.'

'Shall we say eleven? Here, in the bar?'

'I'll be here.'

She swept out of the bar, leaving waves of sensuality quivering in the air behind her, like the reverberations of the last notes of an organ in a cathedral.

*

I spent the night in her room. It was as simple as that. 'I came to Florence all primed to sin,' she said as she undressed, 'and sin I shall.' I don't believe she even asked my name until about 2.30 am.

Despite her imperious manner, she was a gentle and charming lover, undemanding, grateful, and pleasantly lacking in chauvinism. 'There is a large, untapped reservoir of sexual talent in America,' she said at one point. 'The New World to the aid of the diminishing Old. Isn't that nice?'

I was happy to discover that my fears about impotence, nourished by the dreadful Mrs Sloane, were unfounded. I did not think I had to mention to Lady Abbott that my pleasure in her company was heightened by perverse overtones of vengeance.

She was the least curious of women. We talked little. She asked me no questions about what I did, why I was in Florence, or where I was going.

Just before I left her room (she insisted I get out before the help started stirring about), I asked her if she would lunch with me that day.

'If I don't have a telephone call,' she said. 'Kiss the lady good night.'

I bent over and kissed the wide, dear mouth. Her eyes were closed, and I had the impression that she was asleep before I went through the door.

As I went through the baronial halls of the hotel to my room, I felt a surge of optimism. Through Zurich, St Moritz, Davos, Milan, and Venice, nothing good had happened to me, no voice had spoken to me reassuringly. Until this night. The future was far from certain, but there were gleams of hope.

Sweet St Valentine's Day.

Exhausted by the fitful wakefulness of my first night in Florence and my recent exertions, I fell into bed and slept soundly until almost noon.

When I awoke I lay still, staring at the ceiling, enjoying the feel of my body, smiling softly. I reached for the phone and asked for Lady Abbott. There was a long pause and then I heard the voice of the concierge. 'Lady Abbott checked out at ten am. No, she left no message.'

*

It cost me ten thousand lire and a lie to extract the forwarding address of Lady Abbott from one of the assistants behind the concierge's desk. Lady Abbott had left word that, while she wanted messages sent on to her, she did not want the address given out. As I slid the ten-thousand-lire note across to the man, I intimated that the lady had left a piece of jewelry of great value in my room and that it was imperative that I return it to her in person.

'*Bene, signore*,' the man said. 'It is the Hotel Plaza-Athénée, in Paris. Please explain the special circumstances to Lady Abbott.'

'I certainly shall,' I said.

I was in Paris, checking in at the Plaza-Athénée the next day at noon. Before I had time to ask the price of the room, I saw Lady Abbott. She was coming through the lobby on the arm of a hatless, graying man with a bushy British mustache who was wearing dark glasses. They were laughing together. I had seen the man before. It was Miles Fabian, the bridge player from the Palace Hotel in St Moritz.

They did not look in my direction, and went through the front door into the expensive sunlight of the Avenue Montaigne, two lovers in the city for lovers, on the way to an exquisite lunch, oblivious of the rest of the world, oblivious of me, standing just a few feet from where they had passed, with a stiletto in my overnight bag and murder in my heart.

12

The next morning I was in the lobby at eight-thirty. Two
hours later she came through the lobby and went out. In
Florence I had never seen her in daylight. She was more
beautiful than I remembered. If ever there was a lady made
for an American's dream of a wicked weekend in Paris, it
was Lily Abbott.

I made sure she didn't see me, and after she was gone I
went up to my room. There was no way of my knowing how
long she would be gone from the hotel. So I moved quickly. I
had packed Fabian's bag, with all his belongings, the houndstooth jacket on top, as I had found it. I called down to the
concierge's desk and asked for a porter to come to my room
and pick up a suitcase to take to Mr Fabian's room.

I had the stiletto letter-opener in its leather sheath in my
pocket. The adrenalin was pumping through my system and
my breathing was shallow and rapid. I had no plan beyond
getting into Fabian's room and confronting him with his
valise.

There was a knock on the door and I opened it for the
porter. I followed him as he carried the valise to the elevator.
He pushed the button for the sixth floor. Everything happens
on the sixth floor, I thought, as we rose silently. When the
elevator stopped and the door opened, I followed him down
the corridor. Our footsteps made no sound on the heavy
carpet. We passed nobody. We were in the hush of the rich.
The man set the bag down at the door of a suite and was
about to knock when I stopped him. 'That's all right,' I said,
picking up the bag myself, 'I'll take it in. Mr Fabian is a
friend of mine.' I gave the porter five francs. He thanked me
and left.

I knocked gently on the door.

The door was opened and there was Fabian. He was completely dressed, ready to go out. At last we were face to face.
Myself and Sloane's nemesis, riffling cards, afternoon and
evening, at home in the haunts of wealth. Thief. He squinted

slightly, as though he couldn't see me clearly. 'Yes?' he said politely.

'I believe this belongs to you, Mr Fabian,' I said and bulled past him, carrying the valise down a hall that led into a large living room which was littered with newspapers in several languages. There were flowers in vases everywhere. I dreaded to think of what he was paying each day for his lodgings. I could hear him closing the door behind me. I wondered if he was armed.

'I say,' he said, as I turned to him, 'there must be some mistake.'

'There's no mistake.'

'Who are you anyway? Haven't we met somewhere before?'

'In St Moritz.'

'Of course. You're the young man who attended to Mrs Sloane this year. I'm afraid I don't remember your name. Gr – Grimm, isn't it?'

'Grimes.'

'Grimes. Forgive me.' He was absolutely calm, his voice pleasant. I tried to control my breathing. 'I was just about to go out,' he said, 'but I can spare a moment. Do sit down.'

'I'd rather not, if you don't mind.' I gestured toward the suitcase, which I had deposited in the middle of the room. 'I'd just like you to open your bag and check that nothing's missing....'

'My bag? My dear fellow, I never...'

'I'm sorry about the broken lock...' I kept on talking. 'I did it before I realized I had the wrong one.'

'I just don't know what you're talking about. I never saw that bag before in my life.' If he had rehearsed a year for this moment, he couldn't have been more convincing.

'When you've finished and you're satisfied that I've taken nothing,' I said, 'I'd be obliged if you brought out *my* bag. With everything that was in it when you picked it up in Zurich. *Everything*.'

He shrugged. 'This is absolutely bizarre. If you want, you can search the apartment and see for yourself that...'

I reached into my pocket and took out Lily Abbott's letter.

'This was in your jacket,' I said. 'I took the liberty of reading it.'

He barely glanced at the letter. 'This is getting more and more mysterious, I must say.' He made a charming, deprecating gesture, too much of a gentleman to read another man's mail. 'No names, no dates.' He tossed the letter on a table. 'It might have been written to anyone, by anyone. Whatever gave you the idea that it had anything to do with me?' He was beginning to sound testy now.

'Lady Abbott gave me the idea,' I said.

'Oh, really,' he said. 'I must confess, she *is* a friend of mine. How is she anyway?'

'Ten minutes ago, when I saw her in the lobby, she was well,' I said.

'Good God, Grimes,' he said, 'don't tell me Lily is here in the hotel?'

'That's enough of that,' I said. 'You know what I'm here for. Seventy thousand dollars.'

He laughed, almost authentically. 'You're joking, aren't you? Did Lily put you up to this? She *is* a joker.'

'I want my seventy thousand dollars, Mr Fabian,' I said. I made myself sound as menacing as possible.

'You must be out of your mind, sir,' Fabian said crisply. 'Now I'm afraid I must go.'

I grabbed him by the arm, remembering the wall-eyed man in the arcade in Milan. 'You're not leaving this room until I get my money,' I said. My voice rose and I was ashamed of the way I sounded. It was a situation for a basso and I was singing tenor. High tenor.

'Keep your hands off me.' Fabian pulled away and brushed fastidiously at his sleeve. 'I don't like to be touched. And if you don't get out right away, I'm calling the management and asking for the police....'

I picked up a lamp from the table and hit him on the head. The lamp shattered with the blow. Fabian looked surprised as he sank slowly to the floor. A thin trickle of blood ran down his forehead. I took out my paper knife and knelt beside him, waiting for him to come to. After about fifteen seconds he opened his eyes. The expression in them was vague, unfocused. I held the sharp, needle-like point of the stiletto to his throat. Suddenly, he was fully conscious. He didn't move, but looked up at me in terror.

'I'm not fooling, Fabian,' I said. I wasn't, either. At that moment, I would have happily killed him. I was trembling, but so was he.

'All right,' he said thickly. 'There's no need to go to extremes. I took your bag. Now let me up.'

I helped him to his feet. He staggered a little and sank into an easy chair. He felt his forehead and looked apprehensively at the blood smeared on his hand when he took it away. He pulled a handkerchief from his breastpocket and dabbed at his forehead. 'Good God, man,' he said weakly, 'you could have killed me with that lamp.'

'You're lucky,' I said.

He managed a little laugh, but he kept looking at the stiletto in my hand. 'I've always detested knives,' he said. 'You must be awfully fond of money.'

'Average fond,' I said. 'About like you, I guess.'

'I wouldn't kill for it.'

'How do you know?' I asked. I stroked the blade of the little weapon with my left hand. 'I never thought I would either. Until this morning. Where is it?'

'I don't have it,' he said.

I took a step toward him, threateningly.

'Stand back. Please stand back. It's ... well ... Shall we say that I don't have it at the moment, but that it's *available*? Please don't wave that thing around anymore. I'm sure we can come to terms without further bloodshed.' He dabbed at his forehead again.

Suddenly the reaction set in. I started to shake violently. I was horrified at what I had done. I had actually been on the point of murder. I dropped the stiletto on the table. If Fabian had said at that moment that he refused to give me a cent, I would have walked out the door and forgotten the whole thing. 'I suppose,' he said quietly, 'at the back of my mind I realized that one day someone would come in and ask me for the money.' There was an echo there that I could not help but recognize. How had Drusack behaved in his desperate hour? 'I've taken very good care of it,' Fabian said, 'only I'm afraid you'll have to wait awhile.'

'What do you mean – wait awhile?' I tried to keep my tone menacing, but I knew I wasn't succeeding.

'I've taken certain liberties with your little nest egg, Mr Grimes,' he said. 'I've made some investments.' He smiled like a doctor announcing an inoperable cancer. 'I don't believe in letting money lie idle. Do you?'

'I haven't had any money to let do anything before this.'

'Ah,' he said. 'Recent wealth. I thought as much. Would you mind if I went into the bathroom and washed off some of this gore? Lily is likely to come in at any moment and I wouldn't like to frighten her.'

'Go ahead.' I sat down heavily. 'I'll be right here.'

'I'm sure you will.' He got up from his chair and walked unsteadily into the bathroom. I heard water running. There was undoubtedly a door leading from the bedroom into the corridor, but I was convinced he wouldn't leave. And if he had wanted to I wouldn't have done anything to prevent him. I felt numb. Investments. I had imagined various possible scenes while on the trail of the man who had taken my money, but I had never thought that when I finally caught up with him our meeting would take the shape of a business conference.

Fabian came out of the bedroom, his hair wet and freshly combed. His step was firm now and there was no indication that just a few minutes before he had been lying on the floor, senseless and bloody. 'First,' he said, 'would you like a drink?'

'Yes,' I said.

'I believe we can both use one.' He went over to a sideboard and opened it and poured from a bottle of Scotch into two glasses. 'Soda?' he asked. 'Ice?'

'I'll take it neat.'

'Capital idea,' he said. He slipped in and out of being British. White's Club, the Enclosure at Epsom. He handed me the whiskey and I gulped it down. He drank more slowly and sat opposite me in the easy chair, twirling the glass in his hand. 'If it hadn't been for Lily,' he said, 'you probably never would have found me.'

'Probably not.'

'Women.' He sighed. 'Have you slept with her?'

'I'd rather not answer that question.'

'I suppose you're right.' He sighed again.

'Well, now ... I imagine you'd like me to begin at the beginning. Do you have the time?'

'I have plenty of time,' I said.

'May I make one proviso before I start?' he asked.

'What's that?'

'That you don't tell Lily anything about ... well, about all this. As you might have gathered from the letter, she thinks highly of me.'

'If I get my money back,' I said, 'I won't say a word.'

'That's fair enough.' He sighed again. 'First, if you don't mind, I'd like to tell you a little about myself.'

'I don't mind.'

'I'll make it brief,' he promised.

*

As it turned out, it wasn't as brief as all that. He started with his parents, who were poor, the father a minor employee in a small shoe factory in Lowell, Massachusetts, where he was born. There was never enough money around the house. He had not gone to college. During World War II he was in the Air Force, stationed outside London. He had met an English girl from a rich family. Actually, the family lived in the Bahamas, where they were reputed to have large estates. He had been demobilized in England and there, after a hasty courtship, had married the girl. 'Somehow,' he said, explaining the union, 'I had developed expensive tastes. I had no desire to work and no other prospects for leading the kind of life I wanted any other way.'

He had moved to the Bahamas with his new wife and taken up British citizenship. His wife's family weren't miserly toward him, but they were not generous either, and he had begun to gamble to eke out his allowance. Bridge and backgammon were his games. 'Alas,' he said, 'I fell into associated vices. Ladies.' One day there had been a family meeting and the divorce had followed immediately. Since that time, he had made do with his gambling winnings. For the most

155

part he had lived fairly comfortably, although with many anxious moments. During part of the winter season the pickings were not bad in the Bahamas, but he was forced to keep traveling. New York, London, Monte Carlo, Paris, Deauville, St Moritz, Gstaad. Where the money was. And the games.

'It's a hand-to-mouth existence,' he said. 'I never got far enough ahead to take even a month off without worrying. I saw opportunities around me constantly that would have made me a rich man if I had even a modest amount of capital. I won't say that I was bitter, but I certainly was discontented. I had just turned fifty a few days before the flight to Zurich, and I was not pleased with what the future might have in store for me. It is rasping to the soul to be committed to the company of the rich without being rich yourself. To pretend that losing three thousand dollars in one evening means as little to you as to them. To go from one great palace of a hotel to another while you're on duty, so to speak, and to hide in dingy out-of-the-way boarding houses when you're on your own.'

The ski-club group had been particularly lucrative. Almost permanent games had been set up from year to year. He had made himself well-liked, did a minimum amount of skiing to establish his legitimacy, paid his debts promptly, gave his share of parties, never cheated, was agreeable with the ladies, and was introduced to likely prey among the abundant Greek, South American, and English millionaires, all gamblers by nature, proud of their games and careless in their play.

'There was also the possibility,' he said, 'of meeting widows with independent fortunes and young divorcees with handsome settlements. Unfortunately,' he said, with a sigh, 'I am terribly romantic, a failing in a man my age, and what was offered I wouldn't have and what I would have wasn't offered. At least,' he said, with a touch of vanity, 'not on a financially acceptable basis. I know that I am not painting a very heroic picture of myself . . .' he said.

'No,' I said.

'. . . but I would like you to believe that I tell the truth, that you can trust me.'

'Go on,' I said. 'I don't trust you yet.'

'So,' he said, 'that was the man who tried to open a bag that was ostensibly his in the overpriced room at the Palace Hotel in St Moritz and found that the combination didn't work.'

'So you sent down for something to break it open with,' I said grimly, remembering my own experience.

'I had the desk send a man up. When he got the bag open, I saw immediately that it wasn't mine. I don't know why I didn't tell him that the bag belonged to somebody else. Some sixth sense, perhaps. Or maybe the sight of the brand-new attaché case lying on top of everything else. People don't usually pack a case like that *in* their luggage, but usually carry it by hand. In any event, I thanked the man and tipped him.... Incidentally, I didn't have the heart to throw the case away. It's in the bedroom and of course I'll be pleased to give it back to you.'

'Thank you.'

'You're welcome,' he said. Without irony. 'Of course,' he said, 'when I counted the money, I realized that it had been stolen.'

'Of course.'

'It changes the morality of the affair a bit, doesn't it?'

'A bit.'

'It also meant that whoever had carried it across the ocean would not go crying to Interpol to recover it. Would my reasoning seem inaccurate to you?'

'No.'

'I went through the bag very carefully. I hope you'll forgive me if I tell you that I found nothing there to make one believe that the owner of the bag was in anything but the most modest circumstances.'

I nodded. 'You can say that again, brother,' I said.

'I also found no indication of who the owner was. No address books, letters, etcetera. I even looked in the shaving kit to see if there were any medicines with a name on them.'

I laughed, despite myself.

'You must be an extraordinarily healthy man,' Fabian said, approvingly.

'About the same as you,' I said.

'Ah,' he said, beaming, 'you had the same experience.'

'Exactly.'

'I spent the next hour,' he went on, 'trying to recall if there was anything in *my* bag which had my name on it. I decided there was nothing. I had forgotten about Lily's letter, of course. I thought I had thrown it away. Even so, with her usual caution, I knew no names would be committed to the page. The next step was obvious.'

'You stole the money.'

'Let's say I put it to good use.'

'What do you mean, use?'

'Let me go step by step. I had never been in a position before to risk enough to make any coup really conclusive. In view of the circles in which I moved, the amounts I *could* risk were derisive. So that even when I won, as I have more often than not, I never reaped the full benefits of my luck. Do you follow me, Grimes?'

'Partially,' I said.

'For example, until now, I have never dared to play bridge at more than five cents a point.'

'Mrs Sloane told me that you were playing with her husband at five cents a point.'

'That was true. The first night. After that we went up to ten a point. Then to fifteen. Naturally since Sloane was losing rather heavily, he lied to his wife.'

'How much?'

'I'll be frank with you. When I left St Moritz, I had Sloane's check for twenty-seven thousand dollars in my wallet.'

I whistled and looked at Fabian with growing respect. My own poker in Washington dwindled to a pinpoint. Here was a gambler who really knew how to ride his luck. But then I remembered it was *my* money he was risking, and I began to get angry all over again. 'What the hell good does that do *me*?' I asked.

Fabian put up his hand placatingly. 'All in due time, my dear fellow.' I had never expected to be called a dear fellow by a man who had grown up in Lowell, Massachusetts. 'I also did quite well, I am happy to say, at backgammon. Perhaps you remember that handsome young Greek with the beautiful wife?'

'Vaguely.'

'He was delighted when I suggested raising the stakes. A little over nine thousand dollars.'

'What you're telling me,' I said harshly, 'is that you ran my stake up thirty-six thousand dollars. Goody for you, Fabian; you're in the chips and you can give me back the seventy and we'll shake hands and have a drink on it and we're both on our way.'

He shook his head sadly. 'It isn't quite as simple as that, I'm afraid.'

'Don't abuse my patience, man. You either have the money or you don't. And you'd better have it.'

He stood up. 'I believe we both could use another drink,' he said. I glowered at him as he went over to the sideboard. Having refrained from killing him when I had the chance, any lesser threats had depreciated greatly in value. It also occurred to me as I watched his well-tailored back (not my clothes, but from any one of two or three other bags he probably traveled with at all times) that it might all be a lie, a cock-and-bull story to keep me tamped down until somebody – a maid, Lily Abbott, a friend, came into the room. There would be nothing to stop him then from accusing me of annoying him, dunning him for a loan, trying to sell him dirty post-cards, anything, and having me thrown out of the hotel. As he gave me my drink, I said, 'If you're lying to me, Fabian, the next time I see you I'm going to be carrying a gun.' I had no idea, of course, of how you went about getting a gun in France. And the only guns I had ever fired were .22 rifles at shooting galleries at town fairs.

'I wish you would believe me,' Fabian said as he sat down again with his drink, after pouring soda into it with a steady hand. 'I have plans for us two that will require mutual trust.'

'Plans?' I felt childishly manipulated, cunningly outmaneuvered by this man who had lived by his wits for nearly thirty years and whose hand could be so steady just a few minutes after he had escaped violent death. 'Okay, go on,' I said. 'You're thirty-six thousand dollars richer than you were three weeks ago and you say it isn't simple to give me back the money you owe me. Why not?'

'For one thing, I have made certain investments.'

'Like what?'

'Before I go into detail,' Fabian said, 'let me outline in general what sort of a plan I'd like to suggest.' He took a long sip of his drink, then cleared his throat. 'I suppose you have some right to be angry at what I've done...'

I made a small, choking noise, which he ignored. 'But in the long run,' he said, 'I have every reason to believe you'll be deeply grateful.' I started to interrupt, but he waved me to silence. 'I know that seventy thousand dollars in one lump seems like quite a bit of money. Especially to a young man like you, who, I can guess, was never particularly prosperous.'

'What are you driving at, Fabian?' I could not get over the feeling that moment by moment a web was being spun around me and that, in a very short time, I would be unable to move, or even utter a sound.

The voice went on, gentle, almost-British, confident, persuasive. 'How long would it last you? A year, two years. Three years, at the most. As soon as you surfaced, you would be the prey of conniving men and rapacious women. I take it that you have very little experience, if any, in handling large sums of money. Just the primitive – and if I may permit myself a small criticism – the fairly careless way in which you attempted to transfer your hoard from the States to Europe is plain evidence of *that*....'

I certainly was in no position to contradict him about my ineptitude, so I remained silent.

'I, on the other hand,' he went on, thoughtfully twirling the ice in his glass and looking me frankly and directly in the eye, 'have been handling considerable sums for nearly thirty years. Where you, in three years, say, would be stranded, penniless, in some backwater of Europe – I take it that you don't think it would be healthy to return to America...?' He looked at me quizzically.

'Go on,' I said.

'I, with any luck, given this start, would not be surprised if I wound up with well over a million...'

'Dollars?'

'Pounds,' he said.

'I must admit,' I said, 'I admire your nerve. Still, what would that have to do with me?'

'We would be partners,' he said calmly. 'I would handle the ... uh ... investments and we would share the profits fifty-fifty. Starting, I would like to say with the check of Mr Sloane and the contribution of the handsome young Greek. Could anything be fairer than that?'

I made myself think hard. The low, polite voice was hypnotizing me. 'So – in exchange for my seventy thousand dollars, I'd get half of thirty-six?'

'Minus certain expenses,' he said.

'Like what?'

'Hotels, travel, entertainment. That sort of thing.'

I looked around at the room full of flowers. 'Is there anything left?'

'Quite a bit.' He put his hand up again. 'Please hear me out. To be more than fair – after one year, you would be permitted to withdraw your original seventy thousand dollars, if you so desired.'

'What if during the year you *lost* the whole thing.'

'That is a risk we'd both have to run,' he said. 'I believe that it is worth taking. Now let me ask you to consider other advantages. You, as an American, are fully liable to the American income tax. Am I right?'

'Yes, but...'

'I know what you are going to say – you do not intend to pay it. I take it for granted that you have not declared the seventy thousand dollars that is the subject of our discussion. If you merely *spend* it, you would not be in any difficulty. But if you *increased* it, in legal or even semi-legal ways, you would have to beware of the legion of American agents all through Europe, of informers in banks and business houses.... You would always have the fear of confiscation of your passport, fines, criminal prosecution...'

'And you?' I asked, feeling locked in a corner by his logic.

'I am a British subject,' he said, 'domiciled in the Bahamas. I don't even fill out a form. Just one quick example – you, as an American, are not legally permitted to trade in gold, although your government is making certain noises that indicate that will be changed eventually. But there is no such restriction on me. The gold market these days is most seductive. In fact, even while I was amusing Mr Sloane and my Greek with our little games, I put in an order for a tidy amount. Have you been following the rate of gold recently?'

'No.'

'I am ahead – *we* are ahead – ten thousand dollars on our investment.'

'In just three weeks?' I asked incredulously.

'Ten days, to be exact,' Fabian said.

'What else have you done with my money?' I still clung to the singular possessive pronoun but with diminishing vigor.

'Well . . .' For the first time since he had come out of the bathroom, Fabian looked a little uneasy. 'As a partner, I don't intend to hide anything from you. I've bought a horse.'

'A horse!' I couldn't help groaning. 'What kind of horse?'

'A thoroughbred. A racehorse. Among other reasons, which I'll come to later, that was why I didn't appear as scheduled in Florence. Much to Lily's annoyance, I must admit. I had to come to Paris to complete the deal. It is a horse that took my eye at Deauville last summer, but which I was not in a position to buy at that time. Also' – he smiled – 'it wasn't for sale then. A friend of mine who happens to own a racing stable and a breeding farm in Kentucky expressed an interest in the colt – a stallion, by the way, and potentially quite valuable later on at stud – and I am sure he would show his gratitude in a substantial way if I were to let him know that I am now the owner of the animal. Out of friendship, I plan to indicate to him, I'd be ready to part with it.'

'What if he indicates to you that he's changed his mind?' By now, almost insensibly, I had been swept into what just fifteen minutes before I would have considered a gambler's insane fantasies. 'That he doesn't want to buy it anymore?'

Fabian shrugged, rubbed lovingly at the ends of his mustache, a gesture I was to come to recognize as a tic, useful to gain time when he didn't have a ready answer to a question.

'In that case, old man,' he said, 'you and I would have a fine start toward a racing stable. I haven't chosen any colors as yet. Do you have any preferences?'

'Black and blue,' I said.

He laughed. He had a hearty, Guards' officer kind of laugh. 'I'm glad to see you have a sense of humor,' he said. 'It's a bore doing business with the glum.'

'Do you mind telling me what you've paid for this brute?' I asked.

'Not at all. Six thousand dollars. He broke down in training last autumn with something called splints, so he comes as a bargain. The trainer's an old friend of mine' – I was to find out that Fabian had old friends all over the globe and in all professions – 'and he assures me he's as right as a dollar now.'

'Right as a dollar.' I nodded, in pain. 'While we're at it, Fabian,' I said, 'are there any more ... uh ... investments that I happen to have in my portfolio?'

He played with his mustache again. 'As a matter of fact, yes,' he said. 'I hope you're not overwhelmingly prudish.'

I thought of my father and his Bible. 'I would say medium,' I said. 'Why?'

'There's a delightful French lady I make a point of looking up every time I come to Paris.' He smiled, as though welcoming the delightful French lady into his dreams. 'Interested in films. Been an actress in her time, she says. On the producing side now. An old admirer has been staking her. Not sufficiently, I gather. She's in the middle of making a picture at the moment. Quite dirty. Quite, quite dirty. I've seen some of the – I think they call them dailies in the industry. Most amusing. Have you any idea what a movie like *Deep Throat* has brought in for its backers?'

'No.'

'Millions, lad, millions.' He sighed sentimentally. 'My delightful little friend has let me read the script, too. Most literate. Full of fancy and provocation. Essentially innocent in my opinion. Almost decorous from a sophisticated point of view, but a little bit of everything for every taste. Something like a combination of Henry Miller and the Arabian

Nights. But my delightful lady friend – she's directing it herself, by the way – she got the script almost for nothing from a young Iranian who can't go back to Iran – but even though she's making it on a shoestring – some of the most lucrative of these particular works of art are made for under forty thousand dollars – I think *Deep Throat* cost no more than sixty – as I was saying, her bookkeeping doesn't quite match her talent – she's just a slip of a woman – and when she told me she needed fifteen thousand dollars to complete the picture...'

'You said you'd give it to her.'

'Exactly.' He beamed. 'Out of gratitude she offered me twenty percent of the profits.'

'And you said you'd take it?'

'No, I held out for twenty-five.' He beamed again. 'I may be a friend, but I'm a businessman first.'

'Fabian,' I said. 'I don't know whether to laugh or cry.'

'In the long run,' he said, 'you'll smile. At least smile. They're having a screening of what they've shot thus far this evening. We're all invited. I guarantee you'll be impressed.'

'I've never seen a pornographic movie in my life,' I said.

'Never too late to begin, lad. Now,' he said briskly, 'I suggest we go down to the bar and wait for Lily. She can't be too long. We can cement our partnership in champagne. And I'll treat you to the best lunch you've ever eaten. And after lunch we'll take in the Louvre. Have you ever been to the Louvre?'

'I just arrived in Paris yesterday.'

'I envy you your initiation,' he said.

*

We had just about finished a bottle of champagne when Lily Abbott strode into the bar. When Fabian introduced me as an old friend from St Moritz, she did not show, by as much as the blink of an eye, that we had ever gone so far as to shake hands in Florence.

Fabian ordered a second bottle.

I wished I liked the taste.

13

We were eight in the small screening room. My feet ached from the Louvre. The room smelled of twenty years of cigarettes and sweat. The building on the Champs Elysées was a shabby one with creaky, old-fashioned elevators. The peeling signs of the businesses on the floors we passed all looked like advertisements for concerns that were well into bankruptcy and minor evasions of the criminal code. The corridors were dimly lit, as though the people who frequented the building did not wish to be clearly observed as they came and went. With Fabian, Lily, and myself were Fabian's delightful French lady, whose name was Nadine Bonheur. At the console in the rear was the cameraman on the picture, a weary, gray professional of about sixty-five who wore a beret and a permanent cigarette hanging from his lip. He looked too old for this sort of work and kept his eyes almost completely closed at all times, as though he did not want to be reminded too definitely of what he had recorded on the film we were about to see.

Seated together on the far aisle were the two stars of the film, a slender dark young man, probably a North African, with a long, sad face, and a pert, pretty young American girl by the name of Priscilla Dean, with a blonde ponytail, an anachronistic, fresh-faced relic of an earlier generation of Midwestern virgins. She was primly dressed and looked as proper as a starched lace apron. 'It's a pleasure, I'm sure,' she said, her voice pure Iowa. I was introduced without ceremony to the others, the atmosphere businesslike. We might have been assembled for a lecture on the marketing of a breakfast food.

A bearded, long-haired man sitting apart, who was wearing a soiled denim jacket and who looked as though he had just bitten into something extremely distasteful, merely grunted when I said hello.

'He's a critic,' Fabian whispered to me. 'He belongs to Nadine.'

''Appy to make the acquaintance,' Nadine Bonheur said to me, looking up from a clipboard and extending her hand. Her hand was silky. She was small and slight, but with a perky full bosom, half of which could be seen over her low-cut black dress. She was tanned a beautiful even shade of brown. I imagined her lying naked on the beach at St Tropez, surrounded by equally unclothed dissolute young men. 'See what that hassole of a projectionist is doing,' she said to the cameraman. 'We only 'ave the room for teartty minutes.' Her accent in English was the sort that sounds charming to Americans.

The cameraman shouted something in French into a telephone on the desk in front of him and the lights dimmed.

For the next thirty minutes I was pathetically grateful that the room was dark. I was blushing so furiously that I felt that, although nobody could see me, the raw animal heat of the blood in my face must be raising the temperature of the room like a huge infra-red lamp. The goings-on on the screen, in color, were what my father would have described as indescribable. There were couplings of all sorts, in all positions, in a variety of backgrounds. There were triplings and quadruplings, animals, including a black swan, lesbian dalliance, and those caresses which we have been taught by *Playboy* to call fellatio and cunnilingus. There was sadism and masochism and behavior for which I, for one, had no name. As Fabian had said, there was something for everybody. The period seemed to be some time in the middle of the nineteenth century, as some of the men wore top hats and frock coats and the women wore crinolines and bustles, briefly. There were hussars' uniforms, boots and spurs, and an occasional shot of a castle, with buxom peasant girls being led behind bushes. Nadine Bonheur, scantily dressed, with her mischievous, incorruptible schoolgirl face topped by a long black wig, played a kind of mistress of the revels in the film, arranging bodies with the cool grace of a hostess preparing flowers in a salon before the arrival of her guests. Fabian had told me the script was literate, but since there was no sound or dialogue it was difficult for me to judge just how accurate his estimate was. The film was to be dubbed later, he told me.

From time to time, there was a shot of an angelic-faced young man in a long pink robe, trimmed with fur, clipping hedges. Occasionally he stared soulfully off screen. He was also to be seen seated on a throne-like gilt chair in a stone hall lit by candelabra, observing various combinations of the sexes in the throes of orgasm. He never changed his expression, although once, as the action reached a climax, he languidly picked up a long-stemmed rose and sniffed at it.

To her credit, I heard Lily, seated on the other side of Fabian, suppress a giggle.

'The story's simple,' Fabian explained to me in a whisper. 'It takes someplace in Mittel-europa. The young man in the robe with the clippers in a prince. The working title, by the way, is *The Sleeping Prince*. He has just been married to a beautiful foreign princess. His father, the king – that's going to be shot next week – wants an heir. But the boy's a virgin. He's not interested in girls. All he's interested in is horticulture.'

'That explains the clippers,' I said, hoping that proof that I was still capable of speech would somehow pale my blushes.

'Naturally,' Fabian said impatiently. 'His aunt, that's Nadine, has been commissioned by her brother, the king, to stimulate his libido. The princess, his wife, awaits him, weeping in one of the towers of the castle, lying in the unused wedding bed garlanded with flowers. But nothing – and, as you see, every possible attraction is tried – nothing arouses him. He looks on with glazed eyes. Everybody is desperate. Then, as a last resort, his aunt, Nadine, dances alone in a diaphanous gown before him, holding a red rose between her teeth. His eyes lose their glaze. He sits up. He drops his clippers. He moves down from the throne. He takes his aunt in his arms. He dances. He kisses her. They fall to the turf together. They make love. There is cheering in the castle. The king declares the marriage to the princess annulled. The prince marries his aunt. There is a three-day orgy in the castle and behind the bushes to celebrate. Nine months later, a son is born. Every year, to commemorate the occasion, the prince and his aunt repeat the dance, in their original robes, as the church bells ring out. It's all pretty Iranian, if you tell it baldly like this, but it has an earthy charm. There's a subplot, of course, with a villain who is plotting for the throne himself and has a thing about whips, but I won't bother you with that . . .'

The lights went up. I made believe I had a coughing attack to explain the blaze of my cheeks.

'That's it,' Fabian said, 'in a nutshell. It's camp and it's not camp, if you get what I mean. We'll get the intellectuals, as well as everybody else.'

'Miles,' Nadine Bonheur, switching smoothly from her role of incestuous seductress to serious businesswoman, stood up from her chair two rows in front of us and faced us, ''Ow you like it, eh? It will lay them in the haisles, no?'

'It's jolly,' Fabian said. 'Very jolly. We're bound to make a packet.'

I avoided looking at anybody as we trooped out to the elevator. I took especial care not to glance at the American girl, who had featured prominently in all the most lurid scenes, and whom I would recognize, even with a sack over her head, on any nudist beach in the world. Lily, I saw, also showed an intense interest in the floor of the elevator.

As we walked down the Champs Elysées toward an Alsatian brasserie for refreshments, Nadine took my arm. 'The little girl,' she said to me. 'What you think of 'er? Talented, eh?'

'Extremely,' I said.

'She only does these on the side,' Nadine said. 'She is paying 'er way through the Sorbonne. Comparative literature. American girls 'ave more character than European girls. You think so?'

'I'm not much of an expert,' I said. 'I've only been in Europe a few weeks.'

'You think it will be big success in America?' She sounded anxious.

'I'm very optimistic,' I said.

'I'm just afraid maybe we 'ave too much what you call class for the general audience.'

'I wouldn't worry,' I said.

'Miles, too,' Nadine said. She squeezed my arm, her motives ambiguous. 'He is wonderful on the set. A smile for everybody. You must come on the set, too. The ambiance is beautiful. One for all and all for one. 'Ow they work! Overtime, double overtime, nevair a complaint. Of course, the salaries are very small and the stars are on percentages and that 'elps. Will you come tomorrow? We 'ave a scene where Priscilla is dressed as a nun ...'

'I'm afraid I'm in Paris on business,' I said. 'I'm awfully busy.'

'Welcome hany time. Do not 'esitate.'

'Thank you,' I said.

'Do you think it will pass the censors in America?' Again she sounded anxious.

'I imagine so. From what I hear they have to pass everything these days. There's always the chance, of course, that a picture can run into trouble with some local police chief, who can get a theater closed down for a while.' Even as I said it I realized that I was giving myself something else to worry about. If I were a local police chief I'd have the film burned, law or no law. But I wasn't a policeman. I was, whether I liked it or not, an investor. To the tune of fifteen thousand dollars. I tried to sound offhand. 'How about France?' I asked. 'Will it pass here?'

'It is terrible here.' She squeezed my arm illogically again. 'You never can tell. A old fart of a bishop makes a speech one Sunday and hall the theaters go dark the next day. And if the wife of the President or a cabinet minister 'appens to walk by and see a poster ... you 'ave no hidea how narrow-minded French people can be about hart. Luckily, there is halways a new scandal next week to take the pressure hoff.' Suddenly, she stopped, releasing my arm. She moved off two steps and looked searchingly at me. 'To the naked heye,' she said, 'you look very nicely built. Ham I wrong?'

'I used to ski a lot,' I said.

'We 'ave not yet cast the role of the villain,' Nadine said. ' 'E has two very interesting scenes. One with Priscilla alone and one with Priscilla and a Nubian girl ... Maybe it would hamuse you.'

'She's offering you a job, Douglas,' Miles said. His voice seemed to boom out over all the noise of the avenue traffic. 'Protect your investment.'

'It's very good of you, madame,' I said to Nadine, 'but if my mother in America ever saw it, I'm afraid...' I was ashamed to bring my dead mother into this affair, but at the moment it seemed like the quickest way to end the conversation.

'Priscilla 'as a mother in America, too,' Nadine said.

'There are mothers and mothers in America. I'm an only son,' I said idiotically.

'Oh, take it,' Lily said. 'I'll go over your lines with you on the set. And we could rehearse the difficult bits back at the hotel.'

'Sorry,' I said, glaring at her, 'I'd really love to do it. But I may be called out of Paris at any time.'

Nadine shrugged. 'The trouble with this business,' she said, 'there hare nevair henough new faces. Halways the same hequipment, the same horgasms. Some hother time, maybe. You have something – ha kind hof underground sexiness, like a young curé ... Ham I right, Lily?'

'Absolutely,' Lily said.

'It would be beautifully perverse,' Nadine said. 'Hinnocently rotten. A new dimension. The bishops would gnash their teeth.'

'Some other time,' I said firmly.

'I will work hon you.' Nadine smiled her incorruptible schoolgirl smile.

*

The two beers he drank one after the other in the brasserie seemed to have aroused the critic with the beard. He began to speak excitedly in French to Nadine.

'Philippe,' Nadine said, 'speak Henglish. We have guests.'

'We are in France,' Philippe said loudly through his beard. 'Why shouldn't they speak French?'

'Because we're stupid Anglo-Saxons, dearie,' Lily said, 'and, as every Frenchman knows, undereducated.'

' 'E speaks Henglish very good,' Nadine said. 'Very good. 'E was in Hamerica two years. 'E was in 'Ollywood. 'E wrote criticism for *Cahiers du Cinéma*.'

'Did you like Hollywood?' Fabian asked.

'I hated it.'

'Did you like the pictures?'

'I hated them.'

'Do you like French pictures?' Lily asked.

'The last one I liked was *Breathless*.' Philippe swigged at his beer.

'That was ten years ago,' Lily said.

'More than that,' Philippe said complacently.

''E is very particular,' Nadine said. 'Halso political.'

'How many times . . .' He turned angrily on her. 'How many times have I told you the two invariably go together?'

'Too many times. Don't be an *emmerdeur*, Philippe. He likes China,' Nadine explained to us.

'Do you like Chinese films?' Lily asked. She seemed to take delight in baiting the man, in her offhand, ladylike way.

'I haven't seen any – yet,' the man said. 'I wait. Five years. Ten years.' His English was heavily accented, but fluent. His eyes glittered. He was the sort of man who would debate happily in Sanskrit. I had the impression that if he ever got into a conversation with anybody who agreed with him he would jump up and storm out of the room.

'Tell me, old man,' Fabian said, hearty and friendly, 'what do you think of our little opus so far?'

'*Merde*. A piece of shit.'

'Really?' Lily sounded surprised.

'Philippe,' Nadine said warningly. 'Priscilla hunderstands English. You don't want to hundermine her performance, do you?'

'That's all right,' Priscilla said, in her pure corn-fed, high-school soprano, 'I never take what a Frenchman says seriously.'

'We are in the city where Racine presented *Phèdre*, where Molière died,' the critic recited, 'where Flaubert went to court to defend *Madame Bovary*, where they rioted in the streets after the first performance of *Hernani*, where Heine was welcomed because of his poetry in another language, and Turgenev found a home.' Philippe's beard was electric with argument, the great names luscious on his tongue. 'In our own time, in the same medium – film – we have to our credit at least *Grande Illusion*, *Poil de Carotte*, *Forbidden Games*.

171

And what have we gathered tonight to discuss? A comic and distasteful attempt to arouse our basest emotions...'

'Do not sound, *chéri*,' Nadine Bonheur said calmly, 'as though you are too fine to fuck. I could gather testimony.'

The critic glowered at her and waved for another beer. 'What have you shown me? The rutting of an empty-faced American *poupée* and a Moroccan pimp, the...'

'*Chéri*,' Nadine said, more sharply now, 'remember, you are halways signing petitions against racism.'

'That's all right, Nadine,' Priscilla said. She was spooning away at a huge bowl of ice cream with chocolate sauce. 'I never take what a Frenchman says seriously.'

The Moroccan smiled benignly, his English obviously not up to complicated observations on aesthetics in that language.

'Made in France,' the critic said, 'written in France, composed in France, painted in France – You remember—' He pointed an accusing finger at Nadine. 'I ask you to remember what that used to mean. Glory. Devotion to beauty, to art, to the highest aspirations of the human race. What does *your* Made in France mean? A tickling of the balls, a lubricity of the vagina ...'

'Hear, hear,' Lily said.

'English lightness of character,' the critic said, leaning forward over the table, jutting his beard fiercely at Lily. 'The Empire is gone. Now we will emit a Buckingham Palace snicker.'

'Old man,' Miles said amiably, 'if I may say so, I think you're missing the point.'

'If I may say so, sir,' Philippe said, 'I think I am missing nothing. What is the point?'

'For one thing, the point is to make a dollar or two,' Miles said. 'From what I've heard, that isn't *completely* against the French character.'

'That is not the French character. That is capitalism in France. They are two different things, monsieur.'

'All right,' Fabian said good-naturedly, 'let's leave money out of it for the time being. Although permit me to point out in passing that the greatest number of pornographic films and the most – ah – explicit ones – come out of Sweden and Denmark, two Socialist countries, if I have my facts straight.'

'Scandinavians,' the critic said. He snorted, dismissing the North. 'A mockery of the word Socialism. I piss on such Socialism.'

Fabian sighed. 'You're a hard man to do business with, Philippe.'

'I have my definitions,' Philippe said. 'I define Socialism.'

'China, again,' Nadine said. She made a small, wailing sound.

'We can't all live in China, now, can we?' Fabian spoke reasonably. 'Whether we like it or not, we live in a world that has a different history, different tastes, different needs...'

'I piss on a world that needs *merde* like the *merde* we saw tonight.' Philippe called for another beer. He would have a belly like a barrel by the time he was forty.

'I went to the Louvre with my young friend this afternoon.' Fabian waved in my direction, his voice gentle. 'And yesterday I treated myself to a visit to the Jeu de Paume. Where the Impressionists are collected.'

'I do not have to have the museums of Paris described to me, monsieur,' Philippe said coldly.

'Forgive me,' Fabian said. 'Tell me, monsieur, do you disapprove of the works of art in these museums?'

'Not all of them,' Philippe said reluctantly. 'No.'

'The nudes, the embracing figures, the busty madonnas, the goddesses promising all sorts of carnal pleasures to the poor mortals below, the beautiful boys, the reclining princesses ... Do you disapprove of all that?'

'I do not gather what you are heading for, monsieur,' Philippe said, sprinkling beer on his beard.

'What I'm getting at,' Fabian said, all patience and bonhomie, 'is that throughout our civilization artists have presented objects of sexual desire, in one form or another, sacred, profane, lowly, elevated – the stuff of sensual fantasy. For example, yesterday in the Jeu de Paume, I saw, with pleasure, for perhaps the tenth time, the large canvas by

173

Manet, *Le déjeuner sur l'herbe*, the one with the two superb ladies lolling naked on the grass with their fully dressed gentlemen friends watching admiringly and...'

'I am familiar with the work,' Philippe said flatly. 'Continue.'

'Obviously,' Fabian said with relish, 'Monsieur Manet did not mean for the viewer to understand that nothing went before that moment and that nothing would happen *after* the moment. The impression *I* get, at least, is one of delicious familiarity, with all that that connotes.... Are you beginning to follow?'

'I understand.' Philippe was surly now. 'I do not follow.'

'Perhaps,' Fabian said, 'if Manet had had the time, he would have painted some scenes of what went on before that peaceful, suspended moment and what would go on after it. And they might not be so terribly different from some of the scenes that were screened for us tonight. Shall we admit that dear Nadine is perhaps not as great an artist as Manet and that sweet little Priscilla might not be as agelessly attractive as the ladies in the painting, but that in its modest way, Nadine's film springs from some of the same basic motives as Manet's oil...?'

'Bravo,' Nadine said. 'He's halways trying to get me to fuck him hout in the hopen hair. Don't deny hit, Philippe. Remember Brittany last summer? Hall that sand up my hassole.'

'I deny nothing,' Philippe said unhappily.

'Sex, love, whatever you call it,' Fabian rolled on sonorously, 'is never just plain flesh. There is always an element of fantasy involved. Each age looks to its artists for the fantasies that deepen or improve or even make possible the actual act. Nadine, once again in her modest way – forgive me, dear...' He leaned over and patted Nadine's hand in a fatherly way. 'Nadine is trying to enrich the fantasies of her fellow men and women. In this dark, joyless, imaginatively stunted age, I would say that she should be saluted, not criticized.'

'Talk the hind leg off a donkey,' Lily said, in full Cockney, 'that one would.'

'You can say that again, sister,' I said, remembering what Fabian had already talked me into in the space of one afternoon. It suddenly occurred to me that he must be a disbarred lawyer. Disbarred for a very good reason, no doubt.

'Someday, monsieur,' Philippe said, with dignity, 'I would like to have a discussion with you in my native language. I am at a disadvantage in English.' He stood up. 'I have to rise early in the morning. Pay the bill, Nadine, and let us find a taxi.'

'That's all right, Nadine,' Fabian said, waving his hand, although she had made no move toward her purse. 'The refreshments are on us.' The plural did not escape me. 'And thank you for a jolly evening.'

We all stood up and Nadine kissed Fabian on both cheeks. She merely shook my hand. I was a little disappointed. The film had had its effect on me, blushes or no blushes. The touch of her lips would have been bracing. I wondered how the Moroccan boy, who had disported with her as her undeniably willing partner in at least two long scenes, could stand meekly aside and watch her go off with another man. Actors, I thought. They must divide themselves into compartments.

'Do you live near here?' Fabian asked Miss Dean.

'Not far.'

'Perhaps you'd like us to escort you home—'

'No, thanks, I'm not going home,' Priscilla said. 'I have a date with my fiancé.' She put out her hand to me and I shook it. 'G'bye, see you in church,' she said. I felt a small, rolled-up piece of paper in my palm. For the first time I looked directly at her. There was a little smudge of chocolate at the corner of her mouth, but her eyes were a deep sea blue, the tide coming in rapidly, bringing incalculable sunken treasure.

'See you,' I mumbled and closed my hand over the bit of paper as she stepped away.

*

Outside, on the avenue, in the soft wet air of the February Paris night, after we had parted with Priscilla and the Moroccan and the cameraman, I dug into my pocket, where I had dropped the piece of paper. I unrolled it and, by the light of a streetlamp, saw that it had a telephone number written on it. I put the piece of paper back in my pocket and hurried after Fabian and Lily, who were walking ahead of me.

'Glad you came to Paris, Douglas?' Fabian asked.

'It's been a lively day,' I said. 'Most educational.'

'It's only the beginning,' said Fabian. 'There are vistas ahead of you, vistas.'

'Did you believe all that stuff you were spouting back there?' I asked. 'About Nadine and Manet and so on?'

Fabian laughed. 'Not at the start maybe,' he said. 'I was just giving in to my normal reaction when I hear a Frenchman start orating about Racine and Molière and Victor Hugo. But by the end I damn near had myself convinced that I was a patron of the arts. That includes you, of course,' he added hastily.

'You're not going to put your name – *our* name – on it, are you?' I said, alarmed.

'No.' Fabian sounded almost regretful. 'I suppose that would be going too far. We'll have to find a company name. Have you any ideas, Lily? You've always been the clever girl.'

'Up, Down, and Over Productions,' Lily said.

'Don't be vulgar, dear,' Fabian said prissily. 'Remember, we want a review in *The Times*. We'll have to put our minds to it in the calm light of day. Oh, by the way, Douglas, get a good night's sleep. We'll be up at five. We have to drive out to Chantilly for the workouts.'

'What workouts?' I had no idea where Chantilly was and for a moment I thought that it was a special place where actors in pornographic movies kept in shape. From what I had seen that evening, a day's shooting involved as much physical expenditure for man and woman alike as ten fast rounds with a bantamweight prize-fighter.

'Our horse,' Fabian said. 'There was a cable waiting for me at the desk when we got back from the Louvre this afternoon – by the way, you did enjoy the Louvre, didn't you?'

'Yes. What about our horse?'

'The cable was from my friend in Kentucky. Somehow, he

found out about the splints. He's not ready to buy at the moment...'

'Oh, God,' I said.

'Not to fret, dear boy,' Fabian said. 'My friend in Kentucky wants the animal to run in one decent race before he puts his money down. You can't blame the man, can you?'

'No. But I can blame you.'

'I'm afraid you're starting our relationship on the wrong note, Douglas,' Fabian said, hurt. 'We just have to explain matters to the trainer. He has great faith in the horse, great faith. All he has to do is to make sure the horse is fit and pick the appropriate race to enter him in. The trainer's name is Coombs. An English name, but his family's been in Chantilly since the Empress Josephine. He's a wizard at picking appropriate races, an absolute wizard. He's won races with animals they were about to sell to pull junk wagons. Anyway, you'll love Chantilly. No lover of horses should come to Paris without seeing Chantilly.'

'I'm no lover of horses,' I said. 'I hate horses. I'm scared stiff of them.'

'Ah, Douglas,' Fabian said as we reached the hotel, 'you have a long way to go, a long, long way.' He tapped me, old comrade, on the shoulder, as we went in. 'But you'll make it, I guarantee you'll make it.'

*

I went up to my room, looked at the bed, turned down for the night, and stared at the telephone. I remembered some of the scenes in the movie I had seen that evening and decided I wasn't sleepy. I went down to the bar and ordered a whiskey and soda. I drank slowly, then took out the slip of paper Priscilla Dean had put in my hand and spread it out before me on the bar. 'Is there a telephone here?' I asked the barman.

'Downstairs,' he said.

I went downstairs and gave the number to the girl who was on duty there and went into the booth she indicated to me and picked up the phone. There was a moment's silence, then a busy signal. I listened to the signal for thirty seconds, then replaced the phone. So be it, I thought.

I went back to the bar, paid for my drink. Ten minutes later I was in my bed. Alone.

*

The name of the horse was *Rêve de Minuit*. Lily, Fabian, and I were standing with Coombs, the trainer, in the morning mist at the head of one of the *allées* in the forest of Chantilly, watching the exercise boys gallop in pairs and trios. It was seven in the morning and cold. My shoes and the cuffs of my trousers were muddy and wet through. I was hunched in my old, sooty, greenish overcoat, the same one I had when I was at the St Augustine, and I felt citified and out of place in the dripping woods, with the smell of wet foliage and steaming horses all around me. Fabian, ready for any occasion, was wearing jodhpur boots and a smart, short, canvas hunting coat over his houndstooth jacket and corduroy pants. An Irish tweed cap sat squarely on his head and moisture glinted on his mustache. He looked as though dawn was his favorite time of day and as if he had owned a string of thoroughbreds all his life. Anyone seeing him there for the first time would be sure that no trainer would be able to pull any crafty trainer's tricks on him.

Lily, too, was dressed for the scene, in high brown boots and loose belted polo coat, her English complexion brought to its genetic perfection by the dank atmosphere of the forest. If I intended to remain in their company – and by now I would have been hard put to figure out how I could disentangle myself – I would have to rethink my wardrobe.

Coombs, a booted, ruddy-faced, sly-looking, tiny old man with a gravelly outdoor voice, had pointed out our horse to us. He looked like every other brownish horse to me, with wild rolling eyes and what seemed to me dangerously thin legs. 'He's coming along nicely, the colt, nicely,' Coombs said. Then we all had to duck behind some trees as one of the other horses started running backward toward us, almost as fast as if it had been going forward. 'They're a little nervy these cold mornings,' Coombs said indulgently. 'That one's only a wee two-year-old filly. Playful at that age.'

The exercise boy finally got the creature under control and we could come out from behind the trees. 'How are the splints, Jack?' Fabian asked. The connoisseur of paintings and sculpture who had led me around the Louvre and who had discoursed on Manet to the critic the night before was gone now, replaced by a knowing horseman, expert on the fine points and obscure ailments of the equine race.

'Ah, I wouldn't worry, man,' Coombs said. 'He's coming along something splendid.'

'When will he be ready to run?' I said, the first words I had uttered since I had been introduced to the trainer. 'I mean in a regular race?'

'Ah, man,' Coombs wagged his head ambiguously. 'Ah, man, that's another question altogether, isn't it? You wouldn't want to push the colt, now, would ye? You can see he's not totally hardened yet, can ye not?' He had the damndest Irish-English way of talking for a man whose family had lived in France since the Empress Josephine.

'He does look as though another couple of weeks of work wouldn't do him any harm,' Fabian said.

'He still seems to be favoring his off foreleg a bit,' Lily said.

'Ah, ye noticed, ma'am.' Coombs beamed at her. 'It's more psychological than anything else, you understand. After the firing.'

'Yes,' Lily said. 'I've seen it before.'

'Ah, and a pleasure it is not to be having to hold the hand of an anxious owner.' Coombs beamed more widely.

'Could you give us an estimate?' I asked stubbornly, remembering the six thousand dollars invested in *Rêve de Minuit*. 'Two weeks, three weeks, a month?'

'Ah, man,' Coombs said, head wagging again, 'I don't like to be pinned down. It's not my way to raise an owner's hopes and then have to disappoint the good man.'

'Still, you could make a guess,' I persisted.

Coombs looked at me steadily, his little gray eyes, set in a thousand wrinkles, suddenly winter-cold. 'Ay, I could guess. But I won't. *He'll* tell me when he's ready to run.' He smiled jovially, the ice in his eyes melting instantaneously. 'Well, we've seen enough for the morning, wouldn't ye say? Now let's go and have a bite of breakfast. Ma'am . . .' Gallantly, he offered Lily his arm and led the way out of the forest with her.

'You've got to be careful with these fellows, Douglas,' Fabian said in a low voice as we followed along a path through the woods. 'They can be touchy. He's one of the best in the business. We're lucky to have him. You've got to let these old boys make the pace themselves.'

'It's our horse, isn't it? Our six thousand bucks?'

'I wouldn't talk like that where he could hear you, old man. Ah, it's going to be a lovely day.' We were out of the forest by now and the sun was breaking through the mist, shining on the coats of the horses that were ambling in slow strings back toward the barns. 'Doesn't this lift your heart?' Fabian said, throwing his arms wide in an expansive gesture. 'This ancient, glorious countryside in the fresh sunshine, these beautiful, delicate animals . . .'

'Delicate is the word,' I said ungraciously.

'I am full of confidence,' Fabian said firmly. 'What's more, I will make a prediction. Before we're through, we'll make our mark on the sport. And not with only one six-thousand-dollar reject. Wait until you come to Chantilly and see twenty horses working out and know they're all yours. Wait until you're sitting in an owner's box at Longchamps and see your colors parade by before a race. . . . Wait until . . .'

'I'll wait,' I said sourly. 'Happily,' but although I carefully kept from showing it, I, too, felt the attraction of the place and the horses and the canny old trainer. I couldn't go along with Fabian's manic optimism, but I felt the power of his dream.

If speculating in gold and risking huge sums on lunatic pornographic films written by an Iranian and starring a nymphomaniac Mid-western student of comparative literature at the Sorbonne could result in thirty mornings a year like this one, I would follow Fabian gratefully. Finally, the money I had stolen had achieved a concrete good. I breathed deeply of the sharp country air before I went into breakfast at a long table in the Coombses' dining room, where the shelves and walls were reassuringly covered with cups and plaques the stable had won through the years. The old man poured each of us a generous shot of Calvados before we sat down at the long table with his plump and rosy wife and eight or nine jockeys and exercise boys and girls. The aroma of coffee and bacon in the room was mixed with the smell of tack and boots. It was a simpler and heartier world than I had imagined still existed anywhere on the surface of the earth, and when Coombs winked at me across the table and said, *'He'll tell me when he wants to run, man,'* I winked back at him and raised my mug of coffee to the old trainer in return.

14

'I think it is time we thought of Italy,' Fabian said. 'What do you think of Italy, dear?'

'I like it,' Lily said.

We were sitting in a restaurant called the Château Madrid, high up on a cliff overlooking the Mediterranean. The lights of Nice and the coastal settlements far below us twinkled in the lavender evening air. We were waiting for our dinner and drinking champagne. We had also drunk a considerable amount of champagne on the *Train Bleu* down from Paris the night before. I was beginning to develop a taste for Moët & Chandon. Old man Coombs had been with us on the train and most of the afternoon. After more than two weeks of workouts, *Rêve de Minuit* had finally told the trainer he was ready to run. And run he had. He had come in first by a neck that afternoon in the fourth race at Cagnes, the track outside Nice, where they had a winter meeting. The purse had been a hundred thousand francs, about twenty thousand dollars. Jack Coombs had lived up to his reputation for picking appropriate races. Unfortunately, he had had to fly back to Paris immediately after the race, so we were denied the pleasure of his company at dinner. I was curious to see just how many bottles of champagne, interspersed with shots of cognac, the old man could down in one full day.

We had also bet five thousand francs on the nose of *Rêve de Minuit*, at six to one. 'For sentiment's sake,' Fabian had said, as we went to the window. In New York I had been gambling for my life with every two-dollar bet. Obviously, as a guiding principle, sentiment was more profitable than survival at a racetrack.

When we had gone back to our hotel in Nice to change our clothes for dinner, Fabian had called Paris and Kentucky. From Paris he had learned that *The Sleeping Prince* had finished shooting that evening and that, after a showing of the incomplete rough cut the night before, representatives of distributors in West Germany and Japan had already put in substantial bids. 'More than enough,' Fabian told me with some satisfaction, 'to cover our investment. And with the rest of the world still to go. Nadine is ecstatic. She is even contemplating starting on a *clean* picture.' As an afterthought, he mentioned to me that the price of gold had gone up five points that day.

His friend in Kentucky had been impressed with the news of *Rêve de Minuit*'s victory, but wanted to consult a partner before making a firm offer. He would call back later, at the restaurant.

The champagne, the view, the triumph of the afternoon, the price of gold, the news from Nadine, the prospect of a splendid meal, the company of Lily Abbott, sitting between us in all her beauty, made me feel an enormous friendliness toward the entire world, with an especial warmth toward the man who had stolen my bag at the Zurich airport. Enemies and allies, I was discovering, as in the case of the German and Japanese movie people, were interchangeable entities.

If *Rêve de Minuit* hadn't won, I suppose I would have been ready to toss Fabian over the cliff into the sea a thousand feet below. But the horse had won and I looked across the table fondly at the handsome, mustached face.

'Did you mention a possible price to Kentucky?' I asked.

'I said in the neighborhood of fifty,' Fabian said.

'Fifty what?'

'Thousand dollars.' He sounded annoyed.

'Don't you think that's a little steep for a six-thousand-dollar horse?' I asked. 'We don't want to scare him off.'

'Actually, Douglas,' Fabian sipped appreciatively at his glass, 'he's not a six-thousand-dollar horse. I have a little confession to make. I paid fifteen thousand for him.'

'But you told me . . .'

'I know I told you. I just thought at the time that it might be wiser to lead you along gently. If you doubt me, I can show you the bill of sale.'

'I no longer doubt you,' I said. It was almost true.

'How about the fifteen thousand for the picture? Were you leading me along on that, too?'

'On my honor, old man.' He raised his glass. 'To *Rêve de Minuit*.' We all clinked glasses happily. I had grown attached to the animal in the time that it took him to come from dead last at the turn, and then go on to lead the pack in the final three strides, and I told Fabian I hated to see him go.

'I'm afraid you have the instincts of a bankrupt, my friend,' Fabian had said. 'You are not yet sufficiently rich to love horses enough to hold onto them. The same, I may say, goes for ladies.' He looked meaningfully at Lily. There had been a noticeable tension between them in Paris. He had had three or four business conferences too many at odd hours with Nadine Bonheur. For myself, I had carefully avoided going to the studio where the movie was being shot and had not seen any of the people involved in it again. The busy signal on the telephone still tolled its message to me.

'What we'll do,' Fabian was saying, 'is buy a car. Do you have any objection to Jaguars?'

Neither Lily nor I had any objection to Jaguars.

'A Mercedes might be too flashy,' he said. 'We do not wish to appear *nouveau riche*. Anyway, I like to do what I can for the poor old Brits.'

'Hear, hear,' Lily said.

The waiter came with the caviar. 'Just lemon, please,' Fabian said, waving away the platter with chopped hard-boiled eggs and onion on it. 'Let us not dilute the pleasure.'

The waiter spooned mounds of grayish pearls on our plates. This was only the fourth time in my life that I had tasted caviar. I remembered the other three times clearly.

'We will fly to Zurich,' Fabian said. 'I have a little business to do in that fair city. We'll pick up the car there. I think the only honest automobile dealers in the world can be found in Switzerland. Besides, there's a first-class hotel there I'd like Douglas to see.'

Baby, I thought, if they could see good old Miles Fabian back in Lowell, Massachusetts, now. Or if Drusack could see me. Then I was sorry I had thought of Drusack. Fabian had not yet asked me how I had come to be carrying seventy thousand dollars in my suitcase and I hadn't told him. Actually, there were many things we had to talk about. In Paris Fabian had spent most of his time around the movie set. Watching the shop, as he put it, while I wandered around sightseeing, sinking blissfully into the city. When we were together, Lily was almost always present and neither of us, I was sure, wanted her to hear about the details of our partnership, as I now thought of it. As for her, if she considered it odd that her lover of one night in Florence had turned up promptly in another country as the close friend and associate of her lover of some years, she gave no sign. As I was to find out, as long as she was fed and admired and taken to interesting places, she asked no questions. She had an aristocratic disregard for the machinery behind events. She was the sort of woman you could never imagine in a kitchen or an office.

'I would like to bring up a delicate subject,' Fabian said, expertly loading a portion of caviar on his toast, not losing a single egg. 'It is a question of numbers. Three to be exact.' He looked first at Lily, then at me. 'Do you get my drift?'

'No,' I said.

Lily said nothing.

'It is the wrong number for traveling,' Fabian went on. 'It can lead to division, subterfuge, jealousy, tragedy.'

'I see what you mean,' I said, feeling a hot flush begin at my collar.

'I suppose you agree, Douglas, that Lily here is a beautiful woman.'

I nodded.

'And Douglas is a most attractive young man,' Fabian said, his tone paternal and kindly. 'And will become more so as he becomes accustomed to wealth and after we supply him with a fresh wardrobe, which I intend to do as soon as we reach Rome.'

'Yes,' Lily said. She looked demurely down at her plate.

'We must face the truth. I am an older man. I hope nobody is going to contradict me.'

Nobody contradicted him.

'The chances of mischief are plain,' Fabian helped himself to more caviar. 'If there is a lady you have in mind as a fit traveling companion, Douglas, why don't you get in touch with her?'

The image of Pat came immediately to my mind, in a wave of tenderness, mingled with regret. I had rarely even thought of her during the years at the St Augustine. The protective, icy numbness that had come over me that last day in Vermont was melting fast in the company of Lily and Fabian. I had to recognize that, like it or not, I was once again exposed to old emotions, old loyalties, to the memories of distant pleasure. But even if Pat were free, I couldn't imagine her accepting my relationship with Fabian, whatever it was or turned out to be, or his blatantly high style of living. The girl who donated a portion of her small salary as a schoolteacher to the refugees of Biafra could hardly be expected to approve of the man sitting at the table spooning up caviar. Or of me, for that matter. Evelyn Coates was a more likely candidate for our little group and would be an interesting match for both Lily and Fabian, but who knew which Evelyn Coates would turn up – the surprisingly gentle woman of the last Sunday night in my hotel room or the abrasive Washington operator and business-like rapist I had met at the Hales' cocktail party? I also had to consider the possibility that, one way or another, Fabian and I might eventually be exposed. It would hardly do her career as a government lawyer any good if one day she was publicly branded as the consort of a pair of thieves.

'I'm afraid there's nobody I can think of at the moment,' I said.

I thought I detected the ghost of a smile pass across Lily's face.

'Lily,' Fabian said, 'what is your sister Eunice doing these days?'

'Going through the Coldstream Guards in London,' Lily said. 'Or the Irish Guards. I forget who's on duty at the palace.'

'Do you think it would amuse her to join our party for a while?'

'Indeed,' Lily said.

'Do you think that if you sent her a wire she'd be prepared to meet us tomorrow night at the Hotel Baur au Lac in Zurich?'

'Very likely,' Lily said. 'Eunice travels light. I'll send the wire when we get back to the hotel.'

'Is that okay with you, Douglas?'

'Why not?' It seemed terribly cold-blooded to me, but I was in cold-blooded company. When in Rome. Caviar and circuses.

The maître d'hôtel came over to our table to tell Fabian that there was a call for him from America. 'What do you say, Douglas?' Fabian asked as he got up from the table. 'How low are you ready to go? How about forty, if necessary?'

'I'll leave it up to you,' I said. 'I've never sold a horse before.'

'Neither have I.' Fabian smiled. 'Well, there's a first time for everything.'

He followed the maître d'hôtel off the terrace.

The only sound was the crunching of Lily's teeth on her toast, ladylike, but firm. The sound made me nervous. I could feel her looking speculatively at me. 'Were you the one,' she asked, 'who broke the lamp on Miles' head?'

'Did he say I did?'

'He said there'd been a slight misunderstanding.'

'Why don't we let it go at that?'

'If you say so.' There was more crunching. 'Have you told him about Florence?'

'No. Have you?'

'I'm not an idiot,' she said.

'Does he suspect?'

'He's too proud to suspect.'

'And where do we go from here?'

'To Eunice,' Lily said calmly. 'You'll like Eunice. Every man does. For a month or so. I look forward to our holiday.'

'When do you have to go back to Jock?'

She glanced at me sharply. 'How do you know about Jock?'

'Never mind,' I said. She had hurt me with her debonair assignment of me to her sister and I wanted to get a little of my own back.

'Miles says he's never going to play bridge or backgammon again. Do you know anything about that?'

'I have a general idea,' I said.

'But you're not going to tell me what it is.'

'No.'

'He's a complicated man, Miles,' she said. 'He has an abiding fondness for money. Anybody's money. Be careful of him.'

'Thanks. I shall be.'

She leaned over and touched my hand. 'I had a lovely time in Florence,' she said softly.

For a tortured moment I wanted to grab her and plead with her to get up from the table and flee with me. 'Lily . . .' I said thickly.

She withdrew her hand. 'Don't be oversusceptible, love,' she said. 'Remember that.'

Fabian came back, his face grave. 'I had to come down,' he said as he took his seat. He helped himself to more caviar. 'All the way to forty-five.' He grinned boyishly. 'I think we need another bottle of champagne.'

*

I was at the big, carved, oak desk in my room at the hotel. I had said good night at my door to Lily and Fabian. They had the suite next to me. We both overlooked the Mediterranean. Lily had kissed me on the cheek and Fabian had shaken my hand. 'Get a good night's sleep, old boy,' he had said. 'I want to do some sight-seeing in the morning before we take off for Zurich.'

I was feeling a little giddy from all the champagne, but I

didn't feel like sleeping. I took a sheet of the hotel stationery from the drawer of the desk and began to write on it almost at random.

Stake, I wrote, 20,000. Gold – 15,000, Bridge and back-gammon – 36,000 ... Movie?

I stared at what I had written, half-hypnotized. Before this, even when I was making a comfortable living at the airline, I had never bothered to add up my check-book and certainly had not known within a hundred dollars what I was worth or even how much I had in my pocket at any given time. Now I resolved to keep an accounting every week. Or, with the way things were going, every day. I had discovered one of the deepest pleasures of wealth – addition. The numbers on the page gave me a greater satisfaction than I could hope to get from buying anything with the money the numbers represented. Briefly, I wondered if I should consider this a vice and be ashamed. I would wrestle with this at a later time.

I heard an unmistakable sound from the next room and winced. How far could I trust Fabian? His attitude toward money, his own and that of others, was, to say the least, cavalier. And there was nothing in what I knew of his character and background that suggested an unwavering commitment to fiscal honesty. Tomorrow I would demand that we write out a firm legal document. But no matter what we had on paper, I knew I would have to keep him in sight at all times.

When I finally fell asleep, I dreamed of my brother Hank, sat at his adding machines, working on other people's money.

*

In the morning we finally had a chance to talk. Lily was going to the coiffeur to get her hair done and Fabian said he wanted to take me to see the Maeght Museum at St-Paul-de-Vence.

We set out from Nice, with Fabian at the wheel of the rented car. There was little traffic, the sea was calm on our left, the morning bright. Fabian drove safely, taking no risks, and I relaxed beside him, the euphoria of the evening before not yet dispelled by daylight. We drove in silence until we got out of Nice and past the airport. Then Fabian said, 'Don't you think I should know the circumstances?'

'What circumstances?' I asked, although I could guess what he meant.

'How the money came into your hands. Why you felt you had to leave the country. I imagine there was some danger involved. In a way, now, I may be equally endangered, wouldn't you say?'

'To a certain extent,' I said.

He nodded. We were climbing into the foothills of the Alpes Maritimes, the road winding through stands of pine, olive groves, and vineyards, the air spiced and fragrant. In that innocent countryside, under the Mediterranean sun, the idea of danger was incongruous, the haunted dark streets of night-time New York remote, another world. I would have preferred to keep quiet, not because I wanted to hide the facts, but from a desire to enjoy the splendid present, unshadowed by memory. Still, Fabian had a right to know. As we drove slowly, higher and higher into the flowered hills, I told him everything, from beginning to end.

He listened in silence until I had finished, then said, 'Supposing we were to continue to be as successful in our – our operations' – he smiled – 'as we have been until now. Supposing after a while we could afford to give back the hundred thousand and still have a decent amount left for our own use.... Would you be inclined to try to find out who the original owner was and return the money to his heirs?'

'No,' I said. 'I would not be inclined.'

'An excellent answer,' he said. 'I don't see how it could be done without putting someone on your trail. On *our* trail. There must be a limit to wanton curiosity. Has there been any indication that people have been searching for you?'

'Only what happened to Drusack.'

'I would take that as fair warning.' Fabian made a little grimace. 'Have you ever had anything to do with criminals before this?'

'No.'

'Neither have I. That might be an advantage. We don't know how they think, so we won't fall into the dangerous pattern of trying to outwit them. Still, I feel that so far you've done the right thing. Keeping constantly on the move, I mean. For a while, it would be wise to continue. You don't mind traveling, do you?'

'I love it,' I said. 'Especially now that I can afford it.'

'Did it ever occur to you that the people involved might not have been criminals?'

'No.'

'I read in the newspapers some time back about a man who was killed in an airplane crash and was found with sixty thousand dollars on him. He was a prominent Republican and he was on his way to Republican headquarters in California. It was during Eisenhower's second campaign. The money you found might have been a campaign contribution that had to be kept secret.'

'Possibly,' I said. 'Only I don't see any prominent Republican coming into the Hotel St Augustine for any reason whatsoever.'

'Well...' Fabian shrugged. 'Let's hope that we never find out whose money it was, or who was supposed to get it. Do you think you'll ever see the twenty-five thousand dollars you loaned your brother?'

'No.'

'You're a generous man. I approve of that. That's one of the nicest things about wealth. It leads to generosity.' We were entering the grounds of the museum now. 'For example, this,' Fabian said. 'Superb building. Glorious collection, marvelously displayed. What a satisfactory gesture it must have been to sign the check that made it all possible.'

He parked the car and we got out and started walking up toward the severely beautiful building set on the crest of a hill, surrounded by a green park in which huge angular statues were set, the rustling foliage of the trees and bushes all around them making them seem somehow light and almost on the verge of moving themselves.

Inside the museum, which was nearly deserted, I was more puzzled than anything else by the collection. I had never been much of a museum-goer, and what taste I had in art was for traditional painters and sculptors. Here I was confronted with shapes that existed only in the minds of the artists, with splotches on canvas, distortions of everyday objects and the human form that made very little sense to me. Fabian, on the other hand, went slowly from one work to another, not speaking, his face studious, engrossed. When we finally went out and started toward our car, he sighed deeply, as though recovering from some tremendous effort. 'What a treasure-house,' he said. 'All that energy, that struggle, that reaching out, that demented humor, all collected in one place. How did you like it?'

'I'm afraid I didn't understand most of it.'

He laughed. 'The last honest man,' he said. 'Well, I see that you and I are going to put in a lot of museum time. You eventually cross a threshold of emotion – mostly just by looking. But it's like almost any valuable accomplishment – it has to be learned.'

'Is it worth it?' I knew I sounded like a Philistine, but I resented his assumption that it was my duty to be taught and his to teach. After all, if it hadn't been for my money, he wouldn't have been on the coast of the Mediterranean that morning, but back in St Moritz, scrambling at the bridge table and the backgammon board for enough money to pay his hotel bill.

'To me it's worth it,' he said. He put his hand on my arm gently. 'Don't underestimate the joys of the spirit, Douglas. Man does not live by caviar alone.'

*

We stopped at a café on the side of the square of St-Paul-de-Vence and sat at a table outside and had a bottle of white wine and watched some old men playing *boules* under the trees in the square, moving in and out of sunlight, their voices echoing hoarsely off the old, rust-colored wall behind them that had been part of the fortifications of the town in the Middle Ages. We sipped the cold wine slowly, rejoicing in idleness, in no hurry to go anywhere or do anything, watching a game whose outcome would bring no profit or pain to anyone.

'Do not dilute the pleasure,' I said. 'Do you remember who said that?'

Fabian laughed. 'I do indeed.' Then, after a moment, 'On that subject – let me ask you a question. What is your conception of money?'

I shrugged. 'I guess I never really thought about it. I don't think I *have* a conception. That's peculiar, isn't it?'

'A little,' Fabian said.

'If I asked you the same question, what would your answer be?'

'A conception of money,' Fabian said, 'doesn't exist in a pure state. I mean you have to know what you think of the world in general before you can hope to have a clear notion about money. For example, your view of the world, from what you've told me, changed in one day. Am I right?'

'The day in the doctor's office,' I said. 'Yes.'

'Wouldn't you say that before that day you had one conception of what money meant to you and after it another?'

'Yes.'

'I haven't had any dramatic changes of outlook like that,' Fabian said. 'A long time ago I decided that the world was a place of infinite injustice. What have I seen and lived through? Wars in which millions of the innocent perished, holocausts, droughts, failures of all kinds, corruption in high places, the enrichment of thieves, the geometric multiplication of victims. And nothing I could possibly do to alter or alleviate any of it. I am not a pain-seeker or reformer, and, even if I were, no conceivable good would come out of my suffering or preaching. So – my intention has always been to try to avoid joining the ranks of the victims. As far as I could ever see, the people who avoided being victims had at least one thing in common. Money. So my conception of money began with that one thing – freedom. Freedom to move. To be one's own man. Freedom to say, screw you, Jack, at the appropriate moment. A poor man is a rat in a maze. His choices are made for him by a power beyond himself. He becomes a machine whose fuel is hunger. His satisfactions are pitifully restricted. Of course there is always the exceptional rat who breaks out of the maze, driven most often by an exceptional and uncommon hunger. Or by accident. Or luck. Like you and me. Well, I don't pretend that the entire human race is – or should be – satisfied with the same things. There are men who want power and who will abase themselves, betray their mothers, kill for it. Regard certain of our presidents and the colonels who rule most of the world today. There are saints who will commit themselves to the fire rather than deny some truth that they believe has been vouchsafed them. There are men who wear themselves out with ulcers and heart attacks before the age of sixty for the ludicrous distinction of running an assembly line, an advertising agency, a brokerage house. I'll say nothing about the women who allow themselves to become drudges for love, or whores out of pure laziness. When you were earning your living as a pilot, I imagine you believed yourself happy.'

'Very,' I said.

'I dislike flying,' Fabian said. 'I am either bored in the air or frightened. Everyone to his own satisfactions. Mine, I'm afraid, are banal and selfish. I hate to work; I like the company of elegant women; I enjoy traveling, with a certain emphasis on fine, old-fashioned hotels; I have a collector's instinct, which up to now I have had to suppress. None of this is particularly admirable, but I'm not running as an admirable entry. Actually, since we're partners, I'd prefer it if we could share the same tastes. It would reduce the probability of friction between us.' He looked at me speculatively. 'Do you consider yourself admirable?'

I thought for a moment, trying to be honest with myself. 'I guess I never thought about it one way or another. I guess you could say it never occurred to me to ask myself if I was either admirable or unadmirable.'

'I find you dangerously modest, Douglas,' Fabian said. 'At a crucial moment you may turn out to be a dreadful drag. Modesty and money don't go well together. I like money, as you can guess, but I am rather bored by the process of accumulating it and am deeply bored by most of the people who spend the best part of their lives doing so. My feeling about the world of money is that it is like a loosely guarded city which should be raided sporadically by outsiders, noncitadins, like me, who aren't bound by any of its laws or moral pretensions. Thanks to you, Douglas, and the happy accident that led you and myself to buy identical bags, I may now be able to live up to my dearest image of myself. Now – about you— Although you're over thirty, there's something – I hope you won't take this unkindly – something youthful, almost adolescent – unformed, perhaps – that I sense in your character. If I may say so, as a man who has always had a direction, I sense a lack of direction in you. Am I unfair in saying that?'

'A little,' I said. 'Maybe it's not a lack of direction, but a confusion of directions.'

'Perhaps that's it,' Fabian said. 'Perhaps you're not yet ready to accept the consequences of the gesture that you have made.'

'What gesture?' I asked, puzzled.

'The night in the Hotel St Augustine. Let me ask you a question. Supposing you had come across that dead man, with all that money in the room, before your eyes went bad, while you still were flying, still were playing with the idea of marriage – would you have done what you did?'

'No,' I said. 'Never.'

'There's one thing you can always depend on,' Fabian said. 'The wrong man will always be in the wrong place at the right moment.' He poured some more wine for himself. 'As for me – there never was a time in my whole life that I would have hesitated for a second. Well, all that's in the past. We want to move as far away as possible from the original source, to cover it up, so to speak, with so much fresh capital, that people will never speculate about just how we started in the first place. Don't you agree?'

'In principle, yes,' I said. 'But just how do you propose to do it? We can't depend upon buying winning horses every day....'

'No,' Fabian said. 'I must admit, we have to regard that as unusual.'

'And you've told me you're never going to play bridge or backgammon again.'

'No. The people I had to associate with depressed me. And the deception I had to practise made me a little ashamed of myself. Duplicity is unpleasant for a man who, by his own lights, would like to have a high opinion of himself. I sat down every night with the cold intention of taking their money away from them and nothing more – but I had to pretend to be friendly with them, be interested in them and their families, enjoy dining with them.... I really was getting too old for all that. Money...' He pronounced the word as though it were a symbol for a problem in mathematics that had to be solved. 'To get the most pleasure out of money, it is best not to have to think about it most of the time. Not to have to keep on making it, with your own efforts or your own luck. In our case, that would mean investing our capital in such a way as to ensure us a comfortable income over the years. By the way, Douglas, what is your notion of a comfortable yearly income?'

'Fifteen, twenty thousand dollars,' I said.

Fabian laughed. 'Come, come, man, raise your sights a little.'

'What would *you* say?'

'One hundred at least,' Fabian said.

'That'll take some doing,' I said.

'Yes, it will. And entail some risks. From time to time it will also take nerve. And no matter what happens, no recriminations. And certainly no more stilettos.'

'Don't worry,' I said, hoping I sounded more confident of the future than I actually was. 'I'll go along.'

'We share all decisions,' Fabian said. 'I'm saying this as a warning to both of us.'

'I understand. Miles,' I said, 'I'd like something in writing.'

He looked at me as though I had slapped him. 'Douglas, my boy...' he said sorrowfully.

'It's either that,' I said, 'or I'm getting out right now.'

'Don't you trust me?' he asked. 'Haven't I been absolutely honest with you?'

'After I hit you over the head with a lamp,' I said. Tactfully, I didn't bring up the subject of the six-thousand-dollar horse that had actually cost fifteen thousand. 'Well, what's it to be?'

'Putting something in writing always leads to ugly differences of interpretation. I have an instinctive distaste for documents. I prefer a simple, candid, manly handshake.' He extended his hand toward me across the table. I kept my hands at my sides.

'If you insist.' He withdrew his hand. 'In Zurich, we'll put it all into cold legal language. I hope neither of us lives to regret it.' He looked at his watch. 'Lily will be waiting for us for lunch.' He stood up. I took out my wallet to pay for the wine, but he stopped me and dropped some coins on the table. 'My pleasure,' he said.

15

'Well, done and done,' Fabian said as he and I left the lawyer's office and stepped out into the slush of the Zurich street. 'We are now bound together by the chains of law.' The agreement between us had just been notarized and the lawyer had promised to have us incorporated in Liechtenstein within the month. Liechtenstein, I had discovered, which imposes no taxes and where corporate income and outlay are closely guarded state secrets, had an irresistible attraction for lawyers.

There were to be two shares outstanding in the corporation – one owned by Fabian, the other by myself. There was a simple justification for this that I did not understand. For some reason which had to do with the intricacies of Swiss law, the lawyer had appointed himself president of the corporation. We had to choose a name for it and I had offered Augustine Investments, Inc. There had been no dissenting votes. Various fees had been paid.

Fabian had gallantly volunteered to include in the agreement the clause guaranteeing me the right to withdraw my original seventy thousand dollars at the end of a year. We had been to the private bank where Fabian already had a numbered account, and we made it a joint one, so that neither of us could take out any money without the consent of the other.

We each deposited five thousand dollars in our own names in an ordinary checking account in the Union Bank of Switzerland. 'Walking-around money,' Fabian called it.

If either of us were to die, the full assets of the company and the balance in the bank went to the survivor. 'It's a little macabre, I know,' Fabian had said to me as I read the clause, 'but one can't afford to be finicky in matters like this. If you have any misgivings, Douglas, I could point out that I'm considerably older than you and can be expected to be the first to leave the scene.'

'I realize that,' I said. I didn't tell him that it had occurred to me as I read the document that it also offered him the temptation to push me off a cliff or poison my soup. 'Yes, it's very fair.'

*

'Are you satisfied now?' Fabian asked, as we picked our way around a puddle. 'Do you feel protected?'

'From everything,' I said, 'except your optimism.' We had been in Zurich six days under a gray and sullen sky and in those days Fabian had bought twenty thousand dollars more worth of gold, had been in and out of the sugar market, on margin, in Paris, twice, and had acquired three abstract lithographs by an artist I had never heard of, but who was going to skyrocket, as Fabian put it, in the next two years. As he had told me, he did not like to allow money to lie idle.

Fabian had discussed all our deals with me and had patiently explained the working of the commodity markets, where fluctuations were so erratic that fortunes could be made or lost in the space of an afternoon and where we had done incredibly well in sugar between Thursday and Friday. I understood, or pretended to understand, our convoluted operations, but when asked for an opinion could only leave decisions up to him. My own naiveté shamed me and I felt the way I had as a small boy in an arithmetic class when I was called on by the teacher for a question which every pupil but myself was prepared to answer. It all seemed so complicated and dangerous that I was beginning to wonder how I had been able to survive in the same world as Miles Fabian for thirty-three years.

By the end of the six days I wasn't sure anymore that I could stand the daily wear and tear on my nerves. There was cold sweat on the palms of my hands every morning.

As for Fabian, nothing seemed to disturb him. The bigger the risk he was taking, the more serene he became. If there was one lesson I would have liked to learn from him, it was that. For the first time since I was a child, I began to suffer from my stomach. As I swallowed Alka-Seltzer after Alka-Seltzer, I tried to tell myself that it wasn't nerves, but the rich food that we were eating twice a day in the fine restaurants of the city, and all the wines that Fabian kept ordering. But neither he nor Lily, nor Lily's sister Eunice, complained of any distress, even after a most elaborate dinner at the Kronen-halle, a Helvetian monument to hearty food and Swiss diges-tion, where we had smoked trout, saddle of venison with *Spätzle* and preiselberry sauce, washed down first with a bottle of Aigle and later a heavy Burgundy, followed by slabs of Vacherin cheese and a chocolate soufflé.

I was beginning to worry about my weight, too, and my trousers were getting uncomfortably tight around my waist. Lily didn't change by as much as an ounce, remaining glori-ously slender, although she actually ate more than either Fabian or myself. Eunice, who was chubby and cuddly, re-mained chubby and cuddly. Fabian, by some miracle, was losing weight, and looked much the better for it, as though the sudden injection of money into his life had drastically improved his metabolism. No matter how much he ate and drank his eyes remained clear, his skin an even healthy pink, his gait springy, his mustache bristling with virility. Gen-erals who had endured long years of peacetime obscurity must react similarly, I thought, when suddenly put in com-mand of armies for enormous, bloody battles. Looking at him, I had the gloomy presentiment that, like a private in the ranks, I was going to do the suffering for the two of us.

Eunice had turned out to be a pretty, pleasant girl with an upturned nose, vulnerable blue eyes, the flowery coloring of a springtime mountain meadow, a sprinkling of freckles, a figure that would have been more fashionable in the age of Victoria than it was in the 1970s, and a soft, almost hesitant manner of speaking that was the result, it was easy to imagine, of the crisp and authoritative speech of her older sister. It was hard to conceive of her going through the Cold-stream Guards, as Lily had suggested, or any other regiment.

Whenever the four of us went anyplace together, the two women invariably drew intense looks of admiration from the other men in the room, with Eunice getting just about the same time and an equal coefficient of lust as her more spectacular sister. Under other circumstances I would un-doubtedly have been attracted to the girl, but confronted with Fabian's semi-innocent voyeurism and raked by Lily's cold, Florentine eye, I could not bring myself to voice any pro-posals, or even indicate that they might be welcome if they came from Lily's sister. I had been brought up to believe that sex was a private aberration, not a public enterprise, and it was too late to change now. Chastely, ever since her arrival, Eunice and I had said good night in the elevator, without as much as a kiss on the cheek. Our rooms were on different floors.

It was with something like relief that I listened to the com-plaints of the two ladies about staying on in Zurich. They had exhausted the shopping, they said, the climate oppressed them, and they didn't know what to do with themselves in the long hours Fabian and I sat talking in offices or in the lobby of the hotel with the various businessmen, bankers, and brokers Fabian collected from the financial center of the city, all of whom spoke, or rather whispered, English in a variety of accents, but whom I didn't understand any better than either Eunice or Lily would have done if they had been in my place. Unfortunately, I had to stay, both at Fabian's re-quest and because of my grim resolve to be present at all transactions. But the two sisters had entrained for Gstaad, where the sun, according to the weather reports, was shining, the snow good, and the company welcoming. We would fol-low, Fabian promised, as soon as our business was finished in Zurich, which would not be long, he said, and then on to Italy. Fabian gave them the equivalent in Swiss francs of two thousand dollars from our joint account. Walking-around money, he called it, in a phrase I had come to dread. For a man who had led a precarious existence for most of his life, he had lordly habits.

Once the sisters were out of the way, Fabian managed to find time for some of the other attractions of the city. We spent long hours in the art museum, with especial attention to a Cranach nude that Fabian visited, he said, every time he passed through Zurich. He never tried to explain his particular tastes to me, but seemed content enough if I merely accompanied him on his rounds of the art galleries of the city. We went to a concert where we heard a program of Brahms, but all he said about it was, 'In Mittel-europa, you must listen to Brahms.'

He even took me to the cemetery where James Joyce, who died in Zurich, was buried, the grave marked by a statue of the writer, and there wrung from me the admission that I had never read *Ulysses*. When we got back to town, he took me directly to a bookstore and bought me a copy. For the first time I had an inkling of the fact that the prisons of the world might be filled with men who had read Plato and appreciated music, literature, modern painting, fine wines, and thorough-bred horses.

The thought had crossed my mind that he was attempting, for some private reason of his own, to corrupt me. But if so, he was doing it in a most peculiar way. Ever since we had left Paris, he had treated me in a semi-affectionate, semi-conde-scending manner, like a sophisticated uncle entrusted for a short while with the worldly education of an untutored nephew from a backward part of the world. Things had moved so fast, and the future he outlined seemed so bright, that I had had neither the time nor the inclination to com-plain. The truth was that, during those first days, despite my moments of panic, I felt myself lucky to have lost my suit-case to him. I hoped that before long I could manage to behave very much as he did. In other eras the virtues for which heroes were celebrated were such commonplaces as courage, generosity, guile, fidelity, and faith, and hardly ever included, as far as I could remember, aplomb. But in our uneasy time, when most of us hardly know where we stand, cannot say with confidence whether we are rising or falling, advancing or retreating, whether we are loved or hated, despised or adored, aplomb attains, at least for people like myself, a primary importance.

Whatever Miles Fabian may have lacked, he had aplomb.

*

'Something has come up,' Fabian said. 'In Lugano.' We were in the living room of his suite, littered, as usual, with American, English, French, German, and Italian newspapers, all open to the financial pages. He was still in his bathrobe, having his morning coffee. I had had my morning Alka-Seltzer in my room on the floor below.

'I thought we were going to Gstaad,' I said.

'Gstaad can wait.' He stirred his coffee vigorously. For the first time I noticed that his hands looked older than his face. 'Of course, if you want, you can go to Gstaad without me.'

'Is it business in Lugano?'

'Of a sort,' he said carelessly.

'I'll go to Lugano with you.'

He smiled. 'Partner,' he said.

*

We were in the new blue Jaguar an hour later, with Fabian at the wheel, heading for the San Bernardino Pass. He drove swiftly, even when we climbed into the Alps, and hit patches of ice and snow. He said hardly a word until we had gone through the enormous tunnel and emerged on the southern slopes of the mountain range. He seemed abstracted, and I knew him well enough by now to understand that he was working something out in his head, probably just how much he wanted to tell me about the day's business and how much he wanted to leave out.

It had been overcast all the way from Zurich, but we hit another weather pattern when we got out of the tunnel, and the sun was shining brightly, only occasionally obscured by high, fast-moving white clouds. The sun seemed to change Fabian's mood, and he whistled softly to himself as he drove. 'I suppose,' he said, 'you would like to know why we're going to Lugano.'

'I'm waiting,' I said.

'There's a German gentleman of my acquaintance,' he said, 'who happens to live in Lugano. There has been a great influx of Germans, wealthy ones, in that section since the German Economic Miracle. The climate of the Ticino appeals to them. And the banks. You've heard of the German Economic Miracle?'

'Yes. What does the German gentleman of your acquaintance do?'

'Hard to say.' Fabian was dissimulating now and we both knew it. 'A little of everything. Dabbles in old masters. Adds to his fortune. We have had one or two minor dealings. He called me in Zurich last night. He mentioned a small favor I might do for him. He would show his gratitude. Nothing is fixed as yet. It's still very vague. Don't worry – if it amounts to anything, you'll be in on every detail.'

When he talked like that, there was no use in asking any more questions. I turned on the radio and we descended into the green Ticino to the accompaniment of a soprano singing an aria from *Aida*.

In Lugano we checked into a new hotel situated on the lake shore. There were flowers everywhere. The spiky fronds of palm trees waved gently in the southern breeze, and people in summery clothes were sitting out on the terrace having tea. It was almost Mediterranean, and I could understand why the climate of the Ticino might appeal to a northern and refrigerated race. In the glassed-in swimming pool adjoining the terrace, a robust blonde woman was methodically swimming lap after lap.

'All the hotels have had to put in pools,' Fabian said. 'You can't swim in the lake anymore. Polluted.'

The lake stretched out blue and sparkling in the warm sunshine. I remembered the old man in the bar in Burlington complaining that Lake Champlain would be as dead as Lake Erie in five years.

'When I first came to Switzerland after the war,' Fabian said, 'you could swim in every lake, in every river, even.' He sighed. 'Times do not improve. Now, if you'll ask the waiter

202

for a bottle of Dezaley for us, I'll go in and call my friend and make the necessary arrangements. I won't be long.'

I ordered the wine and sat in the late-afternoon sunshine, enjoying the view. The necessary arrangements Fabian was making on the telephone must have been complicated because I had drunk almost half a bottle of wine before he came back. 'Everything in order,' he said cheerfully, as he sat down and poured himself a glass. 'We have a date to see him at six o'clock at his villa. His name, by the way, is Herr Steubel. I won't tell you anything more about him just yet....'

'You haven't told me *anything* so far,' I reminded him.

'Just so. I don't want you to have any preconceptions. You have no prejudices against Germans, I trust?'

'Not that I know of.'

'Good,' he said. 'Too many Americans are still fighting World War II. Oh, incidentally, to explain your presence to Herr Steubel, I said that you were Professor Grimes of the Art Department of the University of Missouri.'

'Good God, Miles!' I spluttered over my wine. 'If he knows *anything* about art, he'll catch on in ten seconds that I'm an absolute ignoramus.' Now I realized why Fabian had been so quiet and thoughtful on the first half of our journey. He had been cooking up a useful identity for me.

'I wouldn't worry,' Fabian said. 'Just look grave and judicious if he shows us anything. And when I ask your opinion, hesitate ... you know how to hesitate, don't you?'

'Go on,' I said grimly. 'What do I do after I hesitate?'

'You say, "At first glance, my dear Mr Fabian, it would seem to be authentic." But you would like to come back tomorrow and study it more carefully. In the light of day, so to speak.'

'But what's the sense in it?'

'I want him to spend a nervous night,' Fabian said calmly. 'It will make him more generous in his arrangements tomorrow. Just remember not to show any undue enthusiasm.'

'That'll be the easiest thing I've done since I met you,' I said sourly.

'I know I can depend on you, Douglas.'

'How much is all this going to cost us?'

'That's the beauty of it,' Fabian said gaily. 'Nothing.'

'Explain.' I sat back in my chair and crossed my arms.

'I'd really rather not at the moment,' Fabian said. He sounded annoyed. 'It would be much better if we just let things work themselves out. I expect a certain amount of taking on trust between us...'

'Explain or I don't go,' I said.

He shook his head irritably. 'All right,' he said, 'if you insist. For reasons of his own, Herr Steubel is breaking up a family collection. He believes that by doing it this way he can avoid lawsuits from distant members of the family. And, naturally, he prefers not to pay the grotesque taxes imposed by various governments on this kind of transaction. To say nothing of the difficulties with customs officials when one attempts to ship national art treasures out of one country and into another....'

'Are you suggesting that you and I are going to smuggle whatever this art treasure is out of Switzerland?'

'You know me better than that, Douglas.' His tone was reproachful.

'Tell me,' I said, 'what are we doing? Are we buying or selling?'

'Neither,' Fabian said. 'We are simply agents. Honest agents. There is a South American of great wealth, who happens to be an acquaintance of mine...'

'Another acquaintance.'

'Exactly.' Fabian nodded. 'I happen to know that he is a lover of Renaissance painting and is willing to pay handsomely for authentic examples. South American countries are noted for their discretion in their handling of the importation of art treasures. There are perhaps thousands of great European pictures that have sailed quietly across the ocean and are now hanging safely on South American walls that no one will *even* hear of for the next hundred years.'

'You said you weren't taking anything out of Switzerland,' I said. 'The last time I looked at a map, Switzerland was not in South America.'

'Don't be witty, Douglas, please,' Fabian said. 'It ill becomes you. The particular South American I have in mind is at present in St Moritz, where all good things abound. He is a dear friend of his country's ambassador, and the diplomatic pouch is always available for his use. He hinted that he is willing to go as high as one hundred thousand dollars. And I believe that Herr Steubel could be influenced to pay a fair percentage of that as our commission.'

'What's a fair percentage in this kind of deal?' I said.

'Twenty-five percent,' Fabian said promptly. 'Twenty-five thousand dollars for merely taking a five-hour, absolutely legal drive through the picturesque scenery of beautiful Switzerland. Now do you understand why I told you in Zurich that Gstaad could wait?'

'Yes,' I said.

'Don't say it so glumly,' Fabian said. 'Oh – incidentally – the painting that we are going to see is a Tintoretto. As a professor of art you should be able to recognize it. You will remember the name, won't you?'

'Tintoretto,' I said.

'Excellent.' He beamed at me. He drained his glass. 'This wine is delicious.' He poured for both of us.

*

It was dark when we reached the villa of Herr Steubel. It was a squat, two-storey house built of stone, perched high on an unlit, narrow road overlooking the lake. No lights could be seen through the closed shutters on the windows.

'Are you sure this is the place?' I asked Fabian. It did not look like the mansion of a man who was in the process of breaking up a family collection of old masters.

'Positive,' Fabian said, as he turned off the ignition of the car. 'He gave me explicit instructions.'

We got out of the car and walked on a path through a small overgrown garden to the front door. Fabian pushed the bell. I heard nothing from within. I had the feeling that we were being watched from somewhere. Fabian pushed the bell again and the door finally creaked open. A tiny old lady in a lace cap and an apron said, *'Buona sera.'*

'*Buona sera, signora*,' Fabian said, as we went in. The old lady led the way, limping, down a dimly lit hall. There were no pictures on the walls.

The old lady opened a heavy oak door and we went into a dining room lit by a heavy crystal chandelier over the table. A huge bald man with a heavy paunch and a beard like a New Bedford whaling captain's was standing waiting for us, dressed in a creased corduroy suit that included a pair of short knickers, under which the man's massive calves were brilliant in red wool stockings. Behind him, unframed, lit by the chandelier, hung a dark painting pinned by artist's tacks to the plain, yellowish wall. The painting was of a madonna and child, perhaps thirty inches wide and a yard long.

The man greeted us in German, with a little bow, as the old lady went out, closing the door behind her.

'Unfortunately, Herr Steubel,' Fabian said, 'Professor Grimes does not understand German.'

'In that case, we will speak English, of course,' Herr Steubel said. He spoke with an accent, but it was not heavy. 'I am happy you could come. Could I offer you gentlemen some refreshment?'

'It's good of you, Herr Steubel,' Fabian said, 'but I'm afraid we haven't the time. Professor Grimes has a call to make at seven o'clock to Italy. And after that to America.'

Herr Steubel blinked and rubbed the palms of his hands together, as though they were sweating. 'I trust the Professor can get through to Italy promptly,' he said. 'The telephone system in that misguided country . . .' He didn't finish his sentence. I had the distinct impression that he didn't want anybody to call anywhere.

'If I may,' I said, taking a step toward the painting on the wall.

'Please.' Herr Steubel stepped out of the way. 'You have the documents, of course?' I said.

He rubbed his hands together again, only harder this time. 'Of course. But not with me. They are in my . . . my home in . . . in Florence.'

'I see,' I said coldly.

'It would be a matter of a few days,' Steubel said. 'And I

understood from Herr Fabian that there is a time element …' He turned toward Fabian. 'Didn't you tell me the gentleman in question was scheduled to leave by the end of the week?'

'I may have,' Fabian said. 'I honestly don't remember.'

'In any case,' Herr Steubel said, 'here is the painting. I am sure I do not have to tell the Professor that it speaks very eloquently for itself.'

I could hear him breathing heavily as I stepped up to the painting and stared at it. If it was Fabian's plan to make the man nervous, he was succeeding admirably.

After about a minute of silent scrutiny, I shook my head and turned around. 'Of course I may be wrong,' I said, 'but after the most superficial inspection, I would have to say that it is not a Tintoretto. It may be the *school* of Tintoretto, but I doubt even that.'

'Professor Grimes!' Fabian said, his voice pained. 'Surely you can't believe – in one minute – in artificial light …'

Herr Steubel's breath was coming in short, labored gasps and he was leaning against the dining-room table for support.

'Mr Fabian,' I said crisply, 'you brought me along to give my opinion. I've given it.'

'But we owe it to Herr Steubel …' Fabian was hunting for words and pulling furiously at his mustache. 'Out of common courtesy … I mean … give it a few hours' thought. Come back tomorrow. In daylight. Why … why … this is frivolous. Frivolous. Herr Steubel says he has documents …'

'Documents,' Herr Steubel moaned. 'Berenson himself has attested to this painting. Berenson …'

I had no notion who Berenson was, but I took a chance. 'Berenson is dead, Herr Steubel,' I said.

'Ven he wass alife,' Herr Steubel said. The chance had paid off. My credentials as an art expert had been confirmed.

'Of course, you could seek other opinions,' I said. 'I could give a list of certain colleagues of mine.'

'I haff no need of any damned colleagues of yours, Professor,' Herr Steubel shouted. His accent had thickened considerably. He loomed over me. For a moment I thought he was going to hit me with one of his huge, club-like hands. 'I know what I know. I don't need any damned small-time, barbaric Americans to tell me about Tintoretto.'

'I'm afraid I must leave now,' I said. 'As you remarked, it is difficult to put calls through to Italy and there may be delays. Are you coming with me, Mr Fabian?'

'Yes, I'm coming with you.' Fabian made it sound like a curse. 'I'll call you later, Herr Steubel. We'll arrange something for tomorrow, when we can speak more calmly.'

'Come alone,' was all that Herr Steubel said as we opened the dining-room door and went out into the dark hall. The little old lady in the lace cap was standing just a few feet away, as though she had been trying to listen to what had been said in the dining room. She let us out of the house without a word. Even if she couldn't have understood what had been spoken in the dining room, the tones she had overheard and the brevity of the conference must have made an impression on her.

Fabian slammed the car door behind him when he got behind the wheel of the Jaguar. I closed my door gently as I slid into my seat. Fabian didn't say anything as he started the engine and revved it savagely. He had to back into a driveway to make the turn to go down the hill toward the lake. I heard the tinkling of glass as he slammed the rear light into a low stone fence. I said nothing. He didn't say a word either until we reached the lake. Then he parked the car and turned the motor off. 'Now,' he said, keeping his voice even with an obvious effort, 'what was all that about?'

'What was what about?' I asked innocently.

'How the hell do you know whether a Tintoretto is a fake or not?'

'I don't,' I said. 'But I was getting bad vibes from that fat Herr Steubel.'

'Vibes! We risk losing twenty-five thousand dollars and you talk about vibes!' Fabian snorted.

'He's a crook, Herr Steubel.'

'What're you and I? Trappist monks?'

'If we've turned out to be crooks, it's by accident,' I said, not completely honestly. 'Herr Steubel's a crook by birth, by inclination, and by training.'

'You say that.' Fabian was on the defensive now. 'You see

a man for three minutes and you invent a whole history for him. I've done business with him before and he's always fulfilled his obligations. If we'd gone through with the deal, I guarantee you he would have come across with our money.'

'Probably,' I admitted. 'We might also have wound up in jail.'

'For what? Transporting a Tintoretto, even a fake one, across Switzerland, isn't a criminal offense. One thing I can't stand in a man, Douglas, and I must tell you to your face, is timidity. And if you want to know, I happen to believe the man's telling the truth. It *is* a Tintoretto, Professor Grimes, of the University of Missouri.'

'You through, Miles?' I asked.

'For the moment. I'm not guaranteeing the future.'

'Transporting a Tintoretto, even a fake one, isn't, as you say, a criminal offense,' I said. 'But arranging for the sale of a *stolen* Tintoretto is. And I'm not having any of it.'

'How do you know it's stolen?' Fabian was sullen now.

'In my bones. You do, too.'

'I don't know anything,' Fabian said defensively.

'Did you ask?'

'Of course not. That doesn't concern me. And it shouldn't concern you. What we don't know can't hurt us. If you've decided to back out, back out now. I'm going into the hotel and I'm calling Herr Steubel and I'm telling him I'll be there tomorrow morning to pick up the painting.'

'You do that,' I said levelly, 'and I'll have the police waiting for you *and* that old art lover, Herr Steubel, at his ancestral mansion when you arrive.'

'You're kidding, Douglas,' Fabian said incredulously.

'Try me and see. Look – everything I've done since I left the Hotel St Augustine has been legal, or approximately legal. Including everything I've done with you. If I'm a criminal, I'm a one-time criminal. If they ever can pin anything on me, it will only be evasion of income tax and nobody takes that seriously. I'm not going to jail for anybody or anything. Get that absolutely straight.'

'If I can prove to you that the picture is legitimate and that it isn't stolen...'

'You can't and you know you can't.'

Fabian sighed, started the motor. 'I'm calling Steubel and I'm telling him I'll be at his house at ten am.'

'The police will be there,' I said.

'I don't believe you,' Fabian said, staring ahead at the road.

'Believe me, Miles,' I said. 'Believe me.'

When we got to the hotel, we didn't say a word to each other. Fabian went off to the telephone and I went to the bar. I knew he would finally have to join me. I was on my second whiskey when he came into the bar. He looked more sober than I had ever seen him. He sat down on a stool next to mine at the bar. 'A bottle of Moët & Chandon,' he said to the barman. 'And two glasses.' He still didn't say anything to me. When the barman poured the champagne for us, he turned to me, lifting his glass. 'To us,' he said. He was smiling broadly. 'I didn't talk to Herr Steubel,' he said.

'That's good,' I said. 'I haven't called the police yet.'

'I spoke to the old lady in Italian,' he said. 'She was crying. Ten minutes after we left, the police came and arrested her boss. They took the painting. It was a Tintoretto, all right. It was stolen sixteen months ago from a private collection outside Winterthur.' He laughed wildly. 'I knew there had to be some reason I took you with me to Lugano, Professor Grimes.'

We clinked glasses and again Fabian's maniacal laughter rang out, making everyone in the bar stare at him curiously.

16

Our business done in Lugano, we set out the next morning in the new dark blue Jaguar for Gstaad. I drove this time and enjoyed the sweet performance of the purring machine as we made our way back over the mountains and then sped through winter sunshine through the gentle rolling hills between Zurich and Bern. Fabian sat beside me, contentedly humming a theme that I recognized from the Brahms concerto we had heard a few nights before. From time to time he chuckled. I imagine he was thinking of Herr Steubel in the Lugano jail.

The towns we passed through were clean and orderly, the fields geometrically precise, the buildings, with their great barns and sweeping, slanted eaves, witnesses to a solid, substantial, peaceful life, firmly rooted in a prosperous past. It was a landscape for peace and continuity, and you could not imagine armies charging over it, fugitives fleeing through it, creditors or sheriffs scouring it. I firmly shut out the thought that, if the policemen we occasionally passed and who politely waved us through the immaculate streets knew the truth of the history of the two gentlemen in the gleaming automobile, they would arrest us on sight and escort us immediately to the nearest border.

Since there was no possible way Fabian could risk any more of our money while we were on the road, I was freed, at least for the day, from the erratic nervousness, that fluctuation between trembling hope and taut anxiety that came over me whenever I knew that Fabian was near a telephone or a bank. I hadn't had to take an Alka-Seltzer that morning and knew that I was going to be pleasantly hungry at lunchtime. As usual, Fabian knew of a beautiful restaurant in Bern and promised me a memorable meal.

The gliding, steady motion of the car, as it so often does, set up agreeable sexual currents in my groin, and as I drove I rehearsed in my mind the gentler moments of my night in Florence with Lily and remembered with pleasure the soft voice of Eunice awaiting me at the end of the day's journey, the childish freckles across her tilted British nose, her slender throat and nineteenth-century bosom. If she had been at my side at the moment, instead of Fabian, I was sure I would not have hesitated to drive into a courtyard of one of the charming timbered inns that we kept passing, with names like Gasthaus Löwen and Hirschen and Hotel Drei Koenig, and take a room for the afternoon. Well, I comforted myself, pleasure delayed is pleasure increased, and stepped a little harder on the accelerator.

As I glimpsed snow on fields high up from the road, I realized that I was even looking forward to skiing again. The days in the heavy atmosphere of Zurich and the dealings with lawyers and bankers had made me long for clear mountain air and violent exercise.

'Have you ever skied in Gstaad?' Fabian asked me. The sight of the snow must have set his thoughts going along the same track as mine.

'No,' I said. 'Only Vermont and St Moritz. But I've heard it's rather easy skiing.'

'You can get killed there,' he said. 'Just like anyplace.'

'How do the girls ski?'

'Like English,' he said. 'Once more into the breach, dear friends...' He chuckled. 'They'll keep you moving. They're not like Mrs Sloane.'

'Don't remind me of her.'

'Didn't quite work out, did it?'

'That would be one way of putting it.'

'I wondered what you bothered with her for. I must say, even before I knew you at all, I didn't think she was your type.'

'She isn't. Actually,' I said, 'it was your fault.'

Fabian looked surprised. 'How was that?'

'I thought Sloane was you,' I said.

'What?'

'I thought he'd taken my bag.' I explained about the brown shoes and the red wool tie in the train from Chur.

'Oh, you poor man,' Fabian said. 'A week out of your life with Mrs Sloane. I do feel guilty now. Did she stick her tongue in your ear?'

'More or less.'

'I had three nights of that, too. Last year. How did you find out it *wasn't* Sloane?'

'I'd rather not say.' As far as I was concerned the story of Sloane's discovering me, with a cast on my perfectly sound leg, trying to put my foot into his size eight shoe and throwing *my* shoe and Mrs Sloane's watch out into the Alpine night was going to die with me.

'You'd rather not say.' Fabian sounded pettish. 'We're partners, remember?'

'I remember. Some other time,' I said. 'Perhaps. When we both need a good laugh.'

'I imagine that time will come,' he said softly.

He was silent for a while. We sped along through admirably preserved Swiss pine forests.

'Let me ask you a question, Douglas,' he said finally. 'Have you any ties in America?'

I didn't answer immediately. I thought of Pat Minot, of Evelyn Coates, my brother Hank, of Lake Champlain, the hills of Vermont, room 602. As an afterthought, of Jeremy Hale and Miss Schwarz. 'Not really,' I said. 'Why do you ask?'

'Frankly,' he said, 'because of Eunice.'

'What about her? Has she said anything?'

'No. But you must admit – to say the least – you've been most reticent.'

'Has she complained?'

'Not to me anyway,' he said. 'But Lily has hinted that she's puzzled. After all, she flew all the way from England...' He shrugged. 'You know what I mean.'

'I know what you mean.' I was beginning to feel uncomfortable.

'You do *like* girls, Douglas?'

'Oh, come on, now.' I thought of my brother in San Diego and took a turn in the road more sharply than necessary.

'Just asking. These days one never knows. She *is* an attractive girl, don't you think?'

'I think. Listen, Miles,' I said, more hotly than I would have wished, 'as far as I understand, our partnership doesn't include my hiring out to stand at stud.'

'That's a crude way of putting it.' Surprisingly, he chuckled. 'Although, I must confess, in my own case, from time to time I haven't been averse to the practice myself.'

'Christ, Miles,' I said, 'I've only known the girl a few days.' Even as I said it I mourned for the hypocrisy into which he was forcing me. I had only known Lily four hours before I had gone to her room in Florence. As for Evelyn Coates ...

'If you must know,' I said, 'I don't like the role of public fucker.' Finally, I was approaching the truth. 'I guess I was brought up differently from you.'

'Come now,' he said. 'Lowell, Massachusetts, isn't all that different from Scranton.'

'Who're you kidding, Miles?' I snorted. 'They wouldn't find a trace of Lowell in you if they went in with drills.'

'You'd be surprised,' he said softly. 'You really would be surprised. Douglas,' he asked, 'do you believe me when I tell you that I've grown fond of you, that I have your best interests at heart?'

'Partially,' I said.

'To put it more cynically,' he said, 'especially when they coincide with my best interests?'

'Ill go along with that,' I said. 'Part of the way. What are you driving at now?'

'I think we ought to put you in the marriage market.' His tone was flat, as though it was a decision that he had worked over and had come to after hard thought.

'You're missing a lot of beautiful scenery,' I said.

'I'm serious. Listen to me carefully. You're thirty-three, am I right?'

'Right.'

'One way or another in the next year or two you're bound to get married.'

'Why?'

'Because people do. Because you're fairly good-looking. Because you're going to seem like a rich young man. Because some girl will want you as her husband and will pick the right moment to make her move. Because as you've told me, you've had enough of being lonely. Because you'll finally want children. Does all that sound reasonable?'

I remembered, painfully, the sense of deprivation, jealousy, loss that I had felt when I had called Jeremy Hale's home and his daughter had answered the phone and the pure young voice had called, 'Daddy, it's for you.'

'Reasonable enough,' I admitted.

'All I'm suggesting is that you shouldn't leave it to blind chance, as most idiots do. Control it.'

'How do you do that? Will you go out and arrange a match for me and sign a marriage contract? Is that the way it's done in the Principality of Lowell these days?'

'Make your jokes if you want to,' Fabian said placidly. 'I know they come out of a sense of embarrassment and I forgive them.'

'Don't be so goddamn superior, Miles,' I warned him.

'The key word, I repeat, is control.' He ignored my little outburst.

'You married for money, if I remember correctly,' I said, 'and it didn't turn out to be so god-awful wonderful.'

'I was young and greedy,' he said, 'and I didn't have a wiser, older man to guide me. I married a shrew and a fool because she was rich and available. I would do everything in my power to prevent you from making the same mistake. The world is full of lovely, lovable girls with rich, indulgent fathers, who want nothing better in life than to marry a handsome, well-mannered, and well-educated young man who is obviously wealthy enough not to be after their money. In a word, you. Good grief, Douglas, you know the old saw – it's just as easy to love a rich girl as a poor one.'

'If I'm going to be as rich as you say,' I insisted, 'what do I have to bother with the whole thing for?'

'Insurance,' Fabian said. 'I am not infallible. True, we have what seems to you like a substantial sum to dabble with at the moment. But in the eyes of men of real wealth, we're paupers. Paupers, Douglas, playing in a penny-ante poker game.'

'I have faith in you,' I said, with just a little irony. 'You'll keep us both out of the poorhouse.'

'Devoutly to be wished,' he said. 'But there are no guarantees. Fortunes come and go. We live in an age of upheaval. Just in my own lifetime...' Contemplating his lifetime in the speeding car, he shook his head sorrowfully. 'We are caught in cycles of catastrophe. Perhaps right now we are in the lull before the storm. It is best to take what small precautions we can. And without wishing to harp on ugly matters, you're more vulnerable than most. There's no way of being sure that you'll be able to go on forever unrecognized. At any moment, some extremely unpleasant chap may present you with a bill for one hundred thousand dollars. It would be cozier if you could pay it promptly, wouldn't it?'

'Cozier,' I said.

'A wealthy, pretty wife from a good family would be an excellent disguise. It would take a leap of imagination on anyone's part to guess that the well-mannered young man, moving easily in the cream of international society and married to solid old English money got his start by swiping a packet of hundred-dollar bills from a dead man in a sleazy hotel in New York. Do I make sense?'

'You make sense,' I said reluctantly. 'Still – you were talking about mutual interests. What'd be in it for you? You wouldn't expect me to pay an agent's commission on my imaginary wife's dowry, would you?'

'Nothing as crass as that, old man,' Fabian said. 'All I'd expect would be that our partnership wouldn't be allowed to lapse. The most natural thing in the world would be that your wife would be pleased if you would relieve her of the burden of handling her money. And if I know women, and I believe I do, she'd much prefer to have you do it than the usual gaggle of brokers and trustees and hard-eyed bankers women usually have to depend on.'

'Is that where you come in?'

'Exactly.' He beamed, as though he had just presented me with a gift of great value. 'Our partnership would continue as before. Whatever new capital you brought in would of course still be reserved to you. The profits would be shared. As simple and as equitable as that. I hope I've proved to your satisfaction that I am of some use in the field of investments.'

'I won't even comment on that,' I said.

'The workman is worthy of his hire,' he said sententiously. 'I don't think you'd have any trouble explaining that to your wife.'

'That would depend on the wife.'

'It would depend on *you*, Douglas. I would expect you to choose a wise girl who trusted you and loved you and was anxious to give substantial proof of her devotion to you.'

I thought back over my history with women. 'Miles,' I said,

'I think you have an exaggerated notion of my charms.'

'As I told you once before, old man,' he said, 'you're much too modest. Dangerously modest.'

'I once took out a pretty waitress in Columbus, Ohio, for three months,' I said, 'and all she ever let me do was hold her hand in the movies.'

'You're moving up in class now, Douglas,' Fabian said. 'The women you're going to meet from now on are attracted by the rich, so inevitably they are surrounded by older men, men who are engaged almost twenty-four hours a day in great affairs, who have very little time for women. Along with them there are the men who *do* have time for women but whose masculinity very often is ambiguous, to say the least. Or whose interests are transparently pecuniary. Your waitress in Columbus wouldn't even enter a movie house with any of them. In the circles in which you're going to move now, any man under forty with an obvious income of his own and who shows the slightest evidence of virility and who has the leisure to have a three-hour lunch with a lady is greeted with piteous gratitude. Believe me, old man, just by being your normal, boyish self, you will be a smashing success. Not the least of the benefits I mean to shower on you is a new conception of your worth. I trust you will ask me to be the best man at your wedding.'

'You're a calculating bastard, aren't you?' I said.

'I calculate,' he said calmly, 'and I intend to teach you to calculate, too. It's absurd that the perfectly good verb, to calculate, should have a bad reputation in the modern world. Let schoolgirls and soldiers wallow in romance, Douglas. You calculate.'

'It all seems so – so immoral,' I said.

'I had hoped you would never use that word,' he said. 'Was it moral to abscond with all that money from the St Augustine Hotel?'

'No.'

'Was it moral for me to hold onto your suitcase when I saw what was in it?'

'I should say not.'

'Morality is indivisible, my boy. You can't select certain

chunks of it, as though it were a pie waiting on a table to be cut up and served. Let's face it, Douglas, you and I are no longer permitted the luxury of morality. Let's understand each other, Douglas; it wasn't morality that made you run from Herr Steubel – it was a huge reluctance to share a cell with him.'

'You've got a fucking argument for everything.' I said.

'I'm happy you think that,' he said, smiling. 'Let me present some further arguments. Forgive me if I repeat myself in assuring you that whatever I suggest is in your best interests. I haven't hidden from you that your best interests are my best interests. I am thinking of the quality of life that you and I are eventually going to lead. You agree, I imagine, that, no matter what we do, we will have to do it together – that we will always have to be close together. Just like partners in any enterprise, we will have to be in constant communication. Practically on a day-to-day basis. You do agree, don't you?'

'Yes.'

'For the moment, except for the little disagreement in Lugano, it has been quite pleasant to wander about as we've been doing.'

'Very pleasant.' I hadn't told him about the Alka-Seltzers and the tightness around my waist.

'Eventually, though, it will begin to pall. Going from hotel to hotel, even the best ones in the world, and living out of a suitcase is finally dreary. Traveling is only amusing when you have a home to return to. Even at your age ...'

'Please don't make me sound as though I'm ten years old,' I said.

He laughed. 'Don't be so sensitive. Naturally, to me, you seem enviably young.' He became more serious. 'Actually, our differences in age are an asset. I doubt if we would be able to continue for long if we were both fifty or both thirty-three. Rivalries would develop, differences in temperament would arise. This way you can be impatient with me and I can be patient with you. We achieve a useful working balance.'

'I'm not impatient with you,' I said. 'Just scared shitless from time to time.'

He laughed again. 'I take that as a compliment. By the way, has either Lily or Eunice asked you about what you do for a living?'

'No.'

'Good girls,' he said. 'Real ladies. Has *anybody* asked you? I mean, since the happening in the hotel?'

'One lady. In Washington.' Good old Evelyn Coates.

'What did you answer?'

'I said my family had money.'

'Not bad. At least for the time being. If the question arises in Gstaad, I suggest you tell the same story. Later on, we can invent a new one. Perhaps you can say you're a managerial consultant. It covers a multitude of murky activities. It's a favorite cover for CIA agents in Europe. It won't do you any harm in most circles if that's what people believe. You have such an honest face, no one will be inclined to doubt anything you say.'

'How about *your* face?' I asked. 'After all, people will be seeing us together all the time. Finally we'll be held responsible for each other's faces.'

'My face,' he said reflectively. 'Quite often I study it for hours on end in a mirror. Not out of vanity, I assure you. Out of curiosity. Frankly, I'm not quite sure I know *what* I look like. Moderately honest, perhaps. What's your opinion?'

'Aging playboy, maybe,' I said cruelly.

He sighed. 'Sometimes, Douglas,' he said, 'frankness is not the virtue it's cracked up to be.'

'You asked me.'

'So I did. I asked you,' he said. 'I'll remember not to ask you again.' He was silent for a moment. 'I've made a conscious effort through the years in a certain direction.'

'What direction?'

'I have tried to make myself look like a semi-retired, English gentleman farmer. Obviously, at least as far as you're concerned, I haven't succeeded.'

'I don't know any retired, English gentlemen farmers. We got very few of them at the Hotel St Augustine.'

'Still, you didn't guess that I was an American by birth?'

'No.'

'A step in the right direction.' He smoothed his mustache gently. 'Have you ever thought of living in England?'

'No. Actually, I haven't thought of living anyplace. If my eyes hadn't gone wrong, I suppose I'd have been happy staying in Vermont. Why England?'

'Many Americans find it attractive. Especially in the country, perhaps an hour or so away from London. A polite, uninquiring race of people. No hustle or bustle. Hospitable to eccentrics. First-class theater. If you like horses or salmon fishing...'

'I like horses all right. Especially since *Rêve de Minuit*.'

'Brave animal. Although I wasn't thinking in exactly those terms. Eunice's father, for example, rides to the hounds three times a week.'

'So?'

'He has a handsome estate which happens to be just one hour from London...'

'I'm beginning to catch on,' I said flatly.

'Eunice is quite independent in her own right.'

'What a surprise.'

'For myself,' he said, 'I find her extraordinarily pretty. And when she isn't under the dominating influence of her sister, a lively and intelligent girl....'

'She's barely looked at me since she arrived,' I said.

'She'll look at you,' he said. 'Never fear.'

I didn't tell him about the lascivious thoughts that had crossed my mind, with Eunice as target, as we drove steadily through the neat countryside. 'So,' I said, 'that's why you asked Lily if she thought Eunice would join us?'

'The notion might have flickered through my subconscious,' he said. 'At the time.'

'And now?'

'And now I would advise you to consider it,' he said. 'There's no great hurry. You can weigh the pros and cons.'

'What would Lily have to say about it?'

'From what she's let drop here and there, I would say that on the whole Lily would react favorably.' He slapped his hands briskly together. We were approaching the outskirts of Bern. 'Let's say no more about it. For the time being. Let us say we'll allow matters to take their natural course.' He reached forward and took the automobile map out of the glove compartment and studied it for a moment, although wherever we went he seemed to know every turn in the road, every street corner. 'Oh, by the way,' he said offhandedly, 'did Priscilla Dean slip you her telephone number that night, too?'

'What do you mean, *too*?' I nearly stuttered.

'She did to me. I'm not vain enough to suppose she was all that choosy. After all she's an American. Unfailingly democratic.'

'Yes, she did,' I admitted.

'Did you use it?'

I remembered the busy signal. 'No,' I said, 'I didn't.'

'Lucky man,' Fabian said. 'She gave the Moroccan the clap. You turn right at the next corner. We'll be at the restaurant in five minutes. They make excellent martinis. I think you can indulge yourself in one or two. And have wine with lunch. I'll drive the rest of the afternoon.'

17

We arrived in Gstaad in the early dusk. It had begun to snow. The lights were just being lit in the chalets scattered along the hills, their glow behind curtained windows cozy and warm in the twilight. In this weather and at this time of day, the town looked magical. There was an instant of nostalgia for the harsher slopes of Vermont, for store signs in English rather than German. I wondered what Pat was doing at this moment.

Fabian had not brought up the subject of Eunice again on the trip from Bern, and I was grateful to him for it. It was a problem I was not yet ready to face. The lunch in Bern had been as good as he had promised, and I had had the two martinis and half a bottle of wine and had felt that my defenses were weakened and I could too easily have been persuaded to take a course of action I might later regret.

We had to slow down on the main street for a group of boys and girls, all in jeans and brightly colored parkas, who were streaming out of a *confiserie*, their laughter ringing bell-like in the icy air. It was easy to imagine the heaps of chocolate cakes and mounds of whipped cream they had just consumed in preparation for dinner.

'That's the nice thing about this place,' Fabian said, as he maneuvered around them. 'The kids. There's three or four international schools here. A ski resort needs young people. It gives an atmosphere of innocence to the sport. And the clothes are designed for youthful bottoms and the climate for adolescent complexions. You'll see them all over the hills tomorrow and you'll mourn that you had to go to school in Scranton.'

The car climbed a twisting hill, the wheels spinning erratically in the new snow. On top of the hill, dominating the town, was the huge fake castle of the hotel. Inside and out, the hotel gave no impression of innocence. 'The standard joke runs,' Fabian said, 'that Gstaad is trying to be St Moritz and will never make it.'

'That's okay with me,' I said. I had no desire ever to see St Moritz again.

We signed in. As usual, everybody at the reception and behind the concierge's desk knew Fabian and seemed deeply pleased to see him. He moved from place to place in waves of welcome.

'The ladies,' the concierge said, 'left a message. They are in the bar.'

'What a surprise,' Fabian said.

The bar was a large dark room, but not so dark that I couldn't see Lily and Eunice at the other end. They were still in ski clothes and they were seated at a table with five men. There was a magnum of champagne on the table and Lily was telling a story which I couldn't hear, but which ended with a loud burst of laughter that made the other people in the bar turn and look at their table.

I stopped at the door. I doubted that either Fabian or I would be greeted with pleasure. 'They haven't been wasting their time, have they?' I said.

'I didn't doubt that they would.' He was undisturbed as usual.

'I think I'll go up to my room and take a bath,' I said. 'Call me when you're ready for dinner.'

Fabian smiled slightly. 'Faint heart,' he said.

'Up yours,' I said. As I left the bar, there was another burst of male laughter. Fabian strolled toward the table.

As I went up to the concierge's desk, a group of youngsters came out into the hall from a doorway that led to a bowling alley. They were a mixed bunch of girls and boys, the boys with long hair, some of them with beards, although the oldest couldn't have been more than seventeen. There was a high-pitched gabble of conversation in French and English. I remembered what Fabian had just said about going to school in Scranton. I felt the wrong age, in the wrong place. One of the girls, the prettiest of the lot, stared at me. She had long, uncared-for blonde hair that almost hid a tiny pink face, and she was wearing skin-tight jeans with flowers embroidered in pastel colors over babyish full hips. She pushed her hair back from her eyes in a languid, womanly gesture. She wore green eye-shadow, but no lipstick. Her gaze made me uneasy, and I turned my back to ask for the key.

'Mr Grimes . . .' the voice was hesitant, high-pitched, childish.

I looked around. She had let the other boys and girls in her group go out the front door and was alone now. 'You *are* Douglas Grimes, aren't you?' she said.

'Yes.'

'You're the pilot.'

'Yes.' I didn't see the need of correcting the tense.

'You don't remember me, I suppose?'

'I'm afraid not, miss.'

'I'm Didi Wales. Dorothea. Of course it was ages ago. Three years. I had buckteeth and had braces that I wore at night.' She shook her head and the long blonde hair obscured her face. 'I wouldn't expect. Nobody remembers a thirteen-year-old brat.' She threw her hair back and smiled, showing that she no longer needed braces. Her teeth were nice, white, young-American teeth. 'Stowe,' she said. 'You used to ski once in a while with my mother and father.'

'Of course,' I said, remembering. 'How are they? Your mother and father?'

'They're divorced,' she said. Of course I thought, I could have bet on it. 'My mother is recovering from her heartbreak in Palm Beach. With a tennis player.' The girl giggled. 'And I'm stashed away here.'

'It doesn't seem like such a hardship,' I said.

'If you only knew,' she said. 'I used to like to watch you ski. You never showed off, like the rest of the boys.'

Boy, I thought. Miles Fabian was the only other person who had called me a boy since I was twenty.

'I could tell it was you,' the girl went on, 'even a mile away on the slope. You used to ski with a very nice, pretty lady. Is she here with you?'

'No,' I said. 'You were reading *Wuthering Heights* the last time I saw you.'

'Kid stuff,' she said. 'You once led me down Suicide Six in a snowstorm. Do you remember?'

'Of course,' I said, lying.

'It's nice of you to say so. Even if you don't. It was my accomplishment of the year. Have you just arrived?'

'Yes.' She was the first person who had recognized me since I had come to Europe and I hoped the last.

'Are you going to stay here long?' She sounded like a little girl who was afraid to stay alone at night when her parents were going out.

'A few days.'

'Do you know Gstaad?'

'This is my first time.'

'Maybe I could lead *you* this time.' Again there was the languid gesture of pushing her hair back.

'That's very kind of you, Didi,' I said.

'If you're not otherwise occupied,' she said formally.

A boy with a beard came back through the door and

shouted, 'Didi, are you going to stand there gabbing all night?'

She made an impatient gesture of her hand. 'I'm talking to an old friend of my family. Screw off.' She smiled gently at me. 'Boys these days,' she said. 'They think they own you body and soul. Hairy beasts. You never saw such a spoiled bunch of kids. I fear for the world when they finally grow up.'

I tried not to smile.

'You think I'm peculiar, don't you?' It was an accusation, sharp and clear.

'Not at all.'

'You ought to see them arriving in Geneva after holidays,' she said. 'In their father's private Lear jets. Or driving up to the school in Rolls-Royces. A royal pageant of corruption.'

This time I couldn't help smiling.

'You think the way I talk is funny.' She shrugged. 'I read a lot.'

'I know.'

'I'm an only child,' she said, 'and my parents were always someplace else.'

'Have you been analyzed?' I asked.

'Not really.' She shrugged again. 'Of course, they tried. I didn't love them enough, so they thought I was neurotic. *Tant pis* for them. Do you speak French?'

'No,' I said. 'But I guess I could figure out what *tant pis* meant.'

'It's an over-rated language,' she said. 'Everything rhymes with everything else. Well, I've enjoyed our little conversation. When I write home, whom should I send your regards to, my mother or my father?'

'Both,' I said.

'Both,' she said. 'That's a laugh. There is no both. To be continued in our next. Welcome to never-never land, Mr Grimes.' She put out her hand and I shook it. The hand was small and soft and dry. She went through the door, the embroidered flowers on her plump buttocks waving.

I shook my head, pitying her father and her mother, thinking, maybe going to school in Scranton wasn't so bad after all. I took the elevator and went upstairs and ran a hot bath. As I soaked, I played with the idea of writing a short note to Fabian and quietly getting on the next train out of Gstaad.

*

At dinner that night, there were only the four of us, Lily, Eunice, Fabian, and myself. As unostentatiously as possible, I kept studying Eunice, trying to imagine what it would be like sitting across the breakfast table from her ten years from now, twenty years from now. Imagining sharing a bottle of port with her father, who hunted three times a week. Standing at the baptismal font with her, as our children were christened. Miles Fabian as godfather? Visiting our son at what would it be – Eton? All I knew about English public schools had been gleaned from books by men like Kipling, Waugh, Orwell, Connolly. I decided against Eton.

The few days of skiing had given Eunice's complexion a pretty flush, summery colors. She was wearing a figured silk dress that clung to her figure. Buxom today, would she be stately later? The old saw had it, as Fabian had pointed out, that it was just as easy to love a rich girl as a poor one. But was it?

The sight and sound of her and Lily surrounded by lolling, arrogant young men (at least they seemed so to me) at the table with the magnum of champagne on it had made me flee from the bar. There was no denying that she was a pretty girl, and there would undoubtedly always be young men of that caliber and class in attendance. How would I take that if she were my wife? I had never really thought about what class I belonged to or what class *other* people might think I belonged to. Miles Fabian could leave Lowell, Massachusetts, behind him and pretend to be an English squire. I doubted that I could ever get rid of Scranton, Pennsylvania, and pretend to be anything but what I was – a grounded pilot, a man trained as a kind of superior technician, dependent on a payroll. What would the guests at the wedding be whispering about me as I stood beside the altar of the English country church waiting for the bride to descend the aisle? Could I invite my brother Hank and his family to the wedding? My brother in San Diego?

Fabian could educate me to a degree, but there were limits, whether he recognized them or not.

As for sex ... Still affected by my reveries at the wheel that afternoon I was sure that it would be, at the very least, agreeable. But the passionate desire which I couldn't help but believe was the only true foundation of any marriage – would I ever be stirred to anything even approximating it by this placid, foreign, hidden girl? And what about the ties of family? Lily, as sister-in-law, with the memory of the night in Florence as a permanent ghost at every reunion? At that very moment I knew I wished the room would empty, leaving Lily and myself alone, untrammeled. Was I doomed always to get close to what I wanted, but never *exactly* what I wanted?

'This really has turned into a smashing holiday,' Eunice was saying, as she buttered her third roll of the meal. Like her sister, she had a splendid appetite. No matter what else might finally turn out wrong with the children, they would be born with at least half a chance of having marvelous digestions. 'When I think of all the poor folk back in bleakest London,' Eunice said, 'I could cheer. I have a lovely idea ...' She looked around the table with her innocent, blue, childish eyes. 'Why don't we all just stay here in the beautiful sunshine until everything melts?'

'The concierge says it's going to snow again tomorrow,' I said.

'Just a manner of speaking, Gentle Heart,' Eunice said. She had begun calling me Gentle Heart the second day in Zurich. I hadn't figured out what it meant yet. 'Even when it's snowing here, you have the feeling the sun is shining, if you know what I mean. In London in winter it's as though the sun has wandered away permanently.'

I wondered if she would have been so eager to continue the quadruple holiday with old Gentle Heart and his friends if she had been able to overhear the cold-blooded conversation about her future that had taken place in the car on the road to Bern.

'It seems like such a waste to go rushing off to crumbling, noisy Rome when we're having such a lovely time here,'

Eunice said, the roll now thoroughly buttered. 'We've all *been* in Rome, after all.'

'I haven't,' I said.

'It'll still be there in the spring,' she said. 'Don't you agree, Lily?'

'It's a good bet,' Lily said. She was eating spaghetti. She was perhaps the only woman I had ever met who could look graceful eating spaghetti. The sisters had come into my life in the wrong order.

'Miles,' Eunice said, 'are you absolutely frantic to get to Rome?'

'Not really,' Fabian said. 'There're a couple of things I want to look into here anyway.'

'Like what?' I asked. 'I thought we were here on a holiday.'

'We are,' he said. 'But there're all sorts of holidays, aren't there? Don't worry, I won't interfere with your skiing.'

By the time the meal was over we had decided that we'd stay in Gstaad at least another week. I said I wanted some air and asked Eunice if she would like to take a walk with me, feeling that perhaps if we were alone for once we could make some sort of overt move toward one another, but she yawned and said that the exercise and the cold air all day had left her exhausted and she just had to fling herself into bed. I escorted her out of the dining room to the elevator and kissed her on the cheek and said good night. I didn't go back to the dining room, but got my coat and took a walk alone, with the snow whirling down around me out of the black night.

*

The concierge had been wrong. It wasn't snowing in the morning, but clear, blue, and cold. I rented skis and boots and had some wild runs down the mountain with Lily and Eunice, both of whom skied with a devoted British recklessness that was certain to land them in the hospital eventually. Fabian wasn't with us. He had some telephone calls to make, he said. He didn't tell me to whom or on what subject, but I knew I'd find out soon enough and did my best not to speculate just how much more of our joint fortune would be engaged in perilous enterprises before we met for lunch. He had told us he'd meet us around one-thirty at the Eagle Club, on a mountain called the Wassengrat, so that we could eat together. It was an exclusive club, with rules about membership, but Fabian naturally had arranged for us all to be accepted there as guests for our stay in Gstaad.

It was a marvelous morning, the air glittering, the snow perfect, the girls graceful and happy in the sunshine, the speed intoxicating. By itself, I thought at one moment, it made everything that had happened to me since the night in the Hotel St Augustine almost worthwhile. There was only one slightly annoying development. A young American, hung with cameras, kept taking photographs of us again and again, getting onto the lifts, adjusting our skis, laughing together, starting off down the hill.

'Do you know that fellow?' I asked the girls. I didn't recognize him as one of the men at the table in the bar with them the evening before.

'Never saw him before,' Lily said.

'It's a tribute to our beauty,' Eunice said. 'All three of us.'

'I don't need any tributes to my beauty,' I said. At one point, when Eunice had fallen and I was climbing back to help her up and put her skis on again, the man appeared and began snapping pictures from all angles. As politely as possible, I said, 'Hey, friend, don't you have enough by now?'

'Never have enough,' the man said. He was a gaunt, easy-speaking young man in baggy old clothes and he continued to click away. 'Back at the paper they like to have a wide choice.'

'Paper?' I said. 'What paper?'

'*Women's Wear Daily*. I'm doing a story on Gstaad. You're just what I need. Chic and photogenic, with your skis together. Happy people, in the height of fashion, not a care in the world.'

'You think,' I said sourly. 'There're lots of other people around who answer to that description. Why don't you work on them?' I didn't relish the idea of having my photograph all over a newspaper in New York with a circulation of maybe a hundred thousand. Who knew what paper the two men who had visited Drusack read every morning?

'If the ladies object,' the man said pleasantly, 'of course I'll stop.'

'We don't object,' Lily said. 'If you'll send us copies. I adore pictures of myself. If they're flattering.'

'They could only be flattering,' the young man said gallantly. I suppose he'd taken pictures of a thousand beautiful women in his career and I was sure he hadn't been shy to begin with. Meanly, I envied him.

But he did ski off, loose and careless over the bumps, and we didn't see him again until we were on the terrace of the club, having a Bloody Mary, waiting for Fabian to appear.

By that time another complication had arisen. Just at noon I noticed a small figure following us at a distance. It was Didi Wales. She never came within fifty yards of us, but wherever we went, there she was, skiing in our tracks, stopping when we stopped, moving when we moved. She skied well, lightly and surely, and even when I put on a real burst of speed, which made Lily and Eunice fly down the hill completely out of control, to keep me in sight, there was that small figure faithfully on our trail as though attached to us by a long, invisible cord.

On the last run down, just before lunch, I purposely waited at the bottom of the lift, allowing Lily and Eunice to go up together, in one of the two-seater chairs. Didi came into the lift building, her long blonde hair now caught in a bow of ribbon at the nape of her neck and falling down her back. She was still wearing the flowered blue jeans and a short, bulky orange parka.

'Let's take this one up together, Didi,' I said as the chair swung into place and she clumped up in her heavy boots.

'I don't mind,' she said. She sat quietly as we swung up out into the open sunlight. The chair mounted silently and we got a view of the whole town spread out in the sunlight. The jagged white peaks, stretching everywhere, were like white cathedrals in the distance.

'Do you mind if I smoke?' she said, starting to get a package of cigarettes out of a pocket.

'Yes,' I said.

'Okay, Daddy,' she said. Then giggled. 'Having a nice day?' she asked.

'Wonderful.'

'You're not skiing as well as you used to,' she said. 'More effort.'

I knew this was true but wasn't pleased to hear it. 'I'm a little rusty,' I said with dignity. 'I've been busy.'

'It shows,' she said matter-of-factly. 'And those ladies with you.' She made a peculiar little noise. 'They'll kill themselves one day.'

'So I've told them.'

'I bet when there's no men with them, if they ever go *any-where* without a man, they snowplow all the way down. They sure have fancy clothes though. I saw them in the stores the day they came, buying up everything in sight.'

'They're pretty women,' I said defensively, 'and they like to look their best.'

'If their pants were one inch tighter,' she said, 'they'd strangle to death.'

'Your pants aren't so loose either.'

'That's my age group,' she said. 'That's all.'

'I thought you said you were going to lead me in Gstaad.'

'If you weren't occupied,' she said. 'Well, you sure look occupied.'

'Still, you could have joined us,' I said. 'The ladies would have been pleased.'

'*I* wouldn't,' she said flatly. 'I bet you're all going to have lunch at the Eagle Club.'

'How do you know?'

'You are, aren't you?'

'It happens, yes.'

'I knew.' There was a note of scornful triumph in her voice. 'Women who dress like that always have lunch there.'

'You don't even know them.'

'This is my second winter in Gstaad. I keep categories.'

'Do you want to join us for lunch?'

'Thank you, no. That's not for me. I don't like the conversation. Especially the women. Nibbling away at reputations. Stealing each other's husbands. I'm a little disappointed in you, Mr Grimes.'

'You are? Why?'

'Being in a place like this. With ladies like that.'

'They're perfectly nice ladies,' I said. 'Don't be censorious. They haven't nibbled a reputation yet.'

'I *have* to be here,' she went on stubbornly. 'It's my mother's idea of where a well-bred young lady ought to be while she pursues her education. Education. Hah! How to grow up useless in three languages. And expensive.'

The bitterness in her voice was disturbingly adult. It was not the sort of conversation one would expect to have with a pretty, plump little sixteen-year-old American girl while rising slowly in the sunshine over the fairy-tale landscape of the winter Alps. 'Well,' I said, knowing it sounded lame, I'm sure *you're* not going to grow up useless. In no matter how many languages.'

'Not if it kills me,' she said.

'Do you have any plans?'

'I'm going to be an archaeologist,' she said. 'I'm going to dig in the ruins of old civilizations. The older the better. I want to get as far away as I can from twentieth-century civilization. At least, my mother's and father's version of twentieth-century civilization.'

'I think you're being a little harsh on them,' I said. I was defending myself, I suppose, as well as her parents. After all, they belonged almost to the same generation as I did.

'I'd rather not talk about my parents, if you don't mind,' she said. 'I'd rather talk about you. Are you married yet?'

'No.'

'I don't plan to get married either.' She looked at me challengingly, as though daring me to comment on this.

'I hear it's going somewhat out of style,' I said.

'With good reason,' she said. We were approaching the top now and prepared to debark. 'If you want to ski with me sometime, *alone* . . .' She accented the word. 'Leave a note for me in your box at the hotel. I'll pass by.' We got off the chair and took our skis. 'Though if I were you,' she said as we walked out of the shed into the sunlight, 'I wouldn't stay here too long. It isn't your natural habitat.'

'What do you think is my natural habitat?'

'I'd say Vermont.' She bent and started to put on her skis,

limber and competent. 'A small town in Vermont, where people work for a living.'

I put my skis over my shoulder. The club was just about fifty yards away, on the same level with the top of the lift, and a path was cleared through the snow to the entrance.

'Please don't resent me,' she said, straightening up. 'I made a decision recently to speak my mind on all occasions.'

On an impulse that I didn't understand, I leaned over and kissed her cheek, cold and rosy. 'Well, that's very nice,' she said. 'Thank you. Have a *smashing* lunch.' She had obviously overheard Eunice and Lily talking. Then she was off, skating expertly on her skis, toward the bottom of the T-bar that led higher up the mountain. I shook my head as I watched the bulky, little, brightly colored figure moving swiftly across the slope. Then, carrying my skis, I walked toward the massive stone building that housed the club.

*

Fabian appeared while Eunice, Lily, and I were having our second Bloody Mary on the terrace of the club. He was not dressed for skiing, but looked very smart in turtleneck sweater and blue, oiled-wool Tyrolean jacket, sharply pressed fawn-colored corduroy pants, and high suede after-ski boots. I was wearing the pair of ski pants and plain blue parka that I had bought off the rack in St Moritz because they had been the cheapest things in the store, and I felt dowdy next to him. The pants already bagged pathetically in the seat and at the knees. I was sure that the other elegant people on the terrace were whispering about us, wondering what someone who looked and dressed like me was doing with such a group. Didi Wales' remark about my natural habitat had had its effect.

High above, in the brilliant blue sky, a large bird soared on motionless wings. It might well have been an eagle. I speculated on what prey it might find to live off in this glossy valley.

'Have a good morning?' I asked Fabian as he kissed the girls and ordered a Bloody Mary for himself.

'Only time will tell,' he said. He enjoyed his little mysteries, Fabian.

I tried not to look worried.

'I hope you don't mind, Douglas,' he said. 'I've made an appointment in town for us after lunch.'

'If the ladies will excuse me,' I said.

'I'm sure they'll find some other young man to ski with,' Fabian said.

'I'm sure,' I said.

'There's a big party tonight,' Lily said. 'We have to go to the hairdresser, anyway....'

'Am I invited?' I asked.

'Of course,' she said. 'I've let it be known that we're inseparable.'

'Thoughtful of you,' I said.

She looked at me sharply. 'I'm afraid old Gentle Heart is not having as good a time as he should.' Now she was calling me Gentle Heart, too. 'Perhaps he prefers the company of younger ladies.' She hadn't said anything, but my trip up on the chair lift with Didi Wales hadn't gone unnoticed.

'She's the young daughter of old friends of mine from back home,' I said with dignity.

'Ripe for havoc,' Lily said. 'Let's go in and have lunch. It's cold out here.'

*

The appointment Fabian had arranged was with a real-estate dealer with a small office on the main street of the town. Before we went in he explained that he had been looking that morning at plots of land that were for sale. 'It might be an interesting investment for us,' he said. 'As you may have caught on by now, my philosophy is simple. We live in a world in which certain primary elements are becoming scarcer and scarcer. Soybeans, gold, sugar, wheat, oil, etcetera. The economy of the planet is suffering from overpopulation, fright, wars, a bad conscience, and an overabundance of available cash. Put these things together and the moderately sensible, ordinarily pessimistic man knows that the scarcity can only get worse and buys accordingly. Switzerland is a tiny country with a stable government and practically no possibility of getting involved in military adventures. Soon they will be selling land here to frightened money almost by the

234

ounce. Among my own friends and acquaintances I know dozens who would love to own even the smallest bit of it. At the moment, because of Swiss law, they are not permitted to buy. But we have a Swiss company, or a Liechtenstein one, which amounts to the same thing, and there is nothing to stop us from buying an option for six months, say, on a nice chunk of this beautiful country and letting it be known that we are considering building a luxurious nice-sized chalet with a number of fine apartments and renting them in advance for twenty-year leases, say. With the loan that we can swing from a bank, we can be the owners of a highly profitable piece of real estate which will cost us nothing finally and where we might even have a little *pied-à-terre* at no expense to ourselves for our own holidays. Does all this make sense to you?'

'As usual,' I said. Actually, it made more sense than usual. I had seen how dizzily prices had risen for small sections of abandoned farmland in Vermont, when ski lifts were put in.

'Dear partner,' Fabian said, smiling. 'Old Gentle Heart.'

By the end of the afternoon we had made an offer for a six-month option on a hilly stretch of ground off the road, about five miles from Gstaad. It would take some time, the agent told us, to arrange the formalities and draw up the contract, but he was sure there would be no important obstacles in our way.

I had never owned anything except the clothes I stood in, but by the time we went back to the hotel for tea I was practically assured, or so Fabian said, of being half-owner of a building that within a year would be worth well over a half-million dollars. The knuckles of my hands showed white with tension as I drove the Jaguar through the town that I now looked at with a new proprietary interest. Fabian merely looked quietly pleased with the day's work. 'We are just beginning, Gentle Heart,' was all he said, as I parked the car in the lot in front of the hotel.

*

I was getting dressed for the party when the telephone rang. It was Fabian. 'Something's come up,' he said. 'I can't go with you. Do you mind taking the girls?'

'What is it?'

'I met Bill Sloane in the lobby just now.'

'Oh. That's all I need.' I felt a prickling at the back of my neck. Bill Sloane had not contributed to my finest hours in Europe.

'Someday you must tell me just what went on between you two.'

'Someday,' I said.

'He's alone. He sent his wife back to America.'

'That's the smartest thing he's done all year. Still,' I said, 'what's he got to do with your not coming with us?'

'He wants to play cards this evening. Starting just about now.'

'I thought you said you were off bridge for life?' Now that Fabian had introduced me to the science of high finance, bridge playing seemed unnecessarily risky. A deck of cards was not like gold ingots or soybean futures or an acre of land in Switzerland.

'He doesn't want to play bridge,' Fabian said. 'He's got the message about bridge, he says.'

'What does he want to play?'

'Head-to-head poker,' Fabian said. 'In his room.'

'Oh, Christ, Miles! Can't you tell him you're busy?'

'I've taken so much loot from him,' Fabian said, 'I feel I owe him an evening. And I also owe something to my reputation as a gentleman.'

'Not to me, you don't.'

'Have confidence in me, Gentle Heart,' Fabian said.

'What sort of poker player are you?'

'Don't sound so worried. I can take care of myself. Especially with Bill Sloane.'

'Famous last words,' I said. 'Anybody can get lucky for one night.'

'If you're so worried, you can come and watch.'

'My nerves aren't that good,' I said. 'And I doubt that Mr Sloane would be charmed by my presence.'

'Anyway, explain to the girls, will you?'

'I'll explain,' I said, without grace.

'There's a dear fellow. Really, Douglas, if you're so skeptical, I'll do it on my own. I'll stake myself.'

I hesitated, tempted, then felt ashamed. 'Forget it,' I said. 'I'm in for half, win or lose.'

'Smashing,' he said.

'Yeah,' I said. As I hung up I knew the party would have to be one of the greatest social events of the year if I was going to enjoy the evening.

18

There were fifty guests at the party, with tables set for groups of six and eight in the enormous living room of the chalet, which was furnished in a cottage and comfortable style, despite its great size. For dinner, there were fresh lobsters flown in that afternoon from Denmark. Two Renoirs and a Matisse, not particularly cottage, hung on the walls. The lighting was low, to flatter the ladies, but not dim enough to make you feel that you were addressing a shadow when you spoke to your dinner partner. The ladies needed no flattering. They all looked as though at one time or another they had been photographed by my cameraman friend from *Women's Wear Daily*. The acoustics of the room must have been expertly planned, since, even when everybody seemed to be talking at once, the total sound in the room never rose above a polite and pleasant hum.

The host, a tall gray-haired, hawkish-looking man, I was told, was a retired banker from Atlanta. A soft, agreeable Southern cadence mellowed his speech, and both he and his young wife, a dazzling Swedish lady, seemed genuinely pleased that I had been able to come to their party. It turned out they were celebrating their fifteenth wedding anniversary. If Didi Wales had been invited, she might have revised her ideas about marriage.

There was a general air of sunburned health and offhand camaraderie among the guests, and through the course of the evening, during which I listened to a good deal of random conversation, I heard no one nibbling away at anybody else's reputation. While I wondered secretly how so many grown men could find the time away from their jobs to achieve the mountaineer bronze that was the standard male complexion, I asked no questions and was asked no questions about my profession in return.

Looking around the candlelit room at the immaculate men and the perfectly turned out women, all of them imperiously privileged and at ease with fortune, I felt with added intensity the power of Miles Fabian's arguments in favor of wealth. If there were rifts, divisions, jealousies here, they were not evident, at least to me. Assembled for celebration, the guests were a joyous company of equal friends, secure against disaster, above petty care. As I seated myself next to Eunice, who was radiant in silk, the peer in beauty and grace of manner of any of the beauties in the room, I regarded her with new calculation. I squeezed her hand under the table and got a warm sensual smile in return.

The talk at the table at which Eunice and I found ourselves was for the most part inconsequential – the usual anecdotes about snow and broken legs that are standard at all ski resorts, interspersed with criticisms of the theater in Paris, London, and New York and the appreciation of recent movies in various languages. The *dicta* expressed around the table even in the space of a half-hour represented an impressive amount of multilingual traveling.

I had seen none of the plays and few of the movies and kept a public silence, whispering from time to time to Eunice, who had also seen all the plays in London and Paris and spoke with authority about them and was listened to respectfully. Lily was at another table, and in her absence Eunice spoke with much more freedom and assurance than usual. It turned out that she had at one time wanted to be an actress and had studied, for a short period, at the Royal Academy of Dramatic Arts. I observed her with fresh interest. If she had neglected to tell me this rather important fact about her life, what other surprises might be in store for me?

The subject of politics came up with the dessert, a lemon sherbet floating in champagne. (I figured, at a rough guess, that the evening must have cost our host at least two thousand dollars, but was slightly ashamed of myself for even thinking in such terms.) Among the men at the table there was a plumpish, smooth-faced American of about fifty who was the head of an insurance company, a French art critic with a sharp black beard, and a burly English banker. The current governments of the three nations were gently but firmly deplored by all three gentlemen. Chauvinism was conspicuous by its absence. If patriotism is the last refuge of scoundrels, there wasn't a scoundrel at the table. The Frenchman complained in nearly perfect English about France, 'The foreign policy of France combines the worst elements of Gaullism – egotism, evasiveness, and illusion'; the English banker matched him with, 'The English workingman has lost the will to work. And I don't blame him'; the American in insurance contributed, 'The doom of the capitalist system was sealed the day the United States sold two million tons of wheat to the Soviet Union.'

They all ate their lobster with relish and kept the waiter busy pouring from a seemingly inexhaustible store of bottles of exquisite white wine. I stole a look at the label on one of the bottles – Corton-Charlemagne – and noted it for future great occasions.

I kept silent, although I nodded gravely in agreement from time to time to show that I, too, belonged at the feast. I hesitated to talk, fearing that I somehow would betray my outsiderness, that a single uneasy word might sound a warning among the other guests, unmasking me as a visitor from the lower classes, contemplating revolution perhaps, the dangerous stain of the Hotel St Augustine, that I had up to now managed to hide, suddenly detectable.

There was dancing after dinner in a huge playroom in the basement. Eunice, who loved to dance, went from partner to partner, while I stood at the bar, drinking, looking at my watch, feeling gloomy and deprived. I had always been a hopeless dancer and had never enjoyed it and certainly wasn't going to make a show of myself on the floor among all those swooping, graceful figures who all seemed to be trained in the latest fashionable steps. I was just on the verge of slipping out and going back to the hotel, when Eunice broke away from her partner and came over to me. 'Old Gentle Heart,' she said. 'You're not having a good time.'

'Not really.'

'I'm sorry. Do you want to go home?'

'I was thinking of it. You don't have to go, you know.'

'Don't be a martyr, Gentle Heart. I hate martyrs. I've had enough dancing anyway.' She took my hand in hers. 'Let's go.' She led me around the edge of the dance floor, avoiding Lily. Upstairs, we got our coats and left without saying good-bye to anyone.

We walked along the snowy path, the night cold and crackling around us, the pine air exhilarating after the warmth and noise of the party. When we had gone about two hundred yards and the chalet was only a small glow of light behind us, we stopped as though a signal had passed between us and faced each other and kissed. Once. Then, walking unhurriedly, we went to the hotel.

We picked up our keys and got into the elevator. Without a word Eunice got off at my floor with me. We made a slow, formal parade of our walk down the carpeted hallway. It was as though she, like myself wanted to savor every moment of the evening.

I opened the door to my room and held it so that Eunice could go in before me. She brushed past me, the cold fur of her coat electric against my sleeve. I went in after her and turned on the lamp in the small hallway.

'Oh, my God!' Eunice cried.

Lying on the big bed, outlined by the light from the hall, was Didi Wales. Asleep. And naked. Her clothes were neatly draped across a chair, with her snow boots primly together beneath it. Her mother, whatever her other failings, had obviously taught her child to be neat.

'Let me out of here,' Eunice said in a whisper, as though afraid of what would happen if she wakened the sleeping girl. 'This is your baby.'

'Eunice . . .' I said forlornly.

'Good night,' she said. 'Enjoy yourself.' She pushed past me and was gone.

I stared down at Didi. Her long blonde hair half-covered her face and her even breathing stirred the ends gently. Her skin in the lamplight was childishly rosy except for her throat and face, darkened by the sun. Her breasts were small and plump, her legs sturdy, athletic, schoolgirl's legs. There was red polish on her toenails. She could have posed for an advertisement for baby foods, although somewhat more fully clothed and without the nail polish. Her belly was a little soft mound and the hair beneath it a fuzzy shadow. She slept with her arms rigidly at her sides. It gave her a curious air of lying at attention. If it had been a painting instead of a live, sixteen-year-old girl, it would have been the essence of nude innocence.

But it wasn't a painting. It was a sixteen-year-old girl whose mother and father were, at least technically, friends of mine, and there was no possibility that her intentions in breaking into my room and lying on my bed were in any way innocent. I had the cowardly impulse to steal quietly out of the room and leave her there for the night. Instead, I took off my coat and covered her with it.

The movement awakened her. She opened her eyes slowly and stared up at me, pushing the hair away from her face. Then she smiled. The smile made her look about ten years old.

'God damn it, Didi,' I said, 'what the hell kind of school do you go to here?'

'It's the kind of school where the girls climb out of the window at night,' she said. 'I thought it would be nice to surprise you.' She was much more in control of her voice than I was.

'You surprised me, all right.'

'Aren't you pleased?'

'No,' I said. 'Definitely not.'

'When you get used to the idea,' she said, 'maybe you'll change your mind.'

'Please, Didi . . .'

'If you're worried because you think I'm a virgin,' she said loftily, 'you can disabuse yourself. I've already had an affair with a man a lot older than you. A lecherous old Greek.'

'I don't want any fancy talk,' I said. 'I want you to get up off that bed and get dressed and get out of here and go climb back through that window of yours.'

'I know you don't really mean that,' she said calmly. 'You're just making proper noises because you knew me when I was thirteen years old. I'm not thirteen years old anymore.'

'I know how old you are,' I said, 'and it isn't enough.'

'Nothing bores me more than having people make-believe I'm a child.' Aside from the gesture to push back her hair, she still hadn't moved on the bed. 'What's the magic date for you? Twenty, eighteen?'

'There is no magic date, as you call it.' I heard my voice go higher and higher with exasperation and sat down across the room from her to retain my dignity and show that I was prepared to be reasonable. 'I'm just not in the habit of going to bed with girls of any age after talking to them for ten minutes.'

'And I thought you were sophisticated.' She put as much scorn into the word as she could manage. 'With those fancy ladies and that Jaguar.'

'Okay,' I said, 'I'm not sophisticated. Now will you get up and get dressed?'

'Don't you think I'm pretty? People have told me my body is delectable. Connoisseurs.'

'I think you're very pretty. Delectable, if you like. That has nothing to do with it.'

'Half the boys in town are trying to get me in bed with them. And plenty of men, if you want the truth.'

'I'm sure, Didi. It still has nothing to do with it.'

'You talked to me for a lot more than ten minutes, so that's no excuse. We had a long conversation on Suicide Six. I remember, even if you don't.'

'This is a ridiculous scene,' I said, as firmly and maturely as I could. 'I'm ashamed for both of us.'

'There's nothing ridiculous about love.'

'Love, Didi!' I exploded.

'I was in love with you three years ago ...' Her voice began to quaver and tears, real or forced, appeared in her

242

eyes, glistening in the lamplight. 'And then when I saw you again. I suppose you think you're too old and too worn out to believe in love?'

'I'm nothing of the kind.' I decided to try cruelty. 'I just happen to have a certain code. And it doesn't include fornication with silly little girls who throw themselves at my head.'

'That's an ugly word for a beautiful emotion.' Now she was frankly crying. 'I didn't think you were capable of talking like that.'

'I'm capable of feeling angry,' I said loudly, 'and feeling foolish. And I feel both this minute.'

'It would serve you right,' she said, through sobs, 'if I started yelling at the top of my voice and got the whole hotel in here and told everybody you tried to rape me.'

'Don't be monstrous, young lady.' I stood up now to threaten her. 'Just for your information, when I came into the room I was with a friend...'

'A friend,' she said. 'Hah! One of those old bags.'

'No matter. If you try anything, she'll tell everybody what she saw when she came into the room – you sleeping naked on the bed. That would fix you and your rape. You'd have to leave town in disgrace.'

'I want to leave this miserable town anyway. And disgrace is something you feel yourself, and I wouldn't feel it.'

I tried another tack. 'Didi, Baby...'

'Don't call me Baby. I'm not a baby.'

'Okay, I won't call you Baby.' I smiled gently at her. 'Didi, don't you want me to be your friend?'

'No I want you to be my lover. Everybody else gets what they want,' she wailed. 'Why can't I?'

I handed her my handkerchief to wipe away her tears. She also blew her nose. I was glad that there was an automatic lock on the door so that nobody could come into the room and see us. I refrained from telling her that when she reached my age she would find everybody didn't get what they wanted. Not by a long shot.

'You kissed me on the hill today, when we got off the lift,' she cried. 'What did you do that for it you didn't mean it?'

'There are kisses and kisses,' I said. 'I apologize if you misunderstood.'

Suddenly she threw the coat off her and sat up in the bed. She put out her arms. 'Try it once more,' she said.

I took a step back, involuntarily. 'I'm leaving,' I said, as convincingly as I could. 'If you're still here when I get back, I'm going to call your school to come and get you.'

She laughed. 'Coward,' she taunted me, 'coward, coward.'

In full possession of the field, she was still repeating the word when I got out of the door.

*

I went down to the bar. I needed a drink. Luckily, there was no one I knew there and I sat on a stool in the dim light, staring into my glass. I had thought I could live by accident, taking everything that was offered as it came along – the long tube on the floor of room 602; Evelyn Coates in Washington; Lily in Florence; the outlandish proposition of that not quite certifiably sane man, Miles Fabian, slightly bloodied from where I had broken the lamp over his head; buying a racehorse; investing in a dirty French movie; dabbling in gold and soybeans; saying, 'Why not?' When Fabian had suggested inviting an unknown British girl to join us; venturing into Swiss real estate; backing him for half, even as I sat there, in a head-to-head poker game against a rich and vengeful American gambler.

But there were limits. And Didi Wales had reached them. I told myself I had behaved honorably – no decent man would take advantage of the freakish, adolescent passion of an unhappy child. But I was nagged, in the quiet of the midnight bar, by a small, disturbing doubt. If Eunice hadn't gone into the room with me to discover Didi lying there, would I be in the bar now? Or still in my room? In retrospect, sitting alone staring into a glass, I had to admit that the girl had been marvelously attractive. Regret played in a little scudding cloud at the outer reaches of my conscience. What would Miles Fabian have done, confronted with a similar situation? Chuckled good-naturedly, said, 'What a charming visit'? Thought, this is my lucky year, and climbed into bed? No doubt.

I resolved not to tell him a word about it. His scorn, tempered only by pity for my scruples, would be unbearable. I could just hear him say, mildly, paternally, 'Finally, Douglas, one *must* learn the rules of the game.'

Eunice. I broke into a light sweat as I thought of the next morning's breakfast, with Lily and Miles Fabian, and Eunice saying, over the orange juice and coffee cups, 'The most extraordinary thing happened last night when old Gentle Heart and I got back from the party...'

I finished my drink, signed for it, and started toward the door. Just as I reached it, Lily came in with three enormous men, not one of them under six feet four. I had noticed them at the party and had seen Lily dancing with one of them. This seemed to be her night for size and quantity. She stopped when she saw me. 'I thought I saw you go off with Eunice,' she said.

'I did.'

'And now you're alone?'

'I am.'

She shook her head. There was an amused glint in her eye. 'Peculiar man,' she said. 'Do you want to join us?'

'I'm not large enough,' I said.

The three men laughed, their laughter resounding like bowling balls off the bottles behind the bar. 'Have you seen Miles?' Lily asked.

'No.'

'He said he'd try to make it for a nightcap by one.' She shrugged. 'I guess he's so immersed in stripping that desperate oaf Sloane of his last penny he can't be bothered with poor little me. Did you like the party?'

'Smashing,' I said.

'It was almost like being in Texas,' she said ambiguously. 'Shall we drink, chaps?'

'I'll order the champagne,' the tallest of the men said, lurching among the tables toward the bar like an ocean liner pulling out of a slip.

'Night, Gentle Heart,' Lily said. 'Persist.' She leaned over and kissed my cheek. Instant memories. I bowed a little and went out.

Ripe for havoc, she had said about Didi Wales. How right she was.

A minute later I was at the door of Eunice's room. I listened, but there was no sound inside. I didn't know what I expected to hear. Weeping? Laughter? Sounds of revelry? I knocked, waited, knocked again.

The door opened. Eunice was standing there in a lace dressing gown. 'Oh, it's you,' she said. Her tone was neither welcoming nor unwelcoming.

'May I come in?'

'If you want.'

'I want.'

She held the door wider and I went in. Her clothes were piled haphazardly all over the room. The window was open and a cold Alpine breeze was whistling in. I shivered a little, my resistance to the elements weakened by the events of the night. 'Aren't you cold?' I asked.

'Remember, I'm English,' she said, But she closed the window. Full-bodied, bare footed, rustling of lace.

'May I sit down?'

'If you wish.' She indicated a little upholstered chair. 'Throw those clothes anywhere.'

I picked up the silk dress she had worn at the party. I imagined it was still warm from her skin. I laid it gently across a little writing desk. I sat down on the chair and she lay back against the piled pillows on the bed, her legs revealed as the dressing gown fell away. She had long legs like her sister, but fuller. Shapelier, I thought. I smelled lightly scented soap. She had scrubbed her face when she undressed, and her skin glowed in the light of the bedside lamp.

I mourned for the evening.

'Eunice,' I said, 'I came to explain.'

'You don't have to explain. Somebody got their appointments mixed, that's all.'

'You don't think I asked that little girl to come up to my room, do you?'

'I don't think *anything*. She was just there. And she's not that little. Well-developed, I'd call it.' Her tone was flat, weary. 'One of us was *de trop*. I happened to think it was me.'

'Tonight,' I said, 'I thought, finally...'

'That was my impression, too.' She smiled wryly.

'I wish I could have been bolder,' I said 'I mean even before tonight. Only I'm not built that way.' I made a small helpless gesture with my hands. 'And then there were always Miles and your sister.'

'Miles and my sister. Didn't my sister tell you there were no preliminaries necessary with me?' Her voice took on a sudden harshness.

'I won't say what your sister told me.'

'She likes to give the impression that I'm the wildest girl in London. Bitch,' she said. 'On the fingers of one hand.'

'What's that?' I asked, puzzled.

'Never mind.' She lay back in the piled pillows and crossed her arms over her face. She talked, muffled, through soft flesh. 'If you must know, I didn't come to Zurich for you. Whoever you might have turned out to be. Though you turned out to be much dearer than I had ever imagined an American could be, Gentle Heart.'

'Thanks,' I said.

'I'm sorry if you're disappointed.'

'We could forget the little accident in my room, you know.'

I could see her head shaking behind her arms. 'Not me. I should really be grateful to that naked fat girl. Because I was coming up to your room for all the wrong reasons.'

'What do you mean by that?'

'I wasn't doing it for you. Or me.'

'Who, then?'

'For Miles Fabian,' she said bitterly. 'I was going to have the most blatant, sexy, public affair with you anyone could imagine – to show him—'

'To show him what?'

'To show him I didn't care a penny's worth for him anymore. That I could be as fickle and callous as he was.' She was weeping now behind her arms. It had turned out to be my night for feminine tears.

'I think you had better explain, Eunice,' I said slowly.

'Don't be dense, American,' she said. 'I'm in love with Miles Fabian. Have been since the day I met him. I asked him to marry me years ago. So he fled. Into the arms of my bitch sister.'

'Oh.' For the moment, it was all I could say.

She took her arms away from her face. The tears had made gleaming silvery streaks on her cheeks. But her expression was calm, relieved. 'If you hurry,' she said, 'maybe that little fat girl will still be there. So the evening won't be a total waste.'

*

But Didi had already gone, leaving a note in schoolgirl handwriting on the desk. 'I took your coat. So I would have a memento. Maybe one day you'll want to get it. You know where I am. Love Didi.'

As I was finishing reading, the phone rang. I nearly didn't answer it. It was not a night on which I could expect good news over the telephone.

I picked it up.

'Douglas?' It was Fabian.

'Yes?'

'I hope I didn't interrupt you at anything serious,' he said with the hint of a chuckle.

'No.'

'I thought you might like to hear how it went tonight.'

'I certainly would.'

There was a slight sigh on the phone. 'I'm afraid I didn't do so well, old chap. Sloane had a phenomenal streak of luck. We'll have to do some banking in the morning.'

'How much?'

'Around thirty thousand,' Fabian said matter-of-factly.

'Francs?'

'Dollars, Gentle Heart.'

'Son of a bitch,' I said, and hung up.

19

The next morning the following things happened to me.

On my breakfast tray, which I called for at ten o'clock, because I hadn't been able to fall asleep until nearly dawn, there was a note from Eunice. 'Dear Gentle Heart, I am taking the nine o'clock train out of Gstaad. I'm sure you understand why I'm doing this. Love.'

I understood.

Miles Fabian called on the telephone and asked me to meet him in town in front of the Union Bank of Switzerland at eleven o'clock.

I was arrested. Or at the time, it seemed that I was arrested.

I was shaving, looking with distaste at my yellowed eyes in the mirror, when there was a knock on the door. With the lather still on my face, I went to the door. One of the assistant managers was standing there, correct in his dark suit and white shirt, with a squat man in a belted dark overcoat and a porcupine head of a gray hair, cut short.

'Mr Grimes,' the assistant manager said, 'may we come in?'

'I'm shaving,' I said. 'And as you see, I'm not dressed.' All I had on was the bottom of my pajamas and I was barefooted. 'Can't it wait a few minutes?'

The assistant manager spoke rapidly in German to the gray-haired man, who said only one word. '*Nein.*'

'Police Officer Brugelmann says it can't wait,' the assistant manager said apologetically.

Police Officer Brugelmann walked past me into the room.

'After you, Mr Grimes.' The assistant manager bowed a little.

I went into the bathroom, got a towel, and wiped the lather off my face and put on a bathrobe. Police Officer Brugelmann stood in the middle of the room, his eyes roaming icily over the bureau, on top of which I had my wallet and money clip and watch, then onto the two suitcases set on stands under the windows.

Didi, I thought; oh, my God, they've found out about Didi. Or believe they've found out. I had no idea what the age of consent was in Switzerland. Probably it varied from canton to canton, like everything else in the country. We were in the canton of Bern. It could be anything up to twenty-one, with all those girls' schools.

'I consider this an intrusion,' I said coldly. 'And I'd like an explanation immediately.'

Again, the assistant manager spoke rapidly in German to the policeman. The policeman nodded. He had an extremely stiff mechanical nod. His neck was thick and rolled over his collar.

'Police Officer Brugelmann has authorized me to explain,' the assistant manager said. 'Briefly, Mr Grimes, a robbery has been committed. Last night. On floor number five of the hotel. A valuable diamond necklace has been reported missing.'

Eunice's room had been on the fifth floor. 'What's that got to do with me?' I asked, relieved. At least Didi Wales wasn't involved.

There was another exchange in German. Before I leave for anywhere next time, I thought, I'm going to Berlitz.

'You have been noticed last night, late, prowling in the halls of the hotel,' the assistant manager said.

'I was visiting a friend,' I said. 'I was not prowling.'

'I was merely translating,' the assistant manager said unhappily. He was not enjoying his task and was probably regretting he had ever bothered to learn English.

The police officer said something softly.

'The lady you were visiting,' the assistant manager said, 'checked out of the hotel at eight-thirty this morning. Do you happen to know her destination?'

'No,' I said. Almost honestly. I had never asked Eunice for her address. The note she had sent me was crammed into the pocket of my bathrobe. I hoped it didn't show.

The police officer rattled out several sentences that sounded unpleasant.

'The police officer asks permission to search the premises,' the assistant manager said. The words seemed to strangle in his throat.

'Does he have a warrant?' I asked, American to the last civil-rights, *amicus curiae,* Supreme Court brief.

There was another exchange in German.

'There is no warrant. As yet,' the assistant manager said. 'If you insist on a warrant, Police Officer Brugelmann says he will have to take you to the bureau of police and keep you there until the warrant is made out. He warns that it may take a long time. Maybe two days. There will be no avoiding publicity, he says. There are always many foreign newspapermen here. Because of the quality and prominence of our guests.'

'Did *he* say all that?' I asked.

'I added some on my own,' the assistant manager admitted. 'So that you can have a proper basis for action.'

I stared at Police Officer Brugelmann. He stared back glacially. It was warm in the room, but he hadn't unbuttoned his overcoat. He was a naturally cryogenic man. Snakes and birds were his blood cousins. 'All right,' I said. I seated myself in an easy chair. 'I have nothing to hide. Let him start looking. But please make it quick. I have an appointment at eleven.'

The assistant manager translated and Police Officer Brugelmann nodded stiffly in satisfaction. Then he motioned for me to stand up.

'What does he want now?' I asked.

'He wants to look at the chair.'

I stood up, admiring, despite myself, the talent for his profession of Police Officer Brugelmann. Naturally, if the necklace was hidden in the chair, I would immediately sit on it. I moved away and watched the police officer run his hand over the cushion, then pick it up and poke down into the upholstery. Then he put the cushion back, patting it neatly, and motioned politely that I could seat myself again.

After that, he went swiftly through all my belongings. When he had gone through the closet, he took out my ski pants and held them up, saying something to the assistant manager, obviously, from his tone, a question. The assistant manager fidgeted nervously with the button of his jacket as he translated. 'Police Officer Brugelmann wishes to know,' he said, 'if these ski trousers are the only ones you have brought with you.'

'Yes,' I said.

'Where it wass you wass before?' the police officer was getting impatient with the business of translation and now showed that he could speak a variant of English.

'St Moritz,' I said, 'Davos.'

'St Moritz? With only *these*?' The police officer sounded incredulous. 'And now Gstaad, too?'

'They do the job,' I said.

'How long you plan the entire holiday iss to endure, Mr Grimes?'

'Three weeks. Perhaps more.'

Solemnly, the police officer hung the pants back in the closet. Then he turned back to me, taking out a black, plastic-covered pad as he did so, and seating himself at the small desk, so that he could write comfortably. 'Now I am afraid I must some questions ask,' he said. 'Permanent address in the United States?'

I nearly said the Hotel St Augustine, then gave him the address on East Eighty-first Street. It was as permanent as anything else and if Interpol, or whoever it might be, inquired, at least they couldn't accuse me of lying.

'Profession?' The police officer kept his head down as he laboriously wrote in his pad.

'Private investor,' I said briskly.

'Bank?'

From the expression on his face I knew that sooner or later I would have to explain this more fully.

The water was getting deep. 'Union Bank of Switzerland. Zurich.' I thanked Miles Fabian in my heart as I said this for having insisted on our opening separate accounts in each of our names there for what he called walking-around money.

'In America?'

'I've given up banking in America,' I said. 'I'm considering moving to Europe. The economy . . .'

'Have you ever been arrested before?' The police officer said.

'Now, see here,' I appealed to the assistant manager. 'I'm a guest in this hotel. It's supposed to be one of the best hotels in Europe. I don't have to answer insulting questions like that.'

'It is only standard police procedure.' The button on the assistant manager's coat was almost off by now. 'It is not personal. Others are being questioned, too.'

The policeman didn't look up from his pad, writing and talking at the same time.

'You know Mr Miles Fabian, don't you?' I said.

'Of course. Mr Fabian is an old and honored guest of ours,' said the assistant manager.

'Well, he's my good friend. Why don't you call him and ask him about me?'

The assistant manager spoke in swift German. The police officer nodded and said, 'Before haff you ever been arrested?'

'No, by God!'

'One thing more.' The police officer stood up. 'I would like your passport.'

'What do you need my passport for?'

'To make sure you remain in Switzerland, Herr Grimes.'

'What if I don't give my passport?'

'Then other measures I would have to take. Like confining you. Swiss prisons are of a good reputation. But they are still prisons.'

'Please, Mr Grimes,' the assistant manager said.

I went over to my wallet and took out my passport. 'I am going to see a lawyer,' I said to Officer Brugelmann, as I gave him the passport.

'You are at liberty,' he said, stuffing the passport into an inside pocket of his black coat. 'Please, keep yourself free for other questions. I belieff that iss all for the moment.' He nodded, working the stiff hinge of his powerful cantonal neck, and went out.

The assistant manager wrung his hands. 'I offer you the sincere apologies of the management. This is terribly embarrassing for all of us.'

'Us?' I said. I had no intention of making things easy for him.

'It is these careless rich women,' he said. 'They have no idea of the value of money. They leave eighty thousand dollars worth of jewelry in the train and then there is hysteria for days while we try to recover it. Luckily, we are in Switzerland...'

'You have no idea how lucky I feel to be in Switzerland, brother,' I said. I now regretted bitterly the option we had taken on the land for the condominium the day before.

'Anything the management can do, Mr Grimes...' the assistant manager said piously. 'We will leave no stone unturned.'

'The management can get my passport back,' I said. 'That's what the management can do. I want to leave the country. Fast.'

'I understand.' He bowed. 'The *foehn* is blowing.' He touched his forehead as though ascertaining the degree of fever he was running. 'The south wind. Everybody behaves curiously. Let me say something personal, Mr Grimes. I, myself, do not believe you are a criminal.'

'Thanks,' I said.

'Enjoy your day's skiing,' he said automatically.

'I'll do my best,' I said.

He backed out, twisting at his button.

*

Fabian was waiting for me in front of the bank in his dapper Tyrolean outfit. He was as healthy-looking as ever and no one could have suspected that he had sat up half the night losing thirty thousand dollars. He smiled charmingly as I walked up to him, then frowned at what must have been the expression on my face. 'I say, old man, is something wrong?' he said.

I didn't know where to begin, so I said, 'Everything is dandy.'

'I heard about Eunice. Leaving, I mean. I imagine that was a blow to you.' He was the essence of discreet sympathy.

'First things first,' I said. 'Let's do our banking.' I would discuss Eunice with him another time, when I had cooled down and there was no danger that I would hit him on the jaw.

'Sorry about that,' he said, as he took me by the elbow and

254

guided me into the bank. 'Sloane had a lifetime's worth of luck last night. I gave him an IOU. He wants it all in cash. I promised it by four this afternoon. I've already called Zurich to send it over, but there are certain formalities...' He shrugged. 'Swiss bankers.'

We went in and were quizzed by a young man in a back room, who then called our bank in Zurich and spoke lengthily in German. He kept looking up from the phone at Fabian and myself, and I gathered that he was describing us minutely. He asked me for my passport number and luckily I remembered it. After about fifteen-minutes' conversation with Zurich, he hung up and said, 'Very good, gentlemen; the money will be ready at four o'clock.'

When we were out of the bank, Fabian said, 'I promised Lily I'd ski with her this afternoon. No need to let her in on the drama, is there?'

'No,' I said.

'I could use a little air and exercise after last night,' he said. 'It wasn't exactly a health cure.' It was the one intimation that the hours of play had not been completely enjoyable. He stopped as we reached the car, which he had parked a few yards away from the bank. 'I say, Douglas, I'm concerned about you. You *do* look glum. It's only money, after all. We're still far ahead of the game...'

'That's not why I look glum,' I said, and told him about the visit of the policeman. I didn't tell him about Didi Wales or Eunice or prowling around the halls.

He chuckled, as though I had told him a mildly funny story. '*Did* you take the necklace?' he asked.

'God damn it, Miles,' I said, 'what sort of man do you think I am?'

'I'm only beginning to know you, old boy,' he said. 'And after all, you *have* been around hotels for quite a few years.'

'One hotel,' I said. 'And the most anyone could pick up there would be a pair of dime-store cuff links.'

'May I remind you that you did better than that?' he said coolly. For the first time I realized that he could believe that I **might** have done it. 'Considerably better than that.'

'Oh, shit,' I said. 'Let's go skiing.'

We didn't speak in the car driving back to the hotel. It was not the happiest day of our partnership.

*

Fabian skied fairly well, making the right movements just a little bit wrongly. He had obviously had a good deal of instruction. He was not reckless, and I kept far enough ahead of him and Lily so that there was no conversation possible between us. Lily had started to ask me about Eunice. 'Really, Gentle Heart,' she said, 'what in the world did you do to my poor little sister to make her skulk away like a thief in the night?'

'Ask your sister,' I said. 'If ever you see her again.'

'Oh, this *foehn*,' Lily said. 'It makes everybody so grumpy.' She, too, with the south wind.

Sloane came into the club while we were eating lunch. He came over to our table promptly, his ski boots making even more noise than ski boots usually make. His face was florid and triumphant and he looked as though he had been drinking. I could hear his heavy breathing two yards away. I put down my knife and fork. Any desire to eat had suddenly left me.

'Hello, folks,' Sloane said. 'Isn't this a great day?'

'Great,' Fabian said, sipping at his wine.

'Aren't you going to invite me to sit down with you for lunch?' Sloane said.

'No,' said Fabian.

Sloane grinned, his eyes eternally, congenitally hostile. 'That's what I like,' he said, 'a bad loser.' He dug into his pocket and dug out a piece of the hotel stationery, with a few lines written on it. 'Fabian,' he said, 'you're not going to forget this, are you?'

'Don't be rude,' Fabian said coldly. 'There's a lady present.'

'Good day, ma'am,' Sloane said, as though he was noticing Lily for the first time. 'I believe we met. Last year at St Moritz.'

'I remember you well, sir,' Lily said, abruptly eighteenth century.

Sloane folded the sheet of paper carefully and put it back

into his pocket. Then he turned his attention to me. He tapped me heavily on the shoulder. 'What the hell are you doing here, Grimes? I thought you broke your goddamn leg.'

'It was a mistaken diagnosis,' I said.

'Break into any more hotel rooms lately, Smart Boy?'

I looked around uneasily. Sloane's voice was loud and clear, but nobody seemed to be listening. 'Only last night,' I said.

'Full of jokes, this boy,' Sloane said. 'He's a shoe fetishist.' He laughed hoarsely, his eyes venomous and bloodshot in their wrinkled pouches. He was the sort of man who could destroy relations between friendly nations in the space of a half-hour. The thought of our having to hand over thirty thousand dollars to this American peasant at four o'clock that afternoon made me ache.

'How's the watch trade, boy?' he boomed. 'Just as thriving as on the other side of Switzerland?'

'Fuck off, Sloane,' I said. As I spoke, I felt new blood coursing happily through my veins and my appetite returning.

He laughed, uninsultable, at least for today. 'Be careful of this feller,' he said to Fabian. 'He's quirky.' He laughed hollowly. 'Well,' he said, 'if I'm not invited to the party, I might as well ski. I stayed up late last night and I have to blow the cobwebs out. See you at four o'clock at the hotel, Fabian.' His tone was no longer joking.

He clumped out of the room. Fabian sighed. 'The people you have to do business with,' he said.

'Americans,' Lily said. Then she put her hand on my arm 'Forgive me, Gentle Heart. I didn't mean you.'

'Americans are like anyone else,' Fabian said. 'Some don't export well. I've seen some English in my time . . .'

'As have I,' Lily said.

'I forgive everybody,' I said. 'Don't you think we ought to have another bottle of wine?' My nerves needed some soothing, and, if I was going to ski after lunch, a good dose of alcohol might prevent me from breaking something. Also, sitting at the table with Fabian and Lily, calmly and composedly working at their food, I felt myself on the verge of

257

launching into a bitter harangue against them both, blurting out the confession of the meeting in Florence, the details of what Eunice had told me in her cold room the night before. The temptation to tell Fabian that I was through with him once and for all was strong and would have given me immense immediate satisfaction, but our affairs were so hopelessly intertwined that to disentangle them would probably take years, if it ever possibly could be done. The gesture would only make it more difficult. So I concentrated on my food and on the new bottle of wine when it came and hardly listened as Fabian and Lily chatted away.

'Mr Fabian, Mr Fabian...' It was a young ski instructor hurrying into the restaurant, his voice strained and high. Ordinarily the ski instructors did not eat in the same room with the guests, and the people at the other tables looked up in non-democratic disapproval from their meals as the ski instructor ran down the aisle.

'Yes?' Fabian motioned for the boy to keep his voice down. 'What is it?'

'Your friend,' the instructor said. 'Mr Sloane. You'd better come. He was just bending down to put on his skis...'

'Not so loud, please, Hans,' Fabian said. He knew everybody's name. It was one of the things about him that made him so popular with waiters and concierges. 'What is it?'

'He just went *poomp*,' the instructor said. 'He dropped like a log. I think he's dead.'

Fabian looked across at me, a peculiar expression in his eyes. I could have sworn it was amusement.

'Nonsense, Hans,' he said sharply. 'I believe I'd better take a look. Lily, I think perhaps you should stay here. Douglas, may I ask you to come along with me?' He got up and walked swiftly, his face grave, with all eyes upon him, toward the door. I followed. Our ski boots sounded like a company of infantry crossing a bridge. A drum roll for a loud American, with an IOU for thirty thousand dollars in his pocket.

A small crowd was grouped around the exit of the chair lift, where people put on their skis to traverse to the T-bar. The afternoon was suddenly very quiet. Sloane was lying on his back, staring up at the sky. Another ski teacher was rubbing snow on his face, which was a terrible purple and green. Fabian got down on one knee beside the body and tore open the zipper of Sloane's anorak and pulled up the sweater and shirt underneath. Sloane's chest was hairy and white. I started to shake in cold, involuntary shudders. I could feel my teeth set like clamps in my jaws. Fabian leaned over and put his ear to Sloane's chest. It seemed hours before Fabian lifted his head. Slowly he pulled Sloane's shirt and sweater down and zipped up the anorak. 'I think we'd better take him down to the hospital,' Fabian said to the two instructors. 'As quickly as possible.' He stood up, rubbing his face as if to hide his sorrow. 'Poor man,' he said, 'he was a heavy drinker. The altitude and the sudden cold ... If you'll carry him to the lift,' he said to the instructors, 'I'll go down with him. Just call for an ambulance to be waiting at the bottom. Douglas, may I speak to you for a moment...?' He put his arm around my shoulders and led me to one side, two friends of the newly departed seeking a moment alone to soften the blow of the tragic loss of a comrade. Right out of an old wartime B movie, I thought, playing my part with conviction. The crowd, which had now grown larger, parted respectfully.

'Douglas, my boy,' Fabian whispered, patting my shoulder as if to console me, 'I will not leave the corpse. I'll get the IOU out of his pocket on the way down. Do you remember which side it was on?'

'That's what I call showing a decent respect for the dead,' I said. 'Left.'

'I admire your attitude, Gentle Heart.' He pulled me to him in a manly embrace, as though to keep me from breaking down. 'I must say, old chap,' he said, 'you *are* Johnny-on-the-spot when it comes to heart attacks.' Then he dropped his arm and said aloud, so that everybody could hear what he was saying, 'I'll leave you to break the news to Lily. She'll be undone. Give her a stiff brandy.'

Then he walked, his head down, along the snowy path to the lift, where the two ski instructors were securely strapping the corpse onto one of the two-seater chairs. Fabian got into the second seat and put his arm protectively around the dead man. He gave a signal and the chair began to move slowly down the hill.

The two ski teachers took the next chair down. Honorary pallbearers, in bright jackets, descending into the valley to help dispose of the dead.

I went back into the club, where Lily was finishing her coffee, and ordered two brandies.

20

When I got back to the hotel, I was told by the concierge that Mr Fabian expected me to come up to his room. It was late in the afternoon. Lily and I had had several more brandies, sitting in silence as the restaurant slowly emptied. Death makes for long lunches.

I had left Lily at the hairdresser's. 'No sense,' she had said, 'in wasting the whole afternoon.' We had taken the chair lift out of a sense of decorum. Skiing down, we agreed, after what had happened, would have seemed frivolous. Neither of us had spoken of Eunice.

'What was the last thing you said to the man?' Lily asked as we swung slowly toward the shadowed valley.

'Fuck off,' I said.

She nodded. 'That's what I thought you said. Hail and Farewell.' She gestured toward the peaks in the distance, still glowing in sunlight. The eagle, if that was what it was, was back on station, patrolling the neutral Helvetian air. 'There are worse places to die.' She chuckled. 'And worse last words. If there's any justice, he cut that wife of his out of his will.'

'I'm sure he didn't.'

'I said, if there's any justice.'

'Do you think your husband has cut you out of *his* will?'

'Don't be so American,' she said.

We left it at that.

On the way back to the hotel I stepped off at a shop and

bought myself a topcoat. Didi Wales was welcome to her memento. It was a small price to pay for her absence.

*

Fabian was packing when I arrived at the suite he shared with Lily. He did not travel light. There were four big suit-cases scattered around the two rooms. As usual, there were newspapers everywhere, opened to the financial pages. He packed swiftly and neatly, shoes in one bag, shirts in another, in crisp perfect piles. 'I'm accompanying the body home,' he said. 'It's the least I can do, don't you think?'

'The least,' I said.

'You were correct,' he said. 'The IOU was in the left pocket. The formalities will all be taken care of before this evening. The Swiss are very efficient when it comes to getting a dead foreigner out of the country. He was only fifty-two. A choleric man. Premature destruction. A lesson for us all. I called his wife. She took the news bravely. She's going to meet us – the coffin and myself – at Kennedy tomorrow. She's making the necessary dreary arrangements. By the way, do you happen to know where Lily is?'

'Getting her hair done.'

'Unflappable girl. I admire that in her.' He picked up the phone and asked for the hairdresser's. While he was waiting for the call to be put through, he said, 'Would you mind driving us down to Geneva tomorrow?'

'If the police let me out of town,' I said. 'They still have my passport.'

'Oh,' Fabian said, 'I nearly forgot.' He took my passport out of his pocket and tossed it onto a table. 'Here it is.'

'How did you get it?' Somehow I was not surprised that he had it. Partially against my will he had established himself in my imagination as a looming father-figure, capriciously powerful, solver of problems and mysteries, mover of men and laws. I thumbed through the passport to see if there was anything added or missing. I could see nothing to indicate that I had been suspected of crime.

'The assistant manager gave it to me when I came in,' Fabian said carelessly. 'They found the necklace.'

'Who stole it?'

'Nobody. The lady had it stuffed in a ski boot for safe keeping and forgot where she'd put it. Her husband found it this afternoon. The assistant manager was writhing in apology. There's a large bouquet of flowers and a magnum of champagne waiting for you in your room as a sign of the hotel's mortification. Hello, hello,' he said into the phone, 'may I speak to Lady Abbott please?' Then to me. 'You don't mind being left alone for a few days, do you?'

'Frankly,' I said 'nothing could please me more.'

He arched his eyebrows. 'Well ...' he said.

'I feel as though I've been running cross-country for weeks,' I said. 'I could use a little holiday.'

'I thought you were enjoying yourself.' There was a touch of reproach in his voice.

'Everybody to his own opinion,' I said.

'Lily,' Fabian said into the phone, 'I have to go to America tomorrow. Two or three weeks, at the outside. Do you want to come?' He listened for a moment, smiled. 'That's my girl,' he said. 'You'd better get back rather quickly and start packing.' He hung up. 'She loves New York,' he said. 'We'll be staying at the St Regis. In case you want to keep in touch.'

'Roughing it, aren't you?'

He shrugged, went back to his packing. 'It's convenient,' he said. 'And I like the bar. Actually, even if this hadn't come up, I would have had to fly over in a day or two anyway. I want to put together the chalet deal and just about everybody I can think of is on the East Coast. I may have to go down to Palm Beach for a week or so, too. After the funeral.'

'Rough country.'

'I sense a certain resentment on your part, Douglas.' He frowned at a cashmere sweater he was folding. 'I don't think I'll need this, do you?'

'Not in Palm Beach, you won't.'

'You make it sound as though I'm going on this trip for pleasure.' Again I heard a mild reproach, 'I assure you I'd much rather go down to Italy with you. As a matter of fact, there's something I'd like you to do for me – for us – after you get to Rome. I've been in touch with a charming Italian gentleman. Name of Quadrocelli. Italians have all the luck

262

when it comes to choosing names, don't they? I'll send the Dottore a wire to expect you. A nice little enterprise that's waiting to be wrapped up.'

'What's that?'

'Don't sound so suspicious.'

'You must admit your last enterprise was hardly a howling success.'

'It worked out all right in the end, didn't it?' Fabian said cheerfully.

'I don't think we can count on *everybody* we do business with dropping dead on payday.'

Fabian laughed, showing his excellent teeth beneath the neat mustache. 'Who can tell? I myself am now approaching the crucial age.'

'It would take an axe to do you in, Miles,' I said. 'And you know it.'

He laughed again. 'Anyway, you can explain the circumstances to Dottore Quadrocelli. Why I couldn't come in person. You'll find him in Porto Ercole. That's just about two hours north of Rome. It's a delightful place. I had hoped to spend at least two weeks there. There's a first-class small hotel overlooking the Med. It's called the Pellicano. An ideal place to hide out with a girl.' He sighed, regretting the first-class small hotel overlooking the Med. 'Lily adores it. Later in the year, perhaps. Ask for the room with the big terrace. The good Dottore has a villa not far from there.'

'What have you got going *this* time?'

'I wish you wouldn't sound so surly, old man. I like contented partners.'

'My nerves aren't as strong as yours.'

'No, I suppose they're not. Wine.'

'What?'

'You asked me what I had going this time. What I have going is wine. With the way the world's drinking these days, being in wine is like having a license to steal. Have you noticed how the prices for any kind of bottle have been going up? Especially in America.'

'I can't say I have.'

'Trust me, they have. Quadrocelli has a small estate outside

263

Florence. He makes a delicious Chianti. So far, on a very small scale. Just for himself and his friends. He's surrounded by a lot of small farmers who also grow wine of the same quality. We played with the idea last summer of contracting to buy the crop of his neighbors, having a pretty label drawn up, and bottling it under his name and selling it in the States directly to restaurant chains. Eliminate all the middlemen. You can imagine the advantages.'

'I can't really,' I said. 'I've never eliminated a middleman in my life. But I suppose it's enough if *you* can.'

'Believe me,' he said. 'It would take a little capital, of course. Mr Quadrocelli doesn't have the necessary and last summer, as you can imagine, neither did I.'

'And now you have.'

'*We* have. First person plural, old man.' He patted my arm in a brotherly gesture. 'Forever and a day. I've been in touch with Mr Quadrocelli and he's working out a set of figures. I'd appreciate it if you'd look them over and call me in New York so we can discuss it. In fact, I think it would be a good idea if you called me every few days, say at ten o'clock New York time. There's always something coming up.'

'That's no lie,' I said.

'Keeps the blood circulating,' he said airily. 'Tell Mr Quadrocelli that on my side I'll be lining up restaurants in the States. Luckily, I have some dear friends who are in the business. Very much in the business. In fact, they've been after me to come in with them as vice-president in charge of public relations. But it would mean going to an office every day. Unthinkable. No matter what the money is. It would also mean smiling all the time. Not my cup of tea, at all. But they'd absorb a lot of wine.'

'Miles,' I said, 'how many other schemes have you got at the back of your head that you're going to spring on me one at a time?'

He laughed. 'I don't like to worry you about projects until they ripen, Gentle Heart. You should thank me.'

'I thank you,' I said.

'After dinner,' he said, 'I'll give you Quadrocelli's address and telephone number. Also the address of my tailor in

Rome. Tell him you're a friend of mine. I suggest a complete wardrobe. I'll also give you the address of a very good shirt-maker. I also suggest throwing away your present wardrobe. It does nothing for our mutual image, if you get what I mean. I hope I'm not hurting your feelings.'

'On the contrary,' I said. 'I understand. By the time you see me again, I'll be a credit to you.'

'That's better,' he said. 'Would you like the telephone numbers of some lovely Italian girls?'

'No. I'll do it alone, thank you, if you don't mind.'

'I just thought you might like to save a little time.'

'I'm in no hurry.'

'Finally,' he said, 'we'll have to try to uproot the old Puritan in you. Meanwhile I suppose I'll have to take you as you come.'

'The way I take you.'

He had been going in and out of the bedroom through all this, coming out with various articles of clothing that he stowed in one bag or another. Now he emerged with the pretty blue Tyrolean jacket. 'This would look very good on you, Douglas,' he said. 'It's a little large for me. Would you like it?'

'No, thanks. I've had my skiing for the year,' I said.

He nodded soberly. 'I understand. What happened today took the edge off Alpine joys a bit.'

'I never wanted to come here in the first place.'

'Sometimes you have to do things to please the ladies,' Fabian said. 'Apropos of that. Do you want to tell me why Eunice decamped?'

'Not particularly.'

'I regret you didn't see fit to take my advice,' Fabian said. 'It was good advice.'

'Oh, come on, now, Miles! Enough is enough. She told me everything.' Somehow, the sight of this handsome, com-pletely composed man, every hair in place, his trousers and shirt fitting him perfectly, his shoes with a high mahogany shine, deftly packing his array of bags, the perfect traveler for the jet age, suddenly infuriated me. 'All about you. Or at least enough about you.'

'I haven't the faintest notion of what you're talking about, old man.' He tucked a half-dozen pairs of socks neatly into a corner of a suitcase. 'What in the world would there be to tell about me?'

'She's in love with you.'

'Oh, dear,' he said.

'You had an affair with her. I'm not in the business of accepting hand-me-downs.'

'Oh, dear,' he said again. 'She said that?'

'And more.'

'Ever since I've met you,' he said, 'I've worried about your innocence. You have a terribly low threshold of shock. People have affairs. It's a fact of life. People you're associated with. More or less permanently. Good God, man, have you ever been to a wedding at which the bride hasn't had an affair with at least one of the guests?'

'You might have told me,' I said, knowing it sounded foolish.

'What good would that have done? Be reasonable. I suggested her to you with the best intentions in the world. For both you and her. I can vouch for the fact that she's a marvelous girl. In bed and out, not to put too fine a point on it.'

'She wanted to marry *you*.'

'A passing whim. I'm much too old for her, for one thing.'

'Oh, come now, Miles. Fifty's not all that old.'

'I'm not fifty. I'm long past that, if you must know.'

I looked at him incredulously. If he hadn't told me when we first met that he was fifty, I'd have found it hard to believe that he was much over forty. I knew he found it easy to lie, but I couldn't see why he would pretend to be older than he was. 'How much past?' I asked.

'I'll be sixty next month, old man.'

'You must tell me your secret,' I said. 'Someday.'

'Someday.' He snapped a suitcase shut decisively. 'Women like Eunice have no sense of the future. They look at a man they've taken a fancy to and they see only their lover, ageless with passion, not an old man sitting by the fire in slippers a few years from then. There's no need to tell anyone what you've just learned, of course.'

'Does Lily know?'

'Not on your life,' he said briskly. 'So, you see, I rather thought I was doing both you and Eunice a good turn.'

'It didn't quite work,' I said.

'Sorry about that.'

I almost told him about Didi Wales lying naked on my bed, but realized in time that it would not increase his esteem for me appreciably. 'Anyway,' I said, 'I think it's better for all concerned that Eunice went home.'

'Perhaps you're right,' he said. 'We'll never know, shall we? By the way, is there anybody you'd like me to call or see while I'm in America? Any messages?'

I thought for a moment. 'You might telephone my brother in Scranton,' I said. I wrote down his address. 'Ask him how he's doing. And tell him all is well. I've found a friend.'

Fabian smiled, pleased. 'You certainly have. Anybody else?'

I hesitated. 'No,' I said finally.

'I look forward to it.' Fabian put the slip with Henry's address on it in his pocket. 'Now, if you don't mind, I have to do my yoga exercises before my bath. I imagine you're going to change for dinner?'

Yoga, I thought, as I left the suite. Maybe that's what I ought to take up.

*

I watched the big plane take off from Cointrin, the Geneva airport, with Fabian and Lily and the coffin on it. The sky was gray and it was drizzling. I had said nothing would please me more than being left alone for a few days and I had thought that I would be relieved at seeing them finally on their way, like a schoolboy at the beginning of a holiday, but I felt lonely, depressed. I had a slip of paper with Mr Quadrocelli's address and telephone number in my wallet and the addresses of the tailor and shirtmaker in Rome and a list that Fabian had made out for me of good restaurants and churches that I was not to miss on my route south. But it was all I could do to keep from going over to the ticket counter and buying passage on the next plane to New York. As the plane disappeared westward, I felt deserted, left behind, the only one not invited to the party.

What if the plane crashed? No sooner had I thought of it than it seemed to me to be probable. Otherwise, why would I have thought of it? As a pilot I had always taken a macabre professional interest in crashes. I knew how easily things could go wrong. A stuck valve, unexpected clear air turbulence, a flock of swallows ... I could almost see Fabian calmly dropping through the deadly air, imperturbably drowning, perhaps at the last moment, before the ocean swallowed him, finally telling Lily his correct age.

I had been involved in two deaths already since the beginning of my adventure – the old man in the St Augustine and Sloane, now flying to his grave. Would there be an inevitable third? Was there a curse on the money I had stolen? Should I have let Fabian leave? What would the rest of my life be like without him? If there had been any way I could have done it, I would have had the plane recalled, run out to greet it, all reticence and reason gone, before it even rolled to a halt.

In the gray weather, Europe seemed suddenly hostile and full of traps. Maybe, I thought, as I walked toward where the Jaguar was parked, Italy will cure me. I wasn't hopeful.

21

On the trip down from Geneva to Rome, I dutifully visited most of the churches on the list that Fabian had given me and ate in the restaurants he had suggested, the slow drive south a confused mingling of stained glass, madonnas, martyred saints, and heaped plates of *spaghetti à la vòngole* and *fritto misto*. There had been no reports of any planes falling into the Atlantic Ocean. The weather was good, the Jaguar performed nobly, the country through which I drove was beautiful. It was just the kind of voyage I had dreamed of since I was a boy, and I should have savored every moment of it. But as I entered Rome and drove across the broad reaches of the Piazza del Popolo, I realized that for the first time in my life I was miserably lonely. At the end, Sloane had had his revenge.

Using a map, I drove slowly toward the Grand Hotel, another of Fabian's choices. The traffic seemed insane, the other drivers wildly hostile. I felt that if I made one wrong turn I would be lost for days in a city of enemies.

The room I was given in the Grand was too large for me, and, although it was sunny outside, dark. I hung up my clothes carefully. Fabian had told me that Quadrocelli was traveling and didn't expect to be back in Porto Ercole until the weekend. It was only Monday. I had four days to enjoy Rome or despair in it.

At the bottom of my overnight bag, as I cleared it, I saw the thick envelope Evelyn Coates had given me to deliver to her friend at the embassy. I had his name and address and telephone number in a notebook. I looked it up. Lorimer, David Lorimer. Evelyn had asked me not to call him at the embassy. It was just past one o'clock. There was a chance he would be home for lunch. I had been alone for almost a week, walled off from all but the most primitive communication by the barrier of language. I hoped Mr Lorimer would invite me to lunch. The contented unsociability of my nights at the St Augustine had vanished. I missed Fabian and Lily, I missed the sound of voices speaking English, I missed a lot of other things, many of them vague and indefinable.

I gave the number to the operator. A moment later, a man's voice said, '*Pronto.*'

'This is Douglas Grimes,' I said, 'Evelyn ...'

'I know,' the man said quickly. 'Where are you?'

'At the Grand,' I said.

'I'll be there in fifteen minutes. Do you play tennis?'

'Well ...' I wondered if he were speaking in code. 'A bit.'

'I was just leaving for my club. We need a fourth.'

'I haven't any stuff with me ...'

'We'll find gear for you at the club. And I have an extra racquet. I'll meet you in the bar. I have red hair. You can't miss me.' He hung up abruptly.

*

The lanky man with red hair came into the bar, his stride loose and energetic. His hair was quite long, at least for a diplomat, his face craggy, with thick bushy eyebrows, also red, and a bold nose. As he had said, you couldn't miss him. We shook hands. He seemed about my own age. 'I found an old pair of sneakers,' he said. 'What size do you wear?'

'Ten,' I said.

'Good. They'll fit.'

His car, a sleek little blue, open, two-seater Alfa Romeo was parked just outside the hotel, constricting traffic. A policeman was standing beside it, a look of pain on his face. The policeman remonstrated gently with Lorimer, his voice musical, as we climbed into the car. Lorimer waved him off good-naturedly and we headed into the traffic. He drove zestfully, like his fellow Romans, and we nearly scraped fenders a dozen times before we reached the tennis club, situated on the banks of the Tiber. Driving, especially at his speed, seemed to require all his attention, so there was no conversation. He spoke only once. 'This is the Borghese Gardens,' he said as we turned into a green park. 'You ought to look in at the museum.'

'I will,' I said. By now I had acquired a small addiction to museums. It would please Fabian when I reported that I had been to the Borghese. He, too, had told me to visit it. 'Pay special attention to the Titians,' Fabian had instructed.

When we swung through the gates of the club, Lorimer parked the car in the shade of some poplars. There were other cars parked along the road, but nobody to be seen. I started to open the door on my side, but Lorimer put out his hand and touched my arm to stop me.

'Have you got it?'

'Yes.' I reached into the inside pocket of my jacket and pulled out the bulky envelope. I handed it to Lorimer. Without examining it, Lorimer stuffed it into the inside pocket of his jacket.

'Evelyn told me you'd turn up eventually,' Lorimer said. 'Thanks for not calling me at the embassy.'

We got out of the car, Lorimer reaching in for a battered old tennis bag. As we walked toward the clubhouse, he said,

'I'm glad you could come. It's hard to arrange games at this hour. I like to play *before* lunch and Italians like to play after lunch. Fundamental differences in two civilizations. Never to be reconciled. We call to each other from opposite sides of an abyss.' He saluted two small dark men who were playing on one of the courts. 'In a minute,' he shouted.

The two men were only rallying, but they looked pretty good. 'I'm afraid I'm going to slow down your game a bit,' I said, watching them. 'I haven't played in years.'

'Don't give it a thought,' he said. 'Just keep moving up to the net. They crack under pressure.' He grinned. He had a nice, friendly, wolfish grin.

The sneakers fit me comfortably and the shorts and shirt approximately, flopping around me a bit, but playable.

'Take your valuables with you to the court,' Lorimer said. 'You could leave them at the desk, but there have been incidents. And don't leave your passport lying around anywhere, or one day you will be surprised to read that a Sicilian by the name of Douglas Grimes has been arrested for smuggling heroin.' I saw that along with his wallet and loose change and his watch, he also took Evelyn's envelope out to the court with him.

I doubt that the two men we played with ever heard my name. Lorimer introduced us, but spoke in mumbled Italian, and I never got *their* names.

I enjoyed the game more than I thought I would. The skiing I had done that winter had kept me in shape and my reflexes were still there. And as Dr Ryan had promised, my eyes were adequate for the sport. Lorimer loped all over the court, blasting everything. He was wild, but intermittently very effective. We split the first two sets with the Italian gentlemen, who, as Lorimer had predicted, cracked under pressure. I developed a blister on my thumb in the third set and had to quit. The blister was a small price to pay for the pleasure of playing in the balmy Roman sunshine alongside the river which Shakespeare had insisted Caesar had swum with all his armor on. It had been a dry season and the river looked small and innocent and as though I could have swum it, too.

While we were dressing, after our showers, the Italians invited us to lunch, which they were having at the club, before going back to their offices. 'Tell me, partner,' Lorimer said to me, 'is this your first time in Rome?'

'First day,' I said.

'We won't eat here then. We'll go to a tourist place. The Tre Scalini in the Piazza Navona.' I nodded. That was on Fabian's list, too. 'Whenever anybody comes to Rome,' Lorimer said, 'I tell them not to pretend to be anything else but a tourist. Do and see all the standard things. The Vatican, the Sistine Chapel, the Castel Sant'-Angelo, the Moses, the Forums, etcetera. They haven't been put in guidebooks for hundreds of years for nothing. Later on, you can pick your own way. For reading, I suggest Stendhal. Do you read French?'

'No.'

'Pity.'

'I wish I could go back to school all over again.'

'Don't we all?' he said.

*

'How do you like your lunch?' Lorimer asked. We were sitting out on the terrace looking across at the great fountain, with the four enormous carved feminine figures of the Rivers. It was certainly a better idea than having a sandwich and a beer at the bar of the tennis club.

'I like it fine,' I said.

'Don't spread it around,' Lorimer said. 'In certain high-toned circles it is accepted doctrine that the food is inedible.' He grinned. 'You'll be marked as a crude yokel for life and you'll only get to meet a *principessa* with difficulty.'

'Well, I can say I liked the view, can't I?'

'Say you just happened to be strolling through the Piazza Navona by accident. At night. If the subject comes up.' He stared thoughtfully at the fountain. 'Dwarfing, isn't it?'

'What's dwarfing?'

'Those big girls. That's one of the reasons I prefer Rome to New York, say. Here you're dwarfed by art and religion, not by the steel and glass fantasies of insurance companies and stockbrokers.'

'Have you been here long?'

'Not long enough. And the sons of bitches are trying to move me out.' He tapped the bulge in his jacket made by the envelope I had given him. He had taken it out, slit it open, and glanced through the pages hastily while we were waiting to be served. When the first course and the wine appeared, he had jammed the pages back into his pocket without comment. 'That's what this is all about,' he said, tapping the jacket for the second time. 'They're after me. I know it and they know I know and we're all waiting for someone to make the wrong move. I sent along some recommendations that were not received – ah – with enthusiasm in certain quarters. I pushed through some contracts. Evelyn was in on it, too, in Justice and her head is on the block, too. We tried to get the money to the right people in this beautiful, lamentable country, with its desperate inhabitants, not the wrong people. A difference of opinion. Possibly fatal. Don't boast that you know me. There're spies everywhere. When I get back to my desk, the papers will have been moved. Do I sound paranoid?'

'I wouldn't know,' I said, 'although Evelyn hinted . . .'

'It happened before,' Lorimer said, 'and it sure as hell can happen again, with what's going on in Washington. What McCarthy did to the old China hands for coming in with an unpopular message will look like a tea party compared to what that bunch in the White House are capable of pulling off. Orwell was wrong. It shouldn't have been nineteen eighty-four. It should have been nineteen seventy-three. Do you think they'll get that second-story man out of the White House?'

I shrugged. 'I haven't been following it closely,' I said.

Lorimer looked at me oddly. 'Americans.' He shook his head sadly. 'My bet is he'll still be there till the next election. With his foot on all our necks. My next post will probably be in some small African country where they have a *coup d'état* every three months and shoot American ambassadors. Come and visit me.' He grinned and poured himself a full glass of wine. Whatever he was, he wasn't frightened. 'I'm afraid I won't be able to devote any time to you this week. I have to go to Naples for a few days. But I can get back for tennis again on Saturday and there's a poker game on Saturday night, mostly newspapermen, nobody from the embassy.... Evelyn wrote you were a devout poker player....'

'I'm sorry,' I said. 'I won't be here. I have to be in Porto Ercole Saturday.'

'Porto Ercole?' he said. 'The Pellicano?'

'As a matter of fact, I have a reservation there.'

'For a fellow who's just arrived in Italy, you know your way around. The Grand in Rome, the Pellicano in Porto Ercole.'

'I've been briefed by a friend,' I said. 'He knows his way around everywhere.'

'You'll love it,' Lorimer said. 'I go up there for weekends whenever I can. They have a nice tennis court. I envy you.' He looked at his watch, then started to pull out his wallet to pay.

'Please,' I said. 'On me.'

He put his wallet back. 'Evelyn wrote you were independently wealthy. Is that true?'

'More or less,' I said.

'Three cheers for you. In that case, it's your lunch.' He stood up. 'Do you want me to drive you back to the hotel?'

'I think I'd like to walk.'

'Well thought out,' he said. 'I wish I had the time to walk with you. But the executioners await. *Arrivederci*, chum.' He strode off, toward his car, brisk and American, the statues looming over him, toward the desk on which the papers had been moved in his absence.

I finished my coffee slowly, paid, and walked leisurely in the general direction of the hotel, reflecting that Rome, as seen by a pedestrian, was a different and much better city than Rome seen from an automobile. For that afternoon, at least. Lorimer's description of Italy as a beautiful, lamentable country, peopled with desperate inhabitants, seemed only partially correct.

I found myself on a narrow busy street, the via de Babuino, where there were several art galleries. Faithful to Fabian, I peered in through the windows. In one of the windows there was a large oil of a deserted street in a small town in

America, the familiar drugstore, barbershop, fake Colonial bank, a clapboard newspaper office, all in what looked like the last faded night of a cold evening in the middle of flat prairie country. It was painted realistically, but realism heightened by an obsessed attention to every smallest detail, which gave the impression of a distorted, fanatical vision of the country, loving and furious at the same time. The name of the painter who was having the one-man show in the gallery was not an American one – or perhaps half an American one, Angelo Quinn. Out of curiosity I went into the gallery. Aside from the man who ran the place, a wispy, gray-haired sexagenarian in a high collar, and a youngish, sloppily dressed man in need of a shave who sat in a corner reading an art magazine, I was the only one in the shop.

All the paintings were of small towns or dilapidated old sections of cities, with here and there a weather-worn farmhouse set on a bleak, windy hill, or a rusted line of railroad tracks, with frozen puddles reflecting a dark sky, the tracks looking as though they were going nowhere and as if the last train had passed that way a century before.

There were no little red stamps on the frames to indicate that any of the paintings had been sold. The owner of the gallery did not follow me around or offer to talk to me, but merely gave me a sad little dental-plate smile when he caught my eye. The young man with the art magazine never looked up.

I left the gallery saddened, but somehow also uplifted. I wasn't certain enough about my taste to be able to pronounce whether or not the paintings were good or bad, but they had spoken to me directly, had reminded me, elusively but surely, of something I didn't want to forget about my native country.

I walked slowly through the bustling streets, puzzling over the experience. It was very much like what I had felt about books at the age of thirty, when I had begun to read seriously, the sense that something enormous and enigmatic was being tantalizingly revealed to me. I remembered what Fabian had said the morning we had visited the Maeght Museum in St-Paul-de-Vence – that after I had *looked* enough I would pass a certain threshold of emotion. I resolved to come back again the next day.

Near my hotel, by accident, I noticed that I was passing the shop that Fabian had told me was the place I should get my suits made. I went in and spent an interesting hour looking at materials and talking to the head tailor, who spoke a kind of English. I ordered five suits. I would dazzle Fabian when I saw him next.

The next day I got a directory of the art galleries in Rome that were having exhibitions that week and I visited all of them before going back to Quinn's show. I wanted to see how the other contemporary works of art on view in the city affected me. They affected me not at all. Realistic, surrealist, abstract, my eye remained unmoved. Then I went back to the gallery on the via del Babuino and slowly drifted from painting to painting, studying each one carefully and critically, to make sure that what I had felt the afternoon before had not been the result of its having been my first day in Rome, following a good lunch with plenty of wine and the pleasure of conversation with a knowing young American after a week of silence.

The effect on me was, if anything, greater than it had been the day before. The gallery owner and the young man with the art magazine were again the only ones in the shop, looking as though they had not moved in the last twenty-four hours. If they recognized me, they gave no sign that they did so. If I can afford to buy suits, I decided suddenly, I can afford to buy a painting. I had never bought even as much as a print before and was unsure about how one went about it. Fabian had haggled with the dealer in Zurich, but I knew I wasn't up to that.

'Excuse me,' I said to the wispy old gallery owner, who smiled automatically at me, 'I'm interested in the painting in the window. And maybe this one, too.' I was standing in front of the oil of the disused railroad tracks. 'Could you give me some idea of how much they might be?'

'Five hundred thousand lire,' the old man said promptly. His voice was strong and steady.

'Five hundred thousand . . . Uh . . .' It sounded monumental. I still suffered from fits of apprehension when dealing with the Italian decimal system. 'How much is that in dollars?' Tourist, tourist, I thought bitterly as I asked the question.

'About eight hundred dollars.' He shrugged despondently. 'With the ridiculous rate of exchange, less.'

I was paying two hundred and fifty dollars for each of the five suits. They would never give me as much pleasure as either of the paintings. 'Will you take a check on a Swiss bank?'

'Certainly,' the old man said. 'Make it out to Pietro Bonelli. The show closes in two weeks. We can deliver the paintings to you then at your hotel, if you wish.'

'That won't be necessary,' I said. 'I'll pick them up myself.' I wanted to walk out of the shop with the treasures under my arm.

'There should be a deposit, of course,' the old man said. 'To confirm ...'

I looked in my wallet. 'Would ten thousand lire do the trick?'

'Twenty thousand would be more normal,' he said smoothly. I gave him twenty thousand lire and told him my name and he wrote out a receipt for me in flowing Italian script. It was Pietro Bonelli. Through all this the shaggy young man had not looked up from his magazine. 'Would you like to meet the artist?' the old man asked.

'If it's not too much trouble.'

'Not at all. Angelo,' he said, 'Mr Grimes, who is a collector of your work, would like to say hello.'

The young man finally looked up. 'Hi,' he said. 'Congratulations.' He smiled. He seemed even younger when he smiled, with brilliant teeth and deep, dark eyes, like a mournful Italian child. He stood up slowly. 'Come on, Mr Grimes, I'll buy you a coffee to celebrate.'

Bonelli was pasting the first red tab on the frame of the painting in the window as we went out of the shop.

Quinn led me to a café down the street and we stood at the bar as he ordered coffee. 'You're American, aren't you?' I asked.

'As apple pie.' His accent was from no particular place in the States.

'Did you just come over?'

'I've been here for five years,' Quinn said. 'Studying the Italian scene.'

'Did you do all those paintings in the gallery more than five years ago?'

He laughed. 'No. They're all new. They're from memory. Or inventions. Whatever you want to call them. I paint out of loneliness and nostalgia. It gives a certain original aura to the stuff, don't you think?'

'I would say so.'

'When I go back to the States I'll paint Italy. Like most painters I have a theory. My theory is that you must leave home to know what home is like. Do you think I'm crazy?'

'No. Not if that's the way they come out.'

'You like them, eh?'

'Very much.'

'I don't blame you.' He grinned. 'The Angelo Quinn *optique* on his native land. Hold onto them. They'll be worth a lot. Someday.'

'I intend to hang on,' I said. 'And not for the dough.'

'Nice of you to say so.' He sipped at his coffee. 'If it was only for the coffee,' he said, 'I wouldn't consider my time in Italy wasted.'

'Where did you get the name Angelo?'

'My mother. She was an Italian war bride. My father brought her home. To a variety of homes. He was a small-time newspaperman. He'd get tired of one job and he'd move on to another god-forsaken, two-bit town until he got tired of that. I paint my father's wanderings. *Are* you a collector, as old man Bonelli said?'

'No,' I said. 'To tell the truth, this is the first time in my life I ever bought a painting.'

'Holy man,' Quinn said. 'You broke your maiden. Keep at it. You've got a good eye, though I'm not the one who should say so. Have another coffee on me. You've made my day.'

I took the check around to Bonelli's the next day and had a good half hour looking at the pictures I'd bought. Bonelli promised to hold them for me if I couldn't get back in time to claim them when the show closed. All in all, I thought, as I drove up toward Porto Ercole on Friday afternoon, I had to consider my first visit to Rome a successful one.

22

There were few guests at the Pellicano and I was given a large airy room, fronting on the sea. I had the girl at the desk call the Quadrocelli home. Mr Quadrocelli was not expected back until tomorrow morning, she told me. I told her to leave word that I would be at the hotel all day.

I had bought some tennis things in Rome and my blister had healed and the next morning I played polite mixed doubles with some elderly English people who were staying at the hotel. After the tennis and a shower, I was sitting on the terrace overlooking the Mediterranean when the girl from the desk came out with a short dark man dressed in shapeless corduroy pants and a sailor's high-necked, navy blue sweater. 'Mr Grimes,' the girl said, 'this is Dottore Quadrocelli.'

I stood up and shook hands with Dottore Quadrocelli. His hand was hard and callused, like a laborer's. He looked like a peasant, deeply tanned, with a round strong body. His hair and eyes were deep black, his movements quick and vivacious. There were deep lines around his eyes as though he had laughed a great deal in his lifetime. I guessed that he was about forty-five.

'Welcome, welcome, my dear friend,' he said. 'Sit down, sit down. Enjoy the morning. What do you think of our magnificent view?' He said it as though the view, the rocky sweep of the coast of the Argentario peninsula, the sunlit sea, and the island of Genuttri that bulked in the distance were all part of his personal estate. 'May I offer you a drink?' he asked as we seated ourselves.

'Not yet, thank you,' I said. 'It's a little early for me.'

'Ah, excellent,' he said. 'You are going to present me with a good example.' His English had almost no trace of an accent and he spoke rapidly, as though his thoughts tumbled over each other in his head and he could only keep up with himself by speaking at top speed. 'And how is the delightful Miles Fabian? What a pity he couldn't come with you. My wife is desolate. She is hopelessly in love with him. Also my three daughters.' He laughed gaily. His mouth was small, the lips curved, almost like a girl's, but his laughter was loud and robust and masculine. 'Ah, what a history of amour his life must be. And unmarried, to boot. Wisdom, wisdom. He has the sagacity of a philosopher, our friend Miles. Wouldn't you agree, Signor Grimes?'

'I don't know him all that well,' I said. 'We've only met recently.'

'Time only improves him. As compared to the rest of us poor mortals.' Quadrocelli laughed again. 'Are you here alone?'

'I'm afraid so.'

He made a little sad grimace. 'You have my pity. In a place like this...' He made a wide gesture, saluting the glory of our surroundings. 'You are not married?'

'No.'

'I will introduce you to my three daughters. One is beautiful, even if it is a doting father who says so, and the others have character. Each soul to its own virtues. But I treat them equally. When Miles called me on the telephone from Gstaad, he spoke very highly of you. He said that you were the best of companions. You possessed intelligence and rectitude, he said. Two characteristics that do not often go together in one person in these naughty days. I would say the same about Miles.'

I didn't think I had to inform my new friend that he was too generous by half in his judgement.

'How did you happen to meet Miles?' Quadrocelli asked.

'We were on the plane together coming from New York.' This was true, even though I hadn't seen him on the flight and he had never mentioned having seen me. But it would help stop further questions.

'And you hit it off together just like that?' Quadrocelli snapped his fingers.

Hit was the appropriate word, I thought, remembering the lamp I broke on Fabian's head. 'Just like that,' I said.

'Like marriages,' Quadrocelli said, 'partnerships are made in heaven. Have you any experience in wine, Mr Grimes?'

'None. Until I came to Europe, I hardly ever touched it. Beer was my drink.'

'Of no importance. Miles has the palate for all three of us. I tell you, it was a day of great honor for my wine when Miles suggested he would be interested in sending it out into the world with my name on the bottle. Every time an American will say, "I would like to order a Chianti Quadrocelli," I will have a little thrill of pride. I am not a vain man, but vanity is not unknown to me. And it will be an honest wine. That I promise you. It will not be mixed with Greek rotgut or Sicilian acid. Ah, the things they do here in Italy. Bull's blood, chemicals. I am ashamed for my country. So much of our wine is like so much of our politics. Debased. Devalued, like our lire. And not only Italy. If the truth would get out about France! You and I and our friend Miles will be able to look any man in the face and say, "You have not been deceived in buying our product." And we will be enriched in the process. Greatly enriched, my dear friend. The thirst is insatiable. I will show the figures after lunch – you will have lunch with me and my wife, please—'

'Thank you,' I said.

'It is one of the few things our idiotic government cannot ruin,' Quadrocelli said. 'My wine. I have a printing business in Milan. You have no idea of how difficult they make it just to keep the head above water. Taxes, strikes, red tape ... Bombings.' His face grew sober. '*Dolce Italia*. I have to have an armed guard at my plant in Milan twenty-four hours a day. I print, at cost, some harmless tracts for some Socialist friends of mine and I am constantly being threatened. Do not believe it, Mr Grimes, when you are told Mussolini is dead. My father had to flee to England in 1928 – there was one consolation, of course – I learned your beautiful language – and I would not be surprised if one day *I* will have to flee, too.

From the right, from the left, from above, from below.' He made an impatient gesture, as though he was annoyed at himself for this show of pessimism. 'Ah, you must be careful not to take everything I say too seriously. I swing from extreme to extreme. My family came from the South. In our family, we all cried and laughed on the same day.' He laughed gaily, fond of his family's range of emotions. 'You are here to talk about wine, not our insane politics. The eternal grape. Not even the politicians and the bully boys can keep grapes from growing. And the yeasts never go on strike. You and Miles have picked the one business that might be considered a reasonable risk in all of Italy. When Miles spoke to me on the phone, he talked of a death.'

I began to see that I would have to be on the alert for sudden switches of subjects in Mr Quadrocelli's conversation. 'A friend of ours,' I said.

'I hope it was not too painful.'

'I don't believe it was,' I said.

'Ah,' he said, 'we are all mortal.' He hugged himself, as if to reassure himself that his body was still there. 'Let us talk of more cheerful things. Have you ever been in Italy before?'

'No.' I didn't think I had to count the trip to Florence hunting for Miles Fabian.

'I will be your guide. It is a wonderful country, full of surprises. Some of them even happy ones.' He laughed. He was not shy at laughing at his own jokes. I had begun to like the man already, his vitality and bouncing health and cynical honesty. 'We are no longer great, but we are the inheritors of greatness. We are poor caretakers, but everything is all there, even if it is crumbling a little. I will take you to my home near Firenze. You will see the vineyards with your own eyes. You will drink your wine in the place where it is grown. I have some bottles in my cellar that will make the tears come to your eyes. That I promise you. Do you like the opera?'

'I've never been.'

'I will take you to La Scala, in Milan. You will be introduced to rapture. Do you plan to stay long in Italy?'

'That depends somewhat on Miles.'

'Do not be in a hurry to leave, I beg of you. I do not want

our relationship to be merely a business one,' he said earnestly. 'I know it sounds foolish, but it will be bad for the wine. Are you a good sailor?'

'I've only been in small boats on a lake back home.'

'I have a twenty-five-foot little power cruiser in the harbor. We will visit Genuttri.' He gestured toward the island, which now looked like a small, wispy cloud on the horizon. 'It is still wild and unspoiled. That is a great deal to say about a place in these naughty days. It is too bad it is too cold to swim. The water is like sapphires. We will take a picnic and get sunburned. You will want to live the rest of your life here. Where is your home in America?'

I hesitated. 'In Vermont. But I move around a lot.'

'Vermont.' He shivered. 'I never can understand why people who do not have to do it live in ice and snow. Like Miles, with his crazy skiing. I have told him that there is a house just next to mine that is for sale. A beautiful house and I could get it at a price. And with his Italian ... He could live like a king. At his age there is a good chance he could live his life out before everything went down in ruins. He seems to have come into some money...' Quadrocelli looked at me shrewdly, his eyes narrowing. 'Am I right or wrong?'

'I don't know,' I said. 'As I told you I only met him recently.'

'Ah, good,' he said, 'you are a discreet gentleman. If Miles wishes to tell me, he can tell me himself. Is that it?'

'More or less.'

'If I may ask, Mr Grimes ... Ah!' He made an impatient gesture. 'What is your first name?'

'Douglas.'

'And I am Giuliano. So that is settled. If I may ask, Douglas, what is your business?'

I hesitated again. 'Mostly investments,' I said.

'I will not pry.' Quadrocelli put his hands out in front of him in a braking motion, as though physically stopping himself from going too far. 'You are a friend of Miles and that is enough for me. Or any man.' He stood up. 'And now it is time for lunch. Pasta and fresh fish. Simple fare. I have never had a stomachache since the day I married my wife. I am overweight, my doctor says, but I tell him I do not plan to be a movie star.' He laughed again.

I got up and he linked my arm in his as we started toward the door of the hotel. But before we reached it, the door opened and out into the bright Italian sunshine stepped Evelyn Coates.

'Lorimer called me,' she said. 'He told me you might be here. I hope I'm not intruding.'

'You're not intruding,' I said.

*

It might have been the springtime Mediterranean weather or the fact that she was on a holiday or merely being away from Washington, but whatever the reason, Evelyn was a changed woman. The harshness and abrasive authority that had offended me in my first introduction to her were no longer in evidence. She was gentler, careful not to wound, relaxed. When we made love, I no longer had the feeling that she was on a desperate search for something she would never find. Even on the last Sunday night in Washington, with all the tenderness, I realized now, there had been the same underlying tension. We spent hours alone together, basking in the sun, holding hands, talking desultorily, laughing easily, childishly, at little things, like our attempts to talk Italian to a waiter or posing for each other in extreme positions in snapshots that we took with a camera that Evelyn had brought along with her.

When she arrived, Mr Quadrocelli had left us tactfully alone, saying, 'You must have many things you wish to talk about with your beautiful American friend. We can have lunch tomorrow, instead of today. My wife will understand. And my three daughters.' He laughed, his rumbling, robust laugh. 'I do not pity you anymore, Douglas.' He winked as he said it. 'Not at all.'

Then he had called during the afternoon, full of apologies, to say that he had received a telephone call, that he had to fly to Milan that evening, there had been sabotage at the plant. 'Imagine,' he said, 'even on Saturday.' But he would return as soon as possible, he said. I was to give his salutations to the beautiful American. His call had come after lunch, when

Evelyn and I were in bed together, in the warm, pretty room overlooking the sea, all our hungers for the moment sated. Although I was sorry Quadrocelli's plant had been sabotaged, I was not sorry that I wouldn't have to spend time with him, nice as he was, time that I otherwise could devote to Evelyn.

The hotel was practically empty in this off-season, and it was like having a luxurious country house, equipped with a friendly and highly efficient staff, all to ourselves. The large terrace that came with our room was shielded from observation, and we lay naked side by side for hours in the warm sunshine, tanning ourselves. It seemed to me that Evelyn's body had grown softer and rounder. In Washington it had been hard and taut, trained for competition, the body of a woman who religiously went through strenuous calisthenics and expensive massages daily to keep in shape. We talked of many things, but never about Washington or her work there. I didn't ask her how long she could stay with me and she didn't mention when she would have to leave. I did not report my conversation with Lorimer at the Tre Scalini.

It was a marvelous, in-between kind of time, sensual and carefree, untroubled by clock or calendar, in a beautiful country whose language we could not speak and whose problems were not our problems. We read no newspapers and never listened to the radio and made no plans for the future. Fabian called me several times to say things were going swimmingly in New York and that we were growing richer daily but that because of certain complications that he wouldn't bother to explain to me over the phone he would have to stay in the States longer than he had expected. Quadrocelli had sent over the figures on the wine deal before he had left, and I had mailed them to Fabian without looking at them. They were fine, Fabian said, and when Quadrocelli got back to Porto Ercole, I could tell him his terms were acceptable.

'Incidentally,' I said, 'how was the funeral?'

'Pure pleasure,' Fabian said. 'Oh – I nearly forgot – your brother came to New York to visit me. He's a very different kettle of fish from you, isn't he?'

'I guess you might put it that way,' I said.

'Still, he says the company you and he are in on looks very promising. He told me about his eyes and I sent him to my man in New York and he's being treated with some new drug and the doctor says he'll be fine. Lily sends her love.'

It was a week in which nothing could go wrong.

*

We drove down to Rome to get my five suits and stayed at a hotel overlooking the Spanish Steps and like good tourists we walked everywhere, had lunch in the Piazza Navona and drank the wine of Frascati and visited the Vatican and the Forum and the Borghese Museum and heard *Tosca* at the opera. Evelyn said she admired my suits and pretended that all the girls we passed were looking longingly at me. I was not blind to the fact that practically all the Italian men we passed looked longingly at *her*.

On one of our walks I steered her to Bonelli's gallery. The painting of the American small-town street was still in the window, with my little red tab on the frame. I didn't tell Evelyn that it belonged to me. I was curious about what she thought about it. She was much more sophisticated than I and, sharing an apartment with a gallery-owner, she must have been exposed, even if it was only by this association, to a good deal of modern art. I stood silently by her side as we both studied the painting. If she said it was worthless, I probably would never claim the painting and never admit that I had bought it.

'What do you think of it?' I finally asked.

'It's beautiful,' she said. 'Absolutely beautiful. Let's go in and see the whole show. I must write Brenda about this man.'

But it was lunch hour or hours and the gallery was closed, so we couldn't go in. It was just as well, I thought. She might not have liked any of the other paintings and Bonelli would have undoubtedly spoken to me, thanking me for the check I had given him and I would have felt diminished in her eyes. I knew that after the days we had spent together since she had arrived at Porto Ercole I wanted her always to have a high opinion of me. In all fields.

The next day, I went down to the gallery to collect the two paintings. Evelyn had an appointment with a friend at the embassy and I was alone. Bonelli seemed happier than when I had last seen him. There were three more red tabs on the paintings on the walls and I supposed that accounted for the improvement in his spirits. As he wrapped my canvas he hummed a tune that I recognized as an aria from *Tosca*. Quinn was not there, 'He has had a sudden seizure of talent,' Bonelli said when I asked about him. 'Since you talked to him, he has been home painting night and day.'

Further wanderings of father, I thought, coming up.

'I think you must take some of the credit, Mr Grimes,' Bonelli said. 'He was very despondent, sitting around here from opening to closing, looking at more than a year's work on the walls and nothing happening, nothing. An artist, especially a young artist, becomes desperate for a little encouragement.'

'Not only artists,' I said.

'Of course you're right,' Bonelli agreed. 'Despondency is not only the privilege of artists. I myself sometimes have days when I wonder if I have not totally wasted my life. Even in America, I suppose...' He shrugged, leaving the sentence unfinished.

'Even in America,' I said.

*

When I got back to the hotel, Evelyn had not yet returned, and I put the paintings side by side on the mantelpiece, with a note on which I merely wrote, 'To Evelyn. In gratitude, Rome,' and the date. Then I went out and walked down to the Via Veneto and sat at Downey's on the terrace, drinking coffee and watching the crowds walk by. I wanted Evelyn to see the pictures and the note without me.

When I got back to the hotel, she was lying on the bed, propped up against the pillows, staring at the paintings. She was crying. Without saying anything, she motioned for me to come over to her and pulled me down beside her and kissed me.

After a while, she said, 'I'm a bitch.'

'Oh, come on now,' I said.

She pulled away from me and sat up. 'I have to tell you why I came over here. To Italy.'

'I'm delighted you came,' I said. 'Let's leave it at that. And I don't want to hear why you think you're a bitch.'

'I'm pregnant,' she said. 'By you. I ran out of the pill the day I met you. You don't have to believe me, you know, if you don't want to.'

'I believe you,' I said.

'I was all ready to have an abortion,' she said, 'when Lorimer called me.'

'I'm glad he did.'

'I've always said I didn't want children,' she said. 'But when David told me where you were ... I suddenly realized I'd been fooling myself. About that. And about a lot of other things, too. I've quit my job. No more government for me. I was destroying myself in Washington. Along with just about everybody else I knew there. I had a cold-blooded lawyer's proposition I was going to put to you....'

'What was that?'

'I was going to ask you to marry me,' she said.

'That's not so awfully cold-blooded,' I said.

'I was going to tell you we could get a divorce after the baby was born. I didn't want an illegitimate child. Big, hot-shot, hardboiled, liberated woman that I am, the scourge of the Department of Justice.' She laughed miserably. 'And I was ready to behave just like a brainless, marshmallowy little flirt just out of finishing school. But then, after this week we've had ...' She gestured helplessly. 'You've been so *good*. The pictures were the final touch. I'll handle it by myself.'

I took a deep breath. 'I have a better idea,' I said. 'Why don't we get married and have the baby and *not* get divorced?' As I said it I knew I was wrong to have done so. There were shadows hanging over me, shadows that had to be dissipated before I could marry anyone. Chief among the shadows was that of Pat. I had almost asked her to marry me, too, and that had come to nothing. I had tried to forget her, but had I? More often than I liked to admit I dreamed about her. Even in bed, with Evelyn sleeping beside me, I had dreamed about her.

It was with relief that I heard Evelyn say, 'Not so fast. Not so fast. First of all, I might be lying...'

'About what?'

'About who's the father of the child, for instance.'

'Why would you do that?'

'Women do, you know.'

'*Are* you lying?'

'No.'

'That's good enough for me,' I said.

'Even so,' she said, shaking her head, 'not so fast. I want no repenting in leisure in my house. No long faces of regret year after year. Save your spontaneous gestures of generosity for lesser events. Think it over for a while. Let's both think *everything* over for a while. Let's both be sure we know what we're doing. Let's give ourselves a couple of weeks.'

'But you said . . .' Her sudden resistance made me irrationally stubborn. 'The reason you came to Italy . . .'

'I know what I said. I know the reason I came to Italy. It's no longer operative. That's a word that's very popular in Washington these days.'

'Why is it no longer operative?'

'Because I've changed,' Evelyn said. 'You were a stranger I was going to use. You're not a stranger any longer and I can't use you.'

'What am I now?'

She laughed, a little sad laugh. 'I'll tell you another time.' She stood up. 'Let's go and have a drink,' she said. 'I need one.'

*

'Remember what you told me the first night in Washington?' Evelyn was saying. We were walking down the Via Condotti, peering idly into the windows. Since the scene in the room in the hotel, we had avoided the subject of marriage. We behaved as though the conversation had never taken place. Or almost as if it hadn't. We were more tender with each other than before, gentler. Our lovemaking had an edge of sorrow to it.

'What did I tell you in Washington?'

'That you were a simple country boy from an enormously wealthy family.'

I nodded. 'Did you believe it?'

'No.'

'You were right.'

She smiled. 'Remember,' she said, 'I'm a trained lawyer. Just what do you do? As your possible future wife I suppose I ought to know, don't you think?'

'Worry not,' I said. 'I make enough to support you.' Without reflecting on it, I kept up the pretense that I was still committed to what I had said to her. I knew it was foolish, unrealistic, but it was the easiest path to follow. At least for the moment.

'I'm not worrying about anybody supporting me,' she said. 'I have money of my own, and wherever we go I can always make a living. Lawyers hardly starve in America.'

'Why America? What's wrong with living in Europe?'

She shook her head. 'Europe's not for me. I like to come on holidays and all that, but not permanently.' She looked at me shrewdly. 'Is there a reason you don't want to go back?'

'No.'

'You're lying to me.' She stopped walking.

'Maybe,' I admitted. A man coming out of a leather shop bumped into me and said, '*Scusi*.'

'Would that be a good way to start a marriage?'

'I'm not asking *you* any questions.'

'Ask,' she said.

'I'd rather not.'

'I have a nice small house near the bay in Sag Harbor,' she said. 'My parents left it to me. I like it there. I could set up a law practice and make a living without running myself into the ground. Whatever your business is, could you handle it living there?'

'Maybe,' I said.

'If I said that the *only* place I would live after we got married was there, would you still want to marry me?'

'*Are* you saying that?'

'I am,' she said. It was the first time since she had appeared on the terrace at the hotel in Porto Ercole that the Washington tone had come into her voice. Plainly, she was going to be no man's meek little wife. We were walking again and I was silent for twenty yards. 'Are you going to answer me?'

'Not right now,' I said.

'When?'

'Tonight, in a few days, in a month ...' She was making me think about America and I was angry with her for it. Angelo Quinn's paintings back in the hotel room were having their effect on me. Ever since I had first seen them, with their harsh and melancholy statement about my native country, I had been fighting the realization that one day I would have to go back. Some people, I had found out, are born to be aliens, luxuriate in being aliens. Not I. That was one thing the paintings had proved to me. Hell, I thought, I'll never learn another language. Not even one other language. Perhaps it had been an accident that I had gone into Bonelli's gallery that day and perhaps it had been an accident that the paintings had been as good as they were, but paintings or no paintings, in the long run, I now knew, whether it was with Evelyn or without her, I would go back. I was sure Fabian would disapprove. I could hear his arguments in advance. 'Good God, man, you'll wind up with a bullet in your head.' But I couldn't spend my life seeking Miles Fabian's approval.

'I'm not saying I won't live in America,' I said. 'In your house in Sag Harbor, if you want. But, everything else being equal, if I told you that there are reasons that I don't want to explain for my preferring to live abroad, reasons I might never tell you, would you still want to marry me?'

'I don't like to accept people on faith,' she said. 'Even you. I don't have all that much faith.'

'Now I'm the one that's asking the question. Would you still want to marry me?'

'I won't answer that now.' She laughed. The laugh was harsh.

'When?' I asked.

'Tonight, in a few days, in a month ...'

We walked in silence again. Crossing the street we were nearly run over by a large Mercedes, speeding to catch a light. Suddenly, I had had enough of Rome.

'By the way,' Evelyn said, 'who's Pat?'

'How do you know anything about Pat?'

'I know that you know a girl called Pat.'

'How do you know it's a girl?' I had been taken by surprise and stalled for time. I had never mentioned Pat to Evelyn. 'It's a man's name.'

'Not the way you say it,' Evelyn said.

'When did I say it?'

'Twice. Last night in your sleep. And the way you said it, it couldn't be a man.'

'Oh.' I had stopped walking.

'Uh-huh. Oh.'

'It's a girl I know. Knew,' I corrected myself.

'You sounded as if you knew her very well.'

'Did I?'

'Yes.'

'I did.'

'Were you in love with her?'

'I thought so. Some of the time.'

'When was the last time you saw her?'

'Three years ago.'

'But you still call out her name in your sleep.'

'If you say so,' I said.

'Do you still love her?' She smiled. 'Some of the time?'

I waited a long time before answering. 'I don't know,' I said.

'Don't you think you'd better see her and find out?'

'Yes,' I said.

23

The trip back to Porto Ercole the next morning was a quiet one. Neither of us spoke much. I was busy with my own thoughts and I suppose Evelyn was busy with hers. She sat far over on her side of the car, her hands in her lap, her face composed and grave. Pat, unmentioned and thousands of miles away in snowbound Vermont, was a dark presence in the sunny Italian morning. I had told Evelyn I would go and see her. 'The sooner the better,' Evelyn had said. I would have to call Fabian and tell him I was arriving in New York. By way of New England.

When we got to the Pellicano, they told me that Quadrocelli had been in looking for me the night before. I asked the girl at the desk to get him for me on the phone. 'Welcome home,' he said, when the connection was made. 'Did you enjoy Rome?'

'Moderately,' I said.

'You are becoming blasé.' He laughed. He did not sound like a man whose plant had recently been sabotaged. 'It is a beautiful morning,' he said. 'I thought today would be nice for the trip to Genuttri. The sea is gentle. Would you like to go?'

'I have to ask my friend.' Evelyn was standing beside me at the desk. 'He wants to take us for a ride on his boat. Do you want to go?'

'Why not?' Evelyn said.

'We'd be delighted,' I said into the phone.

'Fine. My wife will pack us a picnic hamper. She will not accompany us. She despises boats. She has transmitted this trait to her daughters, alas.' His voice was cheerful as he described the non-admiration for life at sea of the women of his family. 'I must always be on the lookout for other companionship. Do you know where the Yacht Club is in the harbor?'

'Yes.'

'Can you be there in an hour?'

'Whenever you say.'

'An hour. I will be there getting the boat ready. Bring sweaters. It can get cold . . .'

'By the way, how bad was the damage at the plant?' I asked.

'Normally bad,' he said. 'For Italy. Do you know anybody who wants to buy a highly up-to-date, slowly failing printing establishment?'

'No,' I said.

'Neither do I.' He was laughing merrily as he hung up.

The idea of sailing to the island on the horizon attracted

me. Not so much for the cruise itself as for the fact that for a full afternoon Evelyn and I would not be alone together. I decided to invite Quadrocelli and his wife to dinner with us. That would take care of the evening, too.

Evelyn went up to our room to change for the outing and I put in a call for Fabian. While waiting for the call to come through, I read the morning's *Rome Daily American*. In a column of social notes, there was an item about David Lorimer. He was being transferred to Washington. A farewell party was being arranged in his honor. I threw the paper away. I didn't want Evelyn to read it.

'Holy God, man,' Fabian said, when I finally reached him. 'Do you know what time it is?'

'Noon.'

'In Italy,' Fabian complained. 'It's six o'clock in the morning here. What civilized human being wakes up a friend at six in the morning?'

'Sorry about that,' I said. 'I just didn't want to make you wait for the good news.'

'What good news?' His voice was suspicious.

'I'm coming back to the States.'

'What's so good about that?'

'I'll tell you when I see you. Private business. Can you hear me? This connection is lousy.'

'I can hear you,' he said. 'All too well.'

'The real reason I'm calling is to find out where you want me to leave the car.'

'Why don't you wait where you are and I'll come over and we can discuss this calmly.'

'I can't wait,' I said. 'And I'm calm right now.'

'You can't wait.' I could hear him sigh at the other end of the wire. 'All right – can you drive the car to Paris? Tell the concierge at the Plaza-Athénée to put it in a garage for me. I have some business to look into in Paris.'

He could have said someplace more convenient – like Fiumicino. He was a man who had some business to look into everywhere – Rome, Milan, Nice, Brussels, Geneva, Helsinki. He was being purposely inconvenient to discipline me. But I was in no mood to argue with him.

'Okay,' I said. 'Paris it will be.'

'You know you've ruined my day, don't you?'

'There'll be other days,' I said pleasantly.

*

When we drove down to the harbor and parked the car, I could see Quadrocelli coiling rope on the deck of his little white cabin cruiser, tied fore and aft to the dock of the Yacht Club. Most of the other boats in the harbor were still fitted out with their winter tarpaulins and the dock was deserted except for him.

'Sailing, sailing, over the bounding main,' Evelyn sang as we walked toward the dock. She had made me stop at a pharmacy and buy some Dramamine. I had the feeling she shared Mrs Quadrocelli's low opinion of the sea. 'Are you sure you're not going to drown me when you get me out on the water?' she said. 'Like what's-his-name in *An American Tragedy* when he finds out Shelley Winters is pregnant.'

'Montgomery Clift,' I said. 'I'm not Montgomery Clift and you're not Shelley Winters. And the picture wasn't called *An American Tragedy*. It was *A Place in the Sun*.'

'I just said it for laughs.' She smiled sweetly at me.

'Some laughs.' But I smiled back. It wasn't much of a joke, but it was a joke. At least it was a sign she was ready to make an effort not to be gloomy for the rest of our time in Europe. The long haul through France would have been hard to take if she just sat in her corner of the car, silent and withdrawn, as she had done on the trip that morning from Rome. After the phone call to Fabian I had told her I had to drive to Paris and asked her if she wanted to come along.

'Do you want me to?' she said.

'I want you to.'

'Then so do I,' she had said flatly.

Quadrocelli saw us as we approached the dock and jumped off the boat spryly and hurried to meet us, robust and nautical in his shapeless corduroys and bulky blue seaman's sweater. 'Come aboard, come aboard,' he said, bending to kiss Evelyn's hand, then shaking mine heartily. 'Everything is ready. I have arranged all. The sea, as you notice, is calm as a lake and the well-advertised blue. The picnic basket is secured. Cold chicken, hard-boiled eggs, cheese, fruit, wine. Adequate nourishment for sea-going appetites...'

We were about twenty yards away from the boat when it blew up. Bits and pieces of wood and glass and wire flew around us as we all dove to the pavement. Then everything became deadly quiet. Quadrocelli stood up slowly and stared at his boat. The stern line had been torn away and the stern was drifting at an odd angle from the dock, as though the boat had been broken in two just aft of the helm.

'Are you all right?' I asked Evelyn.

'I think so,' she said in a small voice. 'How about you?'

'Okay,' I said. I stood up and put my arm around her. 'Giuliano...' I began.

He did not look at me. He kept staring at his boat. *'Fascisti,'* he whispered. 'Miserable *Fascisti.'* People were now streaming out of the buildings across the wide quay and we were surrounded by a crowd of citizens. all talking at once, asking questions. Quadrocelli ignored them. 'Take me home, please,' he said to me quietly. 'I do not believe I trust myself to drive. I want to go home.'

We shouldered our way through the crowd to our car. Quadrocelli never looked back at his pretty little boat, which was sinking slowly now into the oily waters of the harbor.

In the car, he began to shiver. Violently, uncontrollably. Under his tan, his face took on a sickly pallor. 'They could have killed you, too,' he said, his teeth chattering. 'If you had arrived two minutes earlier. Forgive me. Forgive all of us. *Dolce Italia.* Paradise for tourists.' He laughed eerily.

When we reached his house, he wouldn't let us go in with him, or even get out of the car. 'Please.' he said, 'I must have a discussion with my wife. I do not wish to be rude, but we must be alone.'

We watched him walk slowly, looking old, across the driveway and to the door of his house. 'Oh, the poor man,' was all that Evelyn said.

We drove back to our hotel. We didn't say anything about what had happened to anyone. They would find out soon enough. We each had a brandy at the bar. Two dead, I thought, one in New York, one in Switzerland and one near miss in Italy. Evelyn's hand was steady as she picked up her glass. Mine wasn't. 'To sunny Italy,' Evelyn said. '*O sole mio.* Time to go, I'd say. Wouldn't you?'

'I would,' I said.

We went up and packed our bags and were paid up and out of the hotel and on the road north in twenty minutes. We didn't stop, except for gas, until after midnight, when we had passed the border and were in Monte Carlo. Evelyn insisted on seeing the casino and playing at the roulette table. I didn't feel like gambling, or even watching, and sat at the bar. After a while she came back, smiling and looking smug. She had won five hundred francs and paid my bar bill to celebrate. Whoever would finally marry her would marry a woman with sound nerves.

*

Evelyn drove out to Orly with me in the rented car with a chauffeur. The Jaguar was in the garage, waiting for Fabian. Evelyn was going to stay in Paris a few more days. She hadn't been in Paris for years and it would be a shame just to pass through, she said. Anyway, I was going to Boston and she was going directly to New York. She had been carefree and affectionate on the trip through France. We had driven slowly, stopping often to sight-see and indulge in great meals outside Lyon and in Avallon. She had taken my picture in front of the Hospice de Beaune, where we toured the wine cellars, and in the courtyard at Fontainebleau. We had spent the last night of the trip just outside Paris at Barbizon, in a lovely old inn. We had dined gloriously. Over dinner I had told her everything. Where my money had come from, how I had met up with Fabian, what our arrangement was. Everything. She had listened quietly. When I finally stopped talking, she laughed. 'Well,' she said, 'now I know why you want to marry a lawyer.' She had leaned over and kissed me. 'Finders keepers, I always say,' she said, still laughing. 'Don't worry, dear. I am not opposed to larceny in a good cause.'

We slept all night in each other's arms. Without saying it to each other, we both knew a chapter in our lives was coming to an end and tacitly we postponed the finish. She asked no more questions about Pat.

When we reached Orly, she didn't get out of the car. 'I hate airports,' she said, 'and railway stations. When it's not me that's going.'

I kissed her. She patted my cheek maternally. 'Be careful in Vermont,' she said. 'Watch out for changes in the weather.'

'All in all,' I said, 'it's not been a bad time, has it?'

'All in all, no,' she said. 'We've been to some nice places.'

My eyes were teary. Hers were brighter than usual, but dry. She looked beautiful, tanned and refreshed by her holiday. She was wearing the same dress she had worn when she arrived in Porto Ercole.

'I'll call you,' I said, as I got out of the car.

'Do that,' she said. 'You have my number in Sag Harbor.'

I leaned into the car and kissed her again. 'Well, now,' she said softly.

I followed the porter with my luggage into the terminal. At the desk, I made sure I had all the checks for my bags.

*

I caught a cold on the plane and was sniffling and running a fever when we landed at Logan. The customs man who came up to me must have taken pity on my condition because he merely waved me on. So I didn't have to pay any duty on the five Roman suits. I took it as a favorable omen to counterbalance the cold. I told the taxi driver to take me to the Ritz-Carlton, where I asked for a sunny room. I had learned the Fabian lesson of the best hotel in town, if I had learned nothing else. I sent down for a Bible and the boy brought up a paperback copy. The next three days I spent in the room, drinking tea and hot rum and living on aspirin, shivering, reading snatches from the Book of Job, and watching television. Nothing I saw on television made me happy I had returned to America.

On the fourth day my cold had gone. I checked out of the hotel, paying cash, and rented a car. The weather was wet and blustery, with huge dark clouds scudding across the sky, not a good day for driving. But by then I was in a hurry. Whatever was going to happen I wanted to happen soon.

I drove fast. The countryside, in the changing northern season, was dead, desolate, the trees bare, the fields muddy, shorn of the grace of snow, the houses closed in on themselves. When I stopped once for gas, a plane flew overhead, low, but unseen in the thick cloud. It sounded like a bombing raid. I had crossed this stretch of the country, at the controls of a plane, hundreds of times. I touched the silver dollar in my pocket.

I reached Burlington just before three o'clock and went directly to the high school. I parked the car across the street from the school and turned the motor off and waited, with the windows all turned up to keep out the cold. I could hear the three o'clock bell ring and watched the flood of boys and girls surge through the school doors. Finally, Pat came out. She was wearing a big, heavy coat and had a scarf around her head. With her myopic eyes I knew my car, forty yards away from her, was only a blur to her and that she couldn't tell whether anyone was in it or not. I was about to open the door and get out and cross over to her when she was stopped by one of the students, a big fat boy in a checkered mackinaw. They stood there in the gray afternoon light, talking, with the wind whipping at her coat and the ends of her scarf. The window on my side was beginning to mist over from the condensation of my breath in the cooling car, and I rolled it down to see her better.

She and the boy seemed in no hurry to be on their way, and I sat there looking at her for what seemed like a very long time. Consciously, I made myself assess, at that one moment, what I felt on the deepest level, as I watched her. I saw a nice enough little woman, ordinarily pretty, who in a few years would look austere, who had no connection with me, who could not move me to joy or sorrow. There was a faded, almost obliterated memory of pleasure and regret.

I turned on the ignition and started the car. As the car moved slowly past her and the boy, they were still talking. She did not look at the car. They were still standing there, on the windswept, darkening street, when I took a last look back in the rear-view mirror.

I drove to the Howard Johnson Lodge and put in a call for Sag Harbor.

*

'Love, love!' Fabian was saying disgustedly. We were in the living room of his suite in the St Regis. As usual, as in anyplace he lived even for a day, it was littered with newspapers in several languages. We were alone. Lily had had to go back to England. I had driven directly to New York. I had told Evelyn on the phone that I would get to Sag Harbor the next day. 'I thought that you had at least gotten over *that*,' Fabian was saying. 'You sound like a high-school sophomore. Just when everything is going so smoothly, you've got to blow up the whole thing. . . .'

Remembering the morning on the dock at Porto Ercole, I was displeased with his choice of words. But I said nothing. I was going to let him talk himself out.

'Sag Harbor, for Christ's sake,' he said. He was pacing up and down, from one end of the big room to another. Outside there was the sound of the traffic on Fifth Avenue, reduced to a rich hum by thick walls and heavy drapes. 'It's just a couple of hours from New York. You'll wind up with a bullet in your head. Have you ever been in Sag Harbor in the winter, for God's sake? After the first fine flush of passion dies down, what do you expect to do there?'

'I'll find something,' I said. 'Maybe I'll just read. And let you work for me.'

He snorted and I smiled.

'Anyway,' I said, 'I'll probably be safer in America surrounded by millions of other Americans than in Europe. You saw for yourself – I stick out like a lighthouse among Europeans.'

'I had hoped to be able to teach you to blend into the scenery.'

'Not in a hundred years, Miles,' I said. 'You know that.'

'You're not that unteachable,' he said. 'I saw certain signs of improvement even in the short time we were together. By the way, I see you went to my tailor.'

I was wearing one of the suits from Rome. 'Yes,' I said. 'How do you like it.' I flipped the lapel of the jacket.

'A welcome change,' he said, 'from the way you looked when I met you. You got a haircut in Rome, too, I see.'

'You never miss anything, do you?' I said. 'Good old Miles.'

'I dread to think of what you're going to look like after a visit to the barber at Sag Harbor.'

'You make it sound as though I'm going to live in the wilderness. That part of Long Island is one of the swankiest places in the United States.'

'As far as I'm concerned,' he said, still pacing, 'there are no swanky places, as you so elegantly put it, in the United States.'

'Come on, now,' I said. 'I remember you come from Lowell, Massachusetts.'

'And you come from Scranton, Pennsylvania,' he said, and we both should do our damndest to forget the two misfortunes. Righto, marriage. I grant you that. You're pleased at the prospect of having a son. I'll grant you *that*, even though it's against all my principles. Have you ever taken a good look at American kids today?'

'Yes. They're endurable.'

'That woman must have bewitched you. A lady lawyer!' He snorted again. 'God, I should have known I should never have left you alone. Listen, has she ever been to Europe? I mean before this – this episode?'

'Yes,' I said.

'Why don't you make this proposition to her – You get married. Righto. But she tries living in Europe with you for a year. American women love living in Europe. Men chase them until they're seventy – especially in France and Italy. Let her talk to Lily. Then she can decide. Nothing could be fairer than that, could it? Do you want me to talk to her?'

'You can talk to her,' I said, 'but not about that. Anyway, it's not only the way she feels. It's the way *I* feel. I don't want to live in Europe.'

'You want to live in *Sag Harbor*.' He groaned melodramatically. 'Why?'

'A lot of reasons – most of them having very little to do with her.' I couldn't explain to him about Angelo Quinn's paintings and I didn't try.

'At least can I meet the lady?' he asked plaintively.

'If you don't try to convince her,' I said. 'About anything.'

'You're some dandy little old partner, partner,' he said. ' give up. When can I meet her?'

'I'm driving out tomorrow morning.'

'Don't make it too early,' he said. 'I have some delicat negotiations starting at ten.'

'Naturally,' I said.

'I'll explain everything I've been doing over dinner. You'l be pleased.'

'I'm sure I will,' I said.

And I was, as he talked steadily across the small table lat that evening at a small French restaurant on the East Side where we had roast duckling with olives and a beautiful, full Burgundy. I was considerably richer, I learned, than when had watched his plane take off from Cointrin with Sloane's coffin in the hold. And so, of course, was Miles Fabian.

*

It was nearly six o'clock by the time we got to Evelyn's house, the rural, gentle landscape through which we passed neat in the seaside dusk. Fabian had checked into a hotel in Southampton on the way, and I had waited for him while he bathed and changed his clothes and made two transatlantic telephone calls. I had told him that Evelyn expected him and was readying a guest room for him, but he had said, 'Not for me, my boy. I don't relish the idea of being kept awake all night by sounds of rapture. It's especially disturbing when one is intimate with the interested parties.'

I remembered Brenda Morrissey reporting at breakfast on the same phenomenon in Evelyn's apartment in Washington and didn't press him.

As we drove up to the house, the outside lamp beside the door had snapped on. Evelyn was not going to be taken by surprise.

The lamp shed a mild welcoming light on the wide lawn in front of the house, which was built on a bluff overlooking the water. There were copses of second-growth scrub oak and wind-twisted scraggly pine bordering the property, and no other houses could be seen. In the distance there was a satin-

last glow of evening on the bay. The house itself was small, of weathered, gray, Cape Cod shingle, with a steep roof and dormer windows. I wondered if I would live and die there.

Fabian had insisted upon bringing two bottles of champagne as a gift, although I had told him that Evelyn liked to drink and was sure to have liquor in the house. He did not offer to help as I unloaded my bags and picked them up to carry them into the house. He considered two bottles of champagne the ultimate in respectable burdens for a man in his position.

He stood looking at the house as though he were confronting an enemy. 'It *is* small, isn't it?' he said.

'It's big enough,' I said. 'I don't share your notions of grandeur.'

'Pity,' he said, grooming his mustache. Why, I thought, surprised, he's nervous.

'Come on,' I said.

But he held back. 'Wouldn't it be better if you went in alone?' he said. 'I could take a little walk and admire the view and come back in fifteen minutes. Aren't there some statements you want to make to the lady alone?'

'Your tact does you credit,' I said, 'but it isn't necessary. I made all the required statements to the lady on the telephone from Vermont.'

'You're sure you know what you're doing?'

'I'm sure.' I took his arm firmly and led him up the gravel path to the front door.

*

I can't pretend that the evening was a complete success. The house was charming and tastefully although inexpensively furnished, but small, as Fabian had pointed out. Evelyn had hung the two paintings I had bought in Rome and they dominated the room, in a peculiar, almost threatening way. Evelyn was dressed casually, in dark slacks and a sweater, making the point, a little too clearly, I thought, that she wasn't going to go to any extra lengths to impress the first friend of mine she had ever met. She thanked Fabian for the champagne, but said she wasn't in the mood for champagne and started for the kitchen to mix martinis for us. 'Let's save the champagne for the wedding,' she said.

'There's more where that comes from, dear Evelyn,' Fabian said.

'Even so,' Evelyn said firmly, as she went through the door.

Fabian glanced thoughtfully at me, looked as though he was about to say something, then sighed and sank into a big leather easy chair. When Evelyn came back with the pitcher and glasses, he played with his mustache, ill at ease, and only pretended to enjoy his drink. I could see he had had his taste buds ready for the wine.

Evelyn helped me to carry my bags upstairs to our bedroom. She was not one of those American women who believe that the Constitution guarantees that they will never be required to carry anything heavier than a handbag containing a compact and a checkbook. She was stronger than she looked. The bedroom was large, running almost the full width of the house, with a bathroom leading off one side of it. There was an oversized double bed, a vanity table, bookcases, and two cane and mahogany rocking chairs set in an alcove. I noticed that there were lamps, well placed for reading.

'Do you think you'll be happy here?' she asked. She sounded uncharacteristically anxious.

'Very.' I took her in my arms and kissed her.

'*He*'s not very happy, your friend,' she whispered, 'is he?'

'He'll learn.' I tried to make my voice sound confident. 'Anyway, he's not marrying you. I am.'

'One hopes,' she said ambiguously. 'He's power-hungry. I recognize the signs from Washington. His mouth tightens when he's crossed. Was he in the Army?'

'Yes.'

'A colonel? He seems like a colonel who's sorry the war ever ended. I bet he was a colonel. Was he?'

'I never asked him.'

'I get the impression that you're very close.'

'We are.'

'And you never asked him what his rank was?'

'No.'

'That's a funny kind of very close,' she said, slipping out of my arms.

*

Fabian was standing in front of the mantelpiece, on which stood his half-drunk martini. He was staring at Angelo Quinn's painting of the main street. He made no comment when we came down the stairs and into the living room, but reached, almost guiltily, for his glass. 'As for refreshments,' he said, falsely hearty, 'let me buy you two dear children a magnificent seafood dinner. There's a restaurant in Southampton I . . .'

'There's no need to go all the way to Southampton,' Evelyn said. 'There's a place right near here in Sag Harbor that serves the best lobsters in the world.'

I saw Fabian's mouth tightening, but all he said was, 'Whatever you say, dear Evelyn.'

She went upstairs to get a coat and Fabian and I were alone for a moment. 'I do like a woman,' he said, a hard glint in his eye, 'who knows her own mind. Poor Douglas.'

'Poor nothing,' I said.

He shrugged, touched his mustache, turned to look at the painting over the mantelpiece. 'Where did she get that?' he asked.

'In Rome,' I said. 'I bought it for her.'

'You did?' he said flatly, but with a hint of unflattering surprise. 'Interesting. Do you remember the name of the gallery?'

'Bonelli's. It's on the via . . .'

'I know where Bonelli's is. Old man with sliding teeth. If I happen to be in Rome I may look in . . .'

Evelyn came down from the bedroom with her coat over her arm, and Fabian was quick to help her on with it. Somehow, as was the case with any woman whom he considered attractive, his movements at moments like that were caressing, like a lover's, not a headwaiter's. I took it as a good sign.

*

The lobster turned out to be every bit as good as Evelyn had promised, and Fabian ordered a bottle of American white wine from Napa Valley that he said was almost as good as any white wine he had drunk in France. Then he ordered another bottle. By then, the atmosphere had relaxed considerably and he teased me gently about my Roman suits, praised my skiing to Evelyn and told her that she must allow me to teach her, mentioned Gstaad, St-Paul-de-Vence, Paris, all very casually, told two funny, unmalicious anecdotes about Giuliano Quadrocelli, listened seriously as we described the blowing up of the boat in the harbor, did not bring up the names of Lily or Eunice, stayed away from the topic of business, deferred at all times when Evelyn wanted to say something, and in general behaved like the most charming and considerate of hosts. I could see that for better or worse he had decided to win over Evelyn and I hoped he would succeed.

'Tell me, Miles,' Evelyn said as we were finishing our coffee, 'in the war were you a colonel? I asked Douglas and he said he didn't know.'

'Heavens no, dear girl,' he laughed. 'I was the lowliest of lieutenants.'

'I was sure you were a colonel,' Evelyn said. 'At least a colonel.'

'Why?'

'No particular reason,' Evelyn said carelessly. She put her hand on mine on the table. 'Just a kind of air of commanding the troops.'

'It's a trick I learned, dear Evelyn,' Fabian said, 'to cover up my essential lack of self-confidence. Would you like a brandy?'

When he had paid the bill, he wouldn't hear of our driving all the way to take him to his hotel in Southampton. 'And tomorrow morning,' he said to me, 'don't bother to get up early. I have to be in New York by noon and the hotel will find a limousine for me.'

As the taxi drove up to the restaurant, now half-obscured by fog rolling in from the bay, he said, 'What a lovely evening. I hope we will have many such. If I may, Gentle Heart ...' I did not miss the echo ... 'If I may...' He leaned toward Evelyn. 'I would love to kiss this dear girl good night.'

'Of course,' she said, not waiting for my permission, and kissed him on the cheek.

We watched him get into the taxi and the red tail-lights faded wetly into the fog.

'Whew!' Evelyn said, reaching for my hand.

*

That night and the next morning I was glad Fabian was in a hotel and not in Evelyn's house.

He did not make it to the wedding, as he was in England that week. But he sent a superb Georgian silver coffeepot as a gift from London, hand-carried by a stewardess he knew. And when our son was born, he sent five gold napoleons from Zurich, where he happened to be at the time.

24

The sound of hammering woke me up. I looked at the clock on the bedside table. It was six forty. I sighed. Johnson, the carpenter who was working on the new wing of the house, insisted upon giving you what he called an honest day's work for your money. Evelyn stirred in the bed beside me, but did not awake. She was breathing softly, the covers half-thrown back, her breasts bare. She looked delicious lying there, and I would have liked to make love to her. But she was cranky in the morning, and, besides, she had worked late the night before on a brief she had brought home from the office with her. Later, I promised myself.

I got out of bed and parted the curtains to see what the weather was like. It was a fine summer morning and the sun was already hot. I put on a pair of bathing trunks and a terry-cloth bathrobe, got a towel, and left the room, barefooted and silent, congratulating myself for having had the good sense to marry a woman who came complete with a house on a beach.

Downstairs, I went into the guest room, which was now transformed into a nursery. I could hear Anna, the girl who looked after the baby, moving around in the kitchen. The baby was in his crib, gurgling over his morning bottle. I stared down at him. He looked rosy, serious, and vulnerable. He didn't resemble either Evelyn or myself; he just looked like a baby. I didn't try to analyze my feelings as I stood beside my son, but when I went out of the room, I was smiling.

I turned the bolt on the second lock that I had installed on the front door when I moved in with Evelyn. She had said that it was unnecessary, that in all the time she and her parents had the house there never had been any trouble. So far there had been no uninvited guests, but I still made certain the bolt was in place each night before I went to bed.

Outside, the lawn was wet with dew, cool and agreeable on my bare feet. 'Good morning, Mr Johnson,' I said to the carpenter, who was putting in a window frame.

'Good morning, Mr Grimes,' Johnson said. He was a formal man and expected to be treated formally. The rest of the building crew wouldn't arrive until eight, but Mr Johnson had told me he preferred working alone and that his early-morning labor, when nobody was around to bother him, was the best part of the day. Evelyn said the real reason he started so early was that he enjoyed waking people up. He had a Puritanical streak and didn't approve of sluggards. She had known him since she was a little girl.

The new wing was almost finished. We were going to move the nursery into it and there would be a library where Evelyn could work and keep some books. Up to now she had to work on the dining-room table. She had an office in town, but the phone was always ringing there, she said, and she couldn't concentrate. She had a secretary and a clerk, but she always seemed to have more work than she could comfortably handle between nine in the morning and six at night. It was amazing how much litigation went on in this peaceful part of the world.

I circled the house and crossed to the edge of the bluff. The bay stretched out below me, glittering and calm in the morning sunlight. I went down the flight of weathered wooden steps to the little beach. I took off the bathrobe and took a

308

deep breath and ran into the water. It was still early in July and the water was shockingly cold. I swam out a hundred yards and then back and came out tingling all over and feeling like singing aloud. I took off my trunks and toweled myself dry. There was nobody else on the whole stretch of beach at that hour to be offended by momentary male nudity.

Back in the house, I turned on the kitchen radio for the early news as I made myself breakfast. There was speculation in Washington that President Nixon was going to be forced to resign. I thought of David Lorimer and his farewell party in Rome. I sat at the kitchen table and drank my fresh orange juice and lingered over bacon and eggs, toast and coffee. I pondered on the special, marvelous taste of breakfasts that you made for yourself on a sunny morning. In the fourteen months since we had been married, I had become addicted to domesticity. Often, when Evelyn came home tired from the office, I prepared dinner for both of us. I had made Evelyn swear never to tell this to a soul, especially not to Miles Fabian. On his subsequent visits, after the first touchy evening on which they had met, Evelyn and he had come to terms. They would never be friends, but they were not unfriendly.

Fabian had been in East Hampton for three weeks, helping me get ready for the opening. Early in the year, he had gone to Rome and had gotten in touch with Angelo Quinn and made a contract with him for all his output. He had done the same thing with the man whose lithographs he had bought in Zurich. Then he had come out to Sag Harbor and outlined a scheme that I had thought was insane at first, but which, surprisingly, Evelyn had approved of. The plan was to open a gallery in nearby East Hampton and have me run it. 'You're not doing anything, anyway.' he said, which was true at the time, 'and I'll always be available to help you when you need it. You have a lot to learn, but you certainly picked a winner with Quinn.'

' I bought two paintings for my girl,' I said. 'I didn't intend to start a career.'

'Have I steered you wrong up to now?' he demanded.

'No,' I admitted. Among the other things on which he had not steered me wrong, like gold and sugar and wine and

Canadian zinc and lead and the land in Gstaad (the chalet would be built by Christmas and every apartment had been rented), there was also Nadine Bonheur's dirty movie, which had been playing to full houses for seven months, in New York, Chicago, Dallas, and Los Angeles amid cries of shame in church publications. Our names, happily, were not on anything connected with the picture except the checks we received each month. And they went directly to Zurich. My bank balances, both open and secret, were impressive, to say the least. 'No,' I said, 'I can't say that you've steered me wrong up to now.'

'This area is rich in three things,' Fabian went on, 'money, potatoes, and painters. You could have five shows a year just with local artists and you still wouldn't begin to tap the total product. People are *interested* in art here and they have the dough to invest in it. And it's like Palm Beach – people are on vacation and are free with their money here. You can get double the price for a picture that you'd have to sweat to get off the wall in New York. That's not to say that we'd just stick with this one place. We'll start modestly and see how it goes, of course. After that, we could look into the possibilities of Palm Beach, say, Houston, Beverly Hills, even New York. You wouldn't be against spending a month or so in Palm Beach in the winter, would you?' he asked Evelyn.

'Not completely,' Evelyn said. 'No.'

'What's more, Douglas,' he said, 'it would launder a reasonable portion of your money for the tax hounds. You were the one who wanted to live in the States and they're bound to come after you. You could throw open your books and sleep at night. And you'd have a legitimate reason to travel in Europe, on the search for talent. And while you were in Europe you could make the occasional necessary visit to your money there. And, finally, for once you could do something for me.'

'For once,' I said.

'I don't expect gratitude,' Fabian said aggrievedly, 'but I do expect normal civility.'

'Listen to the man,' Evelyn said. 'He's making sense.'

'Thank you, my dear,' Fabian said. Then, to me, 'You

don't object if something that is in both our interests happens to be a project that is dear to my heart, do you?'

'Not necessarily,' I said.

'You *can* be ungracious, can't you?' he said. 'Nevertheless – permit me to go on. You know me. You've tagged along with me through enough museums and galleries to have some notion of what I think about art. And artists. And not just what they mean in terms of money. I *like* artists. I would have liked to be one myself. But I couldn't. And the next best thing is to be mixed up with them, help them, gamble on my taste, maybe one day discover a great one.' Part of this may have been true, part pure rhetoric, for the purpose of persuading me. I doubted if Fabian could have distinguished which was which himself. 'Angelo Quinn is good enough,' he went on, 'but maybe one day some kid will walk in with a portfolio and I'll say, "Now I can give up everything else. This is it, this is what I've been waiting for".'

'Okay,' I said. I had known from the beginning I couldn't hold out against him. 'You've convinced me. As usual. I'll devote my life to the building of the Miles Fabian museum. Where do you want it—? How about down the hill from the Maeght Museum in St-Paul-de-Vence?'

'Wilder things have happened,' Fabian said soberly.

We had rented a barn on the outskirts of East Hampton, painted it, cleaned up the interior, and put up our sign – The South Fork Gallery. I had refused to put my name on it. I wasn't quite sure whether my refusal was influenced by modesty or fear of ridicule.

Now, Fabian would be waiting for me there at nine o'clock that morning, surrounded by thirty paintings by Angelo Quinn that we had spent four days hanging on the barn walls. The invitations to the opening of the show had gone out two weeks in advance and Fabian had promised free champagne to about a thousand of his best friends who were in the Hamptons for the summer and we had arranged for two policemen to handle the parking problem.

I was finishing a second cup of coffee when the telephone rang. I went into the hall and picked it up. 'Hello,' I said.

'Doug,' a man's voice said, 'this is Henry.'

'Who?'

'Henry. Hank. Your brother, for God's sake.'

'Oh,' I said. I had called him when I got married but hadn't seen or spoken to him since. He had written to me twice to say that the business still looked promising, which I took to mean that it was about to go under. 'How are you?'

'Fine, fine,' he said hurriedly. 'Listen, Doug, I've got to see you. Today.'

'I've got an awfully busy day, Hank. Can't it . . .?'

'It can't wait. Look, I'm in New York. You can get here in two hours. . . .'

I sighed. I hoped inaudibly. 'Not possible, Hank,' I said.

'Okay. I'll come out there.'

'I'm really jammed . . .'

'You're going to eat lunch, aren't you?' he said accusingly. 'Christ, you can spare an hour every two years for your brother, can't you?'

'Of course, Hank,' I said.

'I can be there by noon. Where do I meet you?'

I gave him the name of a restaurant in East Hampton and told him how to find it.

'Great,' he said.

I hung up. This time I sighed aloud.

I went upstairs and dressed.

Evelyn was just getting out of bed and I kissed her good morning. For once she wasn't cranky at that hour. 'You smell salty,' she whispered as I held her. 'Deliciously salty.' I slapped her fondly on her bottom and told her I was busy for lunch, but that I'd call her later and tell her how things were going.

As I drove toward East Hampton I decided that I could give Hank ten thousand dollars. At the most, ten thousand. I wished he had chosen another day to call.

*

Fabian was prowling around the gallery, giving little touches to the paintings to straighten them, although they all looked absolutely straight to me. The girl from Sarah Lawrence we had hired for the summer was taking champagne glasses out of cases and arranging them on the trestle table we had set up at one end of the barn. The champagne would be delivered in the afternoon by the caterer Fabian had hired. The two paintings from our living room were on the walls. Fabian had put little red sold tabs on them. 'To break the ice,' he had explained. 'Nobody likes to be the first one to buy. Tricks in every trade, my boy.'

'I don't know what I'd do without you,' I said.

'Neither do I,' he said. 'Listen, I've been thinking.'

I recognized the tone. He was coming up with a new scheme.

'What is it now?' I asked.

'We're underpricing,' he said.

'I thought we'd been through all that.' We had spent days discussing prices. We had settled on fifteen hundred dollars for the larger oils and between eight hundred and a thousand for the smaller ones.

'I know we talked about it. But we set our sights too low. We were too modest. People will think we don't have any real confidence in the man.'

'What do you suggest?'

'Two thousand for the big ones. Between twelve and fifteen hundred for the smaller ones. It'll show we're serious.'

'We'll wind up the proud owners of thirty Angelo Quinns,' I said.

'Trust my instinct, my boy,' Fabian said grandly. 'We're really going to put our friend on the map tonight.'

'It's a good thing he won't be here,' I said. 'He'd swoon.'

'It's a pity the young man wouldn't come. Give him a haircut and a shave and he'd be most personable. Useful for lady art lovers.' Fabian had offered to pay Quinn's way across from Rome for the show, but Quinn had said he wasn't finished painting America yet. 'So,' Fabian said, 'two thousand it is, right?'

'If you say so,' I said. 'I'll hide in the john when anybody asks what anything costs.'

'Boldness is all, dear boy,' Fabian said. 'The breaks are coming our way. I was at a party last night and the art critic from *The Times* was there. He's down for the weekend. He promised to look in tonight.'

I felt my nerves grow taut. Quinn had only gotten two lines in an Italian paper for his show in Rome. They had been appreciative, but they had only been two lines. 'I hope you know what you're doing,' I said. 'Because I don't.'

'The man will be stunned,' Fabian said confidently. 'Just look around you. This old barn is positively glowing.'

I had looked so hard and so long at the paintings that I no longer had any reaction to them. If it had been possible, I would have driven out to the far edge of the island at Montauk Point and stayed there looking at the Atlantic Ocean until the whole thing was over.

There was a tinkle behind us and I heard the girl say, 'Oh, dear.' I turned and saw she had dropped a glass and broken it. I supposed they didn't have any courses on the handling of champagne glasses at Sarah Lawrence.

'Do not grieve, dearest,' Fabian said as he helped pick up the pieces. 'It's a lucky omen. In fact. I'm glad you did it. It reminds me we have a cold bottle of wine in the fridge.'

The girl smiled gratefully at Fabian. In the three weeks she had been working for us, he had won her over completely. When *I* spoke to her, she seemed to be trying to catch a weak message being tapped through a thick wall.

Fabian went back into the little room we had partitioned off as an office and brought out the bottle of champagne. He had insisted upon having the refrigerator put in as an essential piece of the gallery's furniture. 'It will pay its keep in the first week,' he had said as he told the workmen where to install it.

I watched him expertly tear off the foil and unwind the wire. 'Miles,' I said, 'I just had breakfast.'

'What better time, old man.' The cork popped out. 'This is a great day. We must treat it with the utmost care.' His life, I had discovered, was replete with great days.

He poured the champagne for the girl and myself. He raised his glass. 'To Angelo Quinn,' he said. 'And to us.'

We drank. I thought of all the champagne I had drunk since I met Miles Fabian and shook my head.

'Oh, by the way, Douglas,' he said, as he filled his glass again, 'I nearly forgot. Another of our investments will be represented here tonight.'

'What investment?'

'At the party last night, we had a distinguished guest.' He chuckled reminiscently. 'Priscilla Dean.'

'Oh, my God,' I said. A good part of the abuse heaped on our movie had been directed at the feminine lead. Her photograph, in the nude and in the most provocative positions, had appeared in two nationally circulated magazines. Crowds followed her in the streets. She had been booed by a section of the studio audience when she appeared on television. It had added to the receipts of the movie, but I was doubtful of what it would do for Quinn's reputation. 'Don't tell me,' I said, 'that you invited her here tonight.'

'Of course,' Fabian said calmly. 'We'll be in all the papers. Don't worry, Gentle Heart. I took her aside and told her that her – ah – her connection to us must remain a closely guarded secret. She swore by the head of her mother. Dora,' he said, 'you realize that anything we say here is never to be repeated anywhere.'

'Of course, Mr Fabian.' She looked puzzled. 'I really don't understand. Who is Priscilla Dean?'

'A low woman,' Fabian said. 'I'm glad to see that you don't go to the movies or read filthy magazines.'

We finished the bottle of champagne without any more toasts.

*

Henry was waiting for me when I got to the restaurant a little after twelve. He was not alone. Seated next to him on the banquette was a very pretty young woman with long auburn hair. He stood up as I came over to the table and shook my hand warmly. He was not wearing glasses, his teeth were capped and even, he was tanned and healthy-looking and had put on weight. He had dyed his hair and he could have passed for a man of thirty. 'Doug,' he said, 'I want you to meet my fiancée. Madeleine, my brother.'

I shook hands with the lady, choking back questions. 'Hank has told me so so much about you,' Madeleine said. She had a low, pleasant voice.

I sat down, facing them. I noticed that there were no drinks on the table. 'Madeleine has never been out here,'

Henry said, 'and she thought she'd like to take a look.'

'I really wanted to meet you,' she said, staring directly at me. She had big gray eyes that I guessed could be blue in some lights. She did not look like a woman who was engaged to a man who was reputed in some quarters to be impotent.

'This calls for a drink. Waiter...' I called.

'Not for us, thanks,' Henry said. 'I'm off the stuff.' He sounded slightly defiant, as though challenging me to comment. I said nothing.

'And I've never been on it,' Madeleine said.

'In that case, no drinks,' I said to the waiter.

'Shall we order?' Henry said. 'I'm afraid we're presssed for time.'

Madeleine stood up and Henry and I stood up with her. 'I won't be having lunch with you gentlemen,' she said. 'I know you have a lot to talk over. I'll take a walk and look around this pretty little town and come back and join you for coffee.'

'Don't get lost,' Henry said.

She laughed. 'Not a chance,' she said.

Henry's face as he watched her walk toward the door was curiously intense. She had slender legs, a good figure, and her walk was ladylike but sensual. Henry seemed to be holding his breath, as though he had momentarily forgotten to breathe.

'Holy man,' I said, as the door closed behind her, 'what is all this?'

'Isn't she something?' he said, as he sat down.

'She's a lovely girl,' I said with conviction. I didn't say it to flatter either him or her. 'Now, spill it.'

'I'm getting a divorce.'

I nodded. 'It's about time, I guess.'

'More than about time.'

'Where are your glasses?' I asked.

He laughed. 'Contact lenses,' he said. 'That friend of yours, Fabian, sure sent me to the right man. Give him my regards when you see him.'

'You can do that yourself. I just left him.'

'I'd love to. But I have to be back in New York by four.'

'What were you doing in New York this morning?' Somehow, it had never occurred to me that it was possible for my brother to escape Scranton.

'I live there,' Henry said. 'Madeleine has an apartment there. And the business moved up to Orangeburg. That's just about thirty minutes from the city.'

The waiter had come back by now with two glasses of water. Henry ordered shrimp cocktail and a steak. His appetite, as well as his appearance, had improved.

'I appreciate your coming all the way out here to see me, Hank,' I said, 'but what was the hurry? Why did it have to be today?'

'The lawyers want to have a handshake on the deal this afternoon,' he said. 'We've been working on it for three months and they've finally got everything together and they don't want to give the other side time to come up with more objections. You know how lawyers are.'

'Not really,' I said. 'What deal?'

'I didn't want to bother you with it until it was definite,' he said. 'I hope you don't mind.'

'I don't mind. Now if you'll begin at the beginning...'

'I told you the business looked promising...'

'Yes.' Guiltily, I remembered that I had considered the word 'promising' in his mouth as a synonym for failure.

'Well, it turned out to be a lot better than that.' He was silent as the waiter put the shrimp cocktail and my salad in front of us. When the waiter had left, he said, 'Better than any of us ever dreamed.' He dug heartily into the cocktail. 'We had to expand almost immediately. We have more than a hundred people working for us in the plant right now. The stock's not on any of the boards yet, but it's gone way up in value. We've had feelers from a half-dozen companies who want to buy us out. The biggest offer is from Northern Industries. It's a huge conglomerate. You must have heard of them....'

'No,' I said, 'I'm afraid I haven't.'

He looked at me disapprovingly, like a teacher at a pupil who neglected his homework in school. 'Anyway, they're *huge*,' he said. 'Take my word for it. They're the people who're ready to give us the go sign today. They're ready to offer us – our company, that is – a half million dollars.' He sat back and let this sink in. 'Does the figure grab you?'

'It grabs me,' I said.

'We should have the money within a couple of months,' Henry said, resuming his meal. 'What's more, we – the two boys who came up with the idea and myself – retain running control of the business for the next five years – now, listen to this – at three times the salaries we've been paying ourselves, plus stock options. You'd be in on the options, of course, along with me. . . .'

I wished Fabian was there at that lunch. It was the sort of thing he would wallow in.

The waiter brought Henry his steak and he began to wolf it down hungrily, eating a baked potato and a roll, both heavily buttered, along with it. Before long he would have to watch his diet. 'Figure it out, Doug,' he said, through a mouthful of food, 'you put in twenty-five thousand. Our third of the stock will bring us thirty-three percent of half a million. That's one hundred and sixty-six thousand. Your two-thirds of that . . .'

'I can do the arithmetic,' I said.

'That's without taking into account the options,' Henry said, continuing eating. Either the hot food or the chanting of enormous figures had made his face flush and he was sweating. 'Even with today's inflation and all that crap . . .'

I nodded. 'It's a nice bundle.'

'I promised you you'd never regret it, didn't I?' he said harshly.

'So you did.'

'No more other people's money,' he said. He stopped eating and put his knife and fork down. He looked at me soberly. His eyes, through the contact lenses, were deep and clear. The little red furrows on the side of his nose had disappeared. 'You saved me from drowning, Doug,' he said in a low voice. 'I can never thank you enough and I won't try.'

'Don't try,' I said.

'Are you all right?' he asked. 'I mean – well – about everything?'

'Couldn't be better.'

'You look good, kid, you really do.'

'And so do you,' I said.

'Well—' He shifted uneasily on the banquette. 'The decision is finally up to you. Is it yes or no?'

'Yes,' I said. 'Of course.'

He smiled widely and picked up his knife and fork again. He finished his steak and ordered blueberry pie à la mode for dessert.

'You'd better get some exercise, Hank,' I said, 'if you're going to eat like that.'

'I'm taking up tennis again.'

'Come on out here and play sometime,' I said. 'There're a thousand courts at this end of the island.'

'That'd be nice. I'd like to meet your wife, too.'

'Anytime.' Then I began to laugh.

He looked at me suspiciously. 'What're you laughing about?'

'On the way to town this morning,' I said, 'after you called, I made up my mind that when I saw you today I wasn't going to let you have one cent more than ten thousand dollars.'

For a moment he looked hurt. Then he began to laugh too. We were both laughing, a little hysterically, when Madeleine came back to the restaurant to join us for coffee.

'What's the joke?' Madeleine asked as she sat down.

'A family affair,' I said. 'Brother stuff.'

'Henry will tell me later,' she said. 'He tells me everything. Don't you, Henry?'

'Everything,' he said. He took her hand and kissed it affectionately. He had never been an open or demonstrative man, but that, too, I saw had changed, along with the eyes, the teeth, the appetite. If stealing a hundred thousand dollars from a dead old man could put the expression that I saw now on Henry's face, felony became a virtue and I would steal ten times over from ten dead men.

When I took them to their car, Madeleine gave me their address. 'You must come and see us soon,' she said.

'I will,' I promised. None of us had any idea of how soon it was going to be.

*

The show, Fabian assured me, was a great success. At one time there must have been more than sixty cars parked outside the barn. The room remained crowded, as people came and went. The champagne got a good deal of serious attention, but so did the paintings. What comments I could overhear in the din of conversation were enthusiastic. 'All on the plus side,' Fabian whispered to me when we both found ourselves together for a moment at the bar. I didn't see the critic from *The Times*, but Fabian told me he liked the expression on the man's face. By eight o'clock, Dora had put red tabs on four of the big oils and six of the small ones. 'Phenomenal,' Fabian exulted as he passed me. 'And a lot of people have told me they're coming back. What a pity Lily couldn't be here. She'd adorn the room. And she loves parties.' His speech was a little thick. He hadn't eaten all day and he had a glass in his hand at all times. I had never seen him drunk before. I hadn't thought he *could* get drunk.

Evelyn seemed somewhat dazed by it all. Quite a few of the guests were theater and movie people, and there were four or five well-known writers whom she recognized but had never met. In Washington, she had never been impressed by the senators or ambassadors she had known, but this was a world that was new to her and she was almost tongue-tied when she had to talk to a man whose book she admired or an actress who had moved her on the stage. I found it an endearing weakness. 'Your friend, Miles,' she said to me, shaking her head. 'He knows *everybody*.'

'You don't know the half of it,' I said.

Evelyn had to go home early, because she had promised Anna the night off. 'Congratulations, darling,' she said as I accompanied her outside to her car. 'It's been splendid.' She kissed me and said, 'I'll be waiting up for you.'

The night air was cool after the heat of the crowded gallery and I stood outside for a few minutes, enjoying the clear, unsmoky evening air. I saw a big Lincoln Continental drive up and Priscilla Dean get out with two graceful young men. The men were in dinner jackets and Priscilla was wearing a long black dress, with a bright red cape thrown over her bare shoulders. She didn't see me and I didn't think I had to go over to say hello to her. I followed them warily into the gallery. There was a little hush as she entered the room, and eyes turned in her direction, but the conversation rose quickly to normal pitch. It was a polite and well-mannered group, and I guessed that most of the people there, like Dora, were not the sort who patronized the kind of theaters in which *The Sleeping Prince* was playing, or subscribed to the magazines in which Priscilla Dean, unclothed, was so prominently featured.

Fabian himself escorted her to the bar. I didn't see her look at a single painting. By the time all the other guests had left, it was past ten o'clock and she was alone at the bar. Drunk. Very drunk. When there had still been a dozen or so people in the room, the two young men had tried to persuade her to leave. 'We're expected for dinner, Prissy, darling,' one of them had said. 'We're way overdue. Come on. *Please.*'

'Fuck dinner,' Priscilla said.

'*We* have to go,' the other young man had said.

'Go,' Priscilla said, steadying herself against the bar. Her cape had fallen to the floor and a generous portion of her excellent upper body was on view. 'And fuck you, too. To-night I'm an art lover. Fags. My old friend from Paris, Miles Fabian, will take me home, won't you, Miles?'

'Of course, dear,' Fabian said, without enthusiasm.

'He's an old man,' Priscilla said, 'but oo la, la. Nadine Bonheur has spread the word from Passy to Vincennes. A for effort. *Très bien.* That's French, you fags.'

By now, the last of the guests had vanished. I gave silent thanks that Priscilla had arrived on the scene late and that Evelyn had had to go home to mind the baby. Dora was staring at Priscilla with her eyes wide and her mouth hanging open. She had told us when we interviewed her that she was looking for a quiet, clean job where she could catch up on her reading. I avoided Fabian's eyes.

'Stop hanging around, for shit's sake,' Priscilla said to the two young men. 'One thing I can't stand is people hanging around.'

The two young men looked at each other and shrugged. They said good night civilly to Fabian and me and told us how much they had liked the paintings. 'Incidentally,' the older of the two said, 'we're not homosexual. We're brothers.' They made their exit with dignity, and a minute later I heard the Lincoln Continental start up and go off.

Fabian bent to pick Priscilla's cape from the floor. He staggered a little and almost fell, but recovered quickly. He put the cape over Priscilla's shoulders. 'Time to go beddy-bye, dear,' he said. 'I shouldn't drive in my condition—' At least, I realized gratefully, he wasn't that far gone. 'But Douglas will drive us nice and slowly.'

'Your condition.' Priscilla laughed raucously. 'I know what your condition is, you old goat. Give me a kiss, Daddy.' She held out her arms.

'In the car,' Fabian said.

Priscilla held onto the table. 'I won't budge until I get my kiss,' she said.

With an uneasy glance at Dora, who had shrunk back against the wall, Fabian leaned over and kissed Priscilla. Priscilla wiped her mouth with the back of her hands, smudging her lipstick. 'I heard you can do better than *that*,' she said. 'What's the matter – out of practice? Maybe you ought to go back to France.' But she allowed Fabian to lead her to the door.

'Dora,' Fabian called back, 'put out the lights and lock the doors. We'll clean up in the morning.'

'Yes, Mr Fabian,' Dora whispered.

We left her there, not moving, rigid against the wall, as we went out.

Priscilla insisted upon sitting between us in the front seat. 'Cuddly,' she said. She had spilled champagne down the front of her dress and the smell was unpleasant. I rolled down my window before I turned on the ignition.

'Now, dear,' Fabian said, 'where are you staying?'

'Springs,' Priscilla said. 'That's it. Springs.'

'Where *exactly* is Springs, dear?' Fabian said patiently. 'What road?'

'How the hell do I know what road?' Priscilla said. 'Just drive. I'll show you the way.'

'What's the name of the people you're staying with? We

could call them and they could give us directions.' Fabian sounded like a policeman trying to get information from a lost child on a crowded beach. 'Surely, you must know the name of the people you're staying with.'

'Of course I do. Levy, Cohen, McMahon, something like that. Who cares? A bunch of jerks.' Priscilla leaned over and turned on the radio. The music from *The Bridge on the River Kwai* crashed through the car. 'Come on, Mr Clean,' she said angrily to me, 'get this crate moving. You know where Springs is, I hope.'

'Go to Springs,' Fabian said.

I started the car. But two minutes after we had passed the sign that read, Welcome to Springs, I knew it would be a miracle if we ever found the house that Priscilla was gracing with her presence that weekend. I slowed down at every fork and crossroad and every house we passed, but Priscilla only shook her head and said, 'No, that's not it.'

No matter how much money we were making from *The Sleeping Prince*, I thought, as I drove, it wasn't worth this.

'We're just wasting time,' Priscilla said. 'I got an idea. I have two girl friends in Quogue. On the beach. You can at least find the Atlantic Ocean in Quogue, can't you?' She didn't wait for an answer. 'They're fantastic. Original swingers. You'll love them. Let's go to Quogue and have a gang bang.'

'Quogue is an hour away from here,' Fabian said. He sounded very tired.

'So Quogue is an hour away. So what?' Priscilla demanded. 'Let's have some fun.'

'We've had a very long day,' Fabian said.

'Who hasn't?' Priscilla said. 'On to Quogue.'

'Perhaps tomorrow night,' Fabian said.

'Fags,' Priscilla said.

We were running through woods, on a small, dark back road that I didn't recognize, and I wasn't sure how I could get back to town without roaming all over the Hamptons for hours. I had just about decided to try to make my way back to East Hampton and find a hotel room for Priscilla and dump her on the sidewalk, if necessary, when my headlights picked up a car facing me, pulled over to the side of the road, with its hood up and two men looking down into the motor. I stopped the car and called out, 'I wonder if you two gentlemen could tell me where . . .'

Suddenly I realized I was looking into the muzzle of a gun.

The two men came over to the car, walking slowly. I couldn't see their faces in the dark but could make out that they were both wearing leather jackets and fishermen's long-billed caps. 'They have a gun,' I whispered to Fabian, across Priscilla, whom I felt stiffening beside me.

'That's right, brother,' the man with the gun said. 'We have a gun. Now, listen careful. Leave the key in the ignition, because we're going to take the loan of your car. And get out. Nice and easy. And the old guy, too. He gets out on his side. Also nice and easy. And leave the lady in the car. We're going to take the loan of the lady for a while, too.'

I heard Priscilla gasp, but she sat absolutely still. The man stepped back a pace as I opened the door and got out. The other man went around to Fabian's side. I heard him say to Fabian, 'Get over there with your partner.' Fabian came around and joined me. He was breathing heavily.

Then Priscilla started to scream. It was the loudest, most piercing scream I have ever heard.

'Shut the bitch up,' the man with the gun shouted to his partner. Priscilla was still screaming, but she was lying back, with her head on the wheel and kicking at the man, who was trying to hold onto her legs.

'For Christ's sake,' the man with the gun said. He moved a little, as though he was going to get at Priscilla from the driver's side. His gun had drooped a little and Fabian lunged at him. There was an enormous noise as the gun went off. I heard Fabian grunt as I jumped on the man, dragging his gun hand down. Our combined weight was too much for him and he fell back, the gun clattering to the pavement. Priscilla was still screaming. I grabbed the gun just as the second man came around the front of the car in the glare of the headlights. I fired at him and he turned and ran off into the woods. The man who had had the gun was crawling away on his hands and knees, and I fired at him. He jumped up and ran into the darkness. Priscilla was still screaming.

Fabian was lying on his back now on the pavement, holding his chest with his two hands. He was breathing in loud, irregular gasps. There was a little light reflected off the road top from our headlights. 'I think we'd better get me to a hospital, old man,' he said, with long spaces between the words. 'Fast. And tell Priscilla to please stop yelling.'

I was trying to lift Fabian, as gently as possible, into the back seat of the car, when I became conscious of headlights approaching from behind me. 'Sorry,' I said to Fabian, who was half in and half out of the car now. 'There's somebody coming.' I picked up the gun again and stood between Fabian and the oncoming car. Priscilla had stopped screaming and was sobbing wildly in the front seat, hitting her head dementedly against the dashboard. I didn't know which was worse, her screaming or this.

As the car approached, I saw that it was a police car. I dropped the gun I was holding. The car came to a halt and two policemen jumped out, their revolvers in their hands.

'What's going on here?' the one in front asked harshly.

'There's been a holdup. Two men. They're in the woods somewhere. My friend's been shot. We've got to get him to a hospital right away.'

'Whose gun is this?' The policeman asked, bending down to pick it up from where it was lying at my feet.

'Theirs.'

'You jumped a guy with a gun?' the policeman said incredulously.

'Not me,' I said. 'Him.'

'Holy man,' the policeman said softly.

He helped me put Fabian into the rear of the car, while his partner, a thin man with glasses, who looked too young to be a policeman, went to inspect the car with the hood up that the two men had been examining when we drove up. 'That's the car, all right,' he said when he came back. 'We've been looking for it. It was stolen last night at Montauk. We got a description from a gas station at Three Mile Harbor. Lucky for you.'

'Real lucky,' I said.

He looked curiously at Priscilla, who was still knocking her head against the dashboard, but he didn't say anything. 'Follow us,' he said. 'We'll lead you to the hospital.'

With the lights of the police car all flashing and the siren going, we sped down the dark roads. Coming the other way, I saw first one, then another police car racing past us toward the scene of the holdup. They must have sent out a call by radio from the car ahead of us.

*

The operation took three hours. Fabian had lapsed into unconsciousness before we reached the hospital in Southampton. An intern had taken one look at Priscilla and had her put in a bed under heavy sedation. I sat in the anteroom of the emergency ward, trying to answer the questions of the policemen about what the men looked like, the sequence in which things had happened, what we were doing on the road at that hour, who the lady was, whether or not I thought I had hit one or both of the men when I fired at them. It was hard to sort the things out. My mind felt numb, overwhelmed. It was hard to make the policemen understand who Priscilla Dean was and how it happened she didn't know where she lived. They were unfailingly polite and not suspicious, but they kept asking the same questions, in slightly different ways, over and over again, as though what had happened couldn't have happened the way I thought it had. I had called Evelyn as soon as they wheeled Fabian into the operating room and told her Fabian had had an accident but I was all right, not to worry. I told her I'd give her the details when I got home.

It was about midnight when the young policeman came back from using the phone to tell me the two men had given themselves up. 'You didn't hit either one of them.' He couldn't help grinning as he said it. I would have to go to the police station in the morning to identify them. And so would the lady, he added.

When Fabian was wheeled out on the operating table he looked calm and peaceful. The doctor, in his green smock and mouth-mask, now hanging at his throat, looked grave as he pulled off his rubber gloves. 'It's not so good,' he said to me. 'We'll know better in twenty-four hours.'

'Twenty-four hours,' I said dully.

'He's a good friend of yours?' the doctor said.

'A very good friend.'

'Where did he get that long scar on his chest and abdomen?'

'Scar? I never saw a scar,' I blinked. 'I guess I never saw him except with his clothes on.'

'It must have been something fierce,' the doctor said. 'It looks like shrapnel. Was he wounded in the war?' The doctor was young, too, no more than thirty-two or thirty-three, and I wondered, briefly, what he knew about wars.

'Yes,' I said, 'he was in a war. He never told me he was wounded though.'

'Live and learn,' the doctor said briskly. 'Good night.'

When I went out of the hospital, there was a flash in my eyes and I cringed. But it was only a photographer, taking my picture. Wait until tomorrow, friend, I thought, when they get dear old Priscilla Dean down to the police station. There'll be some pictures to be taken then.

I drove home slowly, the road blurring uncertainly before me. Evelyn was waiting up for me and we each had a Scotch as we sat in the kitchen and I told her the whole story of the evening. When I finished, she bit her lips and said, 'That miserable woman. I could strangle her with my bare hands.'

25

In the morning, the story was in the Long Island papers, with my picture. And, of course, Priscilla's. Before I went to the police station, I called the hospital and was told Fabian was resting comfortably. I probably could come and visit him for a few minutes later in the morning. Priscilla got to the police station just ahead of me, with uniformed escort. There must have been ten photographers waiting for us. Inside, we both identified the two men, although how Priscilla could have seen what they looked like in the darkened car with all her screaming and thrashing around was beyond me. They had both confessed anyway, so the identification was really a formality.

The two men looked harmless in the light of day. They weren't men, really. Neither of them could have been much more than eighteen, scrawny and frightened, with bad adolescent complexions and fake-tough mouths that quivered when the cops addressed them. Punk kids, my policeman friend called them contemptuously. It was difficult to believe that just a few hours before they had shot a man and had tried to kill me and I had tried to kill them.

When I left the building, the photographers tried to get me to pose with Priscilla, but I just kept on walking. I had had enough of Priscilla Dean.

* * *

I talked to the doctor before I went in to see Fabian. The doctor was optimistic. 'He came out of the operation much better than I thought he would. I think he'll be around for a while.'

Fabian was lying flat in the neatly made bed, with tubes leading into his arm and somewhere in his chest under the covers. The room was sunny and there was the smell of newly cut grass through the open window. He smiled wanly as I came in and raised his hand in greeting.

'I just talked to the doctor,' I said as I drew up a chair next to the bed, 'and he says you're going to be all right.'

'I'm glad to hear that.' His voice was frail. 'Imagine dying to save the honor of Priscilla Dean.' He laughed faintly. 'What we should have done was *introduce* her to those two boys.' He laughed again, a little rasping noise. 'They could have gone off to Quogue together and had themselves a hell of a night.'

'Tell me, Miles,' I said, 'what possessed you to go for that goddamn gun?'

He shook his head gently on the pillow. 'Who knows? Instinct? My better judgment blunted by drink? Maybe it was just a little bit of old Lowell, Massachusetts, sticking out.'

'I guess that's as good an explanation as any,' I said. 'While we're on the subject, the doctor says you have a great big scar on your abdomen and chest. Where did you get that?'

'A souvenir of a previous engagement,' he said. 'I'd prefer not to talk about it right now, if you don't mind. Could you do me a favor?'

'Of course.'

'Will you call Lily and ask her if she could possibly come over for a few days? I think old Lily would do me a lot of good.'

'I'll call her today,' I said.

'That's a good fellow.' He sighed. 'That was a nice evening, last night. All those polite people. You ought to cable Quinn and congratulate him.'

'Evelyn is doing it this morning,' I said.

'Thoughtful woman. She looked beautiful last night.' I started to get up. 'Don't go quite yet,' he said. 'I believe there's a pad and a pen in that drawer. Will you give it to me, please?'

I opened the drawer and gave him the pad and the pen. He wrote slowly and with difficulty. He tore the top sheet off the pad and gave it to me. 'There's no telling what's going to happen, Douglas,' he said, 'so I . . .' He stopped, as though he was having difficulty choosing his words. 'That note you have in your hand is to the private bank in Zurich. I have an account of my own there, as well as our joint one. The number's on there. And my signature. What I'm trying to tell you is that from time to time I . . . I, well – siphoned off a not inconsiderable sum. To put it plainly, Douglas, I was cheating you. That note will restore the money to you.'

'Oh, Christ,' I said.

'I warned you in the beginning,' he said, 'I was not running as an admirable man.'

I patted his head gently. 'It's only money, friend,' I said. 'The ride was worth it.'

There were tears in his eyes. 'Only money,' he said. Then he laughed. 'I was just thinking – it was a lucky thing I got shot. Otherwise nobody would have believed that it was anything but a publicity stunt to promote Priscilla Dean.'

The nurse came in and looked at me sternly, so I got up to go. 'Don't neglect the shop,' Fabian said as I left the room.

*

Lily arrived the next afternoon. I met her at Kennedy to drive her out to the hospital. She was handsomely dressed for traveling, in the same brown coat I remembered from Florence. She was composed and quiet as we sped east down the highway. But she smoked cigarette after cigarette. I had to stop at a diner to get her two fresh packs. I had told her that the doctor believed that there was a good chance that Fabian would pull through. She had merely nodded.

'The doctor also said' – I broke the silence as we passed Riverhead – 'that Miles has an enormous scar running down his chest and abdomen. He said it looked like shrapnel. Do you know anything about that? I asked Miles, but he said he preferred not to talk about it.'

'I saw it, of course,' Lily said. 'The first time we went to bed together. He seemed almost ashamed of it. As though it somehow lessened him. He's vain about his body, you know. That's why he'd never go swimming and always wore a shirt and tie. I didn't press him about it, but after a while he told me. He was a fighter pilot – I suppose he told you that . . .'

'No,' I said.

She smiled gently through the cigarette smoke. 'He's a great one for selective information to selected people, our Miles. Well, he was a pilot. He must have been a very good one. I found out from older American friends of mine who had known him that he had almost every medal a grateful government could hand out.' Her mouth twisted ironically. 'In the winter of nineteen forty-four, he was sent on a mission over France. It was a ridiculous, hopeless mission in impossible weather, he told me. I wouldn't know anything about that, of course, but on something like that I tend to believe him. He said his wing commander was a stupid, murderous glory hunter. I'm not up on wars, but I have some idea what that means. Anyway, he and his best friend were shot down over the Pas de Calais. His friend was killed.

Miles was taken by the Germans. They took care of him – in a nice, German way. That's where the scar came from. When the hospital he was in was finally overrun, he weighed a hundred pounds. That big man.' She smoked in silence for a while. 'That's when he decided, he told me, that he had done his last deed for humanity. That explains something of the way he lived. Or does it?'

'Something,' I said. 'Did you believe that English act?'

'Of course not. We laughed about it. I coached him on Britishisms. You were involved in quite a bit of business with him, weren't you?'

'A bit,' I said.

'You remember I warned you about him when it came to money?'

'I remember.'

'Did he cheat you?'

'A bit.'

She chuckled. 'Me, too,' she said. 'Dear old Miles. He's not an honest man, but he's a joyous one. And he gives joy to others. I'm not the one to say, but maybe one is more important than the other.' She lit a fresh cigarette. 'It's hard to think of his dying.'

'Maybe he won't die,' I said.

'Maybe.'

We said no more until we reached the hospital. 'I think I'd like to see him alone,' Lily said, as we drove up to the door of the handsome red-brick building.

'Of course,' I said. 'I'll drop your bags at the hotel. And I'll be home if you need me.' I kissed her and watched her go into the hospital, in her smart brown coat.

It was dark by the time I got home. There was a car I didn't recognize standing in front of the house. More reporters, I thought disgustedly, as I walked up the gravel path. Evelyn's car wasn't in the garage and I guessed that Anna had let whoever it was into the house. I opened the door with my key. A man was sitting in the living room, reading a newspaper.

He stood up when I came in.

'Mr Grimes...?'

'Yes.'

'I took the liberty of coming in and waiting for you here,' he said politely. He was a thin, studious-looking man with sandy hair. He was neatly dressed in a lightweight, dark-gray summer suit with a white shirt and dark tie. He didn't look like a reporter. 'My name is Vance,' he said. 'I'm a laywer. I'm here on behalf of a client. I came for a hundred thousand dollars.'

I went over to the sideboard where the whiskey was and poured myself a drink. 'Would you like a Scotch?' I asked the man.

'No, thank you.'

I carried my drink with me and sat down in an easy chair, facing Vance. He remained standing, a neat, small-boned, unmenacing, indoor type of man. 'I was wondering when you'd come,' I said.

'It took some time,' he said. His voice was dry, low, and educated. It would bore a listener in a short while. 'You were not easy to follow. Fortunately ...' He made a little movement with the newspaper. 'You've made yourself into quite a hero out here.'

'So it seems,' I said. 'There's nothing like a good deed for shining in a naughty world.'

'Exactly,' he said.

He glanced around at the room. From the nursery came the sound of the baby crying. 'A nice place you've got here. I admired the view.'

'Yes,' I said. I felt very tired.

'My client has instructed me to tell you that you have three days to deliver the money. He does not want to be unreasonable.'

I nodded. Even that was an effort.

'I will be at the Blackstone Hotel. Unless you prefer the St Augustine.' He smiled, skull-like.

'The Blackstone will do,' I said.

'In the same conditions in which it was found, please,' Vance said. 'In one-hundred-dollar bills.'

I nodded again.

'Well,' he said, 'that takes care of everything, I think. I must be on my way now.'

At the door, he stopped. 'You haven't asked me whom I represent,' he said.

'No.'

'Just as well. I couldn't tell you if you had asked. Still, I can say that your ... your escapade ... was not without its benefits. It might ease the pain of having to return the money to know that it saved several distinguished people ... *very* distinguished people from considerable embarrassment.'

'That makes my day,' I said.

*

It was nine o'clock when I went up in the elevator in the apartment building on East Fifty-second Street. I had left word with Anna to tell Mrs Grimes that I had been called to the city suddenly on business and that I would be gone a day or two. I could have called Evelyn at her office, but I didn't want to have to explain anything.

Henry let me into the apartment. I had caught him just as he was about to go out. He and Madeleine had tickets for the theater, but when I said he would have to wait for me, he said, 'I'll be here.' He looked worried as he opened the door. Madeleine was in the living room, dressed for her night out in New York. She, too, looked worried.

'Maybe it would be better if you and I talked alone, Hank,' I said.

But he shook his head. 'I'd rather she stayed, if you don't mind.'

'All right,' I said. 'It won't take long. I need a hundred thousand dollars, Hank. In hundred-dollar bills. I haven't time to collect it from Europe and I don't have it here. I have only three days. Can you get it for me in three days?'

Henry sat down suddenly. We had all been standing in the middle of the living room. He rubbed his eyes with the back of his hand, in a gesture that was a hangover from childhood. 'Yes,' he said, almost inaudibly. 'Somehow. Of course.'

*

It only took two days.

I called Vance's room from the lobby of the hotel. He was there. 'I'm coming up,' I said. I held the heavy suitcase in one hand while I held the telephone with the other.

'Excellent,' he said.

I waited while he counted the bills. He did it slowly and carefully. I hadn't asked Henry where he had found the money and he hadn't told me. 'That's it,' said Vance, as he snapped a rubber band around the last bundle of bills. 'Thank you.'

'You can keep the bag,' I said.

'That's kind of you.' He escorted me to the door.

*

I drove fast. I wanted to look in at the hospital before it was too late for visitors. I had called at noon and spoken to Lily. Fabian was resting comfortably, she had said. I wanted to tell him that the man had come, as he had predicted, and asked for a hundred thousand dollars and that I had had it to give to him.

When I got to the hospital, the nurse at the front desk stopped me. 'I'm afraid you're too late, Mr Grimes,' she said. 'Mr Fabian died at four o'clock this afternoon. We tried to reach you, but . . .'

'That's all right,' I said. I was mildly surprised at how calm my voice sounded. 'Is Lady Abbott here?'

The nurse shook her head. 'I believe Mrs Abbott has left town.' Even at that moment her American distrust of titles prevented her from saying Lady Abbott. 'She said there was nothing more she could do here. She thought she could catch a night plane back to London.'

I nodded. 'Very wise,' I said. 'Good night, Nurse. I'll be here in the morning to make the necessary arrangements.'

'Good night, Mr Grimes,' she said.

I drove slowly toward East Hampton. There was no hurry now. I did not want to go home just yet. I drove to the barn, dark now, with the newly painted sign, The South Fork Gallery, in small, modest letters above the door. 'Don't neglect the shop,' Fabian had said. I took out my ring of keys and opened the door. I sat on a bench in the middle of the room, without turning on the lights, thinking of the joyous, dishonest, scarred, cunning man who had died that day, and who, by the terms of the contract we had signed that slushy day in the office of the lawyer in Zurich, now had left me free and absurdly wealthy. The tears came slowly.

I got off the bench and went over to the switch and turned on the lights. Then I stood in the middle of the room and looked at the paintings of the wanderings of Angelo Quinn's father, glowing on the walls.

IRWIN SHAW

*All these books are available at your local bookshop or newsagent, or
can be ordered direct from the publisher. Just tick the titles you want
and fill in the form below.*

Prices and availability subject to change without notice.

Hodder & Stoughton Paperbacks, P.O. Box 11, Falmouth, Cornwall.

Please send cheque or postal order, and allow the following for
postage and packing:

U.K. – 55p for one book, plus 22p for the second book, and 14p for
each additional book ordered up to a £1.75 maximum.

B.F.P.O. and EIRE – 55p for the first book, plus 22p for the second
book, and 14p per copy for the next 7 books, 8p per book thereafter.

OTHER OVERSEAS CUSTOMERS – £1.00 for the first book, plus 25p
per copy for each additional book.

Name ....

Address ....

....

Contents

List of Plates

1. Honoré Daumier, *Pose de l'homme de la nature* and *Pose de l'homme civilisé* from *Croquis Parisiens*, 1853. (Bibliothèque Nationale, Paris)
2. Mme Pierre-Paul Darbois, *Mr Henry Rosales*, painted miniature, 1843. (Trustees of the Victoria and Albert Museum)
3. Physiognotrace engraving by Gilles-Louis Chrétien, 1793. (The Kodak Collection, National Museum of Photography, Film and Television)
4. Unknown photographer, daguerreotype portrait in its case. (Trustees of the Victoria and Albert Museum)
5. W. H. Fox Talbot, *Gentleman Seated*, calotype, 1842. (Trustees of the Science Museum, London)
6. D. O. Hill & R. Adamson, *Portrait of D. O. Hill*, calotype, c.1845. (Trustees of the Victoria and Albert Museum)
7. Unknown photographer, *Portrait of a Man with a Tall Hat*, collodion glass negative, c.1860. (Trustees of the Science Museum, London)
8. Charles Lutwidge Dodgson (Lewis Carroll), *Alice Liddell*, albumen print from a collodion negative, c.1858. (Graham Ovenden)
9. Pages from an album of cartes-de-visite of *Prominent French Figures*. (Trustees of the Victoria and Albert Museum)
10. André Adolphe Disdéri, *Carte-de-visite Portrait of Marshal Vinoy*, albumen print. (Trustees of the Victoria and Albert Museum)
11. Gaspard-Félix Tournachon (Nadar), *Gioacchino Rossini*, albumen print. (National Portrait Gallery, London)
12. Pages from an album of Kodak snapshots, 1893–1894. (Trustees of the Science Museum, London)